Home: Interstellar
(2nd Edition)

Ray Strong

Impulse Fiction

Home: Interstellar
(2nd Edition)

Ray Strong

Published by Impulse Fiction, Pleasanton, CA

Cover Illustrations: Vikncharlie at Fiverr.com,
Elementi.studio (99 Designs), and
D.J. MacKenzie (dmacstudios.com) and Kimberly Mah

ISBN-10: 0-9863599-1-2
ISBN-13: 978-0-9863599-1-0
Library of Congress Control Number: 2015908391
LCCN Imprint Name: Impulse Fiction, Pleasanton, CA

Chapter 1
The *Princess*

*"Once in an age, the forces of darkness align to bend the
arc of history..."*
 —From *The Diary of Neuchar de Merlner*, Europa, 2121

In 2177, that alignment broke the *Princess*.

***

"Hurry, Littlebit," Meriel said to her younger sister,
Elizabeth, as they rushed to their ship. They had missed the
boarding siren and cut across the docks, dodging grav-sleds
and puddles to make up time. She lurched to a stop and
yanked her sister behind her to avoid the massive treads of a
cargo loader. Hoisting a crate into the hold, it dripped oily
dirt on their best fatigues.

Beyond the loader, her mother waved from the air lock.
Meriel relaxed; they were home. Before her moored the
Princess, a merchant vessel crewed by seven families
working a circuit between Luyten's Star and Sirius.

At the gangplank, the two girls queued up with their
young shipmates who, juiced on simulators and sugar from
Elizabeth's birthday party, jostled each other to board. When
they reached the air lock, they paused and brushed their
hands past their foreheads in a child's salute to the officer on
deck, their mother and XO, Esther Hope.

"'Mission to come aboard, ma'am," Meriel said, but
Elizabeth remained quiet, distracted by the symbol of a cat's
eye in light blue on the crate.

"Granted," their mother said and returned the salute as dockhands detached the umbilicals behind them.

Once inside the *Princess*, Meriel's world opened up to the familiar bustle of cargo lashing and comm chatter in preparation for the faster-than-light jump through hyperspace to Enterprise Station. With eyes closed, she danced her way to their cabin, running one hand over the nicked walnut railing and the other hand over the fabric walls covered with children's artwork. The tips of her fingers brushed the corner of Tommy's drawing—a fire-breathing dragon melting a knight in armor—and the rough texture of Anita's first creation: her name written with a backward *n* in letters larger than the sunflower drawn just above it. And behind her, little Elizabeth copied every move.

Immersed in the routine background murmur about mass, vectors, and fuel capacity, she dreamed that she captained the *Princess* and plotted their course. With her arms out and eyes still shut, she rode the quantum probability to their first jump point but bumped into something soft. She opened her eyes and looked up at Uncle Ed's smiling face just before her sister collided into her.

"Hey, lassies," he said and reached out his long arms to hug them both. "Course correction needed." He glanced over their heads to her mother behind them. "Sis, we're loading late cargo that will meet our margin requirements."

"Good. Then we'll undock on schedule. What about data?"

Ed shuffled beside her with the two little girls sitting on his shoes and wrapped around his legs. "Still got thirty-Z of memory unfilled."

"What's the bid?" her mother asked, but Meriel stopped listening. Across the promenade, one of the passenger's kids, a snot-nosed snob from white-zone, sneered at her as he would a contract servant. She responded with a polite smile, and he turned to observe the debark through the window.

"He's gotta be rich," Elizabeth whispered with wide eyes. And she was right—hauling mass around the galaxy cost a fortune.

"He still doesn't have to be a jerk," she said, but his contempt stung, and she blushed. Nearly thirteen years old, she couldn't help but compare his handsome clothes to her stained and worn fatigues. That her parents could afford no better did not mean they loved her less, just that her future would be so different from his. He would have a secure future as a station citizen, and she would live with the constant fear of a hull breach or a bad hyperspace jump that stranded them out in the middle of nowhere.

Terror crossed the boy's face as a docking clamp banged and hissed its release. He gripped his guardian's hand and scanned the passageway for an escape route. But Meriel smiled: space was her world, not his, and he was a guest.

Outside the *Princess,* it was just as cold and deadly as outside the home where he felt so safe. But the station's size allowed him to pretend he was coddled in a megastructure on Earth—as long as he didn't look out a window. Seeing the panic in the boy's eyes as the ship drifted away from the station, she knew he could pretend no longer. She was not afraid of the risks in his world or hers, and with her ship, she had a freedom that he would never know. She wanted none of his life, no matter how elegant his clothing.

"OK, girls, on to bed," her mother said, and with a brush of her hand, she shooed them to their cabin.

Thinking no more of him, Meriel took her sister's hand and scurried to their berth. She loved this time most, the quiet time before sleep and jump when their mother belonged to them alone. After slipping into their pj's and sleep nets, their mother joined them and sat near their bunks.

"Did you find Elizabeth's doll, M?" her mother asked and tucked her into her sleep net.

"Yes, Mom, but Liz was a brat and didn't want to come."

Her sister mimed, "Blah, blah, blah," with her fingers and rolled her eyes.

"Hey, birthday girl, your sister's in charge when your father and I aren't around. Hear me now?"

"Yes, Mama," Elizabeth said and leaned over the edge of her bunk. "Where are we going next?"

Meriel kicked the bunk above, where she expected her sister's butt to be. "Enterprise. We're gonna have fun there. Nick will reserve us more time on the dino-sims, and Tommy rigged a saddle for the raptors."

"Time for sleep now, girls. Take your tranq," her mother said and pointed to the tranquilizers on their pillows that would ease the disorientation of the jump. "Which song would you like tonight?"

"'Home,' Mama, please," she said, and her mother began their favorite nursery rhyme.

> *"Soaring past her misty veil,*
> *Seven sisters near her sail.*
> *Round the giant's emerald tail,*
> *She sends a tiny probe…"*

When her mother pointed her finger, Meriel closed her eyes and imagined a planetary fly-by. "What's it like, Mom?"

Her mother took each of the girls' hands in hers. "Well, you can run all day in a straight line through fields of grain and never reach the end. The days are warm, and you can feel the sun on your bare arms. Little insects buzz near your ears, and the air smells of wheat and flowers. Home has two moons, and some nights you can read by moonlight…"

Elizabeth purred, which was her mom's cue that they were both sleeping. But Meriel had palmed her tranq and lay still, faking it.

Her father's voice called on the comm. "Esther. Report for duty, please."

"Aye, Captain," her mother said and kissed her daughters on their foreheads.

When she could no longer hear her mother's footsteps, Meriel rose and followed her to the bridge. There she settled into her usual hiding place behind the communications console and pictured the crew going through their pre-jump checklists.

"…and great work on the late cargo, Ed."

That's Papa, she thought.

"We were lucky, Mike."

And Uncle Ed. He was her mother's brother and the ship's manager. Except for God, he knew more about the financial health of the ship than anyone.

"The shippers seemed to dry up as soon as we got here," Ed continued. "If this happens again, we could lose the *Princess.*"

Meriel gasped. This was her home.

"Don't talk like that," her mother said. "It's not that bad yet."

"The trend sucks, Sis. If we can't—"

"I heard the *Esperanza* was sold out from under them for dock fees," Aunt Joanna said. "The parents are all working on the mining colony on GH343 just to eat."

"God, that's hell," her mother said. "But even a low-g sewer like 343 is better than the organ mills. Where are the kids?"

"Visiting relatives on Wolf Station."

"Not for long. The kids are unskilled and not citizens. What'll happen to them?"

No one spoke, and Meriel shuddered at the image of sunken-eyed children with distorted skeletons. Prolonged periods of reduced gravity and malnutrition in the mines were murder to a growing body.

Her father broke the silence. "We're not as deep in debt as the *Esperanza*—"

"But this could happen again, Mike. We should be looking for a different route now."

"The Pacific League won't just hand us another circuit," her mother said.

A fist slammed on the console. "Damn 'em to hell, then," her father said. "We need a different league."

"You can't just up and switch leagues," her uncle said as footsteps paced the bridge. "They want us to bring them something."

"Like what?"

"Like goods with higher margins. Profits will give us standing with a new league. Without that, we're stuck."

"Drugs?"

"Pharmaceuticals, genomics," her mother said, "and legal."

"Of course, Esther."

"What about Home?"

"Come on, Sis. Those fantasies again?"

"It might be real."

"There's no way someone could keep an earthlike planet so well hidden. Nothing that important could stay off the grid for this long. Besides, you have no clue how to find it."

"Someone does. We only need the orientation. I received something that—"

A muffled gasp caused Meriel to turn and catch her sister hiding behind her.

"It's real!" Elizabeth whispered. Meriel raised a finger to her lips.

Ed continued. "We're spacers, Sis, and not made for the dirt."

"Maybe just a home base, not a home," her mother said. "We have nothing if our route fails. A few bad trips and we're working the docks. And the kids—"

"Then let's not have any bad trips," her father said.

"That's a lot of pressure on me, Mike."

"Sorry, Ed. Esther, we won't solve this tonight. I know it's your dream, but we can't bet on it yet."

"How long to jump?"

"Ten minutes," Aunt Joanna said. "Time to strap in."

The girls snuck back to their berths and crawled into their sleep nets.

"Mom thinks it's real," Elizabeth said.

"No one else seems to. Take your tranq, Littlebit. No faking this time."

Her sister swallowed her pill. "Wow. Imagine running until I drop. What does wheat smell like?"

Meriel tapped her link to combine the scents of wheat and jasmine with the sounds of crickets and the rustle of trees.

Then she held the device between them to share the experience.

"Do you think we'll ever see it?" Elizabeth said.

She reached up to grab her little sister's hand. "If Mom can find it, we'll get there, Littlebit."

Closing her eyes, she imagined running through a field of wildflowers like the pictures she had seen of Earth. But when she did, the ground curved up a few hundred feet away, just like in a space station. Like perspective, gravity on a planet was too hard to imagine without knowing where to find the next handhold in the event artificial gravity failed, and the deck became the overhead. Home was still a lovely dream as long as she didn't examine it too closely.

For a moment, she worried for her poor cousins on the *Esperanza,* and she cringed. But as the *Princess* jumped into hyperspace and far from all her cares, she drifted away with the sweet smells of Home.

***

The claxon woke Meriel as they emerged from jump. She sprang from her bunk netting and reached for her sister in the dim red emergency lights, but her feet never reached the deck; they were zero-g. She grabbed for her bunk to orient herself.

Instead of the background hum of the engines and whoosh of the ventilation, a low pinging rang through the hull. The smell of ozone stung her nose. *Something terrible must have happened.*

"Girls! Come!" her mother whispered from the door of their cabin. Tethered behind her floated all the children on a safety line to which Meriel and Elizabeth now clipped themselves. Through the narrow service corridors, her mother led them to a small hatch behind Maintenance-1 and pushed them inside—noisy and crying.

Her mother cracked a light stick. "Quiet, kids. Your parents will come for you soon." Turning to Meriel, she placed the light in her hand. "Hon, you're in charge when I'm gone." She glanced at Elizabeth. "You hear me, Liz?"

"Yes, ma'am," her sister said and pressed her lips together.

"Mom, what is it?" Meriel asked.

With eyebrows drawn together, her mother scanned the service tunnel. "It's serious. Keep them quiet."

"What about the passengers' kids?"

Esther bit her lip and shook her head. "I'll be back in a few minutes." She left and shut the hatch behind her.

Alone with the children, Meriel tapped the shoulders of those nearest her for attention, who in turn tapped the others.

"Roll call," she signed. Sign language was an accommodation for Little Harry who was deaf and too young for implants. The children raised their hands when she signed their names. Including Elizabeth, there were eight of them: Tommy and Sam Spurell, Penny Hubbard, Erik White, and little Harry in the lap of his older sister, Anita. Except for little Harry, they were all over five years old, so they understood her. But she was only twelve, and being older didn't mean they would mind her. Tears can't fall in zero-g, so she wiped their eyes and noses until the sobs waned to sniffles.

To distract them, Sam suspended his communications link in the air to observe changes in orientation and acceleration. When the maneuvering thrusters fired, the device appeared to spin, though they and the ship rotated around it. The main engines rumbled and gradually restored gravity, which settled the kids and the link onto the deck.

"They'll come soon," she signed. The children began to relax in the familiar one-g until an ejecting escape pod clanged.

"They've gone!" Penny said aloud. "They left us here!"

"No! They'd never leave us, ever," Meriel replied in sign.

A few minutes later, her mother opened the hatch and crawled inside wearing a small lamp attached to a headband dripping with sweat. She breathed in shallow spurts as she handed more lightsticks to Meriel. After sealing the hatch with a hand welder, her mother gripped a cable tray and winced.

"Follow. Quiet," her mother signed and led the children down the service tunnel and around a corner out of sight of the hatch. Once past a rib along the hull, she stopped and gathered them together.

"Your parents will come soon," her mother signed. "Until then, be very, very still. Meriel is my number two. Do what she says." She gasped, squinted, and bit her lip. "Now, we wait for a signal." Gathering their comm links, her mother pried off the talk buttons so they could only receive, and returned them. "Rest now, kids. It may be a while."

Meriel saw the tracks of tears in the dirt on her mother's cheeks and new tears glistening in the corners of her eyes.

Her mother took her arm and drew her close. "You need to grow up fast now, hon." She reached around the back of her neck to unfasten a chain with a pendant and tiny medal. After kissing the medal, she latched the necklace around Meriel's neck.

"It's all here, M. If no one comes, wait at least a half hour. If it grows colder than you can stand, move immediately. Understand?"

"Mom, why would no one come?"

Her mother touched her lips with a finger and then pointed to the dogged portal nearby. "The hatch here opens only from the inside," she signed. "Cargo-2 is on the other side. Go to E-48 next to the galley. Find the alt-bridge behind the panel in the cold locker. The pendant is a key to open the panel. Inside the pendant is a q-chip. Stick it in the nav slot. *Princess* will jump one minute later, so be sure to tell the kids to secure themselves. Tranq is in the drawer under the console. Got it?"

The comfort she had felt earlier evaporated. "Why can't you do this, Mom?"

"I maybe cannot, sweetheart," her mother signed and grimaced again, her breathing raspy and uneven.

"What about Home?"

"It's all on the chip, hon," her mother said aloud. She took Elizabeth's hand to draw her closer. "Help your sister, Liz. She'll need it."

Elizabeth nodded with lips pinched together.

Her mother leaned back on the bulkhead and began to hum the melody of their favorite lullaby. "You remember the words, girls?" The sisters nodded. "Have faith…and never leave them."

After her mother's headlight dimmed, Meriel used the lightsticks to keep all the kids in sight. They sniffled in the murky light while huddling close together in the chilly hold and whimpered when the cargo loaders and hatches banged. Time passed, and the sniffles ebbed. The clanging ended, the children calmed and fell asleep, and she dozed off.

The cold woke her, shivering in the fog of condensed breath. The banging had stopped, and frost covered the surfaces on their hideout and seemed to seep into her bones. Dressed only in their jams, the kids had bunched up against each other for warmth but could not last long without warm suits. They had to move, or they would die. She shook her mother to wake her, but she did not stir. Cracking their last lightstick, she saw her mother's clothing soaked with blood.

Chapter 2
The *Tiger*

Nightmare

Meriel screamed as she sat up in her bunk, panting and sweating, the ten-year-old image of her dying mother as clear as a vid. She grabbed the pendant and medal on the chain around her neck and took slow, deep breaths to calm herself, fighting not to close her eyes again. *No wonder I can't keep a roommate. Damn, I need more boost.*

Still groggy, she took a moment to orient herself. She had just woken up from her first jump on the *Tiger*, a new ship with new routes. It was her first private cabin in her new post as chief warrant officer of cargo, and the first time she had ever slept without someone else's butt a few inches from her nose. Her berth still smelled of disinfectant, and the putty-gray walls bore the shadows of vids and knickknacks of the former occupant.

She rose and gulped down a juice pack from the cabinet. Wetting a towel in the sink, she sat with her head back and the cloth over her eyes to help recover from the disorientation of the long jump.

Based on the ship's clock, they had dropped out of the jump early. Perhaps the nav system dumped them at some obscure singularity known only to the navigators. Being in the wrong place did not worry her the way it had on her last post. The *Tiger* ran a safer circuit, and Molly Vingel, the XO, told her there were five other Marines onboard who could help in a fight.

"Incoming," Meriel said to trigger the communications console. "List."

"Security," it responded.

"Bah." She removed the damp cloth from her eyes for the device to scan her retina.

"Littlebit. Harry, urgent. Bell, Jeremy…" the console recited.

Little Harry. *Damn.* They had torn him away from his older sister, Anita, and the siblings still missed each other. *God, how cruel the law could be for the powerless.*

"Bell. Go," she said.

"Ross Station, ET/2187:98:21." Jeremy appeared dressed in a colorful Hawaiian shirt, lounging on a veranda beside a tropical beach. Behind him, a gull squawked and stole the cherry from his drink.

She pressed the cloth back against her eyes.

"Greetings, Miss Hope, and good luck on your new ship. Regarding the legal issues, I have good news and bad news. Good news: the case for the *Liu Yang* moved up to Court-5. That's the court of appeals on Enterprise." *Liu Yang*. That's what they called the *Princess* now to hide her while her papers showed her scrapped and recycled. "If they rule in your favor, you get your ship back with no more legal hassles, and you can return the registry to the *Princess*. Bad news: Court-5 only hears pleas from licensed representatives, and they are expensive. Not my choice, M. I'm pro bono on this, and I'd do it if they'd let me, but the reps of the court are specialists and do not negotiate. They're cost-plus, and your account balance is insufficient. Estimate attached."

"Pause," she said and peeked under a corner of the cloth and whistled: the estimate was two years of her gross salary. "Damn, I don't have that kind of money." Leaning back again, she shook her head. "Well, *Princess*, I guess we're just gonna have to wait. Play."

"I know what you're thinking, Ms. Hope, but we can't wait. There's more bad news." He waved a vid sheet. "Court says you have twenty-one days to submit evidence the

Princess was not carrying contraband at the time of the attack. If you can't, they're going to auction her from impound to offset dock fees and legal claims."

She jerked her head up, and the cloth fell from her eyes. "What!" she said without thinking, and the device replayed the last sentence and continued.

"Some clerk wants to close the case, and the issue remains unresolved."

"They can't take her. She's ours!"

The playback paused when she spoke.

She stared at the wall with her mouth open. Her ship was their only asset; her only means to reunite the kids and keep her promise to her mother. Without the *Princess*, they would all drift apart.

"Play," she said.

At the edge of the window, Jeremy moved a few fingers, and another vid sheet appeared. To the left of it, a porthole revealed a scene inconsistent with his tropical paradise. Outside the window, the scaffolding of a spaceship-repair station, or perhaps a junkyard, exposed his location as a tiny office with an active wall. With a swipe of his hand, he synced the vid to the window, and the document replaced the beach.

"They towed your ship from the boneyard at YR56 to the impound dock at Enterprise. Except for the patch on that big hole, she's in decent shape; she's still inert at low pressure with supporting electronics asleep. I'm sure that decision saves on dock fees. Lower stress, too."

He leaned closer to the camera. "About the kids and custody, the cases are all weak. The courts would never take children from their fosters without proof of neglect and an alternative, but we could negotiate for visitation. Some are of age now and can make their own decisions, of course, but their contracts have a few more years to run. I'm working on it." He glanced at his link. "I'm leaving for meetings on Lander in a few hours. Give me a call if you're in-system, and we can chat more. Twenty-one days, Ms. Hope. Don't forget."

"End message," the machine said.

With her head in her hand, she rubbed the pendant on her necklace. "Never leave them," her mother had said. But her ship was the means to make that happen. She reached into her kit, removed a vid sheet of the *Princess*, and stuck it into a corner of the mirror.

"It's not fair," she whispered. Without their ship, her dream would die, and her promises to her mother would die with it. Without their ship, the kids would dissolve into the billions of anonymous spacers, lost to each other.

For years she had been content to keep the *Princess's* custody at a low priority and the edge of her attention. All the while, she chipped away at the funding and legal issues. Sometimes, she could even go a week without thinking about her, convinced that things would work out in time. Not anymore.

"Acknowledge," she said, and a reply query opened. "Jeremy, I'll try to meet you on Lander. But how in the hell can we clear her in twenty-one days? We tried for years to prove a negative. See ya. Send." The send queue absorbed the message where it would wait until the *Tiger* synchronized with the next communications beacon.

Meriel touched the vid, and the *Princess's* brochure displayed a white ellipsoid stretched on the long axis. Sleek and featureless as a polished river stone, her shape would feel comfortable in a closed palm.

According to the ship's clock, her shift would not start for hours, but she dressed for work regardless; as the new cargo chief with a logistics-five rating, checking the lashings before and after jump was her responsibility.

From the cabinet, she removed the pack of meds her contract obliged her to take for the nightmares and grumpy moods. She gazed at a pill. *One dose and the terrors and flashbacks will disappear for a few days. No cold sweats, no anxiety attacks. And I won't have to wait until Lander for boost. One dose, and I'll forget about the pirates and freezing and...what I did.*

She rolled the pill between her fingers. *But if I do, I'll also forget about Elizabeth and the* Princess *and stop caring again.*

No, never again. I promised. Crushing the pill, Meriel sprinkled the dust directly into the toilet, just as she had done every morning for seven years.

When zipped, the high collar of her shirt covered the long scar that crossed her chest; a lock of hair hid the white tip that ran behind her ear. To fix her hair in place, she added a visor with an embedded link. She preferred embeds to implants to assure that one of her occasional brain farts would not command a bot to take a shortcut through the hull and space the entire payload.

So, when are we going to hit Lander? She scanned the *Tiger's* roster on her visor's head-up display. *Maybe twenty-five passengers and twenty-five crew.*

"Pilots," she said while buttoning her collar. The visor displayed,

```
        Vonegon,    Jerri.    Senior    Pilot,
    nav-four.
```

"Location."

```
        On duty. Bridge.
```

Damn. "Other nav."

```
        Smith, John. Pilot, nav-four. Off
    duty. Promenade.
```

"Well, Mr. Smith, let's go find out when we'll hit Lander."

Approaching the promenade, a crewman in khaki with a brass circle on his left lapel caught her attention. *He's a nav-four.* She blinked to pull up crew vids. *Let's see: medium tall, brown hair. Smith, John. That's him.*

As she prepared her introduction, the view caught her eye, and she stopped. The window ran the length of the passageway and overlooked a sea of pearlescent green with red filaments of hydrogen weaving through towering pillars of black and gray.

"Makes you want to suit up and go EVA," she said to break the ice.

"Uh-huh," he murmured and stared out the window. After a few moments, he turned to her. "Say, aren't you the new cargo chief?" he asked, and Meriel nodded. "I'm John Smith."

She folded her arms. "So where are we, Mr. Navigator?"

"Well, we jumped from Sector 48, so judging from the show outside, we should be somewhere between Ross and Lalande."

She looked him straight in the eyes before turning back to the field of stars. "You're clueless."

"Well, that's our flight plan."

"So when are we gonna dock at Lander?"

"Wait till my shift starts and give me about ten minutes at the screens, and I'll let you know."

"I heard Jerri's pretty good too," she said, referring to the senior pilot. "Bet you a scotch she gets us moving before you arrive. Say, you don't talk like a spacer. How come you're sitting nav?"

"I grew up on L5, and you do what you need to."

"Damn." It just slipped out of her mouth. Her face softened, and she studied him more closely. For a refugee from L5, she expected disease and deformity and, well, damage. However, the man standing next to her appeared perfectly normal. *Kinda nice, actually, with that smile.* She blushed and looked away.

"Sorry," she said, but before she could say more, his comm link interrupted.

"Bridge to Smith. Your biotag says you're awake. Report, please."

"Smith here. I'm off duty, Socket. What do you want?"

"Jerri told the OOD that we'd jump a lot sooner with your help."

He raised his eyebrows. "She said that?"

"Get over it. Stevens says to report to the bridge stat, or let me know why not. So you coming?"

"On my way," he said with a wink to Meriel.

She smirked at his confidence. "The bet stands. Ten minutes."

"Piece of cake," he said. "See you at sixteen hundred."

"Don't you sleep?"

"A real scotch is worth it. See ya."

"Uh, yeah." *Oops. Did he think I meant real scotch?* Her gaze followed him down the promenade. *He doesn't move like a spacer either; he's heavier on his feet, solid, not afraid of losing gravity.*

"Hello, Meriel."

She turned at the voice and recognized Patrick Ferrell, the ship's doctor, walking toward her.

Oh, crap. "Hi, Doc." She gave him a polite smile but took a step backward. "Sorry, but I'm in a hurry now. I need to check the restraints before some crate turns into a projectile—"

"Then stop for a minute," Ferrell said. "You left me in the middle of our conversation yesterday and haven't been to see me like you promised. I thought we had more to talk about."

"Sorry, Doc." She retreated farther. "No more interviews. I did all my talking on the *Thrace* and with the Troopers a decade ago. There's nothing left to figure out." She paused. "My last skipper had no complaints."

"You're taking your meds, right?"

"Sure," she lied.

"The drugs help you cope."

"I'm coping fine. You see me ripping anybody's head off?"

"Well, I hoped something like that would never cross your mind. The meds help with the blackouts, too. We can't have you passing out on a cargo loader, now, can we?"

She glanced around and stepped back toward him, hoping no one else had heard. "I don't have blackouts. I was a kid and couldn't explain—"

"If you come to see me, we can straighten it all out."

"I just got nervous sometimes." *Crap! I just gave him more ammunition.*

"I understand. I'll make an appointment for—"

Meriel brightened, perceiving the possibility of escape, and retreated again. "Sure, Doc. Before we complete the circuit."

"No, next shift," he shouted after her.

"Right. Next week. OK, I'll be there," she yelled back over her shoulder and ducked around the bulkhead. "Like hell I will," she murmured as she marched to her duty station in cargo.

The Sphere

John took a roundabout way through the mess hall to pick up a mug of coffee from the replicator. Jerri could find their way with the nav computer alone but would require lots of short jumps and fuel. Margins were thin, so the longer he delayed, the more they might appreciate his talents.

He paused at the door to the bridge. "Smith on deck. Reporting for duty, sir."

Lieutenant Commander Ed Stevens, the OOD, signaled him to enter. "Jeez, there you are. You stop for a manicure?"

"Seven twenty-three. Mark the time," John said and walked to the navigation station next to Jerri.

"Sure. Just find out where the hell we are," Stevens said, pacing the bridge. "And move it. If we miss our dock schedule on Lander, it'll screw up our bonus."

Jerri eyed the hot coffee in John's hand and shook her head. When he sat at the nav-b beside her, she turned away to hide her blush. With a few motions of her fingers, her nav-a console projected a star map. Overlaid on the map was what appeared to be an ice-cream cone. The tip of the cone identified the start of their last jump. The scoop of ice cream at the other end represented where they might be now—their sphere of uncertainty. It was huge.

"Sphere's too big to plot a jump," she said and switched the projection to John's smaller nav-b console. "We'd end up in a star."

"Did you try to triangulate the Doppler?" he asked.

"Nope," she said and tapped her foot. "Just waiting for you."

"What's coming in, Socket?" he asked communications chief Suzanne Soquette, or just Socket—a nickname she rather enjoyed. She was beautiful, even for a spacer, and he always had to limit his gaze to avoid staring.

"Some chatter for the buyers and lots of encrypted garbage," she said with an extra flash of her eyes which increased his discomfort. "All EM, clear as a bell. Think anybody's listening out here?"

"Pipe some over to me," he said and turned to Stevens. "Say, I met the new cargo chief in the passageway just now. What's her story?"

"Came over from Jeff's boat, the *Jolly Roger*, saying she didn't like the routes and had trouble sleeping. Jeff said she's the best cargo mate in the sector. Lifetime spacer who knows the boards. Said she could man any seat on the bridge if she wanted, so Molly bought out her contract." Molly was XO and rated exec-four with laser-sharp instincts, so she would know. His link flashed, and he went back to his console.

Jerri leaned over to John with a timid smile. "Is this academic or are you interested?"

"Nothing's academic."

She bit her lip.

"She's too pretty for you," Socket said.

"If you ask me, I think she's got a past," Jerri said. "Something that won't forget her, won't let her go."

"Like what?"

"Well, rumors say it was from a long time ago and bad. Something that needs drugs. I heard pirates, but that's just a horror story. I really don't know."

Done," Socket said and turned to John. "Say, sailor, why don't you just ask her?"

"I'll do that." His nav-b console lit up with comm chatter, and he engaged a parser to extract the time stamps and origins from the packets. "Too many gravity wells to make this exact, but let's give it a go."

On Jerri's star map, he included three rays from the center point representing the vectors of the incoming signals. He rotated the projections until the sources aligned with the three well-known stations. Around the locus of rays, a new bubble appeared—one that was still much too large.

"Not small enough," she said with a smug grin and folded her arms across her chest.

He closed his eyes. "Second law of nav," he mumbled, "everything is moving all the time; nothing stands still, ever. And I flow within them." Based on the time stamp on the EM and time dilation, he adjusted the locations of the sources. This additional data changed the position of the station from where it appeared to be now to where it was when the signal originated. The bubble contracted. Some reliable beacons from Earth and two more sources fine-tuned his calculations, and the sphere shrank to a point with a fuzzy halo. Zooming into the star map, their current most probable location displayed on the console.

"OK, Jerri, check for a match," he said. "Say, anyone hear the score on the outbound?"

"Fourteen to nine, final," Stevens said. "Socket won the pool."

Jerri shifted the data over to her console and matched the major stars by their spectra and red shifts. "There we are." Their actual location lay just outside the original sphere. She glowered at Stevens. "Mass was wrong."

"Are we hauling military?" John asked.

Stevens nodded. "They're gonna get someone killed."

"Who'd know out here?" Jerri said.

"Time seven thirty-one. Eight minutes. Remember that if someone asks," John said and keyed a message to Meriel.

```
    To Hope: 8 min. ETA Lander dock, 15
hrs from jump.
```

"Stick around to check my course corrections," she said.

He grabbed the visualization goggles and reclined with his feet up. "Sure."

Stevens knocked John's feet off the console and threw his coffee in a recycler. "This is Hope's first post as chief, so don't eff it up. And don't startle her. She's qualified marine-three."

Interview with a Marine

"I'm parking the cruiser," Meriel said to Lev Tyler, her cargo-three, who waved in acknowledgment from the cargo-bay console. She backed the power loader against the bulkhead, secured it, and switched the servos to standby. With a half-liter thermos of coffee wedged into the loader's safety cage, she observed Lev complete the data-integrity checks on the ship's memory cargo.

Twenty-one days, and I don't have a clue, she thought and played with the pendant on her necklace that held the quantum-chip. "It's all here," her mother had said ten years ago. But it wasn't all there. The files were unreadable after the police returned the chip to her. She rubbed the medal, a symbol of the Church of Jesus Christ Spaceman, between her fingers. *Is this what she meant? Have faith? No.* Esther believed, but Meriel was sure she implied the q-chip. They would have to try again.

She keyed a message to her only nonspacer friend, a hacker named Nickolai Zanek on Enterprise.

```
    To nz:
    Panic. I need your help. I've got
twenty-one days to prove the Princess
wasn't a mule, or we lose her.
Forever. We need to bang on the q-chip
again. There has to be something. See
you on Enterprise.
    Love, M
```

It would be a week before she could meet him face-to-face. *What can I do until then?*

She scanned the schedules for the other kids. Tommy Spurell's ship, the *Jennifer Edwards*, would dock at Enterprise about the same time as the *Tiger* would. He was twenty now and stable as a rock. She messaged,

```
Let's touch base on Enterprise. M.
```

What else? There's gotta be something we've missed all this time.

The police filed the case as "unexplained," which left everyone with only the wrong explanation—that their cargo was contraband, and that implied drugs. She knew it could not be true, but the slander would stick if she walked away.

OK, then. Space is huge. How could pirates have found the Princess *in deep space? Aunt Teddy might know, but she's not here. How about a navy guy?*

On the cruiser's console, she searched the crew roster for marine qualifications. *Let's see, marine-two, another two, a six.* She whistled aloud. *Wow, a marine-six as chief of security. Charles Cook, Sergeant Major of the Marines. That's fleet rank. How'd this little ship bag somebody that good?*

She left to visit the security office and find him. Instead, she found a note which read, "At the gym."

***

Open mats and the absence of stale sweat made the *Tiger's* gym unusual. On one of the mats, a big man with short blond hair demolished a training droid by kicking it across the gym into the bulkhead. *Fast for someone so large*, she thought and went to the mats to stretch.

She began her kata almost as a meditation, a ritual she'd started as physical therapy for her injuries. Her movements were fluid, except for the strike at the end of each.

He stopped to watch her during her second iteration, and on the ninth position, he intervened.

"May I?" he asked.

Pausing, she nodded, skeptical that he might have useful coaching.

"Your rear knee should be bent, not stiff," he said and touched the outside edge of his hand to the inside of her knee. When her knee flexed involuntarily, he caught her arm to balance her. "And your heel off the mat when you begin your block."

"And you are?"

"They call me Cookie. You're marine qualified?"

"Yes, sir. Name's Meriel Hope."

He raised an eyebrow at her show of respect. "Oh yeah, new cargo chief. Marine-three, huh? Weapons?"

"Blasters, pulse rifles, nothing heavy."

"Combat?" he asked.

"No, sir."

"S'OK. Shooting for marine-four?"

"Not yet. I want to get better where I am."

"Good. Repeat your kata, and I'll oppose you."

"I've never done that before," she said.

"Yeah, that's what happens when you train by holo." He slipped an instrumentation cuff on his forearm. "Now, repeat movement nine beginning from eight."

Lining up in position eight, she rotated both feet for a downward strike with the blade of her hand. He stepped back and blocked with the cuff raised and right hand poised for a punch. She struck his padded forearm, but he restrained his counter.

"Hold that stance," he said and moved to her side. "See, if your heel is down before you begin your strike, the power comes from your muscles. That's weak. We want the power from your center." He slapped his tummy with his palm. "Drop the heel with your center and strike at the same time. Like this." He demonstrated the drop and strike. "Now you."

She imitated his movements, but he frowned and tapped her forehead with his index finger. "Get out of your head and into your center." He patted his tummy again. "Your body knows the pattern."

Meriel repeated the movements until he signaled his approval. She took her stance and struck his forearm again. But this time at the moment of impact, her body from her toes to her hand was one with the deck. Twisting his instrumentation cuff, she checked the readout and stared with wide eyes.

"See. Twice the impact force. OK, next movement."

She pivoted.

"Good. Pivot is fine, but just before the strike, your rear foot is planted, and your body turns from the hips in one motion, like a coiled spring." He took a stance opposing position one. "Again, from the start. And speed it up. Don't think."

This time her kata looked like a fight, each strike countered by a block, each block followed by a punch or kick. He was huge but moved like a lion. At the end, she glistened with sweat, and welts rose on her forearms and shins.

"Don't take the force of my blows," he said as he toweled the sweat from his forehead. "I outweigh you two to one in muscle. Divert my energy, and don't try to absorb it. Blend until your blows count."

"Yes, sir."

They bowed to each other and left for the showers.

"Say, you're marine-three," he said over the shower partition. "You passed zero-g defense, right? Gymnastics and center of gravity?"

"Yes."

"That makes you an optional for my security team," he said. "You OK with that? It'll bump your pay a grade."

"Sure."

"Let's call that your interview."

"Who's on the team?"

"Suzanne Soquette in comm, Nobu Draeger in the galley, and Lev Tyler, who works for you. He's my number two. Staff Sergeant Tyler, actually. Good man. Your marine-three cert will make you a squad leader like Socket. The captain's marine-two rated, but I don't count him."

"Sure," she said. "Say, do they teach you how to attack ships in space?"

"Uh, yeah. Hull breach, hand-to-hand weightless, EMP weapons. History mostly, not practice. Why?"

"How about defense in open space?"

"No. They always tell us that surprise is unlikely, even impossible without betrayal."

She finished her shower to listen. "How so?"

"Well, if you are smaller than a moon, it's too hard to find you in open space unless your attacker knows right where you're going to be." He left his shower stall. "And if your attacker is waiting for you, you can spot him before he spots you."

"How does that work?"

"Relatively fixed targets like stations are easier to find. Nothing at all like sublight or atmospheric." She furrowed her brow, and he tacked. "If you want a better explanation, you need to ask a pilot about coordinating in space and how hard it is. Jerri will know, and Smith would too."

She nodded once while considering the implications. "What about smugglers? If locating each other is so hard, why even try a drug drop in space?"

"Expense and time aren't issues when it's illegal or when secrecy is paramount."

Drugs again. This doesn't help. She finished dressing and saw John's message calling her bet. Then she met Cookie in the passageway.

"Let me know when you want to do this again," he said. "You can usually find me in the gym or the galley."

"Thank you." She smiled, grateful for her good luck, and turned to leave.

"Hey, I don't mean to pry, but is this about the *Princess*?"

Without speaking, she judged his intent. She did not talk about her past or her ship because the first thing people said was "sorry" or "poor girl" or "oh my God!" The last thing she wanted was pity.

"Don't misunderstand, Chief. I got nothing against you. I'm head of security. I read the files. You qualified marine-three and logistics-five, so you're welcome on my team."

"Appreciate it. Just not ready to talk about it."

"No problem. I'm off to the galley. Where you headed?"

"The mess to study. I have a nav-three test coming up.

"Isn't it noisy there?"

"Sure, but studying gets lonely, especially since that's all I do when I'm off duty."

They walked together to the mess hall, and Meriel sat down at a table.

He brought her coffee. "I'll bet Smith can help you with nav," he said with a glint in his eye.

"Uh-huh," she said with a glance which translated to, "Mind your own business."

"Hey, just saying." He smiled and left for the galley.

In the mess, she used her link to cast a holo of her test prep but could not focus; fear of losing the *Princess* and her means to keep the orphans together consumed her. *Calm down. Jeremy will have an idea.*

The five-minute claxon interrupted her, and she returned to her cabin to prepare for the jump. There she drank the nutrients, took the tranq without boost, and had another nightmare.

Chapter 3
Lander Station, Lalande 21185 System

Lander Station—Inbound

The *Tiger* dropped out of jump at the edge of the Lalande system and made a few mini-jumps to sync its velocity to that of Lander Station. Lander was the interstellar hub for the system and another transshipment logistics center. It was also the financial heart of the sector with the highest concentration of wealth outside of Earth and Sirius.

A few hours of one-g deceleration remained until the pilot ships and tugs met them, so Meriel returned to her cabin after checking the cargo. Jeremy, her lawyer, told her he'd be on the station and she keyed a message to him.

```
Will be on Lander by 2300. Where
should we meet? M
```

Then another to John.

```
I owe you a scotch. M
```

To which she received an immediate reply.

```
Ack. On duty. Will collect at
TarnGirl.
```

The Tarngirl was familiar to her: a spacer bar in Lander's blue-zone docks, just around the rim. Her thoughts drifted to John standing at the window gazing at the nebula. *Like a tree rooted to the deck, looking up at the stars.* She shook her head. *No time for that now.*

In her personal log, she added a new association, *attacks in open space,* and included what she learned from Cookie. In her calendar, she set a reminder to talk to John or Jerri about it.

Nav, she thought and fiddled with the pendant on her necklace, which held the jump program that had rescued them a decade ago.

"What were you trying to tell me, Mom?"

She queried the q-chip with her link and queued up the research on Home. It was unreadable, like all of the other data on the chip, but she knew from the name what it was. The holo was the single piece of evidence she had to support her mother's belief in Home. Home: the most sought-after real estate in the galaxy for everyone who didn't already live on Earth.

She retrieved a copy from a conspiracy site that had the same name as her mother's file: "Interview with J. Mouldersen." The vid was a low-res version of a hologram squeezed onto 2-D and might have been recorded by the unsteady hand of a holographer trying to hide. A forest of white jackets filled the foreground, beyond which two men and a woman sat at a table looking haggard, or perhaps tipsy, but smiling. Meriel could not make out any insignia of affiliation.

The woman behind the table stood. "Ladies and gentlemen, I have the most wonderful news. A few years ago, one of our remote survey probes returned and found what we've all been searching for. The data seemed crazy until we located a key. We discovered something marvelous, which—"

A woman's voice interrupted the speaker. "Cut the hyperbole, Jeannine. What did you find?"

"An earthlike object that—"

Loud grumblings interfered again. The conversation was almost inaudible and sounded like they were speaking from inside a locker with their mouths full of bread.

"We've found lots of earthlike objects but not *like* enough to be livable," said another voice.

Livability was the issue. People existed on many habitable bodies in space, but habitable referred to what humans could survive. The best were domed structures like Mars and Moon-1 that had enough wealth and energy to provide continual artificial gravity. The worst were low-g communes or overcrowded arcologies. These were hellholes that stretched the limits of human life.

Jeannine continued. "Really, it's earthlike—liquid water, high-oxygen atmosphere, close to one-g, temperate—" She continued to talk, but her voice disappeared in incomprehensible static and loud mumblings.

"It's bad data, Jeannine," shouted a new voice, "or faulty instrumentation. The probe should have come back with the others decades ago."

"Yeah, how'd it get lost?" someone asked.

"Apparently there's a lot of EM noise and dust nearby," Jeannine said, "and the probe got confused. It took the AI algorithm a while to figure out where it was before it returned home. Clever thing used spectra in the Magellanic cloud to orient itself."

"Did some real-estate speculator sign you up for this?"

"No, no. Have an independent lab audit us." The others at the table with Jeannine nodded.

The image spun and pointed to a blank wall—as if the camera had been placed against a chair leg. Black boots and tailored cuffs shuffled past.

"Meeting over. Stop recording," a man's garbled voice said. A few unintelligible hisses later, the vid cut off, either due to a dead battery or a judgment the rest was just noise.

After her parents' death, this clip, and the hope it represented, gave Meriel something to hold onto and sustained her with the dream of a home for the orphans. She and her little sister dreamed about Home and researched it obsessively. Even after the Troopers hustled them all into protective custody and fostered them out on different ships, they searched the net for vids that could hide additional clues.

But before that first year ran out, the dream was gone. When Meriel was just thirteen and too young to protest, they gave her a psych evaluation and medicated her to control the nightmares. The meds numbed her emotions, and she stopped caring about pretty much everybody and everything and hid herself in her work. She never told Elizabeth she had lost faith in Home, and she excused her apathy by calling the vid an amateur production, a teaser for a screenplay. By then it was too late; the social workers contracted her out to a new ship to split her from her sister, and they drifted apart.

At the thought of Elizabeth, she smiled, returned the device to her necklace, and switched back to her incoming messages.

```
Elizabeth K ET/2187:58:14.3
Hey, M, miss u!
I finished nav-two training and am
ready to solo, not that I really need
to. (I can't rightly tell the test
committee we jumped a starship when I
was ten, can I.)
Met Penny at her last stop at eIndi.
Some pretty face on the Murititius has
turned her into a lovesick puppy. He's
sweet but dull as a bolt.
M, regarding your last question
about my well-being…squawk…hiss…
reception is breaking up. Ha. How am I
doing? Feeling low. My LI (love
interest) swapped ships for a
promotion, and I won't see him for at
least a month. I don't know if it was
me or the new contract, but either
way, he dumped me. That leaves me the
only eligible female on the boat. His
replacement is a horror, some hairy
beast who thinks he's gonna move in,
and I can't be caught alone. There's a
slot in security on the Tjana matching
```

```
my marine-two qual. If the troll
persists, I'll transfer.
    I'll be at Etna about the time you
are, and maybe we can meet. LU always.
Littlebit.
```

Crap! I don't want her dragging spacers out of a drunk tank.

"Reply," she said to the console. "Sis, we want you on the bridge, not in security. Don't volunteer to be in the line of fire yet. Stay with comm for now; it's safer. And use the marine training to tame your admirers." *What can I tell her about the* Princess *that would be helpful? Nothing.* "Bad news from the lawyers. I'll tell you when I see you. Love, M. End reply."

She clicked on the message from twelve-year-old Harry Fisher, who still missed his older sister, Anita. A vid of him popped up. It looked like he lay in his bunk with the covers over his head.

"Meri, I wanna be with Anni," he said on the vid. "I don't like it here. The captain's great, and Ms. Lanceux is OK, but the kids tease me about being a foster. They play pirates all the time, and it's creepy. They don't get it, and I can't tell them.

"I haven't seen Anni in a year, M, and I'm not gonna see her for another month. I want to be with Anni, M. Please, please, please."

God, what do I say to him? His fosters have their own plans, and they'd never risk bringing Anita back aboard.

"Reply. Audio," Meriel said. "Begin. Harry, hon, hang in there. I'm doing what I can. The logs show you at Cygni about the same time as Sam. I'll make sure you two touch base. M. Stop. Send."

Harry's birthday is coming up. That's the worst of this, not having family there at special occasions. It's like celebrating on an asteroid all by yourself. Sure, friends help, but family is different. I'll have to do something memorable for him.

From the replicator, she grabbed a juice pack and chugged it. *Maybe I should have left them alone. Then they could adapt to the separation rather than giving them hope of getting back together again. Now they miss what we lost, and it stops them from finding happiness where they are, especially Harry. He was young enough to bond with a new family, and I keep tempting him with something I can't deliver.*

She shook her head. "Birthdays," she said, and a calendar with everyone's birthdays appeared. *Now, where will the kids be on Harry's birthday?* One of her duties was to post at least one of the other kids at every celebration, or have something special if no one could be there. But she never thought to celebrate her own.

A glance at her link showed another hour remained until dock. *So what can I do now?* she thought, playing with the pendant. *In less than twenty days, the* Princess *will be gone and the kids one misstep closer to hell.*

***

In her ready room, XO Molly Vingel squinched at the active wall across from her desk. There, numbers flashed, representing changing commodity prices for fuel and water on Lander. On the other walls looped pastoral views of the lush vegetation on Enterprise station's agriculture deck. Doc Ferrell's interruption caught her there by surprise.

"Can we do this later, Doc?" she asked. "I'm working."

"Exec, I need Hope's confidential file."

"Why?"

"I think she's off her meds, and that means she's dangerous."

She paused. "The *Jolly Roger* cleared her."

"It was conditional. She's a loose blaster, and if she goes off, it will reflect badly on my tour here."

She remained quiet.

"Do this, or I resign."

Captain Richard Vingel, her husband, leaned in from his adjoining ready room and raised an eyebrow.

She scribbled *untreated narcissist* in her log and held it up to show the captain and then returned to her link. "OK, Doc. Keep this confidential, and focus on her performance. You stir up her past, and I'll write you up—with prejudice. Your tour will be over. Clear?"

"Clear," Ferrell said.

When his wife ended the call, the captain spoke. "You don't trust him?"

She reclined in her chair. "Nope. He's the league's pick and a shrink rather than a surgeon. God help us if we need first aid. We had to take him or the insurance would break us. I'm searching for a replacement."

"Shame Doc Griffin had to leave so suddenly."

"Death in the family, he told me, but I'm not so sure. Griffin is older than dirt and should have outlived all his relatives. And he didn't seem to care about losing his tour bonus, either. He was just in a big damn hurry to leave."

"Let's find out where he went. Send a flier out for his whereabouts," he said and left.

***

In his tiny office next to the infirmary, Dr. Ferrell waited for access to Meriel's file. Confident no one would visit without a serious injury, he wagged a finger to frost the window and lock the door. On the desk in front of him, he placed a small whisky bottle and poured himself a drink.

Rotating his chair, he smiled at a picture of a young girl and raised his glass.

"One more year, Asha. Just one more year and my exile will end."

He tapped his link. "Open private journal. Create new record. Title Meriel Hope. Ship ID. Subtitle summary of confidential file review. Entry. Time stamp."

When the link chimed, he used hand motions to project the data on the wall.

ET/2177:38:57 Enterprise Independent
News Wire: LSM Princess (GCN
13442:88), family merchant ship, found

```
near Enterprise outer beacon, Procyon
system with only one survivor from an
unexplained tragedy. Unfolding.
```

"Well, that's pretty sketchy," he said. A quick search for the *Princess* and survivors located only the same article.

```
ET/2177:38:59 Global News Network:
LSM Princess attacked in deep space
by unknown assailants. Unidentified
surviving minor in protective custody.
Station authorities deny rumors of
piracy…
```

"They buried the story ten years ago. That would have made her almost thirteen."

```
ET/2177:105:19 Meriel Hope:
Daughter of Esther and Michael Hope.
Born ET/2165:85. Residence: family
merchant ship Princess until attack
ET/2177:37:10. Vessel severely damaged
and recycled. Details sealed by order
Superior Court 4, Enterprise, to
protect minor.
ET/2178:102 Meriel X: foster child
in protective custody of Enterprise
Station. Released to unidentified
merchant vessel, Cargo-0 trainee.
```

"Huh. Unidentified vessel. Witness protection? So what did she witness?"

The next item was a news vid dated ET/2181:86:13.

```
This is Lance Freiden of GNN on the
dock of the LSM Thrace. Sixteen-year-
old Meriel Hope surfaced today after
four years in protective custody. Hope
is the only survivor of an attack on
the LSM Princess. Claims of piracy
repeatedly dismissed by authorities…
```

Another search for information about the *Princess* and Meriel found nothing.

"No additional data on the attack. God, what a childhood."

Next, he scanned the training and certification logs.

"Rated nav-two, logistics-five," he dictated. "Ambitious. Only twenty-two and made logistics-five. Admirable. Marine-three. Yikes, is she preparing for a war?"

He waved his hand to skip forward to the arrest record and keyed in his ID for access to her private records.

```
   ET/2181:83 Dexter Station.
Aggravated assault. Ruled self-
defense.
   ET/2183:147 Ross Station. Resisting
arrest. Charges dismissed.
   ET/2184:220 Wolf Station. Disorderly
conduct. Charges dropped.
   ET/2184:259 Lander Station.
Aggravated assault on a bouncer.
Charges dismissed as self-defense.
Treated in blue-zone infirmary and
released to outpatient physical
therapy.
```

He chuckled. "Subject has evidence she is not invulnerable."

```
   ET/2185:315 Ross Station. Disturbing
the peace. Doctor testified as
personal reference. Released without
charges.

   Profile—psych:
```

"Here we are."

```
   Tests: EMR 485. STM 223. KRTT 454,
Briggs and Hall E3R4. MMPI-GAX3.
```

"Tests out as a loner and driven," he said. "E3R4 borderline psychotic. Request data that produced those MMPI scores."

```
ET/2180:115:19.50 LSM Thrace (GCN
23492:06) X. Johansen, PhD.
   Quick learner. Highly motivated.
Gets along well with crew.
   Enduring nightmares of childhood
trauma on Princess. During counseling,
she still speaks of the Princess as
her ship and plans to reclaim it. She
also speaks of getting custody of
supposed orphans from the Princess and
chartering routes in Sector 42.
Requests to the captain for legal
assistance denied. Court records are
sealed. No evidence found of legal
rights to, or existence of, the
Princess or any other survivors…
```

He poured himself another drink. "No evidence of other survivors," he said aloud to his journal. "She was alone but thinks the other kids are still alive. Symptoms of survivor's guilt. Damn, that's tough."

```
   Diagnosis: severe neurotic
delusions, bordering on psychosis.
Becomes agitated when fantasies are
challenged. Well-adjusted teen as long
as fantasy remains intact. Working
with her to adapt to the reality that
all of the crew and her friends on the
Princess were lost.
   Prescribed mandatory antipsychotics.
Psychogel-H (H1804-005) (aka
Aristopine).
```

"Makes sense," he said. "Private journal. Analysis. Adaptation to trauma by creating a fictional reality. Truth too difficult to face head on. Uncertain which world she is living in now."

> ET/2184:115:20 LSM *Commodore Levski* (GCN 65512:43) Dr. Botev.
> Excellent crew member. Commendation for diligence.
> Resistant to counseling and analysis. Not willing to discuss the *Princess* incident. Court records are unavailable, and no evidence to substantiate delusions. Continuing mandatory antipsychotics.

> ET/2186:152:12 LSM *Jolly Roger* (GCN 41223:21) Dr. L. Kustenov.
> Excellent crewman. Eager to work.
> Bailed out on Lockyear Station for illegal tranq boost. Reluctant to discuss it. Resisting therapy and analysis. Will discuss nothing about the *Princess* tragedy. Ongoing antipsychotic medication. Check of comm traffic (Cpt's approval on record) indicates communication with a low-rent lawyer (J. Bell esq. of Ross). Discussions confidential, but believed to regard custody of *Princess* and fictional orphans. While she has that fantasy to structure her reality, she appears in control. Without that, or the meds, her stability is uncertain.
> ET/2186:283 Captain's commendation for exceptional service. Unconditional recommendation.

He paced the three steps across his tiny office. *Damn.*

"Private journal. Summary. Entire crew killed—parents, kids, everyone. She must have been through hell, and maybe still going through it. How could she survive? How'd she jump back to a station?"

He sat down at the console again and drummed his fingers on his desk. "Delusions and barely in control, never lost it on duty, but maybe dockside at Lander Station. Now she's brought this cheap lawyer into her fantasy world? Conclusion. Insufficient information to modify treatment. Personal history is tragic but refuses trauma counseling that might relieve symptoms. Monitor to assure sustained medication. Close private journal."

"Append ship's file, Chief Meriel Hope," he said. "Entry, ship ID, time stamp now, name. Begin. Hope comes highly recommended. No meeting yet to form professional opinion. Continue mandatory medication. Close."

The file blinked out and the console squawked. "Time limit exceeded. Please see administrator for continued access."

He raised his middle finger to the console. Turning back to the picture of Asha, he raised his glass.

"One more year, honey." He frowned. "If Ms. Hope doesn't self-destruct first. I sure hope she opens up to someone about this before it consumes her. Poor kid. It's a shame what happened to her."

He topped off his glass again, which emptied the bottle.

"Append private journal. Reminder to complain about shrinking whisky allocation."

Lander Station—On Station

In the constant drizzle of condensation from the high ceilings and the smells of oil and stale beer, Meriel wrangled her cargo loader. Lander's wide, cigar-shaped cross section made unloading easy for her crew and the faceless labor droids. She stopped the cruiser when a message appeared from her lawyer.

Meet me at Pierre's, w4552. J

White-zone, she thought and looked down at her stained fatigues. *Totally inappropriate.*

Cookie led the off-duty crew out of the lock but slowed near the dockside ramp and waved to her. "Meriel, we're bound for the TarnGirl. Gonna join us? John will be there." He gave her another cagey smile.

"Sure," she said. "But I need to finish up and do some shopping first."

Two hours later, after unloading and a quick shower, she left the *Tiger* via the blue-zone docks heading for the meeting with her lawyer. On her wrist, a more stylish bracelet link replaced her visor. *That's not enough.* White-zone was special, with fancy shops and clubs intended for station administration and finance personnel—all of it too bright and expensive for spacers. She altered course to procure more suitable clothes.

In a green-zone shop, she picked out a versatile, high-collared outfit that covered her scar. The fabric mimicked a range of styles using a tab on the sleeve, including her current selection: the "little black dress" option. Satisfied with her camouflage, she stuffed her fatigues into her bag and headed for the exit. Without thinking, she turned away from the pervasive surveillance cameras, paid with a cash chit, and left the store concealed within a group of women.

Well-dressed adults and children without the lean and nervous look typical of spacers filled the white-zone concourse. When passersby glanced at her, their generous demeanor disappeared, and their eyes narrowed with suspicion. She felt out of place and wondered if her simple frock made her too obviously a stranger. Then she remembered the cold glares might simply be the security scans of android nannies.

At Pierre's, a man in a dark-gray uniform thawed the chill of white-zone with a warm smile. He opened the door for her to a busy public square with a ceiling so high clouds drifted above. Tiny white-and-pink petals from the cherry and plum trees surrounding the plaza danced in the air and blanketed the cobblestones. Between the stones, pigeons pecked at crumbs brushed from café tables. Artists sketched young couples while mimes entertained the children. The scents of coffee and pastries and the sounds of a jazz trio surrounded her. The tension in her body vanished, and she switched the dress option from black to a white sundress with a rose print.

"Ms. Hope," a voice called, and she turned to see a man waving from a small table at an outdoor café nearby. It was Jeremy, looking quite professional in an impeccably tailored business suit. As she walked to him, he pulled out a chair for her. They shook hands, and she blushed: spacers never treated women with this much courtesy. A snap of his fingers brought a waiter with two glasses containing a dark-red liquid.

"Nice, huh?" he said. "It's Montmartre, Paris, on Earth. That's the basilica behind me."

"Is this all for me?"

"Yes, of course, my dear," he said with a smile and a flourish of his arms. "Really, my clients invited me here for lunch." He kept his expression, but his playful mood could not overcome her impatience.

"The impound was supposed to be a technicality and temporary, Jeremy. That's what you're working on."

"Let's order first."

"I'm not hungry."

"I insist." He called the waiter over and ordered something in French. She searched for a kiosk to sync with the dietary profile on her link but did not find it. Smiling, he shook his head.

When the waiter left, she leaned over with her elbows on the table. "She's ours, Jeremy. The *Princess* belongs to us."

"Not for long. The shippers sued to recoup their losses on the stolen cargo. It's not much, but with the dock fees, Enterprise doesn't think your income will cover it. Ever. Frankly, I don't know how your parents could keep your ship operating with such a cheap payload."

"Jeremy, that last jump was profitable. I heard my folks talking about it."

"Then the biggest shippers didn't sue."

"Who were they?" Meriel asked.

"Can't tell without the manifest."

"Right, and that was wiped, along with everything else on the ship. But we were insured."

"The insurance companies denied the claims since the *Princess* is implicated in drug smuggling."

"Scabs."

"If you take responsibility for your ship, then you're responsible for her debts. You'll need to pay or declare bankruptcy."

"Damn, it keeps getting better."

"The station thinks forfeiture will cover the expenses and your liability."

"My folks would never do anything like smuggle drugs. And they never found anything to implicate the *Princess* or the crew."

"No one has adequately explained an attack in deep space, Meriel. A bad drug deal is the easiest interpretation."

"And the most convenient. If they ruled it piracy, the merchant fleets might refuse to fly."

"Yes, yes, and the stations would die without the trade. You're right of course, and it's all circumstantial. If you had disappeared, they would write it off as bad nav or pilot error. Showing up the way you did leaves only piracy or smuggling. Piracy is rarer than a black swan, so they're stuck with a drug drop as the only acceptable explanation."

"But they have no evidence!"

"Absence of evidence is not proof of innocence," he said. "With all else equal, the simplest explanation, the one with the fewest assumptions, is usually the truth. That's how they see this."

"That's Occam's razor, Jeremy. We have science now."

"These are judges, not scientists, and law is much older than science. Most scientists believe everything taught is the truth and build on that; they extrapolate in one direction or another. Judges see scientific theories as temporary agreements that live only until more useful explanations arise. From Newton to Einstein and now Nakamura, science evolves more powerful explanations. The judges have nothing but speculation, but it's the most logical and useful speculation."

"Useful for them."

The waiter returned with two small plates. Gracing hers lay a pastry containing a variety of fruit and vegetable sprouts surrounded by abstract patterns drawn in dark-brown and red sauces. It was beautiful.

Oh my God. She stared with her mouth open. "Is this fresh?" He nodded, and she blanched with fear. "Am I paying for it?"

He grinned at her discomfort. "No."

She sighed, having been saved from a bill she might never be able to pay.

"Enjoy it. My clients paid for it all. Where were we?"

"Jeremy, they have no proof."

"Your parents are guilty until proven innocent. It's Napoleonic law out here, Meriel, not like America before the UNE."

"How can they do this? My folks never did anything wrong," she said while drawing spirals in the sauce.

"They were in debt."

She stopped fidgeting and glowered at him. "Everybody's in debt. They'd never carry anything illegal or dangerous. Papa even did long jumps to keep us near stations."

"It was a big debt."

"Never, J, never!"

"Then prove it."

"We were just kids, Jeremy. We had to depend on the Biadez Foundation investigation, and the private investigators never seemed to dig up anything new. I don't have a lead."

"Find one."

"My ship will stop at Enterprise next week, and I can visit the *Princess*."

He shook his head. "You'll need a court order, and that will take too long."

"Then what the hell can we do now? The police picked apart every bit of data on the *Princess*. They found nothing, Jeremy—the pirates wiped all of it." She held out the pendant. "And they screwed with my chip. The only thing my mom left us, and they ruined it. The police and Troopers examined every inch of our ship, every deck plate and hidey-hole. They found nothing but a pair of counterfeit designer shoes and some unidentified hair."

"That hair came from a stim user, Meriel."

"Not our crew! Not the *Princess*!" She threw down her fork and lowered her head to hide her tears. He laid his hand on hers.

In a soft voice, she said, "The cops took everything, Jeremy, even our stupid toys. Liz and I don't have a single vid of our parents. And now they're taking our ship."

He laid a handkerchief by her hand. "Vids of the adults could be dangerous for the kids, Meriel. They're still in protective custody."

She took the handkerchief and brought it to her eyes. "Well, I'm not. And so what?" Holding out the pendant again, she said, "This and the *Princess* are all my sister and I have to remember our folks and our friends. The other kids got nothing at all." After a deep breath, she shook her head and exhaled slowly. "What about a delay?"

"I tried. Extensions are often automatic...but not this time."

"Can we buy her?"

"No. They got the bid they wanted and closed the bidding. No announcements."

"Is that legal?"

"For an impound that's damaged, yes." He stiffened and leaned over the table. "Ms. Hope, as your attorney, it is my responsibility to inform you a generous settlement has been offered to you first, not to the station." He pulled out a link and displayed the offer letter. The sum, in bold, was a fantastic amount of money.

She whistled. "Almost enough for a new boat."

"But not quite. It's like they're trying to discourage opposition."

"Like me."

"Or our mutual friend."

He means Teddy. "They don't want me to have my ship but will compensate me when they steal her. This stinks."

"I must caution you that you could lose everything if you pass up this offer. If you let the remaining time expire, you'll forfeit your rights, including any remainder from the proceeds. You'll get nothing. Finding exculpatory evidence in less than three weeks is unlikely. Any such information would still be subject to the ruling of the court, which can never be certain."

She remained quiet.

"The settlement can set you up, Meriel."

"You mean buy me off." She was ready to spit or cry but not sure which.

"As your counsel, I advise you to be prudent and take the cash if you can't meet the court's demands. Make your peace with this and move on. Lots of people would say you've been through enough."

"It's not about me, Jeremy. It's about the kids. They have nothing—parents gone, ship in a graveyard, no future. All we've got is the *Princess* and each other. That bid will not go very far divided among eight of us."

"Don't misunderstand, Ms. Hope. The offer is to you, not them. They don't exist except in records sealed by the court."

"But I can't just take it and run."

"It won't free the *Princess*, and it won't buy a working vessel, but it's something, even split eight ways."

"It's not enough to save us from drifting into danger if we're alone," she said. "Did Teddy tell you about when Penny went missing?"

"No."

"Penny is a real pretty kid—" she began to say.

"It runs in your family," he said with a playful grin, but Meriel tilted her head without recognizing his compliment.

"People always told Penny she was pretty, but her mom and pop played it down, hoping she might not let that define her. Well, on her ninth birthday, she disappeared from a play area on Ross."

"What about her biotag? Her link?"

"I'll get to that. Anyway, the kids scoured the station for her with no luck. Sam Spurell, Tommy's little brother, found her. He looked after her because her older brother got spaced on their prior ship. That's why her folks signed on to the *Princess*. Well, Sam knew she wanted something for her mom for Mother's Day, and a holo might be the thing. He spotted her down the boardwalk in a dress-up shop. We all rushed there as soon as he called.

"We found Penny in tears all tarted up with big hair and lots of makeup like she was going on twenty years old—unrecognizable. But Sam recognized her. My father called the police and made a huge fuss. Apparently, the shop owner lured her in with free vids. They had a jammer to mask the biotags, which made her untraceable."

"EtnaVid?" he asked, and she nodded. "I heard of them. Lucky you found her in time."

"Not luck. Family. They closed them down soon after."

"What happened to Penny?"

"Her mom got her out of there before the shouting and took her and us girls to a legit studio. They scrubbed off her makeup, washed her hair, and redid her with a little blush and a French braid. She was gorgeous. The photographer offered to introduce them to an agent, and her folks had the good sense to say no. But he kept a copy of the stills for advertising."

"You saw it?"

"Yeah. The holo is still there. And she's only gotten prettier. You can't hide beauty like hers. We all know she's gonna waltz into a white-zone party when she gets older and walk out with a prince. But I'll bet Sam will be two steps behind him, checking his pedigree." She took a breath. "We almost lost her, and without the family, we would have. We're stronger together, Jeremy. I want this for them."

"It doesn't change things with the *Princess*."

She tried her pathetic kitten look. "There's nothing you can do?"

"Not without being disbarred."

She prepared to suggest something, but he raised his hand.

"I can't help you if I lose my license."

She sighed and stared at her uneaten lunch. "How many days to decide on the money?"

"Ten days, ET."

"Damn. How can they do this? My parents never did anything wrong."

"Prove it. Bring the judges a better explanation—means, motive, opportunity. Give them a story other than their speculations. I'll do all I can to help." The link on his wrist buzzed, and he glanced at it. "Excuse me, Ms. Hope, I have another appointment. Please advise me of your decision as soon as possible."

He rose and took her offered hand in both of his. She blushed again at the attention, but when she tried to pull away, he maintained his hold.

"Now, business aside," he said with a steady gaze, "I did mention the authorities relocated the *Liu Yang* to the impound dock, yes?" When she nodded, he smiled and released her hand. "Great to see you again, Meriel."

She considered his parting words as he walked away. Of course, she knew they had moved the *Princess*. They had just talked about it, and he told her she could not visit legally. *Then why would—*

The waiter interrupted her thoughts with a polite bow. "Pardon me, miss, but is there something wrong with your lunch? I am sure Chef Pierre would be happy to prepare something unique if this is not to your liking. Perhaps an *ile flottante* or raspberry *crêpes* with *crème fraiche*?"

Having no idea what he referred to, she said only, "No, thank you. I'm sure that would be delicious, but I'm just not hungry."

For an instant, one eye squinted and a corner of his lip trembled as if suppressing an insult, but then he granted absolution with a nod. "As you wish. If I may, we will close for the afternoon in approximately five minutes. If there is anything else I can help you with, please signal me."

"Thank you," she said, and he took her lunch plate, the only fresh food she had been served in her entire life, away untouched.

She viewed the busy square and the beautiful day and sighed. The *Princess* settlement would buy her a vacation on Earth, perhaps in the real Paris, but it would only be for her and only for a little while. And when she left, it would all be gone, every physical reminder of her ship, her childhood, and her family. Everything would be gone forever. *Still, I would have something more than I have now.*

With lips pressed together, she surveyed the plaza. *No. This is beautiful, but it's just an illusion. This isn't my life.* She would need to prove the *Princess* was not a mule and her parents were not drug dealers. *But how do you prove a negative?*

As Meriel walked out of the café, the hologram faded away, and the space became featureless gray walls and ceiling. When the doors closed behind her, the waiters and customers, all mindless androids, lined themselves up against a wall and turned themselves off.

Outside, Meriel switched back to the "simple black dress" option and walked to the edge of the torus to avoid the security cameras. There she boarded a tram headed for green-zone—where the regular folk went to relax, and the elites went to tarnish their reputations. Her mission there was uncomplicated: score some tranq boost to dispel her nightmares without taking the meds.

Neon holograms flashed outside the transparent ceramic window. Another tram passed in sync with hers every few moments to balance the mass and smooth the microgravity tremors with a compensating angular acceleration.

The view was the same from the tram on Runner Station in the Ross 128 system, except she remembered the flashing advertisements to be a lifeless gray. That was where Elizabeth found her seven years ago.

***

All of the color was drained from her life then. The vibrant signage of the blue-zone bars and businesses that flashed by outside the window left no impression on her. She was alone—three years after the *Princess* attack. Her parents were dead, and her sister was light-years away.

She knew what she had seen that day and could not forget, no matter how much she wanted to. The anonymous white jackets told her all the reasons why the attack couldn't have happened the way she said. With pleasant smiles, they complimented her on her rich fantasy life and creative imagination.

But the smiles turned cold when she wouldn't align her memories to the stories they wanted, stories of drugs and intrigue that she would never believe. And she couldn't align them. If she went along with their story, it would unmoor her from all reality. The truth was horrible, but it was not crazy and did not slander her parents. The truth was not a fantasy to make her feel better or a lie to make others feel better.

But the truth was too much for her to bear alone.

In their notes, her detailed accounts became delusions that required medication. After months of interviews, therapy, and separation, she doubted herself. Unable to invent a story that made sense to her and them both, she stopped fighting and took the meds.

Now at fifteen, she had no friends and desired none. There was only the job and the biological need to be suitably compliant for the leadership and the young men on her ship. She thought only of getting a part for her power loader. Without that part, she would fail her cargo-two exam and delay the pay bump another year.

Within that lifeless, gray world, a young blond girl boarded the tram accompanied by an older woman who gave her a sad smile. From somewhere, Meriel remembered the faces and returned a polite nod, but there was no emotional tug, and she averted her eyes. It was her sister, Elizabeth, with Aunt Teddy.

Elizabeth sat next to her and took her hand. "I've been looking for you, Sis."

"Uh-huh," Meriel said.

"Where did you go? I miss you."

She shrugged. The briefest memory flickered that once in her life, this young girl meant more to her than life itself, but the thought slipped away.

A tear rolled down Elizabeth's cheek. "We've been at the same docks, and you never come by. You don't answer my messages anymore. It's like you don't remember me at all."

Meriel ignored her and read the advertising on the seatback, wondering when the blond person would leave.

Reflected in the window, she watched Elizabeth reach out to her. But just before touching the scar on her neck, Elizabeth clenched her hand into a fist. She pulled her hand back and rummaged through Meriel's purse. There, she found the meds, Aristopine, the same drug the doctors planned to give her and all the orphans from the *Princess*.

Elizabeth held up the tube of meds. Teddy nodded, tapped her link, and checked the transit map. Four stops later, she waved, and Elizabeth took Meriel's arm.

"Come with me, M," Elizabeth said and stood.

Meriel rose reluctantly. "I need to pick up a part for my cruiser."

"We'll go there next, but first we have to stop here," Elizabeth said and led her from the tram.

Inside the green-zone corridors, Meriel stopped and looked around as if she had just woken up. "Why are we going this way? I need to fix my cruiser."

"Mom said you need my help. You want to do what Mom says, don't you?" Elizabeth said.

"Sure."

"Well, then we need to go this way. Come."

Before entering the rehabilitation clinic, Elizabeth dropped the meds in the recycling chute at the entrance.

Elizabeth and Aunt Teddy stayed with her for a week until the meds had flushed from her system, and she finally cried. The drugs had helped her push the memories of the attack to the depths of her psyche and dragged the kids down there with them. Without the drugs, it all came back in a rush. But it wasn't so overwhelming this time, because her little sister remained with her through it all. It was there she learned techniques to control her symptoms, including conscious blinking and contact with the other orphans to keep her grounded in reality.

When Elizabeth told her that she had shrugged them off, it scared her. She swore to Elizabeth she'd never take the meds again, regardless of the nightmares.

Her ship had noticed immediately because of her noncompliance and recurring night terrors. They tried to get her back on the medications and threatened to suspend her work card and certifications, but after her sister scared her, she understood it was wrong.

Her shipmates didn't help. "Meriel, just go with the flow," they had told her. "Take 'em and get along. Lots of us do it."

At the time, she didn't know what to tell them and kept quiet. What was she, all of fifteen and a half? Now she knew what to say: *Why take pills to adjust to a world that sucks?* It's seductive to take a vacation from reality for a bit, hoping things will be different when you come back to real life, but life doesn't change so easily. *Instead, make the world adjust to you. You don't need to be an ass or a bully, but you don't have to accept the crap either. Our ancestors didn't stay up in the trees and numb themselves to relieve their fear of tigers; they adapted, climbed down, and made spears.*

Her spear was a lie. Behind that lie, they devised ways to fool the psych evaluations and keep Elizabeth and the kids from having the meds forced on them. And part of that meant using boost instead of the meds to quell the nightmares.

But the meds were on her record as a requirement for her to drive cargo equipment. If they found out she was taking boost, they'd know she was not on her meds. They'd ground her, and she'd be working on some hell-hole mining asteroid just to eat. So to score the boost, she had to be discreet.

***

Meriel exited the tram and walked to her destination: Heinhold's, a watering hole for neighbors and upscale stationers with no business in green-zone. It was dark, discreet, and nearly empty.

She sat at the bar, and a huge bartender with a chin the size of her fist approached, drying a glass with a towel.

"What'll it be?" he asked.

"Teddy here?"

Without moving his head, he scanned her, the room, and the door behind her. He settled his elbow on the counter and flexed a hefty tattooed bicep in front of her while polishing the glass, and then eyed her with a cold squint. "No one here by that name."

"Tell her Hope has returned."

"No promises." He walked to the other end of the bar and picked up a link.

Above the bar, a large monitor displayed the latest news from IGB, InterGalactic Broadcasting, one of the few honest networks, and she watched while she waited.

> "In business news, LML Corp,
> representing the Local Merchants
> League, has added new routes to Alpha
> Station in the Alpha Centauri system
> and nearby asteroid habitats. This is
> a result of the redesigned and
> rehabilitated stations at Alpha and
> Proxima Centauri…"

A nicely dressed woman about Meriel's age sat next to her and interrupted her thoughts with a professional smile. "Hey, spacer, need company?"

Meriel recognized a subtle spacer tattoo on her inner wrist. "No, thanks. Bunk's full, but have one on me." She gave her a large tip, about a night's worth. The woman smiled, genuinely this time, laid her hand on Meriel's arm, and then left.

Must have lost her ship or her sailor. Tough life. That might have been Penny in a few years. Or me.

She returned part of her attention to the news.

```
"Top news in Sol System, recently
elected UNE President Biadez pledged
to uphold the United Nations of Earth
charter today at his inauguration
ceremony..."
```

The bartender, still on the link, looked back at her and stared for a few moments before turning away. On the monitor, Biadez began to speak.

```
"My fellow citizens of Earth, we
stand here on the brink of a
resurgence of Earth's influence on the
galactic stage. After decades of
stagnation, the peoples of Sol are
waking to restore the vitality and
prosperity..."
```

Meriel surveyed the bar again. A woman in an expensive business suit now sat at a small table. With black hair pulled back severely, she might have been a CEO or a corporate counsel. Her glasses shimmered slightly—a head-up display out of focus for anyone but the wearer. She waved to Meriel with a broad smile.

Other than Elizabeth, this woman was the only person in the galaxy in whom Meriel could confide: Theodora Duncan, her mother's childhood friend and nav-six—so skilled she could work any boat, even navy.

"Hi, sweetie," Teddy said and signaled for drinks.

Meriel joined her and gave her a hug. As she sat, she tipped her head in the direction of the girl who had approached her earlier.

"What's her story?"

Teddy shrugged. "Don't know. She doesn't work for me. I don't have the heart to stop them. They're all independent. We space pimps around here, and I make sure they know it."

Meriel glanced back at the monitor on which Biadez continued his inaugural address.

Teddy dropped her smile. "He's still your hero, isn't he?"

"Who?"

Teddy wagged a thumb toward the monitor.

"Biadez? Well, yeah, I guess. No one forced him to help us, them, I mean; his foundation didn't have to help us." The Alan C. Biadez Humanitarian Foundation had helped them with their medical bills and relocation costs. They also funded the investigation. "The kids treat him like a grandfather. They still send him Christmas cards. Anonymously, of course."

"Does he ever respond?" Teddy asked through clenched teeth.

"Not really. They reply with those corporate bulk vids. He's a busy guy, and none of us takes it personally. We're not supposed to have any contact at all."

"You know what I think."

"Yeah, I—"

"I think they're a bunch of bastards."

"You're still mad because they cut you out of the custody hearings."

"No. Because they put you on meds so young—addictive meds."

"Those were the shrinks, Teddy."

"Sure, but the foundation paid for them."

The foundation was the biggest donor to the orphans' care. They squeezed out the others, including Teddy, who had petitioned so aggressively for custody that the court issued restraining orders.

"That's why I came, Teddy. Boost. My nightmares flared up again when we started working the old *Princess* routes. They won't leave me now."

"Boost is legal here, you know."

"I can't have a trail that shows I've got 'em. They'll know I'm off the meds and void my work card."

"We'll take care of you." Teddy tapped on her glasses, and the bartender turned to her. She nodded, and he scanned his link.

Teddy brightened. "Say, did I tell you I met Kendal Grannath?"

"Who?" she said and eyed the door.

"Grannath. Doesn't ring a bell?"

She shook her head and played with the miniature umbrella in her drink.

"Her grandpa designed your ship. She told me the *Princess* was her grandpa's favorite. Had a model on his desk wherever he worked. She showed me vids of the original interior. Did you know the *Princess* was a private yacht? It was gorgeous. The cargo bays moored private shuttles." Her smile changed to concern as she waited for Meriel's response. "It's more than the boost, M. What's bothering you? Is Jeremy making progress? I heard he's visiting Lander today."

Meriel looked up with an arched brow and spoke with a brittle voice. "They're gonna take her, Teddy."

"Who?"

"The *Princess*. And I can't stop them."

"No. How?"

"As a drug boat, if I can't prove we were clean."

"By when?"

"The court gave us twenty-one days. Nineteen, now."

Teddy arched her brows. "Is bidding open? Let's buy her."

"Jeremy told me the bidding was private, and it's closed."

"Odd. It's like they were trying to preclude competing bids."

"That's what he said."

"What jurisdiction?"

"Enterprise. She's still in impound."

"I'll talk to Jeremy, M. Don't give up."

"They're trying to buy me off."

"How much?"

She showed her the settlement.

Teddy's eyes narrowed to slits. "This smells fishy. What's your plan?"

"Well, talking to Jeremy and you first."

"Next?"

"Nick."

"Take another shot at the data chip?" Teddy asked, and she nodded. "That's low probability. You need a motive other than drugs, M. They left you and the *Princess* at one-g going nowhere. They wanted you to disappear without a trace."

"Ships disappear all the time."

"Too many to be random or system failures. OK, we need other motives. What else you got?"

Meriel whispered, "If we stop at Enterprise as planned, I may—"

Teddy sat up straight and wagged a finger. Then she said loudly, "I'm sure anything you might consider is unquestionably legal." She lowered her voice. "Let me look into it. You've always got a place here. You know that."

"What about all the kids?"

"The court won't let me near them, M—"

"Yeah, the restraining orders."

"Not unless they come out of protection, and I'm not sure that's a good idea. I'm still not sure it was good for you to come out."

"Then they'll drift."

"We won't let that happen, M."

They updated each other about the kids and friends over a second round of drinks. When the glasses were empty, the bartender gave Teddy a slip of paper that disintegrated a few seconds after she touched it.

"See the man at the fish-and-chips stand around the corner," Teddy said. "Tell him you want the regular. Leave the money with Ed at the bar on the way out. It's not for me; it's for them."

"Thanks. Say, do you ever see Torsten?"

Teddy smiled, and her eyes softened. "Not since May, dear, but he's fine. He'll be here in two weeks."

"You ever think of going back to the *Endeavor*?" That was Torsten's ship, a midsize independent freighter working a vector from Earth to Den 10.

"You know, I bought a ship to chase him once," Teddy said with a drifty look. "A sleek job, real graceful, and I could fly her by myself. Now? Nah. He's got to come to me. He needs to be in space, and I won't have another."

"Thanks, Teddy. I gotta go now." They hugged again, and Meriel left.

***

Meriel made her trade for boost and changed her course to blue-zone for the crew's party. All the while, she pondered how to save the *Princess* and prove she wasn't involved in transporting drugs. Two toughs leaned against the elevator door. She made sure not to make eye contact, but it didn't matter.

"Hey, doll," one of them said. "You got something of mine."

Ignoring him, she turned to find another route.

"Hey, I'm talking to you."

Footsteps behind her quickened, and she prepared to run. But a hulk of a man, wide-eyed and grinning with a stim dose, stepped out in front of her.

"Hey, cruiser," he said while picking his teeth with a tiny fingernail. Her momentum carried her into his range and he swung a fist at her cheek. Without thinking, she dodged and raised her arm to block. His blow hit her shoulder and banged her against the wall. The bag flew from her hands, causing her fatigues to spill out. *You don't punch a woman unless you're willing to kill her.* She looked for an escape but found none.

The three approached her, the biggest first. The rules of street fights flashed through her mind: *if you can't avoid a brawl, strike first and make it decisive, because you may not get a second chance.* In an instant, she sized them up. They outweighed and outmuscled her, but she had one advantage:

they were high on lust and drugs, and she was high on adrenaline. Time slowed down, and she noticed minute details: the unshaven face of the tall lanky one, the stun baton in the hand of the dark one, the small pin with a clover on the big one. And he lunged first.

Muscle memory engaged, and she kicked the mugger in the neck. Holding his throat, he dropped to his knees and gasped as he faded into unconsciousness. The other two cornered her but kept their distance, now more cautious.

A voice to her left spoke. "You owe me a scotch."

Meriel spun, expecting a new assailant. Instead, John Smith from the *Tiger* stood there, flat-footed and unprepared.

"Be with you in a minute," she said and turned back to her attackers, prepared to defend them both.

He surprised her by walking up beside her, and he held up a small tube. "Cover your ears. Trust me. Now."

She dropped her guard to protect her ears while the muggers closed in. John stepped in front of her and squeezed the tube. The air around her assailants quivered and hazed, and a soft pop blew her hair back. The two men fell to their knees, bleeding from their noses and ears. John turned to leave, but Meriel walked over to the attackers, picked up her bag and fatigues, and kicked each man in the groin.

"That was cruel," he said as they walked away.

"What do you think they had in mind for me?"

"You know him?"

"God, no."

"He called you 'cruiser.'"

"I think he was going for 'slut.' What are you doing up here?"

"I could ask the same of you," he said, evading her question.

"Heading for the TarnGirl?" she asked while peering into the shadows for threats.

"I have an appointment first."

Noting his nonanswer and the package under his arm, she stopped. "What's that?"

"Pharmaceuticals and—"

She stared at him. "Son of a…you're dealing drugs."

"No, no."

"What is it? Rejuve? Stim?"

"No, really, they're life enhancing. It's what we do on my colony."

How could I be so wrong in sizing this guy up? "I don't believe you."

"Please, let me explain."

"I can't get caught with you." While backing away from him, she checked for security cameras. "I'll lose the kids."

"Meriel, please. Nothing I have with me can get you into trouble with the law. I promise."

"They're not illegal?"

"Not yet, not until our competitors find out about 'em."

She did not move.

"Please, let me show you."

Still skeptical, she nodded, and they left for white-zone. He led her to a plain building with a small green cross by the door.

"Hospital?" she asked.

"Recovery facility. A clinic for physical therapy and rehabilitation."

He introduced himself to the receptionist and signed them in. Before she had adjusted to the smells of alcohol and disinfectant, a man in a white coat met them.

"You are Mr. Brown?" the man in the white coat said. He took off his name tag and dropped it into his pocket. "And Ms. White?"

John extended his hand. "Yes. Pleased to meet you. Doctor Wo, is that correct?"

The doctor nodded and shook his hand while Meriel rolled her eyes at the charade.

"As part of our quality control, my associate and I would like to review the efficacy of the prior samples left with you."

"Yes, of course. This way, please." The doctor led them down a corridor to a small room where a patient sat covered from head to foot in a gown. A hood protected his face from the harsh clinical lighting.

"This is our burn unit," the doctor said and showed them into the room. "Hello, Phillip. May we see your progress?"

The hood dipped, and the doctor sat on a stool facing him. He took the patient's right hand and rolled the sleeve up to the elbow to expose perfectly normal pink skin. "We're treating him with your product C, I believe." He raised the sleeve to reveal the extensive scarring above the elbow.

"As your associate promised, there is no scarring at the tissue boundaries, and melanin is normal." He took both of Phillip's hands and rotated them together for comparison: badly scarred on the left and fully recovered on the right.

Without thinking, she placed her hand to the scar on her neck and glanced up with a smile. She expected to see the face of a grateful man under the hood, but instead the burned and torn face of her Uncle Ed appeared to her. The smell of charred flesh filled her nose and she gasped, transported back ten years to the horror on the *Princess*.

"Meriel, help me," her uncle said in her nightmares while reaching out a hand to her.

Retreating from the horror, she stumbled backward until she bumped into a table and fell. Instruments crashed onto the clinic floor around her, and she clutched her arms to her chest and neck to hide her scars.

John rushed to her and kneeled. "Are you all right?"

She blinked repeatedly. "Yes. Just some water, please."

He helped her to her feet, and she rejoined Phillip who had lowered his hood farther over his face. Realizing how much she must have hurt him, she laid her hand on his.

"Forgive me, please, and don't be offended. Your injuries reminded me of a close friend who had wounds similar to yours. The memory was very painful for me."

He nodded and patted the back of her hand as a tear rolled down his scarred cheek and fell onto her sleeve.

The doctor was unmoved by the scene. "You can observe the improvement in just two months. With access to the finished product and replicator templates, we will be able to…ah…thank you, Phillip." He took John by the arm and led him out of the room. "Treatment can begin next week if we reach a final understanding."

She frowned at the idea that he might delay treatments for the burn victim because of financial arrangements, but she said nothing.

Dr. Wo steered them to a small court where two athletic women played a version of racquetball. One woman had red cuffs around her left knee and ankle and a thin brown scar running between them on the outside of her leg. Four monitors adjacent to the viewing area showed side and top views of the joints as they moved. It was clear the cuffs were instrumentation for real-time telemetry.

"See," the doctor said while pointing to a graph below the displays of the knee joint, "the tendon stress exceeds the nominal range for her age. She needs to worry the ISA will rule this as a disqualifying enhancement."

"Is she a professional athlete?" Meriel asked, not recognizing her on the sports networks.

"No. At least, not yet. A talented amateur. Her joints were crushed last year in an accident. They told her to forfeit the leg and hip for prosthetics. Your company offered her an alternative. She learned the sport as part of her physical therapy. Now she's considering a professional career."

Meriel wondered if John had some business deal that required continuing treatment for people like Phillip and this woman.

John checked his link. "What about the radiation victim? Mr. Thompson?"

The doctor smiled again. "Released last week." He turned to her. "An impossible case. Mining accident. Just remarkable. Stage IV melanoma spread to his lungs—incurable. He came here to die, where his family couldn't watch as he wasted away."

"Bone-marrow regen," John said.

"Correct. Genetic replication for hematopoietic regeneration. Your company also provided the cancer-cell tagging. The regenerated T-cells wiped out the melanoma completely." He looked back at her, clearly moved. "Death comes easily for some who have nothing to live for. This man recovered remarkably fast and returned to children who loved him." The doctor turned and walked down the corridor, and they followed a few paces behind.

She could remain quiet no longer. "John, it's cruel to withhold treatment for business reasons."

"Yes, I agree that would be immoral and unethical, but the regimen is also extremely expensive." She opened her mouth, but he raised his hand. "That's why their treatments are free."

"Then what's this 'final understanding'?"

The doctor stopped by the door to a small office, and John turned to her. "Excuse us, please. I'll be out shortly."

After waiting a minute, she returned to the racquetball court to watch. There, she studied the screens with interior views of the ankle and watched it flex and extend. The graphs spiked with stress each time she planted her foot or cut in a new direction.

The young woman's faint scar caught Meriel's attention again, and she recalled Phillip's scar-free wrists. She rubbed her shoulder above her left breast. *Maybe his people can heal me.*

John came up beside her. "Well, what do you think?"

"Well, it's not stim. Can…" Her voice trailed off, and she blushed, not wanting to expose her disfigurement to another round of "poor girl" or "oh my God."

"Does the scarring treatment work on…old scars?" she asked.

"As far as I know, yes. Why?"

"Oh, nothing. So what's this 'final understanding'?"

"A trade for marketing. The regimen is personalized to each patient and very expensive until we can move equipment and replicators near the point of treatment."

"Their treatments are free?"

"Yes, and no one else would help them."

Meriel thought she had misjudged him more than once today. She pointed to the women playing racquetball. "Which was your product? The joints or the telemetry?"

"Yes." He smiled and led her back to the entrance of the clinic.

"Which?"

"Both. When we first introduced joint regen, the doctors could not distinguish the performance between the original and the regenerated joint without better instrumentation. So we had to invent that, too. Our competitors all had joint replacements, but no one could heal the bones, nerves, and muscles at the same time. We can. The standard postop goal is mobility. We're changing the target to performance functionality."

"Why so much secrecy?"

Glancing over both shoulders, he led her outside. "Not here." At the promenade, he flagged a personal shuttle which ferried them back to blue-zone.

***

Blue-zone included the docks and had its own shops and bars that were functional, sterile, and resilient because spacers from different ships tended to mix it up. Stationers thought spacers brought vermin with them and were hard on their fragile decor, so they forced spacers back to the facilities near the docks. Station police harassed the blue-zone bar owners with sanitation orders that kept most of them alternating between repair and fumigation.

Meriel and John joined the *Tiger* crew at the TarnGirl in the middle of a raucous party and pulled chairs over to the table. Cookie flirted with a buxom blonde at the next table, which annoyed a large bald man sitting beside her. Their shoulder patches identified them as crew from another ship in their league, the *JSS Rowley*. Both groups had already reached stage five—loud and bawdy—of Meriel's ten stages of a spacer's party. Alf Martin, Socket's alternate, was there investing heavily in a severe hangover and acting surly. Socket sat nearby, enhancing her legend with two muscular escorts.

John scrolled through the list of premium scotches. "What do you think, Alf, a single malt or blended?"

Alf blinked with his mouth open, and Meriel turned away and bit her lip. She let her breath out slowly when John ordered a scotch-flavored alcohol replica.

"So why the secrecy?" she asked.

"Our competitors hunger for information about our products and customers. I can travel under the noses of our competition when I work my passage."

"Competitive products?"

"No, but they control the product buzz and the media. Our tactic is for loyal customers to post testimonials on the net. Then we spread the word before BioLuna and others can suck the air out of our message."

"Who's the 'we' in your story?"

"LGen Inc. You heard of them?"

"No."

"Good. That's the idea."

"What are you selling?"

"Information," he said. "Hauling finished goods is too expensive, so we sell replicator data sets that partners mass-produce locally."

"Everybody does that."

"Sure, but our siRNA mimics an individual's genetic markers—implants are guaranteed nonrejection; drugs are guaranteed compatible; drug blends without contraindications. We just need to have our nanoscale replicators on site to execute the data sets."

"Why haven't I heard of LGen before?"

"The big corporations have a media blackout and embargo to keep us out of retail and force us to sell through their channels. Even BioLuna sells our stuff.

"But they let you sell it?"

"Well, I kinda sneak out."

"A spy?"

"No, just advance marketing. But if they catch me here, they'll lock us down even tighter. It's not so bad, really. The anonymity gives us lots of flexibility."

"How does a small group like yours compete with BioLuna and the other conglomerates?"

"They need us. We're still essential to their R&D," he said. "Most of their technology, the research threads, started with us on L5. You know about L5?"

She remembered he came from there. "Not much."

"What's the matter? Why the look?"

"You seem too normal, too healthy, to come from L5," she said.

John stood and grabbed a pool cue from the wall and then hit his leg with a loud whack without flinching. "Nobody's perfect."

"Prosthetic?"

"That's us—prosthetics, genomics, pharma. They built L5 for research and development of products for mass production back on Earth. Well, L5 got old and worn, and the residents, including my parents, took a chance and left for a colony called Haven. LeHavre is our station."

"Haven't heard of it," she said. *Sheesh, refugees from a condemned habitat moving up to a low-grav hellhole like Ceres.* "Rumor has it L5ers were sterile from radiation and went extinct."

"Nope. We're doing fine." From his link, he flashed a vid of two girls, perhaps nine and eleven, and a woman kneeling between them. The taller girl had a patch over her left eye. "See? I got two of the sweetest and healthiest little girls in the galaxy there. Becky and Sandy."

Meriel raised her eyebrows and smiled. *Good thing he didn't surprise me about that.* "They're beautiful. How old?"

"Twelve and ten ET now."

"Is that their mom in the middle?"

"Yeah. She died some years ago."

"Sorry. People out here don't know anything about LeHavre either." Remembering the many thousands of habitats was impossible, but ignorance of a viable trading port with a competitive product was unprofessional. If it was real, she should already know about it.

"Only LGen ships fly in and out. The catalog coordinates are wrong, and BioLuna keeps them wrong."

"How come?"

"BioLuna thinks they still own us. They want to control immigration and don't want squatters. It's just as well we don't get visitors. The ecosystem can't handle a large influx of immigrants. We'd all like to keep it a secret."

She cocked her head. "If you're trying to keep it a secret, why are you telling me?"

"Ahh...you asked," he said. But his blush told a different story, and he changed the subject. "Back there, what did you mean when you said you'd lose the kids?"

"The kids from my ship when I was young."

"The *Princess?*" he asked, but Meriel remained silent. "Sorry. Word gets around. I didn't mean to pry."

She didn't hear a note of pity in his voice and gave him a friendly smile. "You're not...yet. I try not to talk about them. What did you hear?"

"Only the announcement. The story disappeared pretty quickly."

"Yeah, instantly."

"You're the kid who survived?"

"One of them," she said. "I'm working to get our ship and the other orphans back together.

"They're family?"

"My mom said we're probably all cousins somehow, but the ship records were wiped, so I'm not really sure. There are lots of lawyers involved, and I need to act like I'm a good influence—or at least not a bad one." The buzz from her second drink hit, and she imagined the station's legal staff taking vids of her here.

"Where are the others now?"

I shouldn't be talking openly like this. "I don't know." She lied. "Sometimes, I want to go AWOL to see them, especially my sister and little Harry." The drinks had loosened her tongue, and she had said too much. *Time to change the subject.* "Say, Cookie told me you could help with some questions about coordinating in space."

"OK, shoot."

"How can one vessel ambush another?" she asked. "Cookie says they teach Marines it's impossible."

"Not impossible, just improbable. That's the issue— probability."

"And they don't teach two-body coordination."

"Because they don't do it anymore. Let me get him."

John turned, and she stole a glance at his profile. *A nice face, and honest eyes. But he's not some station hookup. I still need to work with him tomorrow.*

When John turned back to her, the blush returned to her face. Cookie had a similar flush, and she suspected the nearby blonde still held his attention. It appeared the table next to theirs had achieved stage 6 on Meriel's party scale, and at the current rate of alcohol consumption, they would soon enter stage seven.

"You're nav-two, right?" John asked.

"Yup."

"OK, so I'll just take it for granted you learned about jumping and the sphere."

She nodded.

"Before they built all the stations, spacers tried to transfer cargo at jump points but gave up. Bottom line is merchants couldn't make their margins trying to transfer at jump points, and thieves gave up searching for them."

"How so?"

Cookie interrupted. "'Cause you have to know exactly where something's gonna be." He swayed in his chair, oblivious to the balled-up napkins the blonde bounced off his head and the growing annoyance of the muscle beside her. Meriel supposed they had already reached stage seven.

"That's right," John said. "You need to know precisely where something is going to be, and you can't know that with enough precision. Even if they tell you where they *plan* to be, no one can hit the mark with enough accuracy."

"The sphere," she said and considered inviting them to Teddy's to discuss nav with an expert.

"Right."

"Right," Cookie repeated and slapped his palm on the table for emphasis.

Is he gonna fall from his chair? I think I need to reconsider the invitation to Teddy's.

John continued, "For example, say you give your partner the coordinates where you plan to be and your ship jumps first. You can't actually tell where your friend is until their EM broadcast appears on your scopes."

"When they wink-in," she said.

"Right. EM travels at light speed, so you can't detect their signals until then. Let's say your sphere is one AU, which is good for a jump. That's still hundreds of millions of miles. It takes nearly ten minutes before you can spot the signal and still lots more time and energy to reach them. It's much easier to build a hub near the high-traffic routes."

Wedging her way into their conversation, the blonde poked him on the shoulder. "Say, why do we still use AU anyway? Earth is eight light-years away."

"It's just a convention, like meters and feet," Cookie said.

The blonde swung a dainty shoe onto the table in a most undainty manner. "Sure, but we bring our feet with us; we don't bring Earth with us."

Cookie slammed his boot onto the same table, dwarfing hers. "Your foot is different than mine, but we all agreed on what a foot of distance is, just like meters and AU." He removed his boot from the table and turned back to John and Meriel.

Trying to swing her foot off the table, the blonde reclined too far and would have fallen over if not for the nearby muscle, who caught her chair. Meriel guessed the woman would either pass out or be the first to reach stage seven.

"John, what if my ship doesn't broadcast our position?" Meriel said, and Cookie frowned.

"If they wink-in without you broadcasting, they'll need to spot you against the background of stars. Your ship's albedo is tiny at one AU, and it can take hours to compute contrasts and displacements. Hell, at that distance finding anything smaller than a moon is a miracle."

"And we could jump away first…," she said.

John caught Cookie's frown, and they exchanged glances. "So what's this about? The question isn't academic, is it?"

"No, sorry. I'm trying to understand how pirates attacked my ship when I was a kid. They have the same problem you two are talking about."

"Right. Pirates gave up. Too hard to find the victim."

"Everyone says it couldn't happen, but it did," she said. "I just can't figure out how or why."

He dropped his casual smile and studied her. "Are you sure the meeting wasn't…intentional?"

She clenched her jaw and balled her fists at the insinuation of a clandestine drug drop. Restraining the urge to break his nose, she glared at him instead. "Absolutely."

Cookie leaned over the table. "Then someone sent you somewhere your pilot didn't intend." He appeared sober and serious but then blinked twice as if the last drink just reached his brain. The blonde escalated from throwing napkins at him to cocktail olives to draw his attention, but stage seven impaired her aim. Her companion's face implied violence was imminent, but Meriel could not leave yet.

"They couldn't just follow you in," John said. "It would take too long to find you with two spheres. They'd need to set you there and keep you there."

As if he had uncovered a priceless gem, Cookie nodded slowly. "And lock your nav to stop you from jumping away before they got to you."

She fiddled with the pendant on her necklace. "But you can't lock nav, right?"

Cookie smiled and in a boisterous voice said, "Right. Nav is more secure than a hooker's client list." He laughed, but Meriel shook her head.

The blonde turned to him with a jiggle and a wink. "Who you calling a hooker, sailor?"

Apparently, the *Rowley's* crew had all reached stage seven—looking for trouble—and they were looking at Cookie. He opened his mouth but had no chance to reply.

The big man accompanying the blonde stood. "Yeah, who'd you call a hooker?"

Cookie stood up with open arms and a generous smile on his face, but still the guy swung at him. Leaning back, Cookie dodged the punch, but his opponent lost his balance and fell on the table, spilling their drinks and annoying everyone. It appeared as if Cookie knocked him down, and both crews stood and squared off for a cussing match complete with shaking fists and threatening postures. Alf Martin escalated to a pool cue, which started the punches.

Meriel backed away and searched for the door but could not maneuver around the fighters. She grabbed John's sleeve.

"I've got to get out of here, John. I can't get caught in a riot," she said, intentionally leaving out *again*.

"It's just a bar fight. They'll let us all go in a few hours."

"My sheet is too long, and I'm marine-three. If I hurt someone, even by accident, I'll lose my ship. I'll lose the kids."

"We can blame it all on Cookie."

"I'm serious. I gotta leave."

John nodded and led her to the rear of the TarnGirl as the bartenders and bouncers rushed past them to form a cordon in front of the liquor inventory. They found a door behind the bar, and she exited first into a service corridor. He tried to follow, but a bruiser yanked him back and threw a punch. The door slammed closed behind her and would not reopen.

Burning with unanswered questions about how pirates could have found the *Princess*, she leaned against the wall to wait for John. But when the police sirens wailed, she had to leave.

***

To fill the time until she could see John or Cookie, Meriel stopped at an event-planner's kiosk. There, she arranged a party for Harry's twelfth birthday. To avoid triggering the court orders that kept the kids' identities secret, she used aliases; even arranging a party could endanger the kids and jeopardize her legal cases. While giving instructions to the planner, she dreamed about having all the orphans together again, something which had not happened since they left their ship all those years ago.

John and Cookie did not respond to her calls, so she returned to the blue-zone docks. Molly stood at the *Tiger's* airlock, talking to Lev, and hailed her.

"Seems our crew is in jail," Molly said. "How'd you avoid that?"

"I was shopping, ma'am."

"Well, they're not getting out by themselves. Better go rescue them, Chief. I've authorized you for bail, but call me if the damages exceed your allowance."

"Shore patrol is Cookie's job," Meriel said, to hide her suspicion he'd been arrested with the others.

Molly smiled. "He's detained with them."

"OK." Meriel checked her link. The authorization surprised her; it was almost a blank check—limited in purpose but not in amount. She turned to go, but Molly continued.

"Oh, and someone found this in green-zone." She handed her a lapel ID button that read, "LSM Tiger/Cargo."

The ID had fallen off Meriel's shirt when the tough grabbed her purse. She froze to spin a cover story.

"Maybe you can find the owner and return it," Molly said with raised brow and turned to board the *Tiger*.

Meriel borrowed a cargo cart that might accommodate everyone onboard, not just her crewmates who were in jail, and drove the short distance to red-zone and the police station. *She trusts me with the ship's funds. If this is a test, then I need to pass it. How much does she know?*

Entering red-zone required only an involuntary scan of her bio-tag. This ease of entry expedited the representation and removal of detainees, which was her mission today. But security spiders idled by the entrance; their crimson lights blinking to warn everyone they were armed.

Parking the cart next to the police station, she entered a small waiting room. Inside, a video monitor peered down on two wire benches and a single opaque window opposite the door. No doors were visible other than the entry, and she guessed a hazmat team could hose down the entire room and sterilize it without damaging anything—like some bachelor apartments she had avoided.

She approached the window. It seemed to be thick and most likely made of a ballistic ceramic that fogged at ionizing wavelengths. As she transferred her ID from her biotag, the window cleared, and the desk sergeant appeared.

"Here for the *Tiger* crew," she said.

Without raising his head, the officer peered up at her with an asymmetric squint. "Haven't I seen you before?"

"Probably. Bail?"

His gaze returned to his console, but he pointed to a comm button adjacent to the window.

She ran her bracelet near it. "Damages?"

He nodded slightly and waved a finger to display his console data on the window in front of her. She synced the data again. When his screen flashed, he hit a few keys.

"The Rowdy boys are here, too," he said.

Meriel tapped her link. "Exec, they've got the *Rowley* crew here. Can we take them?"

"Yes, but no damages," Molly replied. Meriel synced her approval on the button.

"Wait, please."

After examining the bench for fresh stains and vermin, Meriel sat down in view of the monitor.

```
     In breaking news, elections on the
  Chosho colony on tau Cetu-4 have been
  in turmoil with the late inclusion of
  Fredric Allen on the Senate ballot.
  Allen's candidacy is supported by the
  Archtrope of Calliope. His only
  legislation to date has been to extend
  the domes to include an exclusive
  self-governing commune for followers
  of the Archtrope. Seen as a referendum
```

```
on the Archtrope's involvement,
Allen's…
```

Meriel half listened while she worked on her link. News was so sequential, so linear, and so dumbed-down that she needed something to do between the endless clichés and cultural tics. She composed another message to her hacker friend, Nick.

```
See if you can find anything on a
colony named Haven or a station called
LeHavre.
```

Haven. John. I didn't thank him for helping me out. She stretched out her legs and put her hands behind her head, imagining the two possible outcomes for her—prison or traction—if he hadn't intervened between her and the stim junkies. He did not look like a fighter but seemed competent. *How many other nonlethal weapons does he carry?*

One of the thugs had called her "cruiser" when he first confronted her. Was it simply an insult, or did he know she worked cargo? Her fatigues were hidden in her bag. *They might recognize me as a spacer by my walk or the proximity to the handholds or maybe my nervousness. But why cargo?*

She walked to the window and waved her link near the button. "Excuse me, Officer. Do you have a moment?"

The window clarified. "Is it business?"

"You betcha. You've seen thousands of people come by here, huh?" she said, and he nodded. "So, what do you think I'm rated for?"

The cop grinned. "Well, a pretty young—"

"Way off. Start over."

"OK. Spacer, of course. Right-handed. Study a lot. Marine training; three or four. Let me see your hands." She showed her hands. "Marine three. Got a rough past—no, I don't want to know. Shipside accident with a torch or blade."

"I thought I covered that."

"You still flinch. You're bailing out friends, not just shipmates." He smiled broadly. "Right. And you were with them." Meriel opened her mouth, but he waved his hand. "No need to deny it." He squinted. "Trouble sleeping. Boost—"

"OK, OK. I wasn't asking for a CAT scan. Rating?"

"Hmmm. Not security. Nav? Communications?"

"Anything that would indicate cargo?"

He studied her again and squinted. "Nope. Say, you still insulted when they call you a cruiser? Don't take it personally. Some guy called my wife a cruiser."

"What happened to him?"

"Dunno. Seems he kinda disappeared," he said and fogged the window.

She returned to the bench. *Then why did the thug call me a cruiser? Maybe he saw me dockside. Maybe it was just an insult to throw me off.*

The scene switched to an interview of a tall man in uniform impatiently slapping a riding crop against his leg.

```
General Subedei Khanag of the
Draconian League and follower of the
Archtrope of Calliope has posted his
fleet near Chosho Station. A
spokesperson for the government called
the presence of Khanag's highly armed
ships intimidating and provocative.
The general was candid in a recent
interview with INS news correspondent
Uriah Limets.
   "Why have you brought so many armed
ships into neutral space, General
Khanag?"
   "Merely as a sign of support and
solidarity," Khanag said.
```

Repeated shouts of "Subedei!" rose from the men behind him led by a handsome young man with captain's bars.

```
   "I assure you we only wish
Representative Allen and the Archtrope
the best of luck in this election."
```

"Allen's opponent claims that you
plan a new front in the Immigration
Wars right here on TC-4."

"Nothing of the kind, I assure you.
Such silly rumors should not be
entertained for an instant. As
believers, we value all human life and
would never use our power for ill.
Those battles are for the desperate
and the fascists. We support self-
determination and the will of the
populace to decide their own future."

"General, where will the Archtrope
send you next?"

"Don't misunderstand. The Archtrope
is my spiritual guide and prophet, not
my commander…"

Another battle in the Immigration Wars, and another band of thugs to fight them. If we get the Princess *back, I'll remember to stay away.* She sighed. *So just how am I going to get her back?*

"Chief Hope," the officer said, interrupting her thoughts. "Your crew will be at R258T in three minutes. I'm sure you know the way, yes?"

She waved and walked outside to the detention-center exit, where John emerged leading the crews of the *Tiger* and *Rowley*. Cookie followed, arm in arm with the muscle from the bar, both of them in T-shirts and both sporting similar marine tattoos on their biceps. The blonde who had instigated the brawl squeezed herself between them.

The big man staggered toward her. "Thank your cap'n for us, dearie." He reached his hand out to her, but before she could shake it, he fell backward with the same speed as his extended palm, and it appeared suspended in space. A moment later, he crashed onto the deck and began to snore. Four of his crewmates picked him up, his arm still extended in the air, and they all boarded the cargo cart.

Cookie and the blonde talked softly in the back of the cart on the way to the docks and hugged when Meriel dropped off the *Rowley* crew.

"Who's the blonde, Cookie?" Meriel asked as she drove them back to their ship.

"Ex-wife."

"Whose?" John asked.

"His...and mine. She's the reason I left the Marines."

Meriel just shook her head and knew it would be hours before he or John would be in good enough shape to hold a conversation about hijackings. But the deadline to submit evidence to defend the *Princess* did not change.

Lander Station—Outbound

With her crewmates safely aboard the *Tiger*, Meriel found a small package addressed to her. She logged the mass in her allotment and proceeded to supervise the cargo loading and undocking.

Hours remained until they reached the jump point away from the station's traffic. Meanwhile, she had nothing to do regarding the *Princess* until hearing more from Teddy or Nick. Her sister would want to know, but Elizabeth could do nothing but worry. The package beckoned, but she had to respond to the messages before they synced again and went to the mess.

A message from nineteen-year-old Penny Hubbard topped the queue. Penny had heard that Sam Spurell, Tommy's kid brother, had been beaten up on eIndi.

```
...The Snapdragon crew did it, but I'm
sure his crew set him up. They all
seem so happy to see us get hurt. The
second we let it slip we're trying to
crew together on another ship, they
start accusing us of disloyalty and
lack of commitment—all kinds of lies.
Can you reassign him? I'm afraid they
are going to arrange an "accident" and
hurt him bad. Please, M. Please.
```

Sam didn't mention that. Toughing it out and not whining, I bet. So, what can I say to her that she doesn't already know?

```
    Sorry, but Sam's under contract for
another six months. We don't have
enough to buy him off and don't have
another ship to billet him. Sam knows
all that. I'll send him a note. M.
```

The *Princess* vid shimmered, and she glanced at it. *I'm screwing up, Mom. We're falling apart. We're all split up, and I can't do anything about it.* Meriel rested her head on her arms and wanted to cry. *Crying won't help. Eighteen days of crying and the* Princess *will be gone forever, and I'll have no chance of getting us all together again.*

After sending another message to her hacker friend, Nick, she searched on "L5," where John said he grew up. She knew the gist of the story—it was the first corporate habitat in Earth's L5 libration point.

The article projected a hologram of a garbage can with slits along the sides running parallel to the axis. The holo panned out to show the station poised against the edge of Earth and the rising sun to add drama to its shape. Some shots inside presented an idyllic planet Earth with farms and buildings and playgrounds. That was when it was brand new.

L5 grew steadily with success. To house the growing population, parks became high-density arcologies, and farms became hydroponics tanks. Over the course of a century, the beauty was eradicated. When business weakened, the bond ghouls withdrew their financing and abandoned it with the inhabitants onboard. The L5ers revolted and declared their independence. A few years later, they disappeared. *According to John, they were med-geniuses and turned up on Haven. So, what about the colony they occupy now?* Galactipedia had nothing on Haven and LeHavre, and she gave up; she would need to wait for Nick to find something.

Meriel opened the package and found a book with a handwritten note within.

> Your mother gave this to me when I
> went through a rough patch some years
> back. She said it was her favorite
> book and that her mother had left it
> to her. I'm sure she would want you to
> have it, especially now.
>   "Be not the stone upon which the
> wave of history crashes; be the wheel
> around which it turns."
>   T.

From Teddy. My grandma's book. Physical books were rare now that photons were free and fuel was expensive. She laid the book on her desk. It fell open to a dog-eared page and she began to read.

> *"Once in an age, the forces of darkness align to bend the arc of history.*
>
> *"And once in an age, the arc of history bends around the wheel of one committed person who, acting from his or her own virtuous interests, changes the course of history: the child who raises the flag above the barricades; the mother who thrusts the picture of her murdered child before the dead eyes of the tyrant; the girl who refuses to deny her love for God while her flesh burns at the stake—individuals who grip a shred of civilization with both hands and will not give it up…"*

Meriel finished the passage in tears. *Thanks, Teddy.*

***

Eight light-years away, a tight-beam laser carried a very private conversation.

"We're on a schedule, and the pieces are moving into place. We need this closed, Benedict."

"We can't force this earlier than the twenty-one days. The courts won't let us," Benedict said.

"How much more are they asking?"

"It's not about money now. There were too many policy changes, and the authorities are suspicious. There have been…inquiries, and our friends are afraid of exposure."

"The forces are in motion. We can't delay." There was a pause on the line. "What about just blowing it up?"

"It's an option, sir, but it would endanger Enterprise. Are you willing to risk the viability of the station?"

"Hmm, not yet," he said, but conviction was absent in his voice. "What about the orphans? Are they still quiet?"

"Yes."

"Then watch them closely to make sure something does not…remind them, chiefly the older one. What's her name?"

"Hope, sir," Benedict said. "Why not just terminate her now?"

"She has a connection to us, which might draw attention to our plans. The quiet disappearance of either the ship or the girl would be optimum."

"We have someone close to her now, sir."

"How close? Never mind. I don't want specifics. He has discretion to…terminate?"

"His talent is cleverness rather than wet work."

"Then please make sure his cleverness has a backup and she does not put this together. An early and quiet end to this is preferred."

"If she does put it together?"

"We drop the hammer on her and anyone connected to her."

"Collateral damage control?" Benedict asked.

"Our concern is publicity, not body count," he said and ended the communication.

Chapter 4
Free Space

Training

Lev glanced up during the data integrity checks in Cargo-A. "You're whistling again, Chief."

"Again? Sorry," Meriel said. She had woken from jump without nightmares and felt better than she had in months. *Thank God for boost.*

"I wouldn't mind if you could hold a tune."

"Thanks. That will show up on your readiness report. Hey, I'm taking a break."

Using the cruiser's console, she scanned the messages they had picked up at the outbound comm beacon before the jump. They were light-years from another to sync with, so there was no hurry to reply.

The arrangements for Harry's party seem OK, and it will take place even if I'm not there in person. Only Anita's boat is in the sector. Says here it'll be parked on asteroid X44t, not too far from Enterprise. She might make it. Wow, Harry would love that.

```
From nz: ping me when you are on
station.
```

She sighed, not realizing how much she depended on him. "Acknowledge."

Using a training app that displayed a grid with names and ratings achieved, she checked the orphans' progress. *OK, let's see what we got. Harry won his logistics-two rating.*

Wow! What can we do to celebrate? His boat will commend him, but he needs something from us. Elizabeth had marine-two and almost nav-two. *No one has a galley rating. I need to tell the kids to train, or we'll need to hire a cook. Erik has qualified for nav-two, and he's only seventeen: he must have the gift, like Teddy.*

When they were young, little Erik would join her and her father, Tommy, and little Elizabeth in the holo room to play the stellar navigation game "Where's Teddy?" The room would project a 3-D starfield as if they were EVA. The challenge was to find out where you were and jump to the nearest fuel-and-food source. Every player's link gave them the specs on each star: brightness, spectrum, red shift...but not its name or location. Instead, you could just point to it, and a callout would appear; nav simulators worked the same way but did most of the work for you. Using your personal link meant you could keep your speculations a secret from the others. If you named one of the stars or clusters, the program would flag it. One step was to choose three stars, or two stars and the sector. Then the image would zoom out and show you the five nearest stations along with your current location. To win, you had to pick the station that met your fuel needs and had food for you and cargo to earn your way. Often picking two stars correctly was enough as long as you remembered the nearby stations. Erik always remembered, and he usually won.

She frowned at the training log and rested her chin on her palm. *To fly her, we need level four or five ratings on all bridge posts, but we only have a few threes. We're not ready and won't be for years. Oh well.*

Pulling up *Galactipedia*, she continued her research on L5.

```
     In 2162, financial interests behind
 L5 partnered with GSPX Galactic [link]
 to build another station, much larger
 and intended for the asteroid
 trade...GSPX traded the L5 orbit for
 cargo haulers with old FTL technology
```

```
and the deed to a speculative
destination about twenty light-years
from Earth. Within two years, seventy-
five thousand residents left, telling
people only that they were "going
home" and have not been heard from
since...
```

No word since? If John is right, BioLuna's gag on the news is tight. Traveling twenty light-years with so many people might have taken years in biological time. Must have used some kind of sleep and swapped crews.

She leaned against her harness. *Going home, they said.* Without thinking, she touched the pendant on her necklace again.

Only seventeen days remained to save the *Princess* and six to accept the buyout offer. Her mind was made up: legal or not, she would find a way to search the *Princess* on their next stop on Enterprise. If she found anything that would help, anything at all, she would decline the offer and work to clear the *Princess*.

***

Alone on the *Tiger's* bridge, John made good on his offer to help Meriel with her nav exam.

"I'm confused," she said. "I understand the laws of nav and relative position and the uncertainty in jump and all, but visualizing relative motion confuses me."

"You should be confused. It's not human. To think of the way things move makes you dizzy. Really, you get dizzy. Here—imagine you are on a moon watching the motions of the planets and a sun." He dimmed the lights and displayed a hologram of Jupiter and nearby space. "Here's a view of Sol system from Europa." Ribbons followed the relative paths of Sol and Saturn and inner planets, fading as they traveled to illustrate their relative speed. The ribbons twisted and spun, and soon the room filled with epicycles and helixes. "OK?"

She squinted and nodded.

He smiled. "Oops, I cheated. Here's what it looks like with Europa rotating."

Chaos hijacked the paths. Her stomach churned as her brain tried to make sense of it, and she shut her eyes. "Whoa."

After freezing the projection, he softened the lighting. "It's OK now."

She peeked with one eye before opening them again.

"Before Copernicus, that's how people saw things and calculated those complex paths."

"Why did they even bother?"

"Navigation and agriculture. Back then, concepts like *where* and *when* were different. They started with Earth as the point of reference to make sense of it all. But you saw what they ended up with. So Copernicus changed the point of view to make it simpler." He brought up another series of projections. "When you view the orbit of a moon, you stand on the planet it orbits; for the orbit of a planet, you stand on the sun it orbits."

"The center of mass, otherwise we get dizzy," she said, following his hands as they moved over the console controls. *Rough hands, not like a spacer pilot who'd spent his life on the boards.*

"Right. So when you track the movement of stars, you place yourself in the middle of the galaxy. Here's Sol and its planets from the galactic ecliptic."

The disk of the Milky Way appeared. He zoomed into a bright sun, which dived below and surfaced above the plane of the ecliptic, like a dolphin racing a sailboat. Around the sun, eight smaller objects spiraled.

"Everything is moving," she whispered, hypnotized by the motion. *The first law of nav.*

"Thinking that computers can do this automatically and with complete accuracy is tranquilizing, but that kind of thinking can drive you into a star. A computer that could do that exactly would not fit on a ship and would take too long to calculate positions. And before it finished, some mass would perturb your vessel or your destination, and your uncertainty would increase again."

He displayed a hologram of the Milky Way with callouts for the Sol, Lalande 21185, and Procyon A star systems.

"Here's our current course," he said, and a sequence of arcs appeared between Lander and Enterprise. The scene changed to follow the arc of their path with suns moving all around them. "To think you cannot know where you are precisely, ever, is scary. It's better to focus on your destination." His words drifted away into the stars, and she stopped listening.

"I feel like I'm riding a light wave," she said, as the stars and nebula rushed past, and Procyon A in front of her moved forward as expected. However, when she glanced behind to Lalande, it seemed to recede. *Oh, right, we're FTL,* she remembered.

"Don't forget this isn't a trajectory. We're like quanta now, just a probability with a series of possible destinations if we jump back into real space early."

"Sure," she said, but knowing did not change her feelings of exhilaration. She wanted to extend her arms like wings and fly the path of light without a ship's hull around her. "How do I do this?"

"That's what nav-three is about."

"This is profound, isn't it?"

"Yup. Earthers don't see it like that. They're born to see their position as fixed, first on Earth, and then on Sol, or some galactic center."

"Self-centered."

"Right. Spacers don't do that. They orient themselves within an ever-changing starscape of moving objects. Earth still publishes all our star maps relative to the Earth ecliptic, but the farther you travel from Earth, the worse the maps are. All the nav computers translate to the galactic ecliptic now. And that's where we live."

She nodded. "The less self-centered you become, the more you see, the more sense it all makes."

He moved again to rest his arm on the back of her chair, and she warmed to his attention. For a moment she wondered if Molly would approve of them using the bridge for a date, but then she relaxed and enjoyed the ride on the flight path. She reached out to touch the stars as they passed, but then she stopped and sat up.

"John, can you overlay our sphere as we travel? And show that it expands larger as we move forward?"

"Sure, but it'll be small on an interstellar scale." He flipped a key, and a gauzy bubble showed around their position. Then he changed their point of view to a few light-years perpendicular to their path. As they traveled, the bubble became exponentially larger.

"Can you add a ship along the same path but leaving ten seconds later?"

He complied, and now a new cone followed the first in a contrasting color and along a slightly different axis.

"Now try a third vessel leaving from a separate station," she said.

"Are all the clocks ET?"

"Yeah, and they are trying to meet at the midpoint."

He did as she requested, and they watched the three flight paths converge. As they approached each other, a new bubble appeared, this one larger than the others and in a new color.

"The new sphere includes the uncertainty in ET from different stations that are light-years apart," he said.

"OK, stop them when the paths intersect. How large is the sphere, now?"

"A hundred AU. Let's ignore this third one. The variations in station time make the sphere much too large."

"The closest is the trailing ship, right? Then how long would it take for them to come into contact if they broadcast their positions? You know, short jumps with inertial glide."

He waved his fingers above the console.

"They need to touch, but not collide. Exponential approach."

"About three hours twenty, minimum, if they sync speeds. That's four sigma. And that assumes they can locate the target as soon as the EM reaches them, which is very unlikely."

She sat back in the chair and smiled broadly. "It's not enough."

"What?"

"There's not enough time. The *Princess* jumped less than three hours after the hull breach. Even if they agreed to meet, pirates couldn't have reached us before we jumped away. A deep-space rendezvous wasn't possible. It was either a short jump that Papa would never do, or there wasn't enough time." The whole scenario damning her family as drug dealers could not have occurred. "John, can we save this? Package it up to send it to the court on Enterprise?"

"I can try, M, but it will take a nav-four to understand it."

"We'll arrange for an expert witness," she said. *And Teddy will be perfect.*

"Thank you, John. This could save the *Princess*." She circled her arms around his neck and kissed him. And when the kiss was over, she gazed up at him and smiled.

He pulled her closer and leaned over to return the kiss, but the comm light blinked with a request from the galley.

She turned and tapped the console. "I'm busy, Cookie."

"Hey, guys. Come on down to the forward mess. I've got something special for ya."

"What kinda special?" she said.

"A party. It was supposed to be a surprise. And bring your date."

"Who?"

"John, of course. Alf is on his way to relieve you."

"Acknowledged," she said and cleared the comm line.

With a finger to her chin, John turned her head back to face him. "Let's stay a bit longer." He moved in for a kiss, but a surly Alf Martin entered and logged in.

"I'm feeling happy. Let's go have some fun," she said and tugged him from his chair.

When they reached the corridor, he pulled her toward his cabin, but she resisted.

He frowned. "I was thinking of a different kind of fun."

"Slow down, sailor," she said and led him toward the party.

Rounding the corner to the mess, he turned to her. "Nav-three may be easier for you than you think, M."

Mardi Gras

Meriel and John found the mess hall crowded with most of the passengers and off-duty crew. Everyone seemed happy, and a few of the passengers' kids ran between the legs of the adults. They walked over to Cookie, who wore a strange hat that appeared to be a colorful octopus with bells on the end of each tentacle.

"What's the occasion?" she asked over the clamor.

Cookie handed noisemakers and masks to them and smiled. "Nothing. They call it Carnival, some old annual Earth excuse for a celebration. I'll get you drinks."

Cookie left for the bar, and Meriel followed John to the window for a breathtaking sight: a wash of blue and red with an orange halo and a scattering of stars floating within it.

"This is a bit off course for Enterprise," he said. "Jerri must have brought us here just for the view."

"This must be what it looks like near the Orion nebula," she said.

"Reminds me of sunrise on a cloudy sky."

She had never seen a sunrise except in some vids from Earth. *Why would he make that connection? Had he watched the same vids?*

When Cookie came back with their drinks, John asked, "Why is everyone so happy?"

He pointed a thumb at the nebula outside. "Clear space and lots of fireworks. Nothing in the way and nothing coming at us. Just life. Relaxing. I think it's biological, but I don't care. Enjoy the mood."

Someone produced an instrument and began singing bawdies, which forced the passengers to remove their children.

"This 'speculative destination' you L5ers ended up at was Haven?" she asked.

"You've been reading. Yup. We made LeHavre from the transport ships."

"Habitable?"

"Close enough to make a go of it and enough resources to be self-sustaining. It surprised us. I think it surprised BioLuna, even though they did the initial survey."

Haven. Habitable. She fiddled with the pendant. *What if Mom copied something about Haven on the chip in one of the corrupted files?* "What's the gravity?"

"About fifteen percent more than Earth."

"Artificial?"

"No. Natural."

That's a sizeable mass. Maybe Mom's Home is a dead end, and our home base could be Haven. "Did you ever hear of a planet called Home?"

"Only the myth," he said. "Don't need it, frankly. We're happy with what we got."

Especially after L5. "So BioLuna just sold it to you clear?"

"A trade for the L5 libration point. I think they hoped we'd just die there, and they'd reclaim it. We didn't die, and they tried to take it back."

"I didn't read about that."

"Cookie might know," he said and waved to invite him over to their table. "BioLuna tried twice to steal it back using hired mercenaries. They kept it real quiet."

"You didn't complain?" she asked, as Cookie turned a chair around and sat with his arms propped on the back.

"Sure did," John said. "Lawsuit filed in court of Lander, and we won a cease-and-desist order and preliminary injunction, but there's no one out here to enforce a judgment."

"There *is* no law unless you enforce it," Cookie said.

John nodded. "Too far from Earth for the UNE Navy, and BioLuna is too rich and too well connected."

She turned to Cookie. "So you know about mercenaries and Haven?"

"Mercs offered me a command for a major deployment, but they never mentioned where. I declined 'cause I was on my honeymoon."

"Want to tell me about it?"

"Hell, no. Say, why aren't you kids dancing?"

"Well, I...," she stammered.

Cookie took both of them by the arm and led them to a clear spot between tables as a slow song began to play. John rested his hand on the small of her back and started to dance.

She was nervous, afraid of falling for a crew member, but she liked this man. *Just relax, girl. A dance isn't a commitment.* Lying her head on his chest, she listened to his heartbeat.

When the music stopped, Cookie played another slow song to keep them dancing. The crowd melted away to prepare for jump, but the pair stayed. At the end of the song, she glanced up at John and closed her eyes, inviting a kiss. She relaxed in his arms and drifted away with the moment. *It'll be OK; I'll just keep the lights off. But what if the emergency light cycles on?* A memory hit her of a prior time she felt this way and she stiffened. *What if he sees my scars and pushes me away like those boys did when I was a teenager? I can't go through that again.* She opened her eyes quickly and pushed him away.

"I'm sorry, John," she said and ran to her cabin.

She'd had her fill of men who could never love her, anonymous spacers on station layovers who didn't care about the scars and only wanted sex. After the first time, her heart hurt too much. And with those who might love her, the scars were like a wall she could not shatter. The scars would still be with her, with them, even if she were in love.

If I take the meds, I'll forget or at least not care. She banged her fist on the bulkhead. *God, it's always the damn meds.* Taking her boost instead, she laid her head on her arms and cried until the *Tiger* jumped.

Chapter 5
Enterprise Station, Procyon A System

Enterprise Station—Inbound

Meriel woke from jump, woozy but without the nightmares again. The *Tiger* had just come out of hyperspace at one-g inertial on approach to Enterprise. The station dominated this sector of space as the hub for manufacturing and materials from the nearby systems. It was not the prettiest station, or the wealthiest, but the gaudy and rich looked to her for stability. Sure, it was big, but that's not what people said about it. It was the rock that other stations orbited around: a sector hub with influence reaching all the way to Sol. And it was the only station her parents had thought of as "child safe."

After inspecting their cargo, she checked her link. First in the queue was a message from John.

```
On duty. Sent nav program of
Princess scenario to GRLs you provided
on Lander and Enterprise. What
happened at the party?
```

She sighed, grateful for his help. From their working together, she finally had something. Though not quite proof of innocence, it was evidence the prevailing theory, the slander that her family made a drug deal in deep space, was wrong. But how would she explain to him why she ran away without sounding pathetic or needy? There it was again, the big wall she could not climb.

Allowing a few extra minutes for sync with the communications beacon, she downloaded the latest news and messages passed from other ships and stations.

```
From Liz: Looking forward to seeing
you on Etna...

From J. Bell Esq.: No progress. Send
money.
```

He must send the same note to every client, every day, automatically, she thought.

```
From nz: sure. come by. loiter near
g2440, and keep your link live. i'll
track you.
```

Green-zone. He's moved. "So,   what trouble are you avoiding now?" she murmured.

```
From T. Duncan:
Re: Ship status intractable.
Contacted Jeremy and court on
Enterprise. Something's going on
that's much larger than your problem.
Someone has spread big money around
quietly. Not giving up.
```

"Reply," she said. "Sent analysis indicating theory of intentional meeting is wrong. Transmitted nav scenarios via Smith to illustrate. Please review. LU, M."

Teddy will receive that soon. Lots of merchant traffic hopped between Lander and Enterprise, which meant nearly real-time communication, allowing for light speed to the beacons, of course.

No message appeared from Tommy, and she checked his ship's schedule: the *J. Edwards* undocked early, making their meeting impossible.

She tapped her visor. "Hey, Socket. Can you aim a tight-beam at Enterprise? I've got a friend outbound on the *Edwards* about now."

"Sure, M," Socket replied. "Jerri, can you spot them?" Muffled voices came through the link, then, "On secure E."

Meriel switched channels on her head-up display and scanned the roster. Tommy appeared, sitting nav backup on the largest bridge console she had ever seen.

"Ping," she said.

"Oh, hi, M. Sorry I missed you. What's up?"

"Bad news. They want to take the *Princess* from us."

"How come?"

She explained the lawsuit and the settlement.

"You don't want the money, huh," he said. "You prefer the fantasy of getting us together again."

"I want our ship back. I want what we had as kids." She turned away.

He sighed, and his voice softened. "You can't bring them back, M."

"I coulda done something, Tommy. Maybe it would have been different. Maybe if I—"

"Hell, that's fantasy. You were twelve; the rest of us were younger. You did what you could and more."

"I just want the future our parents wanted for us. Is that such a fantasy?"

"The fantasy is you remember our childhood better than it really was. The foundation folks got involved because we looked so pathetic. And our ship was a beat-up wreck your uncle kept patching up."

That hurt. Sure, she took lots of trips with Uncle Ed to the outfitters and recyclers scrounging for parts to fix the *Princess*. Until a few years ago, she thought all ships needed that kind of care.

"You're just saying that because your ship is so big and new and perfect. I know we didn't have much money, but we were happy together, right? Or was that a delusion, too?"

"No. That was real. But kids adapt to anything, M. They've got happy kids on the mining asteroids who don't know any different. Things sure picked up when Nick got us passes to the sims, though." He sighed. "Did you tell Liz?"

"Not yet. I want a face-to-face. You'll cross paths first. Can you tell her?"

"Uh, well…"

"What's up, Tommy?"

"We've got history. She doesn't want to see me. Maybe you can put in a word for me."

"Jeez, you drama queens."

"I know what you're asking. Sure, fight for the ship if you want. I don't need the money, and it wouldn't last long anyway. And the *Princess* might be my shot at chief of engineering before I'm sixty. But think about it, M. We're not kids anymore. We can't go back. If you take the cash, we might set up a trust fund to use if one of us has problems."

"I'll think about it. Thanks, Tommy."

They said their good-byes, and she rested her chin on her palm.

Is he right? Am I doing this to re-create a childhood we never had? I can't believe the Princess *was a wreck like he says or that we were so pathetic. That would make us needy and powerless to change things, like those big-eyed kids in the cartoons.*

Walking to the mess hall to find company, she thought about what her life would be like if she laid down her burden. At the promenade window, a hollowness in her gut caused her stomach to cramp. She grabbed a handhold, leaned over, and rocked to stop the empty feeling, a feeling that returned every time she thought about life without her sister and the kids. The emptiness dissolved when she imagined Elizabeth, Tommy, and Harry with her.

She stood again and gazed out the window at the approaching station, where the *Princess* languished.

With a smile she thought, *Hope returns*.

Enterprise Station—On Station

Meriel took a tram to green-zone to see Nickolai Zanek, avoiding security cameras along the way to protect his privacy. A year older than her, Nick had been on the net his whole life. He haunted security, a ghost in the machinery— anonymous and paranoid. If anyone could help her with her mom's data chip, he could do it.

Before the trouble on the *Princess,* she and Tommy met him in a simulator where they teamed up. Nick was a master of the game and took pity on them. At the end of the session, he surprised them by rolling out in a wheelchair. "You don't need legs for this," he had said. After they split the orphans up, he coded asynchronous games that they played together from across the space lanes to stay in contact. He was shy and never talked about his childhood, but somehow he learned how to love. Every Christmas, he made electronic toys for her and Elizabeth, all of which were impounded as possible evidence along with their ship. Other than Teddy, he was the only person who sent condolences to her when her parents died. Other than her sister and Teddy, Nick was the only person she thought truly loved her.

Entering the G2440 neighborhood, her bracelet buzzed.

Across the street.

On the other side of the street, a door stood ajar. She knocked and entered a dark hall. The door closed behind her, the lighting dazzled, and Nick wheeled up with a big smile and open arms. They hugged a bit longer than she expected: she had missed him more than she realized.

"How ya been, M?"

"Good, Nick. I need your help."

"Come." He led her into a small room stocked with threadbare old furniture suitable for a low-rent hacker, then offered her a beer from a cooler.

"I saw Teddy on Lander," she said. "And Harry has a birthday party on Wolf next week. You're invited."

"That might be difficult given my travel restrictions."

She nodded but remained silent.

"I found nothing about Haven or LeHavre. The net's dark, but there's a halo around those words together, like someone is scrubbing the net continuously."

"A friend said BioLuna had a media blackout. He said the L5ers ended up there."

"No kiddin'? I thought the L5ers went extinct. Well, if there's a blackout, it's tight. And that means expensive." He stopped, but she did not fill the silence. "That's not why you're here, is it?"

She held up her necklace. "No. I think Mom tried to tell me something."

"Can't let it go, huh? Like what?"

"I'm not sure. Maybe something about the attack. I think the location was wrong. I still think there's something here that will tell us."

"We've tried, M. For years. Your q-chip is toast. Someone altered the quantum lattice. They corrupted the data, intentionally. The damage is just too precise, too surgical."

"We've gotta try, Nick. We've only got fifteen days before I lose the *Princess*."

"I tried, M. I won't be able to stumble on a matrix that will invert it in less than a few hundred lifetimes."

"Then I'll lose the *Princess*. And if I lose her, I lose everything."

He dropped his gaze and released her hand. "Not everything."

She took his hand again. "You know what I mean. My promise to my mom and to the kids. Without it, we're nobodies."

"You'll never be a nobody."

"Nick, please."

He sighed. "M, I think they tried to destroy the *Princess* with you on it. Your showing up was a mistake."

"That's what Teddy thinks, but she always had trust issues."

"Yeah, she's not much into randomness or the hand of God. Did you read her paper? The one on disappearances?"

"No," she said.

"Well, she pretty much proved that system failures don't explain all the ship disappearances. Something else is going on."

"The bogeyman?"

"I'm serious."

She stopped listening. "Teddy's brainiac theories won't save the *Princess*.

"You sure you can't pry anything off the chip?" she asked, and he nodded. "Then can you do me a favor?"

"Sure."

"I need a pass to the impound dock."

He paused.

"I'm not wired," she said.

"I know. I trust you. The place is shielded anyway."

"Then what is it?"

He furrowed his brow and studied her. "Any security breach is regarded as terrorism."

"Impound is low security."

"It's still security, M. They'll throw you in prison. Forever. Or space you."

"You do it all the time."

"I never bring my body near enough to get caught."

"You did once," she said.

***

Nick had breached security for her once, and she could never tell anyone. It was the one time he had risked his anonymity, and he had done it for her.

Just before the *Princess* attack, he had invited her and Tommy to one of his caves of high-tech equipment, and Elizabeth tagged along.

The setup did not impress Tommy. "Sorry, pal. I'll bet you got more compute power here than the whole navy, but I couldn't live like this. I need the stars."

Nick had smiled. "Come with me," he had said and led them to a service elevator. Hacking access using an ID from a card deck he carried, they exited at the hydroponics sector. Then he produced a visitor's ID badge for himself and borrowed some brown coveralls meant for agricultural workers for Meriel and her crewmates. They followed him through a small section of the huge expanse of vats and pipes while he lectured them about food processing.

No one but the techs wanted to know how they recycled organics for food. Most people contented themselves with idyllic vids of pastures and barnyards with intact animals. Just as no one wanted to see how Earthers once made bacon, no one wanted to know how station agri made neu-bacon now. Today, he had a captive audience to whom he explained it all.

Up another elevator and through a security bulkhead, they reached the upper level of white-zone, the most secure area on the entire sector. In front of them stretched miles of arboretum and fresh-food farms, a sea of green curving up around the torus with no horizon. *This must be what Earth looks like*, she had thought.

"Stay under the trees," he said. "We've got ninety minutes before the drones pass by." He wheeled over to a huge tree and held out his hand to invite her closer. "Touch." He took her hand to place it on the tree.

To her, the bark felt cold but alive.

"This is a redwood. It's over sixty years old and a hundred feet tall now."

Tommy reached for a wild raspberry.

Nick shook his head. "We can't take anything out with us, including what's in our stomachs. It will show in the effluent monitors, and they'll know we've been here."

In the distance, through the trees, an expanse of green surrounding large buildings caught her eye. "Is that wheat?"

"It's grass, a lawn," he said.

"Why? That's not a crop."

"People think it's pretty. It's the first thing people seem to plant when they have land."

"It's like the African savanna on Earth," she said.

He cocked his head, as if seeing it for the first time. Reconfiguring his wheelchair, he joined them lying on their backs in a circle with their heads in the center. Together they gazed at the arc of the torus and stars through the trees above them.

"I stay here for this," he said.

Tommy nodded. "And you've got the stars here too."

That was Nick's home, not the caves of high-tech equipment below, and if security learned about their visit, he would lose it all. He had trusted them and didn't need to say they could never tell anybody what they saw, ever: no vids, no stories, no nothing. He never had to mention that if security caught wind of what they had done, they would all be shipped to a child-labor colony—him first.

***

"You breached security once before," Meriel said again, "for me."

"I admit nothing." He frowned and softened is voice. "There was less at risk then."

"I don't have a choice."

"There's always a choice, M."

"Don't give me clichés. I aim to keep my promises."

"Are you sure?"

"Can you pry the data out of the chip?"

"Nope."

"Then I have to try."

He sighed and tapped symbols on his link. "OK, a pass? You'll need an embedded-security ID to board the *Princess*." After moving the icons around, he crossed his arms. "But I can't get you on the shuttle that takes you there."

"Why not?"

"The bioscreening is too rigorous. We'd need to surgically modify you."

An expression that asked "Is that all?" crossed her face.

"It's that important?"

She nodded.

"No. I'm not gonna do that. Give me a second."

He wheeled around her with his chin in his hands. "I'll need to outthink the TechMasters in Security. Where's your tag?"

"My biotag? Hell, I don't know."

Grabbing a wand from a drawer, he ran it outside her body until it beeped just below her right rib cage. Then he tapped a link. "I'll drop something in a locker at the Greylight terminal near red-zone, number forty-eight. It'll be keyed to your thumb."

"How about a schedule for the security rounds?"

He brought three fingers to his temple. "Yes, I have a premonition someone will call in sick today. Give me an hour or so. No less. You gonna visit me later?"

"Yup."

"Head on over to red-zone, and I'll send something."

***

Ferrell barged into Molly's ready room without knocking and took a chair opposite her. She did not raise her head from her work.

"Ahem," he said.

She tapped on her console but did not raise her head. "What can I do for you Doctor?"

"I need to examine Chief Hope."

"Why? Her file wasn't enough?"

"To see if she's still on her medication."

"Right. More of that loose blaster stuff?"

"She's been avoiding me, refusing appointments."

"Has she missed an appointment?"

"Not really. She's avoiding making—"

"They're voluntary unless you show cause, right?"

He narrowed his eyes but nodded.

With a motion near her console, Meriel's duty schedule popped up. "She's rather busy, Doc."

"XO, she's dangerous and—"

"I need more than your speculations to change the ship's routines. This is a working vessel, and she's paying your wage. She can't do that if she's on your couch."

"This is my professional judgment—"

"And this is my ship. Bring me evidence."

"That's a no?"

Molly rose and advanced to his side of the desk. "I understand your concern, Doc. But you need to understand mine. Bring me something substantial and I'll rearrange her schedule."

He sneered and turned to leave. "Thanks for the conversation."

"And next time knock or we won't have a conversation at all."

Back in his office, Dr. Ferrell studied the ship's roster. Like many of the crew, Meriel had signed out and was not expected to return for hours. Carrying a journal and stylus for camouflage, he walked down the passageway of the *Tiger* while glancing back at each turn to see if someone had followed him. After passing her cabin, he looked around the intersecting corridor and then retraced his steps to her door.

A standard biolock with fingerprint reader secured her door. It was flimsy and no match for an uninvited but determined guest. Every spacer knew there was no real privacy onboard, and locks were simple reminders of the ethics of never entering without an invitation. But Ferrell ignored the courtesies, jiggled the handle hard, and the door popped opened. He entered and closed the door behind him.

Within the cabinet, he found the tube of meds and the imbedded schedule verifying compliance. The desk and drawers contained nothing unusual for a cargo chief. Turning to leave, he noted the console on her desk and paused. An open session would allow him to see her activities, even if he could not read the files. Without Meriel's biotag in proximity, the bioquery came up. To fool it he held his link to the console and played holos of her retina and voice patterns.

The device returned a table with a list of names: Elizabeth, Tommy, Sam, Anita, and Harry and rating qualifications displayed to the right of each. Bridge, nav, comm... *A training schedule?* he guessed. *So who are they?* He took a vid of the screen. Another window appeared— messages from an Elizabeth, an Anita, and a Jeremy Bell. The last message asked for more money. *J. Bell—is he the lawyer mentioned in her confidential file?*

He checked a few more files, but they all had additional encryption. Afraid he would leave a trail of his snooping, he restored her cabin to the state he had found it in and left.

Back in his office, he synced his link to his console. Retrieving the list of names, he compared them to a roster from the *Princess*, a roster sealed by court order and one he should not legally have.

***

Meriel shopped for regulation-blue overalls and a utility belt based on information Nick had sent to her. She then hurried to the locker just outside red-zone to pick up the ID. Inside the locker, she also found a bag containing a small pistol, a burner link, and a spray bandage. A note displayed on the link read,

```
leave your link here and take the
burner. wrap the sticky foil around
your waist to jam your biotag. use the
pistol to embed the capsule in your
forearm. it will hurt. two id's are on
the module. press it to toggle between
maintenance (blue) and security (red).
don't confuse them, and don't key the
security option until you need to.
once you come out, you can't go back
in. turnover is high, and they are
unlikely to care about a rookie. dock
m22, zero-g, diagram included. no
toilets. module will dissolve in situ
after final exit.
```

This was part of his solution to the security problem: two embedded IDs. No stranger to the game, she knew two IDs would not be enough. If a security ID appeared at the dock without logging her path to this point, alarms would go off and they'd shut down the docks until they caught her. *He'll figure out something.*

```
only monthly inspection. every hour,
they cycle through with motion
```

```
detectors and cameras looking for
anything larger than vermin, which
would be you. use the corridors and
the galley and the mess hall. ignore
the schedule. begin at 17.96 on this
link, and it will tell you the next
place to be or not be.
```

"So what's the bandage for?" she mumbled.

After reading the note she entered a bathroom stall to change. Covering her waist with the foil, she dressed in the blue shirt and coveralls. She pushed the pistol against her wrist to install the capsule and pulled the trigger. With a slight puff of gas, the device tore into her flesh.

"Ow!" she cried out. He was right. It hurt a lot.

"OK in there?" someone outside asked.

"Sure," she said while rubbing her wrist. And she would still need to press the wound each time she wanted to activate it. She frowned at the spray bandage and applied it over the ragged cut, then buttoned her shirt cuff to cover it.

Just before entering red-zone, she stopped at a hydration kiosk to survey the area. The security dock extended down a long corridor with police and trooper offices to port. To starboard lay the wharf where shuttles would take her to the impound docks.

This was it. She had not broken the law yet, and her clothing and preparations were still legal. However, when she engaged the ID module or stepped onto any of the shuttles, she would cross the line. If caught, her career would be over, the *Princess* would be lost, and she might never see the kids again—if they didn't space her. But she had made up her mind; her life meant nothing to her without a purpose, and the purpose she chose was to give the kids a future.

Cringing with pain, she pressed the bandaged wound until the blue glow from the maintenance ID appeared under her skin, then strolled to the red-zone entrance.

A note on the burner link interrupted her thoughts.

```
From nz: u sure about this?
```

She replied.

```
Yes
```

Entering the security zone did not require announcement; if her ID did not respond to the RF query with the proper permissions, the security spiders that patrolled the entrance would stop her. They wouldn't kill her; they would just restrain and sedate her, but that would be enough to destroy her life.

Past the heavily guarded entrance to the shuttles, she waved her wrist near a small panel, and the door to the maintenance shuttle opened. The panel flashed yellow to acknowledge her permission. She entered and left for the impound dock.

The shuttle first stopped at dock N21, where two officers in red helmets and IDs boarded. The larger officer turned and inspected her. *What would he expect? Should I meet his gaze or cower?* Meekness seemed more appropriate to maintenance personnel, so she lowered her head.

"New here?" he asked, still watching her.

She nodded.

"Anyone give you the tour?"

"No, sir."

He dropped his tone to a theatrical bass. "Ahh, good. Then let me welcome you to the graveyard of the most infamous vessels in the galaxy. Lurking here are warships that sterilized entire colonies. Between them are tiny vessels used for drug smuggling and petty murders. If any of these ships went missing, they might return to plaguing humanity." He glanced down at her and smirked. "Did they tell you the ghosts of the killers and psychopaths who manned those ships still walk these docks?"

She shook her head.

He pointed to a big ship. "See the big one? That's *Helmut's Inferno.* That boat transported human slaves to the mines on G27H. Helmut stitched together his own cyborgs and sold the human parts to the organ trade. Ownership is still in litigation. Somebody actually wants to use the bloody thing as a theme park."

A shudder ran through her body at the thought of G27H, another of the mining colony hellholes. The mines needed no Pied Piper to fill their roster with slaves and crippled organ donors. It wasn't necessary. The excess population drifted there naturally, like water flowing downstream. The healthy bodies with dull minds or bad habits drifted there, or Etna, or the other stagnant cesspools where the meat grinders were more likely to set up shop. Visions came of Penny and the kids caught in the vortex, and her pulse raced. Stars sparkled in her vision. *Breathe, girl. The kids are safe.*

"That one's my favorite." The guard pointed to an ovoid with a needle nose and huge jump fans. "It smuggled Rejuve after they banned it. That ship left psychotics in its wake for a decade until the Troopers finally cornered it."

"Ever hear those wild tales of piracy?" he said and pointed to the end of M22 dock. "See those two ships being dismantled?" Bright lights and plasma arcs flashed within a spider web of scaffolding around two dismantled ships. "That's what's left of a fleet of hundreds of pirates captured by the Troopers."

"And that little white one. The one's that's next on the block for recycling. They say a kid murdered her entire family there. Imagine the ghosts haunting *that* dock."

Her heart leaped in her chest. "I thought they…" she began but held her tongue and her emotions.

"Thought what, newbie?"

"Nothing," she said but wanted to scream. He pointed to the *Princess*.

They approached the M26 dock, and the security officer's face turned cold. "I know you got a job to do, newbie, but don't go poking around and wake up anything, ya hear? The rest of us have to work here and don't want more stories to tell." He turned and elbowed his companion out the door.

As the shuttle approached the M22 dock, Meriel gazed out the window at the *Princess*. There she lay, a white ellipsoid, her jump fans stowed close to the hull like the wings of a dove. Unlike the other hulks, no jets of condensation leaked from the hull to signal weak seams that might blow when normal pressure returned inside. Her ship was safe, for now.

Exiting the M22 air lock, Meriel pushed herself across the zero-g connecting tube to the service console. Packed amidst the scores of other small ships, she located the berth for the *Liu Yang*, the *Princess's* alias.

Getting there without gravity would be easy: jump, dodge, and repeat, like all the drills during her childhood. The test of skill was how far you traveled without touching the walls. Like any spacer, she could jump farther than any passage on a merchant ship and end with a half somersault and tuck. The dock passageways here were wide and designed for zero-g, with rounded corners to accommodate the clumsiness of those more accustomed to a steady gravity.

A few long jumps and turns later, she reached her ship. From the panel outside the air lock, she checked the status. *N₂/Argon 95/5. Inerted for preservation. Nice of them but deadly as carbon dioxide if I'm not careful. Pressure at 0.5 bar, high enough to avoid the bends. 0-Power/S4* meant some devices had reserve charge to help them power up, but otherwise the electronics were cold.

After installing fresh O_2 cylinders, she donned a warm-suit stowed nearby. The extras she stuffed in her bag should give her about forty minutes—twice as long as she expected to need. With the control module on her suit's forearm, she set monitors for the oxygen levels and respiration rates. She closed her visor, turned on her headlight, and pushed the entry-request button on the door. The door would not respond to her, and she guessed her ID had failed. Wincing, she pressed the wound again until a yellow glow flashed under her skin. *This must be the rest of Nick's access solution*, she thought while she waited. *He must have found an exploit in the security database*. Now she must wait until he modified the database to log her route.

A few seconds later, her wrist flashed red. When the whoosh of exchanging gasses stopped, the door dilated. It was cold and dark when the door shut behind her. The suit's head-up display registered N_2/Ar and lowered pressure as the lock adjusted to the ship's atmosphere. The hard contrast from the headlamp made the shadows appear sinister, and she changed the lamp from beam to flood.

On the day of the attack, she and her sister had entered this way. Her memory of it was vivid and showed her what her headlight did not.

The *Princess* was the foundation of her life then, as transparent as a mood, the only world she knew. Her memories of it slumbered deep below her conscious life of study and entertainments. That foundation remained unnoticed until they ripped it from her, along with the rest of her childhood. Now it returned to life as familiar as her breath. The *Princess* was no pragmatic merchant ship. This was her home.

Through gloved hands, the textures of polished-walnut railings and padded handholds came to her from memory. Earth's animals covered the fabric walls next to nebulas and fantasy landscapes—children's artworks in progress. Holographic displays that once cycled through the finest art and architecture of human antiquity lined the walls of the promenades.

The craft studio was next door, and she could not resist entering. Inside she found a sketch of a big-eyed puppy by little Elizabeth still pinned to the wall alongside Tommy's drawing of a dragon chewing on a navy battleship. Gliding down the passageway, she remembered the deOx drills and low gravity games, and then drifted past the mess hall, where Uncle Ed made snacks while they watched vids. Her mouth watered at the memory of the last cake her mother had replicated for her sister's birthday party: a cake frosted like a planet with deep-blue water and green land. Near the port window, she passed her nine-year-old self memorizing constellations with Mom. As she coasted, her fingertips slipped along the bulkhead. The *Princess* was not dead, just dreaming.

Gliding into the bridge, she recalled sitting next to Mom at the nav console and visualizing the stars. She stopped breathing again. Just past the decompression doors, she noted the rainbow discoloration around a hasty weld job that patched the hull breach. She touched her chest where the q-chip hung, and her mother's voice came to her. "It's all here."

Esther had stood bridge watch XO at the time of the attack, and Meriel traced her mother's path; first from each of the kids' bunks and then to their cabin. It was just the way they had left it: null-g and painted with tigers and porpoises, not the putty-gray she had lived with for the last decade. Her headlamp panned to the foot of her berth, where a net held the toys Nick had made. Next to them lay Elizabeth's doll, the birthday present she'd received that day.

Stretching out on her sleep net, she closed her eyes. A child again, she wished only that her life be as it was, before the murders, the pain, and the drugs. She gripped the blanket and felt the softness from memory that the gloves did not allow. *What would I miss out there? Nothing but responsibility.* With a smile, she reached up to feel her mother's hand and the certainty it promised that every tomorrow would be happier than today.

This was her safe space; the place the therapists told her to remember whenever she felt threatened and couldn't cope. But the shrinks would not believe her story about what had happened.

The claxon blared and the cabin glowed red with the emergency lighting. Jerking up, she opened her eyes and the vision disappeared.

There is no safe space. Every nightmare starts here.

Her oxy monitor beeped the half-full alarm, and she had to go. She reached for the toys in front of her but stopped: she could not take anything out with her.

Retracing their path to the Maintenance-1 hold where they first hid, she examined the hatch that her mother had welded shut from the inside. The hold itself was empty and appeared to have been sterilized. She took another passageway to Cargo-2 and found it empty as well. The hatch to the small service tunnel where they had exited remained open, and she knew why: to remove her mother's body.

Stars sparkled in front of her eyes again when she tried to step into the hold. Her stomach cramped, and her hands shook. The head-up display flashed red with a blood CO_2 crash, and the breath-rate alarm sounded: symptoms of hyperventilation. *I don't remember being this afraid*, she thought, but her body remembered.

Tears can't fall in zero-g, and she saw the world through the eyes of the children in the freezing hold ten years past: cloudy, surreal, disorienting—like looking through a nebula. But she was too afraid to cry then, too afraid of what would happen to them if she let go even a little, too afraid of what would happen to her and her world. She had to keep that world together, or it would wash away with the tears and be lost forever. Still she could not let go and rubbed the tears from the corners of her eyes on the padding of the visor hinge and floated to slow her breathing.

When her blood-gas monitor approached normal, she climbed into the hold and pushed back to where they first entered in maintenance-1. Finding nothing, she returned to the open hatch. There, she remembered all of the kids in their pajamas and Sam suspending his link in the air to distract them.

A translucent, dull brown covered the deck below her: dried blood, her mother's blood. *They never cleaned this.* "Have faith," she heard in her mother's voice.

The suit monitor alarmed again. *Breathe,* she told herself. Tears came again, halting her progress. A new alarm alerted her: only three minutes of oxygen remained on the tank. She breathed much too fast, the excess humidity etching the inside corners of her visor with frost.

Nothing caught her attention in the hold. Frowning, she switched the headlamp to spot, and looked down into the accessway—nothing. She cycled through the headlamp's wavelengths used to expose service marks and carbon fiber fatigue. Each time, she scanned the hold and accessway—still nothing. When she turned to leave, she caught a glint off something under the dried blood. A bright blue from her headlight exposed it: a symbol like a four-leaf clover enclosing an open circle. Her mother must have drawn it while the kids slept, and her blood covered it. Having no idea what it might signify, she took a vid and copied the symbol on her glove.

Mom left us for a while and came back with the qchip. She stopped at the alt-bridge to program the chip. The shortest path there would take her past the next room—the infirmary, where the pirates had slaughtered the adults.

A dark cloud filled Meriel's vision, obscuring the passageway. Repeated blinking did not dispel the visions. She folded her arms across her chest and tucked her legs in, trying to return to the safest place she could remember, her mother's arms.

"No, not now. Stay here. Don't freeze up, girl. Think. What do you need to do?" With a deep breath, she untucked and changed course.

If her mother had gone that way, the pirates would have captured her. *No, Mom left through Maintenance-1 and welded the hatch shut when she returned. So the kids and I left through Cargo-2.*

While turning to take another route, her link buzzed: the security sweep. The next compartments were too far away. She jumped into the infirmary, entered a utility closet, and turned off her headlamp. The light in the room came on, allowing her to peek through the louvers, and she groaned.

It was still there, the blood covering the deck and splattered on the walls. They had not cleaned it but only removed the bodies and devices to log as evidence. Closing her eyes did not help; flashbacks filled in every detail of the scene for her.

"It's not real," she whispered. "It's not real." The heavy copper odor smothered her, and stars glittered in front of her eyes again. Nausea reached her throat, and to relieve the symptoms, she massaged the tendons of her right wrist. It did not work, and she grabbed a service bag from her hip and opened her visor to retch. The cold shocked her, and she inhaled only the N_2/Ar environment. She fought to breathe, which shut down the nausea symptoms, and lowered her visor again, but there was no oxygen left within it. After inserting her last canister, she took a deep breath and ran the safety drill. *Half the reading plus half the reserve: ten plus three minutes...ten and three.*

Near-suffocation reengaged her rational thought processes. The incessant drills they ran as kids snapped her back from the flight response. Like her kata, the drills helped make her next steps automatic—biological—so conscious thought was unnecessary. She still breathed too fast, so she took a few slow breaths.

Able to breathe again, she prepared to leave the closet when the lights dimmed. A narrow curtain of light cut through the dark as she peered through the louvers. A new sound echoed through the infirmary: the skittering and clicking of a security spider. If it found her, that would be enough to arrest her and kill her dreams. Nick did not tell her spiders were aboard. *Sloppy,* she thought, and made a note to bitch.

She ducked below the louvers as the light shone through them. The spider scraped the door, testing the handle, but she gripped it tight from the inside and held her breath. A probe snaked through a louver and felt its way around but could not reach the handle. *The probe is a sniffer, not a camera: it can't tell for sure I'm here.* The stars reappeared in front of her eyes, and the nausea returned.

A part of her wanted to let go, to let the spider tranq her. She took a shallow breath. *Is this really worth it? All this just so the kids can have a chance at something more than a spacer's funeral?*

Yes.

The probe withdrew, the light beam moved on, and the skittering sounds faded to silence. She took a breath but needed to move or risk running out of air—but where? *Mom was away when we heard the escape pod eject.* Meriel turned and pushed herself to the evac bay and ePod berths.

No one believed the parents had attempted to abandon their kids using an ePod, so the empty berth presented another mystery. ePods were rather useless. With few survival rations and no ability to jump, survivors had to depend upon someone being nearby to hear their EM screamers. Unless you ejected near a colony or a busy shipping lane, an ePod was a casket, and you would be buried alive. Many spacers chose not to use them after hearing graphic tales of what rescuers had found inside them.

On the empty ePod hatch, she discovered another four-leaf clover symbol and open circle drawn within. Drops of blood, long dried, were spattered below it. *An ePod will not eject without at least one living person onboard, but all the crew was accounted for—adults killed and kids safe. What happened?*

The suit O_2 alarmed again, and time was running out. *Alt-bridge, that's where Mom went next.* She took the long way to the cold locker next to the galley, but the door was locked. Opening her suit momentarily to access the key on her necklace, she unlocked the door to the coldest, most functional room on the entire ship, the only room without ornamentation or any other sign of the children who flew her. In this compartment, their lives were saved.

Unlike the other compartments, someone had cleaned and polished the alt-bridge and emptied all of the drawers below the console. All signs of habitation had been removed, along with the gum and other detritus common where kids perched for a few milliseconds. *I need to find something,* she thought, shaking her head. *But what do I expect to find that trained investigators missed?*

With the press of a button, she booted nav. The OS remained, but no data or apps. *Why would they wipe the apps? Police wouldn't do that.* She slapped her hand on the console. *Damn. Nothing. Fifteen days left and nothing. What did Mom do?*

Meriel slid the chip into the nav slot. A few of the lights blinked and the chip headers appeared. A message popped up. "Invalid coordinates. Cannot process." *So the OS recognized the header. It wasn't physically damaged, but was corrupted: as Nick said, tampered with intentionally.*

The O_2 alarm sounded again. *Two minutes plus three. Just enough time to exit.* She hesitated, knowing if she left now, she would have nothing. A dim glow at the base of the chip slot and a tiny blinking icon stopped her from removing the chip. "Click," she said.

"Backup incomplete. Continue verify?" the system said.

Did Mom pull the chip out early? "Yes."

"Thank you, Meriel. Verify invalid. Recopy?"

Recopy? That meant the copy buffer might still contain data. The I/O buffers were an integral part of the operating system, and the OS was not wiped. An image of her mom's information might still exist in the system, and no one would know unless someone inserted a chip with the correct header.

"Verify invalid. Recopy?" the console repeated. A recopy would wipe out all similar files on the chip. If it saved the old, a recopy still might erase anything that nav did not associate with another file. That might null everything except the headers, but she did not have another chip or the time to search for one.

She crossed her fingers and cringed. "Archive old. Recopy."

"Thank you again, Meriel." The copy icon came up and spun. Meriel's O_2 now blinked red and beeped. She was out of air and sucking dust. *Zero plus three, zero plus three,* she repeated to herself.

"Countdown from three minutes," she instructed her suit.

"Copy complete," the console said.

Again, there was not enough time to verify. She removed the chip and stuck it in again to check its integrity.

"Destination: Enterprise," the console said. "Initiating jump prep. Begin proximity check." Lights winked and the nav computer behind the smoked plastaglass wall lit up.

"Negative! Abort jump!" She had forgotten that her mom gave her a self-executing nav program.

"Countermanding. Idle," the console announced and dimmed its lights. "Continue validation?"

Yes or No? A check of the suit's countdown clock indicated less than a minute's worth of air. "No," she said, gasping for breath as the rebreather only scrubbed out the CO_2 now. The chip could be trash, but she was out of air. She'd need to take a leave from the *Tiger* to get another shot at this. By then it would be too late.

She scrambled to the air lock and tried alternative O_2 cylinders but found only empties. Struggling for breath, she dropped to her knees and glanced back to the alt-bridge, but there was no time left to return and validate the chip. With a slam of her fist on the exit-request button, the door opened and she lunged inside. Opening her helmet, she gasped for air, which flooded the lock.

After wiping the warm-suit to remove hair and sweat and to contaminate any residual DNA, she launched herself back toward the maintenance shuttle to return to Enterprise. At the turn of a bend, she spotted two service techs headed in her direction from an adjoining passage. She neared the shuttle wharf, expecting the door to open, but the door remained shut and did not acknowledge her ID. *Did the module dissolve already?* The others would be here soon. If the door did not open, they would know she did not belong and alert security.

The security ID. Nick had not cleared the ID this far, and she did not reset it when she left her ship. She jabbed the capsule, which loosened the bandage, and blood leaked from the edge. The jabbing exhausted the local anesthetic on the bandage, and her wrist throbbed with pain.

Turning her back on the approaching workers, she watched as her wrist continued to blink in the wrong color.

"Hey, newbie," someone behind her said. "Having problems?"

Just then, her wrist blinked blue and the door opened. She turned to the voice. "No. Just not in a hurry to get back home."

"Better have that seen to," the other said, pointing to the blood soaking her shirt cuff.

"Will do." She dripped with sweat and breathed too fast as she entered, gripping the handhold to steady her until the artificial gravity settled them onto the deck. With gravity restored, the blood flowed preferentially downward to the edge of her cuff and a small drop fell to the floor of the shuttle unobserved. The three rode back to Enterprise in silence.

Leaving the security area as fast as possible was imperative, but she would not make it like this, clammy and faint. She rushed to the bathroom across the hall. Once inside, she splashed cold water on her face and washed the blood from her shirt cuff. A tight grip on the sink helped to steady her, but did not relieve the nausea, and she ran into a stall and threw up. *God, what am I doing here*? When she could walk again, she staggered back to the sink and wiped the drek off her coveralls, but they still reeked.

The bathroom door opened, and a security squad entered. She turned away and held her breath.

"Phew," one said. "What sewer did you crawl out of?"

"Drunk tank," Meriel mumbled.

"I suggest burning those blues."

Leaving the bathroom, she walked out of red-zone to green, recycled her coveralls and the service bag. She picked up her bracelet link from the locker and hurried back to Nick's. This time when she pressed the wound on her wrist, it did not flash.

Exhausted, with aching sides and throbbing wrist, she placed her hand over her necklace. For the first time in a decade, she might have the clues to what had happened to her parents on the *Princess* and save her ship from the recyclers.

***

Monitors subdividing the three active walls filled the Enterprise security substation. Bunks framed an arms locker on the other wall. In the middle of the room, a uniformed guard tipped his chair back and put his boots on a desk to finish his lunch. A glob of neu-mayo fell on his shirt, and he flicked it off with his little finger.

When the alarm arrived from the impound docks, he jerked up and tapped the desk to activate a tight-beam laser aimed at a shuttle touring the docks.

"What is it now, Bob?"

"She was here."

"We haven't heard anything for years. How do you know?"

"The spider got a holo." Bob transferred the vid of Meriel exiting the *Princess*.

"Damn. Is she still there?"

"She left."

"Take care of her."

"She's still too visible, and the timetable is too close," Bob said. "Our job is to keep this under wraps for a few more weeks."

"Make her disappear before this gets worse. Now. One more misstep, and it will be out of our hands and…and more aggressive forces will intervene."

***

When Meriel approached Nick's door, her link displayed "G2445rt." That was one level higher than where they had met before and in a much nicer part of the station. Taking a people mover, she found herself at a luxury office complex. A business located at the address, Enterprise Cyber Security, ECS, provided specialty security services to corporate clients. Behind the reception desk sat a stunning android secretary.

However, the *rt* suffix indicated a service entrance in an alley around the corner where garbage would be picked up. She smiled without questioning his paranoia.

As soon as she appeared near the door, Nick waved her inside and inspected her with a worried look. "Are you OK?"

Nodding, she slumped into a chair.

He reached out his hand to her, palm up, and she offered hers in return, but he shook his head. "The link, M." Before she could stop him, he grabbed the burner, ground it into sand in a shredder, and sprinkled it into the soil of a potted ficus. His eyes stopped on her bloody cuff and he turned to retrieve a spray tube from a drawer under the plant. "Did it hurt?"

The painful memories mixed with the agony of her recent visit, and she frowned. "Yeah."

With one hand he raised her stained sleeve and with the other sprayed a bandage to reseal the wound on her wrist. While he worked, she peeled off the metal foil from her waist. He took her other hand in his. "So, what have you got for me?"

Her eyes widened. "The alt-bridge recopied the data, Nick. And the jump coordinates checked out. It might all be here."

"Really? Come on then." He spun his chair, and she followed.

Beyond the foyer, they passed a living area with sparse but stylish furniture and entered a closet where an assortment of wigs and glasses hung. A false door at the end hid a room filled with racks of shiny equipment and blinking lights, spotlessly clean but disorganized. Cables and patch cords snaked between everything. All his money was in this room.

"My new cave," he said.

A variety of replicators for different materials lined the walls. Along one, molecular printers with the cases off and guts exposed busied themselves with prototyping. Cryogenic equipment with chugging vacuum pumps occupied another corner, and she wondered if he burned his own chips. Next to it lay a stack of prosthetic limbs. All of his equipment was modularized for rapid relocation using nested crates stacked in an adjoining room. With all the tech that might amuse and distract any genius, the jars of body parts drew her attention first.

He raised his hand to stop her. "Don't touch. That might become a functioning liver in a few more months."

"I know someone you should meet," she said, thinking of John.

Without looking, he held out his hand again. "Give."

She removed the q-chip from her necklace.

"Do you know what's on it?" he asked.

"No. Like before, only the headers. My link is too slow to read the nav format. I checked the coordinates, but I can't tell." She handed him the chip. "Careful. We're not likely to get another chance at this."

He played with the little device he had touched many times. "You sure about this? They tampered with it, M. That means someone does not want us to know what's on it."

She nodded.

He set the chip on the workbench and rolled to a corner of his lab. Extending his chair up to the top shelf, he retrieved a box. After rummaging through the pile of electronics, he surfaced with an ancient nav script programmer and a clear-plastic box ingrained with a fine metal mesh. Placing the system inside the cage, he connected the cord and attached it to another box.

"Is that relic the one you used last time?" she asked.

"Yup. It's the slowest, most addled reader that has the embedded Riemann–Hilbert transforms rather than software emulations. But it will allow us to read the alt-bridge format in real time." He let the system boot.

"What's the cage for?"

"To stop any potential signals from escaping. The box is a filter to protect my house power."

"Why so cautious?"

"The data chip is from the scene of a crime, M, and could turn all my darlings into zombies. I've got to totally isolate it."

"We didn't do this last time."

"We were fools last time. Exec mode," he said. "That should stop the self-executing nav program." He stuck the device into the chip reader and closed the door of the cage. "OK. Here goes. List contents."

The equipment responded to his voice command, and the screen flashed. The familiar network headers appeared on the association map, beginning with the jump coordinates for Enterprise. "I recognize these. List first." A scrolling string of numbers and symbols popped up.

"They work," she said. "The alt-bridge asked me if I wanted to jump there, here...wherever. Next?"

Nick double clicked on the *Home* header to highlight the news announcements about her mother's obsession, the myth called Home. Clicking on the *Personal* header, he found video files and expanded the icons.

She leaned closer. "Liz and I thought we lost these forever."

He patted her hand and then flicked his hand to enlarge each icon in turn.

"Wait," she said. "That one. Click." The vid played her mom in a hard-suit without her helmet. By her side stood a young girl with her helmet still on, but she could see the wide smile and starry eyes through the visor. "That's Liz after her first EVA. She must have been nine. She was so thrilled she couldn't stop talking about it for days."

"That's not Liz, M. That's you. Zoom."

He was right: brown hair, not blond, and the stars glittered in her own green eyes. It was Meriel, and the happiest she had ever been.

"Mom drilled me for weeks on the safety protocols, but I still couldn't remember. The first thing she did before we entered the air lock was to tether us together. We left the lock for one of the deadliest environments in the universe, but I never felt safer. Outside we just drifted and watched a nebula. Mom pressed her helmet against mine, and we talked about space without the communicators, like we owned it all, like we belonged there just as much as the stars." Meriel turned to catch Nick with the sweetest expression on his face.

"Make me a copy of this, OK?" she said, unaware of the tears in her eyes. "We still need to search for something that will save my ship."

"Data," he said. "Top. Double click. Is this anything?"

She squinted to study the lattice of content, and then she gasped. "Cargo manifest. Oh my God, that's from our last flight! Let's see: replicator data, data-feed updates, prototype jump engine, medical prototypes, bio proteins, organics—all standard stuff. At the end. Zoom. I don't recognize those strings of numbers."

"Last. Double click," he commanded to list the contents of the numbered items. A small panel on the display opened in the corner and began to scroll symbols. Behind it, the screen flashed.

"It's a virus, taking over; replicating. We need to end this." He tried to turn off the device without success. "It won't shut off." The cage started to glow. "It's trying to induce a current in the cage. It needs to communicate. Yikes!"

Yanking the cord from the power supply had no effect, and the system kept running. Next, he wheeled around the lab throwing circuit breakers but not before the device flashed QR and UPC codes. He threw a towel over the cage to stop the video signals and then opened the door and flipped the reader to remove the battery. The instant he opened the cage, it shrieked atonal bits and bleeps. "Sheesh, it's trying to communicate by audio."

One of his other computers turned on and beeped. He slammed his palm on a big red button on the desk, and all of his electronics shut down except the infected device. Returning to remove the battery, her bracelet squawked in reply.

"Turn it off, M!" he shouted."

Meriel tried and could not, then peeled the cell off her bracelet to kill it. He succeeded in tearing out the sick device's battery, and darkness filled the room. A moment later, the emergency lights tinted them a dim red, and he slumped back into his chair.

"So…what just happened?" she asked.

"Damn. This virus is aggressive." He let out his breath slowly as he surveyed the chaos. "You bricked it, M. And I'm not sure what else it burrowed into."

After placing the pendant in his pocket, he threw the nav reader into a box with a Tesla coil, and the room lit up with blue flashes and lightning. When wisps of smoke leaked from the box, he used tongs to throw the smoking ruin into a mangler, which ground it to dust. When the racket subsided, he switched the machine off and sat.

"Feeling safer now?" she asked.

"Not yet. When the refuse is broken down into its constitutive elements by the recycler, then I'll feel a little better."

"Sorry for the trouble, Nick."

"Part of the job. Oh, and your link is probably infected, so you better leave it with me." She gave her bracelet to him, and he handed her another burner link. "Here. This doesn't have much memory, but it synced with your biotag. Use it until I can scrub yours, if I can."

"This could be our break, Nick. The manifest might tell us what the *Princess* carried that was worth stealing—something other than drugs. Can you send a copy of what you find to Jeremy Bell on Ross? He's my lawyer."

He nodded. "If anything is useful, I'll find it."

"I hope so. I can't go back."

"What do you mean?"

"You should have warned me about the security spider," she said, but he remained silent. "You didn't know?"

He shook his head. "You should have told me about this earlier. I might have been…more reluctant to read the chip."

"Why?"

"If I didn't know about the spiders, then station security didn't know. Which means someone else wants information on the *Princess*. They must be private, and that's expensive and illegal. You need to be more careful."

"It didn't see me."

"You sure?"

"Yes," she said, but now wondered. "I'm out of options, Nick. I only have fifteen days left to deliver evidence to the court."

"We'll make it."

He made a copy of her q-chip and wagged the original in front of her. "This chip is a loaded weapon. You should leave it with me."

"It's all I have left from her, Nick. I'm not leaving without it."

He smiled but kept the chip.

"Yeah, yeah," she said and took it.

"Then never try to read it, especially near anything on the ship's network. If you do, it'll take over in less than a second, and we don't know what will happen. From now on, think of it as jewelry—pretty and only for show. I'll figure it out from the copy."

She returned it to her necklace. They hugged, and he watched her walk out the door.

Outside, her link buzzed with a message unable to reach her within Nick's shielded domain.

        We're at the Gear Case for lunch.
    Doc is here looking for you.

Uh oh, she thought and slowed her pace.

The significance of their find struck her. Without thinking, she touched the pendant. *Maybe our cargo was worth stealing and the manifest can tell me what it was. That would challenge the whole idea the crew was involved in a drug deal.*

Remembering the clover symbols she had found on the *Princess,* she checked her palm. Her hand was clean—she had drawn the pattern on her glove but wiped it down and left it on the M22 dock. Still, she had a vid on the link. But when she removed it to check, she held a different link—the link with the vid was mulched and decomposing under Nick's ficus. The bracelet that might have synced she had left with him to disinfect, leaving her with the cheap, anonymous device she might have bought in a candy store.

She stopped. There was nothing to show she had visited her ship or Nick. Sparkles appeared again, and she leaned against the wall for support. *Breathe. It wasn't a dream,* she thought, but now had doubts.

I was there. I have the q-chip with the data…but I can't check it, just like yesterday. So what changed in the last five hours? If not at Nick's or the Princess, *where have I been?* The wound on her wrist was real and hurt like hell. She peered at it. *And how else did I get this?*

Nick did not answer her call. Turning, she walked back to the service entrance but the door was flush against the wall and she could not find the seam—as if the door had never existed. She knocked on the wall, but there was no answer.

"Hey, you!" called a security guard at the entry to the alley. "What's your business here?"

"Sorry, just looking for a bathroom," she said, being careful of Nick's privacy.

He glared at her with one hand on the butt of a stunner. "Back to blue-zone, spacer."

Hurrying away, she passed a man with no distinguishing traits who turned to peer into a shop window. He appeared vaguely familiar, but she could not place him. Using Nick's burner link, she took a vid of him and left to meet John.

On the lookout for Ferrell, Meriel approached the docks to join the crew for lunch. Just past the pressure doors dividing green-zone from blue, the doors to the Gear Case Café appeared. The café was noisy but well lit, which had advantages when dining with spacers. At a table by the windows sat John, Cookie, Jeri, and Socket. She signaled to John, who came over to her.

"Doc left. We told him you were shopping and…" He paused. "You OK?"

"Yeah," she said, unaware of her ashen complexion. "Just tired, I guess. Busy day." *Understatement.*

He took her arm and led her to the table. "Can we talk? Privately?"

She sighed and rubbed her painful wrist. "Maybe later, John."

Passing the bar, a familiar face in dress blues with three stripes and a star on his sleeves sat with a beautiful woman in a business suit. Meriel leaned over to John. "Isn't that Stevens at the bar?"

John nodded. "He doesn't like to drink with the non-coms."

"Who's he with?"

He grinned. "She's a league rep. He's likely politicking for a command of his own."

John brought a chair for her and inserted it between himself and Jerri, evoking a pout from her but a snicker from Socket. Meriel caught the looks but said nothing.

With her eyes a bit unfocused, Jerri turned to her. "What does Doc want with you?"

Meriel frowned. "A psych evaluation."

"Not a physical?"

Socket leaned toward the other women. "He's pretty, that guy, but cold as a glass hull. I'd stay away from him if I were you. He'd talk the wings off an angel."

Jerri smiled at Socket. "Did he?"

"Not yet. He still thinks it's his decision."

"He's a drunk with a license," Cookie said. "Avoid him."

"You're jealous, Sergeant," Socket said.

He shrugged. "The military has lots of functional drunks. I know the type."

While her crewmates roasted Ferrell, Meriel's throbbing wrist competed with her aching sides and grumbling stomach. Her stomach won. The burner link did not store her dietary preferences, so she keyed them into the kiosk. After her biotag rejected a peanut curry, she ordered a pasta and cream sauce with shrimp.

Socket drew her head back. "Damn, child. You're gonna blow an artery eating like that."

"This isn't Earth," Jerri said.

She was right. This wasn't Earth. Out here, the references to foods like chicken, beef, or fish implied flavors rather than the actual animal protein served. It did not really matter—anything she might order would be a hydroponically grown soy-mush blend with artificial flavors and colors combined with indigestible roughage for structure and texture. She knew that because the disclaimer appeared in small print at the bottom of every menu in the galaxy.

Delight over her discovery competed with fatigue from her ordeal, and she debated whether to dance or nap. She wanted to confide in John, but admitting to a security breach sounded like a bad idea.

Too exhausted to engage in the conversation, she scanned the café. Next to their table, the IGB news played on an overhead display.

    "...Alan Biadez, seen here proposing
increased immigration to tau Ceti-5.
The UNE/IS approved the action, but
residents of tC-5 oppose it. TC-5 has
agreed to accept ten thousand healthy
and productive immigrants into the
sector each year by lottery. However,
complaints claim the UNE/IS does not
check the health status of emigrants,
and winning lottery numbers are being
openly sold to criminals. They also
charge that the IS will not pay for
return passage..."

Jerri sneered and mumbled, "Weasel."

"Why do you say that?" Meriel asked.

"He's been dumping Earth scum on the colonies, and he takes a cut. Everyone knows. There are enough people in the immigration lottery to hide tons of graft and kickbacks."

"Yeah," Cookie said. "The funds got him elected, and then they wouldn't prosecute him." He appeared woozy and swayed a bit in his chair, unhappy about something. Smoke writhed down the sides of the large glass as he drank, while the iridescent contents swirled within like a demon fighting to escape. She assumed the booze was some blend of tasty poisons that would kill a smaller man, and she made a mental note never to order one.

Jerri raised an eyebrow. "You seem shocked."

Meriel bit her lip. "I thought he was one of the good guys."

A cynical laugh slipped out. "Better look elsewhere, hon. Biadez tried to force Alpha Centauri into the UNE to dump convicts on the asteroid settlements."

"How can you know that, Jerri?"

"I grew up there." She sighed. "I can understand how you wouldn't see this. Nothing leaves Earth without UNE's say so, including news."

"Earth is the jewel of the galaxy. Why do people want to emigrate?"

"The UNE controls everything now through regulation. If you don't like it, there's no choice but to leave or take adjustment drugs, and they won't let the useful people leave." The corners of Jerri's lips turned down. "It's all run by the bureaucrats, so no one knows who to blame anymore. They're like lobsters in a tank, dragging all the good people back down."

Meriel wondered if the adjustment drugs she spoke of were the same as they gave her. "But it's so beautiful."

"Tourist advertisements and old vids. Tourism is the only real industry left, but they don't let off-worlders see anything. It's all sims in the visitors bureaus. Every other business exists just to maintain the populace, like food and housing."

"And wiping each other's butts," Cookie said.

"You've been there?" Meriel asked.

Jerri nodded. "Right after school. Everyone in the sector thinks they need to visit Earth to prove how successful and sophisticated they are. It's like a pilgrimage, and my family believed. I started graduate school in astrophysics." She shook her head. "But real science is dead there now, just another tool of politics."

With his face hovering over his drink, Cookie mumbled, "Poor baby."

Jerri punched him in the arm and took another drink. "They're all focused on entertainments and surgical body enhancements. BioLuna is making a fortune."

Cookie frowned. "They traded their freedom for empty promises. People who disagree are drugged into compliance."

"They're all like little flowers down there," Jerri said, "nodding in the breeze, telling themselves how meaningful their lives are, and filling their time with entertainments. When winter comes, the little darlings will all die."

He sneered. "Yeah, yeah. Everyone who's left plays nicey nice with each other and prays for the government to protect them from Sol and the weather and the sniffles. Some asteroid is gonna smack 'em into the Stone Age while they're all singing 'Kumbaya.' Next time, it won't crater a country like Brazil in '83; they'll lose the whole f'ing planet." He looked as if he would spit and swayed in his chair like a tree in the wind.

"Why should we give a damn about them anyway?" Meriel said. "We're way out here."

"Don't be naive, Meriel," Jerri said. "Don't you read?"

"I've been busy." Meriel dropped her gaze, unable to tell them she had been drugged or sequestered for much of the last decade.

With a frown, John intervened. "Leave her alone, Jerri."

As if she'd been slapped, Jerri recoiled but would not be silenced. "We give a damn because billions of them would escape if they could. Everyone out here is living on the edge, and we can't handle a billion refugees. That's what the wars of immigration are all about. You think Wolf station can absorb another million helpless people and survive? Earth wants to crush us into submission by overwhelming us with immigrants."

"And make a buck at the same time," Cookie said. "So who's buying the next round?" Before anyone answered, he laid his head on the table and began to snore.

"What's eating him?" Meriel asked.

"He got bad news from his sister on Earth," Jerri said. "His favorite niece overdosed on adjustment drugs. He tried for years to bring her out here. Seems she was brainy, and Earth wouldn't let her go."

"That's rough."

No one noticed as two drunks staggered past their table to the bar.

"And get this," Jerri said. "They sent his sister a check. The niece isn't a burden on the healthcare system anymore, so the family got a rebate. It's eating at him, like they put a bounty on her life. His sister burned the check and sneaked the vid to him to post on the net."

"Can't she post it there?" John asked.

"No. They'd pull it down and arrest her. But they will see it out here."

"Maybe it will stop the UNE. They can't use the navy way out here."

"Biadez will find a way. Some of 'em even think we're heathens. Their goddess, Gaia, does not bless us out here, and that justifies treating us like savages."

"My mom told me we followed God out here, and he was waiting for us," Meriel said.

Jerri leaned over the table. "My dad said our struggle with Earth is a battle between our gods, Gaia and Prometheus, Earth versus progress, and—"

"Jeez," Socket interrupted, "you girls need to get laid." She turned to Meriel and John and smiled, and then to Jerri. "Say, the Blue Note next door has some fresh stationers. Let's go find ourselves some dates."

Jerri wagged a thumb at Cookie, who snored loudly. "What are we gonna do with him?

"Bring him along," Socket said and began to wrestle him to his feet.

Standing, Jerri did not help. "Sure, but first I need to hit the head." She left, and Socket dropped Cookie back in his chair.

When Jerri was out of earshot, Meriel turned to John and whispered, "You got history with Jerri?"

He sighed. "Long time ago. Didn't work out."

Crap, more complications. "Does she see it that way?"

"Ah, the *Tiger* is kinda cramped, Meriel."

"Uh-huh." *Target of opportunity?* Disappointed, she turned toward the bar to see Stevens approaching the exit with the woman on his arm. At the door, he stopped and spoke to her after which she frowned and shook her head. He left her and walked toward their table while the woman crossed her arms and tapped her foot.

As he approached them, Socket smiled. "Two birds, sir?"

Stevens leaned on the table. "Pardon?"

"Never mind, sir. What brings you slumming?"

"Don't mean to disturb you," he said. "Just a heads-up in case you're planning a little business. XO said we're stopping at Etna this circuit."

An opportunity for contraband. A useful tip and unusual coming from a senior rank.

"And we're undocking an hour early, so if you have some plans, better start now." He looked at her and John, and she blushed.

Socket nodded. "Thank you, Sir. Much appreciated."

"Carry on, sailors."

Turning to leave, Stevens bumped into one of the drunks from the bar, who fell over Jerri's empty chair and onto their table. The drunk rose and swung an arm, which Meriel ducked and parried. Cookie woke from his stupor and, without thinking, aimed a fist at the drunk. After the wet snap of a broken nose, the man staggered back to his companion, and the two hurried away.

None of this was unusual in blue-zone, and no one noticed Stevens rub the scratch on his hand or the needle-tipped ring that had fallen under the table.

Enterprise Station–Outbound

During the slow hours, while the *Tiger* crawled its way out of Procyon A's gravity well, Meriel studied in the mess. Nav without visualization was boring, and she could not concentrate. Cookie's familiar puttering in the galley and the steady flow of crew and passengers for snacks did not bother her. What distracted her was Jerri's condemnation of Biadez at lunch back on Enterprise. It was as if she'd spoken of a different man. *How could she say that? Have I been so entirely wrong*?

She queued up a vid of one of his speeches from a packet the foundation gave to the kids after the *Princess* attack. The boilerplate she projected on the wall introduced the charity and its humanitarian works.

Biadez stood at the podium in an impeccable dark suit and heavy coat while cherry blossoms drifted past in a mild breeze that tossed his hair. It must have been spring on Earth—or a perfect studio set. He appeared much younger than at his recent inauguration, as if the years between weighed heavily upon him. A beautiful blond woman with a smug look stood behind him—his wife, perhaps. With a wave of his hand to quiet the audience, he began to speak.

> "Throughout history, humans have lived on the brink of extinction, on the razor's edge between starvation and annihilation, at the whim of the unforgiving hand of nature and subject to the universe's existential lack of concern..."

A fresh mug of coffee appeared in front of Meriel, and she turned to see Cookie sit next to her.

"We conquered the threats from Gaia and in so doing became her protector…"

"Thinking about what Jerri said?" he asked.
She smiled. "You remember?"
"Yeah, sorry."
"Sorry about your niece."
He nodded.

"Outposts of humanity cling to life in the stars but only human life, and even the richest habitats cannot support self-sustaining ecosystems with diverse species. And our experiment is still young; it is still not clear if these colonies can survive without their roots planted firmly in the soil of Earth, the single planet which supports human life. I implore us to change that."

He pointed dramatically to the sky.

"…Earth is our home, but our future is out there. We must expand the quantity and diversity of Earth life on the colonies and stations to protect it from the whims of nature. We must affix anchors on other worlds and build ecosystems upon them which will support Earth life. We must make the stars our home. Humanity must rise to the challenge or suffer annihilation.

"Join me, and let us populate the stars!"

The vid ended, and a banner screen from the Biadez Foundation popped up. She picked up the coffee, letting it warm her hands.

"He understood," she said. "How could he be the person Jerri talked about?"

"Maybe once, but power corrupts, Meriel."

"So do ideologies," Jerri said from behind her and walked to the replicator. "I think you should hear the whole speech." After filling her coffee cup, she joined them and queued the vid to an earlier section. "Here."

Biadez spoke again.

```
   "We conquered the threats from Gaia
and in so doing became her protector…
   "The sacrifice of personal liberty,
the limitations of technological
innovation, the strict regulations of
how we live and where we live were all
necessary to achieve this victory over
ourselves—necessary and painful but
for the common good."
```

"He meant that speech for Earthers, M," Jerri said, "to remind them what humans sacrificed to conquer their spirit. He never said what it meant to tame your god."

Meriel cocked her head, not understanding.

"It's an apology for tyranny, and it's gotten worse."

"But it's a democracy. They can change it if they like."

"Not really. They're plebiscites now, with the same power as a survey. Only the children pretend to vote now."

"But we weren't part of that."

"The *Princess*?" Cookie asked.

She nodded. "His people got us orphans onto fine ships. Every one of us. We might have ended up in an organ farm or a mining colony, but we all got great fosters." She shook her head. "I can't believe he's who you say he is."

A cold expression washed over his face. "Do you believe me?"

She had no answer for him.

Jerri sat up. "We don't understand Earthers any more, Meriel. None of us do. And they don't understand us." She leaned over with her elbows on the table. "Did I tell you I visited Earth?"

Meriel grinned.

"Oh, yeah, at the Gear Case. Well, my classmates laughed at me when I went through the debark checklist before leaving a shopping mall. They never for a moment thought to stop at a closed door and verify that a breathable atmosphere existed on the other side. They didn't understand why I had trouble sleeping without a net or felt uncomfortable at the beach without a tether."

"I hadn't thought of that," Meriel said, but Cookie nodded.

"None of us do. We pity those poor low-grav miners on Ceres, but on Earth, that's how they think of us. Stations are bastions of civilization to us. But to Earthers, they are primitive outposts, one step from extinction. One referred to me as a noble savage. She presumed it was a compliment, like my citizenship on a backward station was somehow charming and virtuous."

"Alpha C isn't backward."

He smiled. "What did you do?"

"She was my fiancé's mom, so I didn't kill her. I was an oddity, and she paraded me around to her society friends." Jerri looked her in the eye. "They act like Earth citizenship makes them the center of the universe, like all life slides downhill from there, and we're on the bottom out here. She talked like she reached into a sewer to clean me up."

"What happened to him?"

"He stayed with his mom."

"You're set," Meriel said. "You're a citizen of Alpha C."

"I'm not so sure anymore," Jerri said. "Our breakup wasn't...cordial, and I had to leave Earth in kind of a hurry. My folks might not want me back. To Earthers, living on Alpha C is almost as low as being a spacer."

"There's a lot farther down to go than this," Cookie said.

"I know. I just can't see how people would give up their freedom for citizenship there or any station for that matter."

"It's safer," Meriel replied.

Jerri pursed her lips. "Not you too, M. Life is dead there."

"I just want a place for us. A safe place I don't have to worry about the kids."

The claxon sounded, announcing twenty minutes to jump.

Meriel turned off the vid. "I'm not stupid. I just don't understand how a bad guy could be so kind to us."

Jerri sighed again. "We're different now, M. You're thinking they're like spacers, and they're not. We just don't understand them."

"We all understand greed and corruption," he said and walked behind the counter to the galley, leaving the women alone in the mess.

Jerri's link buzzed, and after a tap, a holo of Molly's face appeared. "Aye, ma'am."

"Report to the bridge, pilot. I want you sitting nav this jump."

"Aye, ma'am. How come? I'm supposed to be off."

"Stevens is down, and I want you to check John's program."

Cookie leaned in from the galley. "What happened to Stevens?"

Molly's holo turned to him. "He turned up sick. Had to stay on station."

"So, what happened?" he asked.

"Seems he collapsed on the way to a sleepover. Almost didn't make it. He's still there in intensive care."

"He'll be alright?"

"With some nerve regeneration and therapy."

They all looked at each other, and Meriel voiced their concern: in close quarters such as a ship or a station, disease and contamination were terrorism vectors. "Infectious?"

"No. A toxin. If we got it, we'd know by now. Doc said they closed the Gear Case and the police are investigating."

"Security will be going nuts," Cookie said and returned to the galley.

"When's he coming back?" Jerri asked.

"We'll pick him up on the next circuit."

"That'll be a few months."

"Doc says he'll need it. Five minutes, pilot."

"Aye, ma'am," Jerri said, and the holo disappeared. She rose to leave, but Meriel touched her hand.

"So, you and John had something?" Meriel asked.

An angry squint crossed Jerri's face for a moment but melted. "Yeah, it was good for a while."

"How long was a while?"

"Long enough for me to think it might be more than a sleepover." She looked away. "He's not really a spacer, you know. You've seen it, like he's walking on a station all the time without fear of losing g."

"Like he's got roots in the deck."

"Yeah. Wherever his colony is, it's got some mass." A timid smile crossed her face. "He's sweet and kinda naive. And he hated station sleepovers: too impersonal. He said it took the love out of love, which didn't leave much left."

"What happened?"

Jerri dropped her gaze. "I knew he'd go home to his kids, and I felt like I didn't belong there."

"He told you about Haven?"

"Yeah. Says he's building a farm there."

"You think it's as nice as he says?"

"Nothing can be as nice as he says. But he's a marketing guy and should be able to spin any story."

Like being advance marketing rather than a spy or a farmer. "All I really know is that he's sitting nav on our boat."

"Me, too. I was just hoping his colony had more than a half g so his girls weren't physically challenged. Then we could take them with us."

"Did it get that far?"

"Not really. Just in my head."

"Would you have gone?"

"Maybe. That's the problem, M. I'm a spacer and not a mom. I didn't feel like…like I had a place in his future." She turned, but Meriel caught the hurt in her posture. "Honestly? He didn't invite me."

"It's a small ship, Jerri."

Jerri smiled at her. "I'm OK. Go ahead."
Meriel's link buzzed.

```
   From Socket: Doc is trolling for
 you.
```

"Thanks, Jerri. Sorry. Ferrell's coming. I gotta run."
"Sure. Oh, and John likes to make his move on the bridge in the dark."
Meriel smiled. "Thanks for the tip," she said, but she already knew that. She turned and used the service corridor to return to her cabin for the jump.

***

Ferrell drummed fingernails on the desk and poured himself another drink, while keeping his eyes glued to his console. It beeped with an incoming message.

```
        Treatment    for    LCDR    Stevens
   proceeding as discussed. Will advise
   when therapeutic progress indicates
   return to duty. We'll take good care
   of him. Don't worry.
        Neurotoxin    profile    attached.
   Markers imply a genetic design.
   However, staff still unable to match
   toxin profile to station personnel.
   As discussed, Stevens would not be
   alive if the toxin was targeted for
   his DNA. Please advise if you can
   identify target.
        Regards,
        CDR S. Khan, MD, DSM, PhD
        Emergency Care Unit
        Disease Control Center
        Enterprise Station.
```

Another beep indicated data sync completion.

Ferrell emptied his glass. With a swipe of his fingers, he ran the toxin profile against Stevens's medical records to confirm the DCC's diagnosis.

```
     Probability  of  toxin  target  to
LDCR E. Stevens, 26%.
```

The genetically targeted poison was not meant for Stevens.

He poured another drink and glanced at the picture of his daughter. "We're not safe yet," he said. "Run profile against all crew records."

```
     Highest    probability   of    toxin
target  to  any  crew  of  LSM  Tiger,
43%.
```

He smiled and poured another drink and poised his finger over the console to close the records. Then he frowned. "Recall symptom spectrum."

```
     Anemia,    disorientation,  hearing
loss,  lack  of  eye  coordination....
```

"Stop." He slapped his palm on the desk. "Damn! Run crew mitochondrial DNA against toxin profile."

```
     Highest    probability   of    toxin
target  to  any  crew  of  LSM  Tiger,
97%.
```

His sighed and shook his head. After emptying another glass, he transferred the video of his daughter to the active wall.

"Sorry, Asha. It wasn't supposed to go this way."

The console displayed the name of the crew member the neuro-toxin was designed for, the single person he could not disclose.

Chapter 6
Free Space

The *Tiger* coasted in deep space midway to Wolf 359 while Jerri optimized the final jump. Meriel and Lev checked the lashings and ran the data-integrity checks in a cargo hold, which is where Ferrell found her.

"You shouldn't be here, Doc."

"Medical emergency."

"Whose?"

"Yours. There's still the issue of your..." Ferrell paused and glanced over to Lev.

She looked around. "So, what is it?"

"You're still taking your meds?"

"Of course," she lied.

He raised his voice. "File says they were for delu—"

"OK. OK. You win." She turned to her cargomate. "Lev, take five," she said and tapped her fingers on the data module. When he exited the cargo bay, she turned back to Ferrell. "Get it off your chest, Doc. So, you've read my files. So what?"

Ferrell nodded but showed no emotion. "It's my responsibility, Meriel. The meds?"

She lied. "They were for the pain."

"An injury?"

"During the attack, I...was hurt."

"I'm sorry. What happened to you and your family was terrible." His brow furrowed. "The file didn't mention an injury."

Something in his voice told her he understood, and she relaxed. She opened her shirt collar to expose a few inches of the jagged scar which ran from her waist, across her chest, and up her neck to her ear. "It's mostly healed now."

He studied her scar.

He doesn't care. He looked right at it and didn't wince or avert his eyes, like the scars aren't part of me and don't matter at all. Maybe I misjudged him, she thought, unaware of her blush.

"LGen has a new treatment for scarring." She had exposed more of herself than she had intended and dropped her gaze.

With a tender smile he rested his hand on her shoulder. "The deepest wounds may not be visible on the surface."

Her body warmed at his touch, and her distrust melted into his blue eyes. *Maybe he's right. Maybe if...*

"Make an appointment, Meriel. When you're off duty."

"Sure, Doc." Still entangled in his words, she watched him turn and leave.

He didn't care about the scars, she thought again. But when he turned the corner, his aura turned the corner with him. She flushed with shame and stared at the empty doorway.

As he left, her nose winkled at the smallest hint of bitter orange.

"Soberal," she whispered. *Cookie was right. Ferrell's a functional drunk.* Realizing she had thought of him as a man, not as an enemy with the power to destroy her future, she flushed with shame.

Lev reappeared and caught her closing her shirt. "Ah, the wolf targets another willing lamb." He shook his head and returned to work.

"He's a doctor," Meriel said to his back, but her voice betrayed her. *Who am I kidding? I'm nothing special, and he wouldn't be squeamish around scars.*

She keyed a message to Molly.

```
    Tell Ferrell not to bother me when
I'm on duty. It's dangerous.
```

Molly's reply was quick.

```
    Dangerous to the cargo? For the
crew?
```

Meriel replied.

```
    Dangerous for Ferrell.
```

***

After completing her watch, Meriel walked back to the galley, grabbed a snack, and sat with her feet up on the neighboring chair. Searching for a message from Nick, she wondered what she could do until he safely read the chip. *If hijackers had attacked the* Princess *for the cargo, then what was worth stealing? Who would have done it?* The answers might be on the chip, but she would need him to disarm it first.

Remembering the plain-looking man on Enterprise, she found the vid on Nick's loaner link and zoomed the image on her visor. He was a graying, middle-aged man: a little severe, as though he'd just cleaned himself up from a lifetime in the sewer. A close-up exposed a long, thin scar over his left temple. She forwarded the clearest images to an app with the galaxy's facial-recognition database.

"Search all," she said and set the ship's computers to work in the background.

An incoming message beeped, one that arrived just before they jumped from the Procyon A system.

```
    From nz: i'm working on the chip in
a clean room. in the meantime, i've
scrubbed the files in the home and
personal groups. too much to send
without more time. attached is the vid
you wanted along with another file i
think will interest you. i cleaned up
```

```
the audio. i also improved the
resolution at the end. the original
uses a noise reduction algorithm that
overmodulates the signal. that's why
the common version is 2-d and so hard
to understand. tell me what you think.
```

She tapped her visor's head-up display to view the still of her and her mother after her first EVA. Then she queued up the vid that Nick wrote would interest her. When she saw the header, she questioned his judgment.

The header identified the vid as the familiar Mouldersen interview about the discovery of an Earthlike body, the same one she had dismissed as amateur theater. However, this was a full holovid.

"Play."

The garbled voice was much clearer now, and she could make out every word. She turned her head to observe different parts of the room, then rose, and walked through the audience displayed by the holovid. The faces were out of the camera's view, and she spotted nothing more of interest. She played it through to the usual scuffling when the recorder fell under the chair, but she had learned nothing new.

"Meeting over," the voice on the vid said, but the speaker stood out of sight. "Everyone back to work, please, and thank you very much for attending. Director, a word."

This was the same script she had heard many times. Expecting the holo to end when the others did, she picked up her trash and walked to the recycle chute. However, the vid did not end, and she stopped in her tracks, trash still in her hands.

"Pause. Duration." The vid reported eight minutes. Other copies of this video quit at about two.

She sat in the nearest chair. "Play." The camera still pointed to the ceiling, but muffled voices caused her to turn up the volume.

"You can't withhold news like this," Jeannine said.

"Of course you are right, Ms. Aldersen," a man's voice responded.

Meriel sidled over to the closest table and sat. "Pause." *Hmmm. Aldersen, not Mouldersen.* "Search Jeannine Aldersen." Her visor displayed a brief obituary: scientist for BioLuna, found alone in her apartment on Europa, apparent victim of starvation due to brain damage during a multimonth Stim bender. *She forgot how to eat. Huh, a responsible astrophysicist and team director suddenly develops a Stim addiction. Killed by sudden success?* "Play."

"Of course you are right, Ms. Aldersen, but all in good time. This is wonderful news, but something so momentous needs subtlety in the presentation. The great news for you is the chairman has a special project and would like a word with you. He suggested you might be the perfect representative to the UNE/IS regarding this magnificent discovery."

"Well…" Jeannine stammered, "this is so sudden."

"The timing is splendid for you. This news will impact all of known space and must be handled with care to avert panic and a land rush. This position will require technical expertise and discretion like you have exhibited during this project."

"But I—" Jeannine said, but the man interrupted again.

"Come now. *Carpe diem.* Some opportunities must be grasped when they arise. Officer, please escort Ms. Aldersen to the chairman's office. Good day, Director."

A door closed, and the voice returned, but now much less charming. "You, clean up. Leave nothing."

More doors closed, followed by a long silence. There was much more to the recording, so she waited. After a few minutes, someone picked up the camera and went behind the table, where Aldersen had stood during her announcement. The camera scanned the empty table and then focused on a clipboard under the table.

Meriel stopped the holo and zoomed in to the SDS, the Survey Data Summary, developed by the probe. The holographer tore off the summary sheet and scribbled "TTL-5B" in the margin.

A loud, "Hey, you!" on the holo startled her. The vid jerked abruptly and ended.

She was very familiar with the torn-off summary. It was famous, or rather infamous, and available everywhere on the net. She and Elizabeth had found many copies on conspiracy sites. It was considered one of the greatest frauds of the century.

The summary revealed an Earthlike atmosphere, gravity, nitrogen-rich soil, and two moons. The data was so explicit and self-consistent that people believed it on sight. And in a galaxy hungry for land, it drove a frenzy of speculators and prospectors to stake their claims. But when they arrived, they found only a dead rock. People condemned it as a sophisticated fraud or theoretical exercise, but they could not figure out who would benefit. They wrote it off as a prank and stopped searching, never knowing why someone would go to all the trouble.

She backed up the holo to a shot of the SDS on the clipboard and froze it. *Well, Nick, let's see how much you've improved the resolution.* "Zoom, two x," she said. Still, the image remained too small and too distorted by the lighting in the mess hall. "Four x." The sheet filled her low-res head-up visor, but the subject remained too fuzzy.

She got up, threw her trash away, and hurried to the entertainment center. Near the controls for the high-resolution holographic projector, she waved her link. The SDS appeared on the deck, full size but still a bit blurred. "Times eight," she said. And there it was.

The designation was TTL-5B3, not TTL-5B. That would make it a moon, not a planet: the third satellite orbiting the second planet. People expected a livable planet but found a cinder instead. Still, they would not likely miss a habitable moon nearby after traveling all that way. Her mother had not seen this but still believed. *What did she guess?*

If I presume everything printed on the sheet is correct, then what do I have? If the data were real and the coordinates were correct, then the origin or orientation must have been off. Jeannine mentioned the survey probe could not orient itself for a return to Earth and used the Magellanic cloud to get its bearings. That meant it could not see Sol. Which also meant Sol could not see TTL-5.

"A new star," she said aloud. The coordinates were referenced from somewhere other than Earth or Sol.

She looked at the image on the deck again. The SDS specified the location in the declination, right ascension and distance. However, the little boxes for EQS or EES, specifying the Earth equatorial or Earth ecliptic system, remained unchecked.

"And not referenced from Earth."

A handwritten note above the boxes, a note not included on the torn-off sheet circulating throughout the galaxy, read: "ref: DXC." *DX? DX Cancri. That's Dexter Station.*

She sighed. "Everybody had hunted in the wrong place and for the wrong thing." She translated the coordinates from DX Cancri to Earth ecliptic. Nothing appeared on the charts; dust clouds obscured observations from Sol and the large stations like Jeannine had said. But you could see it from DX Cancri. They called the star Jira-1, but no one knew the system surrounding it. And no one there would care: Dexter Station was another low-grav logistics hellhole, where no one had time to think about anything other than staying alive long enough to escape.

Jeannine's genius had placed her on that survey probe. She had peered through its eyes and found an Earthlike habitat. The probe had to figure out its location while unable to see Sol through the dust. So it used another star to orient itself, a star it knew well—DX Cancri—and posted the location relative to the DXC ecliptic rather than to Earth's. That's what the scientists celebrated—they had solved the puzzle.

Mom almost found Home and would have if she'd had time to open the latest holo. Using TTL-5B as clues, she almost found TTL-5B3, a moon in the Goldilocks zone, a place with all of the major requirements for human life. The speaker on the vid was right to be afraid of a land rush. It was unique and priceless.

There was one thing she knew—this was not Haven. TTL-5B3 was a moon, and John said Haven was a colony. *Maybe I should ask. Nah. He'll think I'm crazy or some conspiracy nut if I tell him he's living on the biggest fraud in the galaxy.*

So, has anyone been to 5B3 since the survey?

"Damn, I need to celebrate," she said aloud and called John without answer. *Hell, I can't tell him until I verify this, but he doesn't have to know why I'm so happy to enjoy it with me.*

"Jump in ten minutes," Jerri announced on the PA system.

She walked back to her cabin. After taking the nutra-pack and boost, she reviewed her other messages, including one from Teddy.

> Meriel, impressive work on the nav program and congrats to Pilot Smith.
>
> However, scenarios you provided only exclude the possibilities of coordinating from a different station and random encounters.
>
> To meet within the duration available (2:48), the two ships would need to a) coordinate their jumps, b) leave from the same point at about the same time, and c) jump short before the sphere gets too large. Meeting is conceivable, but too improbable unless the ships coordinated intentionally. This means someone on the *Princess* must have programmed nav with the same jump coordinates. Sorry.
>
> I provided similar information to the court ten years ago. Courts hate technical information like this. They concluded the meeting was intentional and coordinated, not what I intended or what you intend now.
>
> Jeremy stopped by, and he offered this: There is no technical difference

```
between someone forcing you to go
somewhere, or you agreeing to go. You
end up at the same place. However,
there is a big difference in
culpability for what happens when you
arrive. Focus on means and motive.
   LU, T
```

Meriel mentally appended Jeremy's guidance to include, "Send money."

Crap. Nick needs to find something more on the data chip, or we won't have enough to reopen the bidding.

"Reply. Teddy, what if the traitor is nav, not a crew member? What if nav got infected somehow? Send."

And she knew how: an aggressive virus in the cargo manifest, a manifest they would review before every jump.

"Transcribe message to Jeremy Bell. Begin. Jeremy, please be alert for information from Nick Zanek. Info regards mil-tech virus found within the manifest at the time of the *Princess* attack. Means and motive may be there. Send." And she made sure not to disclose how that miracle had occurred.

Another message had come in from Nick with a GRL. She tapped the reference:

```
   "Improbability of Nav-RR9I
 Complicity in Ship Disappearances."
   Interstellar Journal of Navigation.
ET/2174:26
   Theodore Duncan, C:Navigator-Six
   Abstract: The frequency of ship
disappearances per light-year traveled
is gratefully low. However, the losses
are much higher than predicted by
analysis of the reliability and
failure modes of current generation of
nav systems (Nav-RR9I) and the vessels
themselves. This paper reviews the
state of the art, estimates the
anticipated disappearances due to
```

```
infrastructure failures, and
speculates on other causes.
```

That was written in 2174—years before the Princess *attack. Teddy proved the ships did not vanish by accident but did not know the cause. But I know pirates tried to kill our ship. Maybe there are more pirate attacks than anyone knows about.*

***

Cookie scooped up the poker chips and added them to his stack. Of the four at the table, he and Socket appeared the least affected by the copious quantities of alcohol consumed.

"You're slipping, pal," he said. "I've got nothing showing to your pair, and you didn't bluff."

From across the table, John looked at him and blinked. Collecting the cards, the sleeve on Socket's blouse hiked up to expose a fresh tattoo.

"Say, you gonna make that one permanent?" Cookie asked.

"Hell, no. I'd feel like it owns me," she said and began to shuffle. "Ante up."

Cookie grabbed Alf Martin by the hair and lifted his head off the table. But Alf drooled from a slack mouth. "He's out this hand," he said and dropped Alf's head back on the table.

John added too many chips.

"He's loaded, Socket," Cookie said.

"Shush," she replied. "His money is still good."

"You'd take advantage of a drunk?"

"This is poker, Sergeant, and the rules are sacred. He's still awake and sitting at the table. We'll leave him his pants." She hit John again. "So where's Meriel?"

"Busy," he said and frowned. His head bobbed, and he blinked in slow motion.

"I thought you guys had a thing."

John wobbled in his chair. "Work in progress."

"You oddballs are meant for each other. You're the only spacers I know who don't like station sleepovers."

He sighed. "She's always busy trying to get her kids together." He slammed his drink on the table. "Damn. I want someone like her, someone true."

Socket rolled her eyes. "Jeez, John. You're gonna drown in your own BS. She's young and hot. Don't confuse yourself."

"All spacers are hot," he said. "This one's got a purpose. She's building a future for the kids from the *Princess*."

"I didn't think spacers thought that far ahead," Cookie said while peering over his cards.

Socket scowled. "What do you mean by that?"

"Sorry, nothing personal. Just that spacers seem to live only for the next station or the next bunk; like every moment it's all going to diffuse like air in a vacuum.

Her scowl faded to a frown. "Most of us live with death a few millimeters away our whole lives."

"But not her," Jon said. "Can you imagine being loved like that?"

Socket held the deck of cards but did not deal. "Yeah, I had that once." After a moment's pause, she dealt the three of them the hole card in a round of five-card stud.

"Keep at it," Cookie said but watched Socket. "She'll come around."

Oblivious, John continued. "And she has this dream of a place out there she calls Home." He raised his arm and seemed to point to something outside the porthole.

"That old myth?" she said.

"Yeah ..." he began to say, but his eyes closed, and his arm drooped slowly to his side. His head fell back, and he started to snore.

Cookie bet and frowned when she took a few chips from John and threw them into the pile. They continued with two more rounds of betting on two up cards.

"You ever have someone like that?" she asked.

"Like what?"

"Someone true who loved you completely and only you."

He nodded. "For a while." He slipped his hole card under the others and stretched with his hands behind his head. "She was like a comet blowing through my life. Lit me up like a star for a while and made me feel like a teenager."

"What happened?"

"She followed her orbit back to the stars. I just couldn't hold on to her. You met her."

She smiled. "Really? The blonde?"

"Yeah."

"You old fart. You find a love like that again, and it'll burn you to a cinder."

"So what? And what about you?"

"Coulda' been," she said. "His boat disappeared on a long haul to Seiyei station. It was a humanitarian run to an asteroid colony with a rare plague. Never heard from."

"Accident?"

"No one knows." Her face softened as she checked her hole card. "They sent me his medal."

Cookie smiled at the reflection of the cabin lights in her eyes. "Yeah. You compare everyone to him."

She stared at her card and bit her lip.

"But you'd do it all again," he said and patted her hand. "Regardless of how it ends."

She grinned with every inch of her face. "In a heartbeat." After dealing the fourth card to each of them face up, she added more of her chips and took some from John. "He raises."

Cookie pushed his chips into the pot. "I know she likes him. Maybe she really loves him."

She dealt the fifth card. "You're a romantic, Sergeant. She's a spacer."

He peeked at his cards and frowned. "Yeah, I know. But I can hope. They look good together." With a sigh, he flipped his cards onto the stack. "Fold."

John's link buzzed, and a holo of Meriel popped up for a moment.

"She's gonna break his heart," Socket said.

"That's what hearts are for."

She nodded and threw a few more chips on the stack.

Jerri's voice blared over the PA system. "Jump in ten minutes."

He took the same chips from John's stack without looking at his cards. "He calls."

She flipped her cards to show two pair, jacks over tens. He turned over John's cards to expose three fours, the winning hand.

"Damn. You can't bluff a sleeping man," she said.

He pushed the pile over to John. "He's a lucky guy. Both of them are."

"How can you say that? John's girls don't have a mom, and she lost her ship and her whole family."

He smiled. "It's their hearts, lass."

She nodded and rested her hand on his. "So, you believe her?"

After examining her through narrowed eyes, he relaxed. "I've seen enough combat fatigue and PTSD. There's something traumatic in her past."

"How can you tell?"

"It's in her eyes, in the way she moves. And I don't think she could make up a story like that. Unless it's hiding something worse."

***

The nondescript man surprised the two security guards when he entered their office.

"Hey, bozo," said a guard with a black eye and a bandage on his nose. "You're not supposed to be in here."

"I see you took the antidote in time, Bob."

Bob lost his smirk. "Yeah, so what's it to you?"

"Yes, what is it to me. You failed. The attempt at the café was clumsy. Did you know a combat Marine sat at that table?

Ignoring his partner's elbow for silence, he crossed his arms and sneered. "So what? I got a black eye for my mistake. Why are you here?"

"You were instructed to contact me before acting." The intruder drew out the fleschette pistol from the holster in the small of his back. "The toxin dose was ten times too high. It put a bystander in the hospital and alerted security. You were identified at the scene."

"Mistakes happen."

"Not with me. You are someone else's mistake, and I am here to correct it."

"Right," Bob said. "I didn't see you trying to help."

Without turning around, the intruder locked the door. He touched a button on his link, and the security console went dark. Bob lunged for him but staggered backward and fell on his back, gasping for breath with a circular pattern of red dots flowing together on his chest. Bob's partner hit the red security-breach alarm button repeatedly, but it did nothing. He then ran for the backdoor and found it locked.

"That will not help." The nondescript man proceeded with his task, knowing no one outside the security office would hear the screams.

"Only one other loose thread to cut," he mumbled. But he would need instructions before proceeding.

Chapter 7
Wolf Station, Wolf 359 System

Wolf Station—Inbound

Rushing through the cargo integrity checks, Meriel kept one eye on the comm light on her visor. They were inbound to Wolf Station, and she looked forward to a busy day. A few hours from now would be Harry's birthday party, which would take her full attention. But before then, she hoped to share her revelations from the Aldersen vid with John and celebrate. But he was on duty now and would be unavailable until dock.

The beep on her visor indicated sync with the inbound comm beacon. She idled her cruiser, anxious to hear from Nick and Teddy about the *Princess,* but Harry's party came first.

```
From Harry: I'm here. The crew kids
are ready to go. Call us when you're
on your way.
  LU!
```

Yikes, I forgot to ask how many crew he invited. I hope they don't empty the bank account. This was all from the *Princess* corporate funds, of course. That's what she called her savings account. It was minimal by any standard, but she needed to do this for him.

```
From Anita: My ship docked at mining
asteroid X44t…
```

Right, a few hours away.

```
   ...and I took a shuttle to Wolf. Just
debarked. I hope I didn't miss Harry's
party. Give me a call, and we can pick
him up. A
```

What a wonderful surprise! Harry will be thrilled.
A message from Nick interrupted her musings, and she
leaned back to read it on her visor.

```
   m, if you are alive to read this,
you did not touch the encrypted files,
and your ship did not jump into a
star. good. reply to confirm you're
still breathing.
   virus is mil-tech. very aggressive.
your bracelet is a zombie, and i
mulched it. the next time you turned
it on, it would have taken over
whatever computing power it could
command to communicate with its
handler, whoever that is. code will
continue replicating until it gets a
response from the handler, after which
it will die. until then, its first
priority is to do the virus's bidding.
   ok, so what's on the manifest? i
copied it here, by hand, thank you
very much—text only, no code, no
metadata, and without the virus. maybe
you can figure it out. the item that
triggered the virus is on the bottom
of the list.
   By the structure, this is a military
id. the xe prefix is mil-spec r&d. to
find out more, you need r&d need-to-
know clearance, likely secret at some
level.
   i strongly advise not searching for
these numbers, as they may expose you
to unwanted attention. when I write
```

```
"strongly advise," i mean do not do
this unless you are prepared to give
up your life or your freedom. i am not
ready to do either and therefore
decline this adventure.
```

Well, he's being dramatic, she thought.

```
    if you are in the mood, please tell
me who decided to add mil r&d to your
cargo.
    oh, and attached another vid i think
you'll like. you once told me about
what happened that day.
```

Meriel scanned the IDs from the manifest and noted the xeM446 prefix, but caution stopped her from querying while on the *Tiger*.

The icon for the attached vid showed a picture of her with her sister, each snuggled into one of their father's arms. She played the vid, and turned up the volume to listen to his snoring.

***

When Elizabeth had turned nine, she had finally grown tall enough, and Meriel and Tommy Spurell took her to the dinosaur park simulator. It was all fun. They kept a running score for evading the carnivores—living even their allotted half hour was a challenge. To survive, they had to make weapons and a first-aid kit from raw materials scattered throughout the sim so they could protect or heal themselves.

Unknown to them, players could "die" in the game by being eaten, injured severely, or poisoned by snakes or bugs. No one died, of course, but the sim would eject them early. They had not died before, too fast and stupid to get caught.

That day with Liz, a raptor family chased them, and Liz could not find a climbable tree fast enough. She froze. Tommy and Meriel jumped in front to protect her, and the raptors got all three of them. The game ejected them, but the ejection point dropped them away from where their parents were waiting. Meriel thought she remembered how to return to their parents but got them lost instead. Park security found them and took them to Child Services, exhausted. Liz held her hand and did not let go.

Tommy regarded it all as a great adventure, but Meriel panicked that they might cause the ship to miss its departure window. That could mean penalties for late arrival and destroy their margins, or even delay the entire circuit and drive them into bankruptcy.

At Child Services, kids from white-zone threatened them, especially Liz because she was small. Tommy stood, ready to defend her, but Liz punched one of the bullies in the nose and made him cry. Just then, Papa arrived to pick them up. He found Liz standing with her fists on her hips, glaring at the bullies, and Tommy and Meriel squared off on each flank.

Papa had smiled ear-to-ear, never saying a word about them getting lost, and took them for ice cream with the other kids as though nothing had happened. But Mom's eyes were red and puffy.

Her father never left them that day. The early ejection from the dino-simulator gave them lots of time, so the *Princess* was not at risk of missing her departure window.

After dropping off Tommy, they went to their parents' cabin, and she and Elizabeth told them every detail of their exciting day. There, they fell asleep in their father's arms.

Watching the vid, she knew why she always felt peaceful when she heard a man snoring.

Wolf Station—On Station

Wolf was a small station, efficient and wealthy but with limited dockage, which caused the *Tiger* to dock late and Meriel to worry about Harry's party. Since she had prepaid, they would not lose the reservation, but their ships had rigid departure times. With no time to shop for a new link and her visor inappropriate for a cabbie, she took Nick's burner link.

She signed out and rushed to the restroom, where she quickly changed into the clothing of a station cabbie. Then with cash and a phony name, she rented a van. Care was needed now—seeing any of the orphans was a violation of court orders and could land her in jail. It also could make them a target for whatever had hit them on the *Princess*. Harry's fosters were OK with contact with Anita, but they needed to be discreet.

Her pulse raced, and shimmering silver stars appeared in front of her, causing her to pull over. *God, calm down. Breathe or you'll pass out. Wouldn't Ferrell love that, proof of blackouts.*

When her head cleared, she picked up Anita. After some hugs, they drove to the *TanaMaru*'s dock where Harry waited with some of his shipmates. Seeing the van park, he gathered his mates behind him and approached without recognizing either of them. Halfway there, he stopped and stared wide-eyed. Then he ran to them and jumped in to hug Anita. They held hands and talked every moment of the ride to white-zone.

At the play area, the other kids leaped from the van before it stopped and dashed to the simulators. Harry led his sister to a bench to talk, and Meriel sat nearby. *Look at that. Even with all the amusements so close by, time with each other is what they want most.*

While she watched her friends, one of the bigger boys tried to nudge Harry to the side and dominate Anita's attention. Meriel signaled her, Anita excused herself, and Harry went to play with his crewmates. The annoying boy glared at Meriel as Anita walked away, but when Anita turned back to Harry, the fellow changed his expression to a charming smile. *Snake.*

Meriel used sign language to ask her, "Who's the muscle?" Sign had been their private language since childhood, and the kids still used it to mock adults or to hold private conversations. No one else signed anymore; no one needed to. Implants, cochlear or cortex, were common from childhood on—Harry got his when he was nine. Other than each other, sign was the single thing they took with them from the *Princess*. It belonged to them alone and bound them together.

"He's why they kicked me off the *TanaMaru*," Anita signed in reply.

"So that's him," Meriel signed. This toad had caused the problems that forced the siblings apart. She was barely fourteen when this guy, the captain's son, messed with her, and she hurt him bad. The ship would not renew her contract and took her from her little brother.

"Want me to talk to him?" Meriel signed.

"No thanks. That would only make it worse for Harry," Anita said aloud and glanced back at him.

Meriel noticed Anita covering her hands and clenching her fists in her lap. She took one of Anita's hands in hers and opened her fist to see fingernails bitten to the quick. Anita withdrew her hand and lowered her head.

"Worried, hon?" Meriel asked.

She nodded. "His ship almost didn't make it."

"What happened?"

"They got behind on the maintenance, and the *TanaMaru* broke down near Gliese 6. The league wouldn't give them a loan."

"Why not?"

"Couldn't prove they could pay it off, too much overhead."

"Sounds fixable."

Anita shook her head. "They've got too many kids."

"Weren't they training them?"

"Not well enough. Other ships wouldn't take them. They're dead wood, including the muscle, but he's the captain's son."

Kids filled the large family vessels like the *TanaMaru* because they allowed parents to escape the strict population controls on all habitats. On family ships, you could have as many kids as you wanted. That is, as long as you could feed them and stay one jump ahead of the social workers. But vessels with uncontrolled populations ended up running the dangerous routes or taking on too much debt trying to support everybody. Risky routes endangered the lives of everyone onboard. Debts dragged your boat to the auction block and your crew—your family—to the mining colonies like the naive and foolish.

"But they're flying now."

Anita nodded. "The Troopers drafted the seniors as cadets, but the ship is still running close to failure."

"He didn't tell me they were in trouble, Anni. Good you got off when you did."

"Not so good with him still stuck there." She patted Meriel's hand. "Thanks, M. I really don't have anyone to talk to." Turning, she spotted a group of older boys from Harry's ship. "I'll take care of the muscle," she said and walked toward them. A few minutes later, the largest had the bully up against the wall for a "talking to," and Anita returned to sit safely with Harry.

She's learning, Meriel thought and smiled.

With a serving of ice cream and cake, Meriel sat by herself again to avoid the security camera. Anita and Harry brought birthday cake and sat with her while a crewmate snapped vids of them together with Anita's link.

"Happy birthday, kid," Meriel said, and Harry jumped into her arms and kissed her.

"Show M the present from Nick," Anita said and turned to Meriel. "It was waiting at the dock when Harry's ship arrived."

He placed a tiny cube on the table and tapped the corner. A holovid popped up of him and his sister with their mother and father onboard the *Princess*. Anita wore a dress and beamed at little Harry, who ran around her while their parents sat close by. The two of them watched the holo now and grinned.

"That was his second birthday," Meriel said. *Nick must have found it on my q-chip.*

Anita beamed at Harry. "I remember."

That week, the *Princess* had stopped near Sirius for a layover, and Uncle Ed had held a movie marathon. One of the vids was an adventure movie her father liked, about a young princess who rediscovered her home in a land that floated in the sky. God knew how old it was. The kids converted the mess hall into a castle and acted out every scene with the adults playing the roles of enormous robots. Her father told her they named their ship after the heroine of the story. No one told the children the nearby asteroids were embroiled in an immigration war, and the *Princess* had to stay close to the station for safety.

"Harry's never seen our folks before, M," Anita said, wiping tears from her eyes. "Remember, Harry, this is just between us. Don't show this to anybody."

"Sure, Sis."

"Hey, kid, I saw your new qualification," Meriel said. "Good work. This is from all of us in your future crew." She handed him a small box, which he immediately ripped apart. Inside lay a brass collar pin signifying his logistics-two qualification and a small service ribbon for his formal uniform. He hugged her again, and Meriel melted into it.

"You OK now?" she signed.

"Sure, M," he signed in reply. "They're all right to me. I just miss everyone so much, 'specially my big sister."

Anita leaned over and hugged him. "We'll be together, Harry, but it will take some time." She bit her lip and turned to Meriel. "M, maybe you can contract us out on the same ship."

"I'm trying, hon," Meriel said. "I'm trying. Your fosters don't want to leave the *TanaMaru*, and I'd never post you back there, ever. I'm just glad he's a youngster. We'll reassign him as soon as we can. Say, you're still in with your fosters, right? Do you think they'd crew with us when we get our ship back?"

Anita smiled at the suggestion. "I think they want to be near us, yeah."

"Great. We'll need skilled adults we trust to fill our roster, and who better than people who love us. Is that OK with you?"

The siblings nodded.

Meriel took a party favor as a reminder of the day. Then, from the corner of her eye, she caught the manager hovering nearby who tapped his wrist.

"Time's up," she said. "Gather your crew, kid."

Harry rounded up his shipmates, and they all got into the van and drove back to the *TanaMaru*. His crewmates boarded, but he would not let go of his sister's hand.

"It's OK, M," Anita said. "I'm going to say hi to my old foster folks. I can find my way back to the shuttle."

"Thanks, M," Harry said. "This was my best birthday ever." He kissed Meriel again and dissolved her fears with a hug.

***

Heading for a public kiosk to investigate Nick's cargo ID numbers, Meriel stopped. She remembered his warning that it might trigger an alarm and realized she was unprepared. At a salvage store she bought used clothing, a metal cosmetics case, and a cheap game player. After a change of clothes and hair, she walked back to a green-zone coffee shop, carefully avoiding the security cameras.

Using a cash app at the café, she paid for her coffee and sat at a corner table. She transferred Nick's copy of the manifest to the game player and set Nick's burner link in the case. As extra precaution, she covered the player's built-in camera with the sticker from her coffee.

Feeling secure in her precautions, she scanned the manifest for the distributors who supplied the *Princess's* cargo that last stop. Her brow furrowed at a few unfamiliar names—Apex Logistics, Sector Systems, Alkmanide Shipping. Correlating the list against Jeremy's list, these same shippers had declined to file insurance claims on their lost cargo. None of those shippers appeared on an up-to-date list of the Pacific League's authorized shippers. *Well, companies go bust all the time, and it's been ten years.* But the cargo items that worried Nick were delivered by those shippers.

She keyed in the number "M446," and the search returned millions of hits and counting. "Mil xeM446" still produced thousands of hits. A longer sequence of the ID displayed "research…communications, wide-field disruption with narrow-band tunneling…read more *here.*" Complying, she clicked *here*, and the player responded with a pop-up holo.

```
Please wait a moment while we
retrieve your data.
```

The camera flashed under the sticker, and she knew she'd triggered something—they wanted her picture. With her head down, she flipped the device over and stripped off the battery. Using its dying breath, it squawked, and every device in the coffee shop beeped a reply as she walked out.

Meriel went into a bathroom to change back into her uniform and peeled open the device. Removing the core with the memory module, she made sure not to expose the camera. As she caught a tram back to the docks, she threw the pieces in different trash chutes, keeping the core.

On the way back to the *Tiger*, the public tram stopped by the *TanaMaru*, but Anita and Harry had left. The dock was empty, and the marquee blank. She wondered for an instant if the party was a dream. Reaching into her pocket, she checked her link for the vids of Anita and Harry. However, Nick's loaner link had not synced with Anita's and had not copied the vids. Then she searched the other pocket for the party favor, but found nothing. Perhaps she had dropped it when she changed clothing. *Or was it just another daydream*? The entire party might have been a fantasy, but she had a more immediate problem: the bot she triggered when searching for the mil-tech.

Why would a mil-tech inventory number be used on the manifest? The answer came to her immediately—to find out if anyone cared and then to detain him. *Crap! I didn't listen to Nick. Still, I should be OK. Even if they can trace the search to this station, no one has the resources to search every inch of the station and connect that query to me.*

Meriel was wrong.

***

A flashing blue light and pleasant tone awoke Benedict. It had been a long trip and a long day trailing his quarry.

The alt-bridge of the *Liu Yang*, a ship no one should care about and had no recorded owner except an escrow account, had been activated. That meant enterprise security had failed to keep its identity a secret. He had cleaned up the mess, but it was not over. Just now, an anonymous query for obscure mil-tech R&D codes tripped snares set a decade ago.

Sitting at the desk in the small hotel room, he turned on the lamp. Police files for the Jeannine Aldersen case, files he should not have, appeared on the active wall. The files held the investigation report, the evidence of Stim abuse, and the ruling of suicide. He knew it had been a contract murder. That secret was well kept, to be sure, without the loose ends of the *Princess* affair; this, he convinced himself, was because they had engaged him early. Secret or no, exposure of either might reveal a more important secret.

The link beeped again, indicating it had located where the search for the mil-tech ID had begun. The reply was many hours sooner than he expected—sooner meant closer. The source was a small café on Wolf.

"How convenient." He was also on Wolf, following a young woman who might have information he wanted. Within a few minutes, he found a surveillance vid near a café showing a woman with a primitive device at a table. Zooming and isolating the image, he ran a biorecognition program through his private database. In seconds a familiar name appeared.

"Well, well. Time we became better acquainted."

His coded messages to his associates spiked traffic between the UNE and BioLuna with the keywords *Isis* and *Haven*. On these channels, *Isis* was a code word for Meriel Hope, and those keywords in proximity to each other signaled danger. His instructions arrived a few minutes later and were clear.

"The hammer falls," he said, "and I have my part to play."

He noted the *Tiger* undock schedule on the security feed and checked the time. Realizing he could not rendezvous with her, he proceeded to make other arrangements to her next port-of-call. From the drawer he removed two stunners of legal charge; one he placed in a well-worn shoulder holster and the other in his sock. To the belt in the middle of his back, he attached a fleschette pistol, the weapon he had used to eliminate two corrupt security guards. As he rose from the desk, a reflection of the nondescript man Meriel had seen on Enterprise appeared in the mirror.

Wolf Station—Outbound

Back onboard the *Tiger*, Meriel headed for her cabin to send Jeremy a message regarding the settlement—or rather, the bribe—for the *Princess*. Her ten days could expire before her message made the trip to him, and he needed a reply. She had more to tell him now and much more to worry about.

"Message to Jeremy Bell. Jeremy, decline settlement for *Princess*. Pursue appeal of forfeiture with information provided by Nick Zanek, which should be in your possession by now. *Princess* cargo included military R&D xe…M446. A net search for any information about this triggered a surveillance bot. Believe we have the motive. Send."

After sending the message, she searched for Cookie and found him in the locker room with John.

"Cookie, if I wanted to find out what some mil-tech ID signifies, how would I go about it?"

"Did you search the net?"

"Keep a secret?" she said, and they nodded. "I did a query on a subset of the ID. It woke up a bot that zombied my game player."

"Where's the device now?"

"Dismantled," she said and showed them the core.

"And the rest of it?"

"Being destructively recycled."

Cookie frowned. "Tell me more."

She took a moment to prepare her thoughts. "The mil-tech ID was listed on the cargo manifest on my chip, the one my mother gave me."

"Why didn't you check it before?"

"I couldn't read it. I just got a hacker to decode it." *Which is close enough to the truth*.

"And?"

"I think the *Princess* was carrying mil-tech when the pirates hit us. I want to learn if our cargo had something to do with it."

"And you triggered a bot when you searched for information about the ID?" Cookie asked, and Meriel nodded. He sneered. "So they want to discover who's inquiring. Did you learn anything before the bot took over?"

"They called it wide-field communication disruption with some kind of tunnel or something."

John frowned. "Narrow-band tunneling?"

"Yeah, sounds about right."

He stared at her and sighed. "When was the *Princess* attacked?"

"About ten years ago."

"Do you have the ID number of the equipment?"

She handed him her link and listed the XE items. John skimmed the numbers and shook his head. "No need to query. I know what this is. It's a Global Communication Executive, a GCE."

Cookie whistled. "A Hydra."

"What's that?"

"A Blackout-Box," John said. "It turns communications to stone, so an entire station will go dark but allow a few encrypted channels." He gave the link to Cookie. "Only line-of-sight laser targeting works when this is engaged."

"How do you know?" she asked.

"Mercenaries tried to use it to invade Haven."

"The M88Ds are semiautonomous drones," Cookie said as he scanned the list. "Antipersonnel, on channels allowed by the Hydra. The M446s are communications."

"How can this Hydra thing be so important?" she asked. "It's just communications, not like missiles or lasers."

"Wars are lightning fast now. You can't coordinate complex technologies and tactics with smoke signals. If you control communications, you can focus all your firepower to the right spot while your enemy is blind and deaf. They're not aware you're shooting at 'em until too late. You can also manage the news feeds going out, so people won't even know they've been invaded." He scanned the rest of the list. "Others here are drone replicators, power supplies, and some parts too hard to produce using replicators."

"My folks would not have carried this knowingly."

"Certainly not knowing what would happen."

"Why not use fully autonomous drones?"

"They don't use them much anymore. They tend to bite their masters."

She pursed her lips. "So, my ship carried military tech that pirates hijacked. And the cargo conveniently turned up in the hands of mercenaries invading Haven."

"Seems like."

"John, who funded the mercenaries who attacked Haven?" she asked.

"BioLuna and some partners we didn't identify."

"Then BioLuna stole the mil-tech?"

"Or bought it from the thief," Cookie said.

"If it was mil-tech and secret, how could BioLuna know?"

John reached over and took her hand. "Someone betrayed you, Meriel, like Cookie said."

Jerking her hand away, she stood up and glared at him. "No one on our ship could do that. We were all family." Her voice softened, and she dropped her gaze. "And they're all dead."

"Someone escaped, Meriel."

Through clenched teeth, she inhaled and closed her eyes. After a moment, she sighed and shook her head. "No one escaped. Only us kids."

"How can you be sure?"

She opened her eyes to stop the visions of the horror. With her face turned to hide her agony, she rose and crossed her arms. "I...I'm sure."

"Then it was your client."

"So, who put that box on our boat?"

"Financial transactions should match the cargo," John offered.

She fiddled with the chip on her necklace. *One of the files might be the financials. But she could not check them yet.*

Cookie lowered his brow. "I suggest you not query that number again. Let's see. A military order would be required to move that machine out of R&D."

"Military. Government," John said. "Do you hear this? The UNE, the navy. They have the monopoly on the legal use of force."

"Big force," Cookie said. "Who else knows about this?"

"Only a very paranoid hacker," she said, withholding Nick's name.

"I hope he's paranoid enough," Cookie said and rose to leave. "And you need to be more careful. I'm off to the gym. You coming, John?"

"In a minute," he said and waited for Cookie to turn the corner. "Meriel, you've been kinda distant since...since the Mardi Gras party."

"Sorry, John. I called when I could. I've been busy working to keep the *Princess* and my job."

"I'm only trying to help, but the *Princess* registry says she was scrapped."

She sighed. "John, it would be nice if you believed me and took all this on faith. But then you'd be crazy or moonstruck and not worth a damn. So, let's just leave this, OK?"

"I think we—"

"Look, hon. I got lots of baggage, and I don't think your kids need that."

"You think we're needing a nanny?"

"No, lucky for you," she said with a smile and took his hand. "Give me time, John."

He frowned but nodded, and turned to follow Cookie to the gym.

"Wait," she said. "The judgment you got on Lander after the invasion. Who were the parties?"

"LGen versus BioLuna."

"Thanks," she said and raised her hand to dismiss him. When John left, she tapped her visor again. "Append message, Jeremy Bell. Jeremy: Mil R&D in *Princess* cargo was used for invasion of Haven colony. See lawsuit on Lander, LGen v. BioLuna. We may have the *who* as well as the *why*. Send."

***

Down the passageway, Doc Ferrell received a message.

```
From Kadvi:
Subject: Revised deadline for
contraindication, 38h elapsed.
```

Chapter 8
Free Space

Between jumps, Meriel studied for her nav-three rating in the mess hall with the IGB news feed droning in the background.

One of her bots chimed on her visor. "Periodic net search for *Esperanza* crew complete."

"Debrief. Status?"

"One mention. Rosanna Tran."

She smiled at the thought that one of her cousins finally surfaced after a decade of searching. "Status?"

"Died Etna station of unknown cause."

"Damn. Who identified the body?"

"Coroner. Biotag DNA profile match to Pacific League records."

"Disposition?"

"Cremation."

That meant fertilizer. "Associations?"

"No data."

No data. It had been this way for years now. Her searches for her cousins on the *Esperanza* retrieved only a few hits and now no information at all on the parents or children. They had slid into the abyss of the mining colonies or nameless jobs somewhere off the books just to survive. Etna was often one of the stops along the way down, but it was Rosanna's last. She shuddered that this could be herself and the orphans if they ever screwed up.

"Hey, Chief," Jerri said as she and Socket entered the room.

Meriel raised her head and waved. Socket sat across from her while Jerri dialed the replicator for the latest fad in caffeine ingestion.

"Studying?" Socket asked.

"Nav-three." Meriel popped up a holo of her current lesson.

"She's going after your job, Jerri," Socket said, but Jerri concentrated on the news on the active wall.

```
"Surprising developments on tau
Ceti-3. Seiyei Station has invited
immigrants from Ceres and Sol
asteroids to populate a new habitat
built for medical research…"
```

Jerri waved her arms. "That's BS!"

"IGB says they were invited, dearie," Socket said.

Jerri brought their drinks to the table and sat. "There's no way they would invite anybody, especially from Sol. They built that colony for themselves."

"No mention of a coup."

"Right. The winners write the news." Jerri peered into her cup. "Damn, I need something stronger."

Meriel wondered if there was more than one Hydra weapon when the captain's voice echoed over the PA system.

"Attention all hands, Captain Richard Vingel speaking. All first timers on Etna, report to the forward mess hall for orientation. Crew and passengers both. No exceptions. If you don't attend, you will not be allowed to disembark."

"We've heard the 'Pleasure Island' lecture before," Socket said. "See ya, Chief."

On the way out, Jerri turned to her. "Say, Ferrell is hunting for you."

"Thanks."

Collecting her study materials, Meriel moved to the galley to hide where she could still hear the captain. He arrived soon after with Cookie, Socket, and Lev in security vests and pulse rifles looking uncomfortable. When Ferrell joined them, she ducked down behind the counter to avoid his notice.

"Check your links," the captain said to the crowd of passengers. "A waiver of liability should appear, and you must confirm the waiver, or we cannot let you disembark. Understood?"

Heads bobbed.

"OK, then. How many of you have heard about Etna?"

A few raised their hands.

"Whatever you've heard, it's much worse. Murder and suicide rates are off the scale compared with other habitats. They don't publish them anymore."

A passenger waved his arm. "It's because of the lack of light."

Captain Vingel narrowed his eyes. "Sure. Etna's in the middle of a dust cloud. But I don't care why. They have different laws there. The morality is…more flexible to entice people to work there. Hedonism and drugs are pretty much all legal as long as it's consensual, and absence of consent is hard to prove. Everything you can imagine is there— simulators, androids, and the real thing." He studied those in the room. "Advertisements began as soon as the bots registered your destination. Temptations begin the moment you hit the docks, mostly with free samples…of everything."

He paused and scanned the room. "OK. The rules. One: no one under eighteen will be allowed off the boat, even with parents."

One man griped. "Hey, they're our kids. You can't hold them."

"Read your ticket," the captain replied. "Leaving the ship is evidence of parental incompetence, and the *Tiger* takes legal custody."

"You can't enforce that!"

The captain pointed to Cookie's team. "They can. You gave us consent when you purchased your ticket. Your children will be turned over to Child Protective Services on our next stop. You deal with them. Two: green-zone is dangerous and off-limits for crew. Copy that, Hope? Ferrell?"

"Aye, sir," Ferrell said, looking around for Meriel.

"Passengers, green-zone is at your own risk," the captain continued. "Three: black-zone is off-limits to anyone onboard."

"We're not crew," another passenger interrupted. "We don't follow the rules for crew."

"These are rules for everyone. Read your ticket next time. If you return from black-zone alive, do not expect to board the *Tiger*. Got that?"

Heads bobbed.

"Four: legal counsel is on you for anything and everything. We're under no obligation to save you from yourselves if anything happens to you. Understood?"

A few nodded while others grumbled.

"The rules are all in the waiver," the captain repeated. "Personal advice now: I advise you all to stay onboard. You can't get much here except scars on your soul. Some of the residents like it here—avoid them. Who's getting off for work?"

The hand of one young man rose.

"Son, wait a moment. The rest of you are dismissed. Make sure to consent to the waiver if you plan to debark." The captain retired, and the crowd dispersed.

One of the last to leave, Ferrell glanced back as an attractive passenger towed him away and down the passageway.

Meriel returned to the mess hall to study. A few tables away, the captain talked to the young man who had raised his hand.

"What's your name, son?"

"Elliot. Elliot Goodwin."

"Your folks know you're here?"

"Ain't got none, sir. Recycled on Ceres."

"Any other family?"

"No, sir."

"Are you going to work on station or in the mines?"

"Mines, sir."

The captain nodded. "I understand the pay is good, son, but you might reconsider. Life is real different here. Tours of duty are short, but miners tend to spend all their money on station. They never save enough to leave, and die here. I'd hate to see that happen to you, son."

"No, sir."

"Any convictions on your record? Drugs?"

"None, sir. "

"You must have some big value-add to ship your mass here. What's your rating?"

"Cybertronics-three."

"So, here's my offer: free passage to the next station if you change your mind and cancel your contract. I'll recommend you to stationside on Ross. Got that?"

Elliot raised his eyebrows and nodded.

"It may not be much to start. You work hard, and things will come. They still believe in merit and hard work on Ross. You can build a life there, not like on Etna. It's a good deal, son. My word means something there. But once you set foot on this station, the offer goes away. Understood?"

"Yes, sir."

Captain Vingel clapped the young man on the shoulder and left.

Elliot stayed at the table and stared at the wall.

That could be any one of the kids if they lost their ship—if they angered the wrong captain or crew chief, or the routes went stale. Or me if they catch me for any one of my regular infractions.

"Excuse me, Elliot."

"Sure, ma'am."

She smiled, not realizing she qualified to be a "ma'am" just yet. "Call me Meriel. I think I overheard the captain offer you a recommendation to a post on Ross Station. You're not a born spacer?"

"No...Ms. Meriel."

"Out here, a captain's recommendation is as rare as...well, it's damn rare. If I were you, I'd take it."

"I got nothing, Ms. Meriel. Lost everything with my folks. Ceres was...not good for us." He scowled at his clenched fists. "The colony advanced me the fare to get here. I think just to be rid of me, but I still owe 'em."

"Take the captain's offer, Elliot. I've been to Ross, and it's nice enough."

Elliot nodded, gave her a weak smile, and walked away.

Her link buzzed.

```
From Lev: Ferrell is here looking
for you.
```

She packed up her stuff and left to find a place to hide until the jump.

Chapter 9
Etna Station, Etna 320 System

Etna Station—Inbound

Meriel hurried down the promenade where she'd first met John on her way to a cargo check. The spray of stars typical of the approach to a station was absent, and she presumed the radiation shield had deployed. As she passed the window, a few points of light caught her eye. She glanced out the window and stopped. Disoriented, she backed up to the opposite side of the corridor to grab a tether.

Star system Etna 320 skirted the edge of nowhere in the middle of the Ciberitus Sink. As opaque as the Coalsack nebula, the Sink dropped Etna's apparent brightness down an order of magnitude. The captain had warned them of Etna's oppressiveness, but his warning did not prepare her for it on a biological level. Now she understood why hedonism and religion were so prevalent here; they served as spiritual negation to hopelessness.

Before inspecting the cargo with Lev, she checked messages picked up on the comm sync as the *Tiger* entered the Etna system. Two were flagged "urgent," and she opened the one from a resident of Moon-C.

> From Anonymous:
> Ms. H: We've never met, and I am not sure I am contacting the right person, but please be patient until you read my story.

```
   I found your name in the archives of
a trading vessel which had problems a
decade ago ET. If this is not you,
dispose of this message. If you crewed
on such a vessel, please retrieve a
package at the Greylight Station
disembarkation lounge, Etna, under the
name of Seafarer.
```

Cryptic. She opened the second urgent message, this one from an unknown GRL on Etna.

```
   From Blue Dragon:
   M, Come get me please! I'm hiding
and can't go back to my ship. I may
have killed someone. Can't go to the
police. When you debark, call 44-9045
and say "M's here." Liz.
```

Crap. She might have killed someone but isn't sure? She's scared, though, stuck on a station where death is amusement. If she's hiding, then her ship refused to protect her, those creeps.

Meriel grabbed a stunner from her hidey-hole under the deck plates and called Lev from her cargo crew.

"I'm off shift, Chief," he said.

"Sorry. Lev, I need a favor. Can you supervise when we dock? I need to take care of some personal business. You can take your leave after unloading."

"Yeah, boss, but let me sleep until then."

"Sure." She clicked off.

Someone knocked on her cabin door.

"It's open," she said.

John walked in. "Got time?"

"I'm in kind of a hurry, John."

"What's goin' on?"

She motioned for him to close the door. "Can you keep a secret?"

"Depends, M. Is this about the mil-tech?"

"No, no." Pausing, she considered how much she wanted to tell him. Actually, she didn't know much. "My sister is in trouble, and I can't fix it."

"She's here on Etna?"

"Yeah, hiding from some bad guys."

He tipped his head. "Why not call the police?"

"The police may be the bad guys."

"Why not tell the captain?"

"How could he help?" Meriel asked and took his hand. "I'm really worried about her."

"OK, what can I do?"

"Well, for one, you can keep this quiet. For two, can you run an errand for me?"

"Sure."

After instructing him how to pick up the package under the name Seafarer, he nodded. He lingered a bit, but she rushed to the air lock.

She signed the waiver to leave the *Tiger*, which required checking boxes for each rule. One of those boxes included the prohibition against entering the green and black zones, though she did not yet know where her sister was holed up.

Etna Station—On Station

Tapping her fingers on the air-lock door, Meriel waited for it to open and listened to her pulse race. Less than ten days left to save the *Princess*, and she had no news from Nick or Jeremy. That wouldn't matter if something happened to Elizabeth.

Her link buzzed.

```
Hope, you sure about leaving the
ship?
  XO
```

Meriel messaged back.

```
Yes, ma'am.
```

She took a deep breath and exhaled slowly to calm herself. Then she sprinted to a rent-a-link near a bar in blue-zone and made the call with video off. What sounded like an old woman with a heavy accent and a creaky voice answered her call.

"M's here," she said.

"What was her doll's name?"

Searching her memory, she only thought of, "Dolly?"

Over the link came muffled voices and a laugh.

"Pink sector concourse," the voice croaked. "Sit near the jukebox in the Pink Palace. We'll contact you."

Meriel followed the instructions to the Pink Palace, an ancient amusement that also served something in a tiny bun—a something that could be anything. Still, the place was huge and crowded and anonymous. She used her link to search for what a jukebox looked like, found it, and sat nearby.

While she waited, she worried. What if they could not straighten out the problem on station? Could she stow her sister somewhere on the *Tiger*? Maybe in the cargo hold? She could bring her water and food, but the hold had no plumbing. *What if I bunk with John and leave her in my cabin? He'll suspect me if I push myself at him like that.*

She could not think of any option better than stowing her sister away in her cabin. Getting her aboard without anyone noticing would be tough. But once inside her berth, Elizabeth could fit in the hidey-hole—most spacers were part-time smugglers and had hidey-holes; hers was just a bit larger than most.

Her sister had not mentioned injuries, and she wrote coherently, but what if someone messaged for her? *God, what if I sneak her aboard, and she's too torn up to survive a jump? A concussion or internal bleeding might worsen when we're all tranqed.*

Teddy's voice came to her. "Before you take the big steps," Teddy had told her, "always have mitigation plans for the possibilities with the direst consequences. Forget the little stuff; plan for the dire stuff. And if you can't develop the mitigation plans, then wait." *That advice presumes I have a choice. If Liz is hurt badly, we need to seek stationside medical assistance regardless of a possible arrest.*

Attempting to make notes, her vision blurred and her cold hands shook. *Breathe, girl,* she told herself, checking to see if anyone noticed her wooziness. *Thank God, we're all anonymous here.*

Then she saw him, a man more anonymous than the others. He resembled no one in particular, just as plain as the man she had seen on Enterprise. She turned away but took a vid of him.

While she concentrated on the nondescript man, a withered Asian carrying an order of take-out food passed and slipped her a note. "Follow. Not close," it read.

She followed the old man around a few corners and past a small EtnaVid studio. A rat-faced, tattooed woman leaned against the doorway, picking her teeth with her little finger. Meriel glared at her, and the woman sneered back.

Around another corner, the old man entered an alley, and she followed. At the end, a sign announced the transition to black-zone, and she gripped the stunner in her pocket. But before he stepped into black-zone, the old man slipped into the side door of a Chinese herbal apothecary.

The shop was tiny and narrow, smaller than those typical of pink-zone and much smaller than those near the duty-free areas. In the corners of both doors and in each of the narrow windows was the same symbol engraved on the medal on her necklace: the oval and cross of the Church of Jesus Christ Spaceman. Shelves bearing small drawers covered the walls from floor to ceiling. Kanji figures or pictograms of flowers or animals identified the contents of each drawer. One caught her eye: a four-leaf clover surrounding an open circle.

An old woman stood behind the counter, her chin level with the countertop. Before Meriel could ask her about the clover, the old woman spoke.

"Can I help you?" the woman asked in the familiar croak.

"I have instructions to pick up a package for M."

The old woman scrutinized her for an awkward few moments, then held her finger on the window to cloud them and   locked the doors. After rapping on the wall, she signaled Meriel to follow her to the back of the shop through an old light curtain. Another knock and the fake wall dissolved. On the other side sat a young man and next to him, her sister.

"Oh, M!" Elizabeth cried and ran to hug her.

"Hey, Littlebit." Tears and dirt hid the bruises on her sister's face, but they became more obvious as she approached. "Damn, hon. What happened to the cruiser that hit you?"

"In the hospital. He's a cargo-three on station here."

Meriel sighed and relaxed when she heard 'he is' rather than 'he was.' "So what happened?"

The young man brought tea and sat nearby.

"He came on to me at the bar and got me in a corner. I couldn't breathe, and it was dark and cold, like…" Elizabeth's eyes became wild. "I couldn't help it, M."

"You whaled on him?" she said aloud and then in sign language, "Trust them, yes?"

"Yes, trust," Elizabeth responded in sign. Aloud she said, "They had to drag me off him. He's big but stupid. Now he's in the hospital. I'm AWOL, and my ship jumped. The cops are hunting me, M. One of the cops is the brother of the a-hole and claims I tried to roll him."

"I'll take you to admin as soon as you're ready."

Elizabeth shook her head. "His mother's a lawyer here. I'm nearly marine-three and—"

"Self-defense won't work."

"They'll space me, M."

"Well, then, let's get you off the station and away from their influence. Pack up."

The young man raised his hand. "Wait, Liz. Your sister may have picked up a tail." On the wall, he displayed a vid of an unrecognizable shape in a dark corner.

"How can you tell?" Meriel asked.

"Same profile as at the Pink Palace."

"He could be following the old man."

"Uh, huh."

"*Tīshēn,*" the old woman said, and he left. She tapped her wrist and turned to Meriel. "You wait. Watch." The wall converted to a multi-display that covered the apothecary and down the adjoining streets. A whisk of her fingers scrolled through more views of unfamiliar dark passages and then a close-up of the shape that might be the tail. A minute later the old man left the shop, and soon after a woman approximating Meriel's size and hair color exited. The shadow followed.

The young man rejoined them, and the old woman waved toward the door.

"Now," the old woman said.

Elizabeth rose and opened her clenched fist to place a small pin on the table. The object caught Meriel's eye, and she reached out and picked up what appeared to be a clover with a circle in the middle.

"Where did you find this?" Meriel asked.

"It fell off one of my assailant's friends in the tussle. Why?"

"Your assault might not have been spontaneous." Meriel turned to their host. "Have you seen anything like this before? This clover?"

The old woman nodded. "*Bu mo, Inshu.*" She made the sign of the cross on her chest.

The young man translated. "Not clover, poppy—an old symbol for heroin. Drugs."

"*Shushoa,*" the old lady said. "Bad men. Real bad. Drugs here. People disappear."

"*Shushoa?*"

"*Shushoa! Shushoa!*" the old woman repeated, while holding one arm out and pulling the other across her chest.

"Archers," the young man said.

"I don't understand."

"Archers. The cult that runs the illegal drug and organ trade here—smugglers."

Meriel shrugged.

"Archers. The Archtrope."

Oh crap. "General Khanag?"

The young man nodded.

"What do we do now, Sis?"

"We run. How do we show our appreciation to your friends here?"

"The Chens are Teddy's friends," Elizabeth said and beamed at the young man. "Brian here is a TechMaster."

"I'm honored," Meriel said and shook his hand.

"I met them a few tours ago, M. I had nowhere else to go. Teddy will take care of them."

"OK, then let's get outta here." She gave instructions to their hosts and turned to her sister. "Time to pack up."

While Elizabeth stuffed her few clothes into a small spacer's duffel, Meriel bowed to the Chens. "*Xièxiè,*" she said, and they bowed back. She turned to leave, but the old woman grabbed her arm and tapped the medal on Meriel's necklace.

"You believe?" the old woman asked and stared at her as if their lives depended upon the answer.

"Kinda. Just haven't had much time."

The old woman gripped her arm until it hurt. "Now time."

***

A buzzing woke Ferrell, and he raised his head. Unable to focus on the blinking light on his desk, he took a dose of Soberal and lay his head back and closed his eyes. A minute later he opened them again to read the message.

```
From Kadvi:
Subject: Immediate action
Will bring you home immediately if
you retrieve requested information
within 6 hours.
```

"Home," he whispered and glanced at the picture of his daughter. He scanned the duty roster and hurried to the cargo holds to find Meriel. Instead he found Lev.

"Where'd she go?" Ferrell asked.

"Dunno," Lev said. "I'm filling in. What do you need?"

"Her."

Ferrell checked for John's location, which recorded him entering the *Tiger* from dockside. He ran to the lock and spotted John with a small package in his hand.

"John, have you seen Meriel?"

"Not since dock."

"It's about her health and very important."

John did not respond.

"I think she's skipping her medication. This is serious."

He took a deep breath. "Can I confide in you, Doc? With doctor-patient confidentiality?"

With a warm smile, Ferrell laid his hand on John's shoulder. "Of course."

John scanned the area and whispered, "She went on station to see her sister."

Ferrell frowned. "What did she say exactly?"

"She told me her sister was in trouble and needed help."

"Come with me for a minute." He led John to his office, closed the door, and poured drinks for them both.

"What's this about, Doc?"

"How much did she tell you about her background, her childhood?"

John shook his head. "Not much, really. She mentioned her old ship, the *Princess*, a few times. And she talked about getting it back and the kids together, including her sister."

"I don't want you to confront her about this. XO's orders."

"Ah…OK."

"John, this is all Meriel's fantasy."

"What is?"

"Her sister, her ship. They are all gone."

"What are you talking about?"

"They're delusions," Ferrell said. "They're all gone, but she can't accept it. She can't handle the loss of all her family and friends."

"She talks about them all the time."

Ferrell paced around the small room. "She's on meds as a condition of working here on the *Tiger*. Antipsychotics because of the nightmares and delusions. I think she stopped taking them. We need her back on her medication before she hurts herself or someone else."

John took a few seconds to absorb the doctor's information. "I don't believe you."

"It's all in her file. Meriel had a psychotic break after they found her on the ship alone and everyone else…dead."

"Even the kids?"

Ferrell nodded. "She's got this whole fantasy world set up with a training schedule for them. Her ship is gone. They're all delusions. Some shyster lawyer is stringing her along for her money." He opened the door. "I'm off to warn the XO. Call me as soon as you hear from her." He grabbed John by the arm. "We need her back on those meds. Understand?"

John sat in the chair, stunned. "Ah…sure," he said, and Ferrell left.

***

Doc Ferrell knocked on Molly's ready-room door and entered without permission.

"XO, Meriel is off her meds."

Molly studied him with a squint. "And you learned this how?"

"She's telling stories about the kids from the *Princess*. She dreamed up a training chart, and now she says she is off to see her sister, the one who died ten years ago."

Molly remained silent but studied him.

"We must get her back on her medication," Ferrell said.

"She's doing her job just fine, Doc."

"Yeah? She's derelict from her cargo shift and wasn't there to unload when we docked."

Tapping her console for the duty roster, she frowned. "Her job is to see it gets done, not to do it. I don't have a complaint, and her job is my business, not yours."

"My job is the health and safety of this ship, Exec."

"OK, I'll talk to her."

"Talk, crap. She's psychotic, living in a dream world, and she's qualified marine-three. She's a killer."

Molly restored her squint. "You mean *could* be a killer, right?"

"I don't know, Exec. Maybe her illness began before the *Princess*."

"What are you saying, Doc?"

"Piracy is always an inside job, or was."

"Yeah, so what are you saying?"

His face reddened, and he slapped the desk. "The *Princess* was an inside job, and she's the only one left inside is what I'm saying."

Molly leaned forward and cocked her head. "You're implying that it wasn't pirates or drug dealers but *Meriel* who killed everyone?"

"No one mentions pirates in a hundred years outside of bedtime stories, and somehow she's the only survivor of a pirate attack? Maybe she was sick before—"

"That's ridiculous, Doc. She was twelve for God's sake. You keep ungrounded crap like that to yourself, you hear? You know what she's been through. She's giving it a go, and I don't want you stirring things up. She's never hurt anyone intentionally, and—"

"It's the *un*intentional that should concern you, Molly, not the intentional," he said.

"No one is that crazy."

"Better take a closer look at your cargo chief." He spun and stormed out.

Captain Vingel, Molly's husband, stood in the doorway. "What do you think, Exec?"

"I think he's fulla crap. And I bet he thinks he's never been wrong."

"Sure," he said without emotion, "but let's check her meds, OK?"

"Roger," she said and tapped her console. "Chief Hope, report to XO, stat." With no response, she tapped again. "Find Chief Hope."

The ship's surveillance monitors cycled, and the soothing voice of Molly's console replied. "Chief Hope is not onboard, ma'am."

"Check on station."

A moment later, it reported. "No location. No ID."

She rose and paced her ready room. "Locate Registration, Light Speed Merchant *Princess*. Relevant association Meriel Hope."

"LSM Princess, GCN 13442:88. Located."

"Status?"

"Decommissioned. Dispositioned as scrap, Enterprise Station, YR56."

She sat on the edge of her desk and scanned the ceiling. "Identify registrations with similar cargo volume, mass, and engine type."

"Specification details?"

"Just ship names."

Without pause her console reported, "Yacht class. Five thousand identified and counting."

"Stop. ID only registrations after *Princess* decommissioned."

Crossing her arms, she waited for the response.

"Two-hundred twenty-six. List?"

"List those most proximate to *Princess* decommissioning."

"Two weeks. LSM *Liu Yang* GC—"

"Stop." She stood again and faced the active wall. "Display vid."

"No video available."

"Silhouettes?"

"None available."

"End search." She leaned over her desk and tapped an icon. "Message. *Jolly Roger*. Attention Captain Jeff Conklin. Jeff. A favor. Please record and forward jump-field spectrum of LSM *Liu Yang*." She glanced at the console. "GCN 14993:026. Molly V."

That would be proof—no two FTL drives were identical.

She did not know the *Liu Yang* was impounded at Enterprise.

***

Meriel rushed back to the *Tiger* pushing a packing crate on a grav-sled with Elizabeth hidden inside, hurrying to beat the crew returning from leave. Once she reached the ship, she scouted the passageways, unloaded her sister, and showed her the hidey-hole.

"Hurry, Liz. I need to return the crate to the dock and finish loading."

"They'll find me here, eventually. The captain will have to turn me in or risk losing his ship, and he'd never do that."

"I wouldn't ask him to. But we don't need to hide you forever, Liz, only until we jump. Once we're at a different station, you can turn yourself in. You can claim asylum there and fight them where they are weaker."

"But the Troopers will indict them for helping me escape."

"Not if the captain didn't know."

"But you know, M. They'll hang you."

"We'll fight it, Liz. You didn't do anything wrong." She did not add, *And they'd have killed you if you stayed.*

Etna Station—Outbound

Once Meriel had stowed the grav-sled and crate, she checked the export paperwork and then fumigated the incoming passengers and personal articles onboarding from Etna. Molly signed on extra fares this trip, which would crowd the corridors.

When the *Tiger* undocked and the umbilicals were stowed, her neck and shoulders relaxed, as if mooring ropes had been cut and rats could no longer scurry aboard. That was fantasy, of course. One word from the station police or the Troopers near the beacon, and the captain would turn around. Elizabeth would end up in jail—and dead.

The trip to the jump point would be inertial, which meant long; a long time in the depressing dust cloud without the stars and open space to cheer them. Plenty of time to update her sister on the *Princess* forfeiture.

"You're jumpin' like a plasma arc, Sis," Elizabeth said after Meriel returned. "Why the panic?"

"We have only nine days to save the *Princess*, or they're gonna salvage her."

"Don't sacrifice yourself for this, M."

"I promised Mom I'd keep us together."

"We'll find a way. What's this new evidence?"

Meriel told her sister what she had learned about attacks in space and the *Princess* cargo of military R&D used to invade the Haven colony. As she told the story, Elizabeth's face grew darker.

"Mom and Pop would never put us in danger."

"I'm sure, Liz. I'll bet they didn't know. But I think it's connected to your assault on Etna. I think those people meant to hurt you."

"What do you mean, M?"

"I triggered something when I tried to find out more about the mil-tech. Your friends attacked you soon after."

"But I knew the guy."

"You didn't know his buddies. They're connected to Khanag and the Archtrope."

"That's a guess."

"It's more than that. Remember the symbol on the pin you picked up?" she said, and her sister nodded. "Mom drew the same symbol on the hold where…where she died. And I saw another near the ePod."

Elizabeth opened her mouth with a question, but Meriel brought a finger to her lips. In sign language, she said, "I went to the *Princess* last week and found the symbols there."

"Legal?" Elizabeth signed.

She shook her head and replied in sign, "I copied Mom's data chip." Then she took her sister's hand. "I have the family—"

A knock on the door and rattle of the door latch interrupted.

"M?" It was John's voice.

"Just a moment," she called from inside. A few moments later, she edged out of her cabin and closed the door behind her. But she remained standing in front of it.

"Why the lock?" he asked.

"Can't a lady have her privacy? Did you pick up my package?"

He handed her a small envelope. "M, we need to talk about this."

"Sure, let me read it first, and—"

"No. Your sister."

Meriel's jaw dropped, but she bluffed it out. "Oh, that. Nothing to talk about. Just a mix-up with station administration. It's all cleared up now. She took the next bus out and is on her way to Wolf."

He tilted his head. "Meriel, I still think we should—"

"Well, sailor, if you insist," she said with a wide smile. "I'll meet you at your place in twenty minutes, and we'll go over this." She unsettled him with a kiss and went back into her cabin and leaned against the door. After his footsteps faded away, she locked the door again, sighed, and turned up the ventilator fan to cover their voices.

Elizabeth grinned. "You've been holding out on me."

"Just a real nice guy, hon."

"Uh-huh. A nice guy you like a lot."

"Maybe. It's too complicated now."

"It's only as complicated as you want it to be, Sis. A little sack time is no complication at all."

"Love is more than an itch to scratch, Liz."

"Oh, so it's love now?"

Meriel flushed brightly and changed the subject. "I might have found Home." She pulled up the data sheet on TTL-5B3.

"5B? Not that rock again, M."

"Not 5B, 5B3, and coordinates relative to DX Cancri ecliptic."

Elizabeth stopped grinning, and Meriel queued up the high-res Aldersen holo from the q-chip that Nick had enhanced.

"Come on, M. The TTL-5B survey again? We chased every thread to dead ends."

"No, wait." Meriel fast-forwarded the vid and played the new part, including the close-up of the data summary.

"No kidding, the DXC ecliptic." Elizabeth dropped her gaze.

"You OK?"

"Yeah, it's just that we hunted so hard and didn't find it before."

"I'm sorry we didn't discover this together, hon."

Elizabeth nodded. "So, has anyone been there?"

Meriel shrugged. "OK now, let's see what's in our mysterious package."

The envelope contained only a small message chip, which she picked up and turned in her fingers. Remembering the experience with Nick, she assembled a wire cage and within it set her link and the chip. After booting, she scanned the chip's contents to find only three files: one text, one graphic, and one encrypted. They read the first together.

> Dear Ms. H:
> I hope this note finds you well and my concerns for you are unfounded. If you have retrieved this, I have engaged your interest. This package comes to you by a circuitous route, and you will soon understand why. Please read my story, and if you remain interested, continue with the attached file.
> About a decade ago ET, my husband, Leo, (God rest his soul) left me a message. The police found his body a few hours later, the apparent victim of a random street crime. (No, dear, I did not believe it either.) The message he sent read, "Send this to the princess." There was an attachment. At the time, I did not understand what he meant. I think I do now.
> Yesterday, men from my husband's former employer visited and asked if I had ever made contact with the crew of a certain merchant vessel. Of course,

I had not, and had no idea to what
they referred. My response did not
satisfy them, and they threatened to
cut off my survivor's benefits and
pension if they learned otherwise. I
honestly told them I'd had no contact.

Later that night, I remembered my
Leo's message and made the connection
to some old newscasts. I do not know
if my deductions are correct, but I do
not like being threatened, and the
corporate thugs pissed me off to no
end.

"I like this lady," Elizabeth said.

I can say nothing about the contents
except that I do not understand them.
The legal tone is consistent with my
husband's scope of responsibilities.
He often worked on highly sensitive
political matters as a representative
of the largest biogenetics firm on the
moon. I cannot say to whom he reported
at the time of his death. However, he
was an upper-echelon executive and
might be of particular interest to
you, if you know what I mean.

I pray the sensitivity of the
attached document will not cause
further harm to come to you. I am not
concerned for myself; I am old, and my
kids are safely away and ignorant of
anything but my love for them. If you
choose to read the attachment, the
password is someone close to you.

Please do not respond to me by any
means, as that might bring us both
unwanted attention.

God bless you and safe jump.
Moira V. Com-5S

"Hmmm, not a spacer, but stationside comm," Meriel said. "She knows the drills." After rereading the letter, she smiled. "'The largest biogenetics firm on the moon.' You got that?"

"Yup, BioLuna. Moira scrubbed it for keywords. Nothing is identifiable except her name, but we understood. A security scan wouldn't raise a flag. Smart woman."

"And she sent it by courier, not transmission. This must have cost her a small fortune." She opened the graphics file labeled "Leo.V," and a man's face appeared.

"Familiar?" Elizabeth asked.

"No. He must be Moira's husband." When she attempted to open the encrypted file, a password request popped up. She typed in 'someone close to you,' but that did not work.

"Try me."

She tried "Elizabeth." The decryption icon spun, and the file opened to the surprise of both of them.

```
            Top-Secret Eyes Only
     Please direct inquiries to
   chairman's office, UNE Commission on
   Immigration Services, UNE/IS
     Title: Interim Treaty of Haven,
   binding residents of Haven (Haveners);
   the orbital station, LeHavre; the UNE
   (United Nations of Earth); and named
   parties.
```

"Haven, that's John's colony," Meriel said.

```
     Article 1: Scope, Responsibilities
   and Intent
     A1.1 This treaty binds the residents
   and legal associations of the LeHavre
   Station, the UNE, and parties
   specifically named in this document
   heretofore...
```

"Blah-blah-blah," she mumbled and scrolled ahead.

```
Article 2: Political Boundaries
A2.1 Haveners agree to retain title
to the region of Ferrizan and reside
there hereafter and renounce all
claims to the remainder of Haven.
```

"I wonder how large that is," Meriel said.
"Or if it's habitable."

```
A2.2 The region of Terni will be
under control of the Archtrope of
Calliope and no other external entity.
```

"So this Archtrope guy can do whatever he wants there with no interference," Elizabeth said. "What do you know about this guy?"

"Not much. The news seems to say he's involved in the immigration politics on Chosho. Your friends on Etna say his disciples run the drugs and sex there."

```
A2.3 Remaining habitable regions
other than Ferrizan and Terni remain
under the guidance of the UNE office
of Immigrant Services (UNE/IS) with
the Interim Governor serving the
Commissioner of UNE/IS. The Office of
Interim Governorship (OIG) will be
maintained until free elections can be
conducted safely.
```

"They control everything until they can hold elections safely," Meriel said. "That sounds like forever to me."

```
Article 3: Trade
A3.1 All trade issues, exports,
imports, tariffs, duties, quarantine,
quality, safety, standards of
compliance, foreign exchange, and all
transactions on and off Haven will be
```

```
under UNE/IS administration and
regulatory guidance [1]…
```

"The UNE/IS is essentially in charge of all trade and finances," she said.

```
[1] Until such time as regulation
and administration is in place to
facilitate safe trade and transport
on, from, and to LeHavre and all
outlying stations within one (1) AU,
trade will be conducted by and at the
discretion of BioLuna.
```

"So, the corporations have a monopoly on Haven and everything nearby," Elizabeth said. "What makes it worth the headache?"

"Yeah, I thought it was a rock," Meriel said, "or a cesspool like Ceres."

"No one would go to all this trouble for a rock."

"I think we need to learn more from John."

"Did you ever hear of this before?"

"No."

Elizabeth queued up *Galactipedia* to begin a search.

"No, Liz. We shouldn't make another inquiry they can trace to me."

"But there should be lots of info. An Earthlike habitat with three habitable regions should be the hottest topic in the galaxy."

"John told me BioLuna is trying to bury info on Haven, and Nick could only find signs of the burial."

"They don't want us to know."

"Right. And simply searching for information might trigger the wrong interests, like I did with the *Princess* manifest."

Mention of their ship hit them both and silenced them.

Elizabeth signed, "Why didn't they just kill us?"

"I think they thought they had. They tired of searching for survivors and pointed us at a gas giant or something. If Mom

hadn't given us a jump program, we would have died there."
She arched her eyebrows. "Wow. Imagine their faces when
we showed up still breathing. Now, we're either more useful
alive or too dangerous dead."

"I'm guessing the former," Elizabeth said. "Nothing
personal, but we're nobodies. They must need us for
something."

"I'm thinking the latter. Killing us would shine some light
where they don't want it."

"We don't exist, remember? Court orders. Who'd put the
puzzle together?"

"I would." Meriel gazed at the wall. "I did."

Elizabeth rested her hand on her sister's hand. "Then they
should take you out first."

She nodded. "They would want to know how much we
know before that. Then they'll kill us quietly—all of us,
every last one."

"Again."

Elizabeth fetched juice packs from the cooler, and Meriel
added a vodka pill.

"OK, so ten years ago, some corrupt interests got together
to divvy up John's colony, thinking it was easy pickings.
They wanted help from some top-secret military
equipment—equipment which rode on our boat. Pirates
found out, stole it, and sold it to them. To do that they would
need knowledge of what it was and who carried it."

"Cookie thinks someone who knew about the R&D told
the thieves."

"Who's Cookie?"

"Sergeant Cook. He's security chief here."

"It wasn't contraband?"

"No. Confidential—secret, perhaps—but not contraband."

"Someone set us up, not pirates but contractors,
privateers?"

"Maybe someone shipped the weapon with us
legitimately, and he was sold out too," Meriel said. "From
what Teddy says, they'd still need to coordinate jumps to
find us.

"No one in our crew could do that."

She nodded. "I'm thinking a worm or a control virus. Like the one Nick tripped on."

"This is nasty business, M. Who would benefit?"

"Those named in the treaty, I guess. Who ran the UNE/IS back then?" She searched the *Galactipedia*, and her mouth fell open when she read the name. Leaning back in her chair, she closed her eyes to stop the tears.

"What is it?" Elizabeth asked and read the article. "Crap. Alan Biadez headed Immigration Services until four years ago."

"And he's the current president. Damn. He's one of the good guys, Liz. How could he be involved in all this? His foundation helped us after…after…" She stared at the deck, unable to continue.

Her sister gritted her teeth and laid her hand on Meriel's arm.

Meriel did not want to believe the inference. "Maybe he was just trying to keep track of us."

"Maybe you, in particular."

"Wow. That shatters an image."

"We can't be sure he's part of this."

"And we can't be sure he's not," Meriel said. "Regardless, these people are much too powerful for us to approach or oppose. I need to see John about this." She removed the chip to archive the files and slipped it into her pocket.

"Whoa, Sis. Stop by the galley and grab some snacks for me on the way back. I'm starving."

***

With Moira's message in hand, Meriel knocked on John's door.

"Meriel, I'm glad you stopped by. I wanted to talk to you. Did you hear the Exec's order?"

"Yeah, yeah, soon. Take a look at this first." She synced the chip with his console, and the Treaty appeared,

"Interim Treaty of… Where did you get this?"

"Widow of a BioLuna fixer. He died about the time the *Princess* was hit."

"Fixer?"

"A corporate lawyer type who does 'special projects.'"

"Legal?"

"I'm sure that's what they would say if the press found out."

After reading the whole document, he rubbed his forehead and sighed. "Damn. I thought this was between us and BioLuna." He converted his console ID to anonymous with a proxy at the communications beacon, and then did a search. "Biadez was also a member of the UNE/MAC, the Military Appropriations Committee."

Meriel covered her mouth with her hand and read the rest of the article. There it was. Biadez would have knowledge of the mil-tech devices and the logistics—he would know the *Princess* carried it. He might set up some other bureaucrat to send it, but he'd know where and how.

"The client behind the client," John said.

Space got a whole lot colder for her. She clenched her fists but had no one to strike. "We thought he was looking out for us." *What would the kids think if their hero was brought down to size? What will they think of me if I am the one doing the downsizing?*

"Can you find the other MAC members?"

He examined the list, and the connection was obvious to both of them: General Adam Miyamoto, the MAC chairman at the time, killed in a shuttle crash of mysterious cause the day of the attack.

"They murdered him before he could talk," she said.

"This isn't proof. None of this is proof."

She nodded. "So why all this fuss over Haven?"

A broad smile crossed his face. "I told you. You didn't believe me."

"Go on."

"It's gorgeous. The most Earthlike colony anyone has settled so far."

Compared to Mars, that wasn't saying much. "Moons?"

"Two."

Meriel stopped. In her mother's song, Home had two moons, and so did TTL-5B3. Then again, so did Mars and Celesta, and she had already excluded Haven as a possibility for Home. *He'll think I'm crazy.*

"Any connection?" he asked.

"No. Just an old fairy tale," she said, but now she had doubts. "You told me BioLuna wants to keep your colony hidden?"

He nodded but stared at the wall. "So that's what was going on. We suspected something, but nothing so elaborate, so well connected." His attention drifted away.

"John?"

"My wife, Annie, my kids' mom, died at Kilgore when the mercenaries attacked."

"They used the Hydra?"

"They tried. Annie died deactivating it. After that, we offered the mercenaries land to settle on. The mercs complained BioLuna violated their contract and joined us. They're loyal to Haven now."

"What about the box?"

"Still broken. We tried to fix it and couldn't. No one knows how."

"How many of your people did you lose?"

"About one in ten. We're scientists and engineers, M, not fighters."

"But clever."

He found a vid of the BioLuna CEO and played it.

```
CEO of BioLuna, Cecil Rhodes, is the
largest shareholder of a conglomerate
with diverse interests which spanned
the galaxy...named chairman and CEO
after consolidation of rivals to
monopolize lunar manufacturing...
```

"Wait," she said. "Zoom in. See the guy behind Rhodes? To his right?"

He nodded.

Returning to the vids on Moira's message chip, Meriel placed the image next to the man near Rhodes. The vids matched.

"He's the fixer, Leo V. Looks like he worked for the CEO. Leo sent a copy of the treaty to his wife just before he died, and she sent a copy to me." She peered into the vid, and another man seemed familiar, but she could not place him.

"So BioLuna and Alan Biadez planned to confine us on a tiny reservation and divvy up the rest. And they hired someone to steal mil-tech from your ship to make it easier."

"That leaves the Archtrope. I don't know much about him, except they say his people run the drug business on Etna. Some of his followers attacked my sister."

"He's a fanatic. His envoy visited and told us—*told* us, mind you—that he was our savior, and we should prepare for his spiritual leadership or prepare for the apocalypse."

"And one of his disciples is General Khanag," she said. "Sounds like a threat to me."

"We thought so, too. All we had to do to satisfy them was to provide the space and infrastructure for his millions of worshipers to pilgrimage."

"Let me guess. You told him no."

"Right, and they didn't like it," John said. "The emissary swore we would submit to the Archtrope's vision in time."

"When was this?"

"Right after BioLuna made its first demands—about eleven years ago." He located a news clip.

    ...the Archtrope of Calliope, seen
    here being escorted from tau Ceti-4.
    The Supreme Court agreed to bring
    indictments against his followers on
    charges of treason and conspiracy. His
    most visible representative, Fredric
    Allen, is seen here in restraints
    after his failed coup and attempt to
    suspend the Constitution. Riots
    continue in some wards of...

"Drugs, human trafficking, and terrorism," he said. "Not a good neighbor. They profess piety and abstain from all vice, but they feel no remorse about selling vice to their neighbors." The video continued.

    His Holiness is seen here boarding a
    ship with General Khanag, a former
    colonel in the UNE Space Marines, to
    return to his theocracy on Calliope.
    The Calliope Foundation is listed as a
    nongovernmental organization by the
    UNE and was nominated for a seat in
    the General Assembly, a first for an
    NGO...

At the ship's portal, Meriel noted the handsome young captain again, this time bowing to the Archtrope.

"It's a cult and a criminal conspiracy," John said. "Somehow, violence always shows up when they want something. Crimes are never directly linked to the leader, but people know if you oppose the theocracy, you risk your life."

"What did this guy do to earn his place at the trough?" She paused to consider the question, and the answer came to her—piracy.

"Oh, no," Meriel gasped. *Whose core business was smuggling contraband and contract executions? Pirates and terrorists. Who had the resources? Drug smugglers with a galaxy-wide network of ships and contacts.*

She teared up and couldn't talk. *Everyone killed and the kids still suffering because of a piece of junk that got blown up on some stupid little colony. And Biadez was mixed up with them.*

John moved next to her and embraced her.

"We were just in the way," she said and melted into his chest. When her tears stopped, she sat up. "This is the last piece of the puzzle, John. This could clear my family and the *Princess*."

"This isn't proof, M."

"No, but it's pretty strong inference. If this is made public, President Biadez, the Archtrope, and the BioLuna executives would have big problems trying to explain it. The treaty puts their fingerprints all over this."

He nodded. "This is too big for us."

She remembered her sister's comment about the Biadez Foundation tracking the kids—"Maybe just you." And she recalled the plain-looking men at the Pink Palace on Etna and on Enterprise. Queuing up her vids, she played them side by side. The vids showed the same man.

"Oh God," she said.

"Who is this guy?"

"Oh, no. I'm being followed," she said. "Here. To the *Tiger*."

"Who is he?"

"Don't know." She pulled up the vid with the CEO of BioLuna.

"Objects," she said, and glowing edges appeared around each item in the holo, each annotated by a numbered flag. "Focus eighteen. Full screen." Her subject filled the image but appeared fuzzy, and his head was turned away. "Clarify," she said, and the app analyzed shadows and searched for reflective surfaces that might reveal the man's face.

A flashing number in the lower corner stopped at 28 percent and beeped. "Reconstruct full frontal and compare." The image clarified and emerged adjacent to the other vids. They were similar.

"Who is he?" John asked again.

"I don't know, but he was there with Leo, and Leo's dead. Molly needs to know." She jumped to her feet.

"About the conspiracy?"

Meriel ignored him. "If he's part of this, they'll be coming back in force." From her link, she checked the *Tiger's* cargo manifest for viruses and quarantined anything that might trigger one.

He opened his mouth to speak, but she raised her hand to silence him. The report was free of malware, but something could still be sleeping. She needed to talk to Cookie, which meant warning Molly first.

She dashed for the door. "I need to go."

"Wait, about your sister," he called, but Meriel had rounded the corner.

***

Meriel knocked on Molly's ready-room door.

"Ah, Chief," Molly said and signaled her to enter. "A word, please. The—"

"XO, I think the *Tiger* may be in danger because of me."

"How so?"

"Someone followed me here."

"As a pretty young woman, you should be flattered. How does that endanger us?"

Meriel fidgeted uncomfortably. "Well…,"

"Sit, Chief."

She sighed and began, "You know about the *Princess*, right?"

When Molly nodded, Meriel told her about the conspiracy without mentioning Cookie or John. Then she displayed the treaty.

Molly raised her hand. "Where did you get this?"

"From the wife of a BioLuna executive."

"This is all very elaborate. How do you know it's legitimate?"

Meriel opened her mouth in defense, but had nothing to offer. The document had no routing information to verify the provenance. That meant it had never been transmitted and was either the original or a copy. It also meant she could have created it a few minutes ago—if she were crazy enough.

"I…trusted the source," she stammered, realizing how unreliable that sounded.

"You think they followed you and will attack the *Tiger* to get to you?"

"Maybe not me. But the information? Yes."

"How will this threat materialize?"

"I don't know, ma'am. The *Princess* had an aggressive military-grade virus in the manifest. I checked the *Tiger* manifest and found nothing. Please, don't accept any late data."

"Acknowledged. Stay, please." She tapped an icon on her desk. "Captain. Sergeant. Be on alert this trip for a security breech."

"What do you expect?" the captain said.

"If we're lucky, a distraction. If not, a hijack."

"On it, ma'am," Cookie said.

"Sergeant, please scan our systems for aggressive viruses, mil-tech. And check the bonafides on our new passengers."

"Aye, aye," Cookie said, and Molly turned to her.

"Thank you," Meriel said.

"I've always been straight with you, Chief. I need the same from you."

"Yes, ma'am."

"Are you taking your meds regularly?"

The question came unexpectedly, and Meriel betrayed herself with a blush. "I'm not making this up. Really. I have it all here, the treaty, the vids—"

"Doc stopped in and mentioned you had some daydreams about your old ship and the kids you grew up with."

Meriel wondered how Doc had found out. She examined her hands in her lap and could barely speak. "I only talk to very few people about them anymore." *Apparently not few enough*, she thought.

"The meds are a condition of your work card, Meriel. Promise me you're taking them."

"Yes, ma'am. I am," she lied again.

"Dismissed, Chief," Molly said, and Meriel left.

Outside the door, Meriel stopped and leaned against the bulkhead to check her link for Cookie's location. When she heard her name, she raised her head to listen.

"Doc, any particular reason why Chief Hope might be feeling anxious about being followed?" Molly asked.

"If she's off the meds, she's delusional," Ferrell replied. "A paranoid fantasy would fit her symptom profile."

"Acknowledge. Out."

Meriel clenched her fists and hurried away. "Damn, he is *not* my friend," she murmured.

Elbowing her way through the overcrowded passageways to the galley, she found Cookie checking the *Tiger's* systems for mil-tech viruses.

"I did an Hff4 virus sweep of the manifest and data sets," she said while loading up a tray of food for her sister. "Nothing sophisticated—no hot links in the manifests. Cargo memory is cold."

Cookie nodded. "I stopped two passengers from boarding whose DNA swab didn't match their ID. The rest are clear." He raised an eyebrow. "You're hungry."

"Yeah, girl stuff, real snackie," she said to shut him up.

"Eat fast and report back here. I'm rallying the security team. Five minutes. And try the applejack," he said, and she grabbed some pastries.

Inside Meriel's cabin, Elizabeth tore into the food. "You left me starving."

"Sorry. Took longer than I planned, but I learned a lot." She described what she and John had pieced together about Haven, the treaty, and the conspirators.

"You're kidding," Elizabeth said with her mouth full of pastry. "So Haven is Earthlike? Makes sense they'd try to steal it. Earthers will kill to leave Sol for a little freedom."

"The people doing this—Biadez, the Archtrope, the BioLuna CEO—they're on top of the system, fat and happy. They want to exploit everyone else who is trying to emigrate."

"Those are voracious carnivores, M. You remember the dino-sims on Enterprise?"

"Yeah, it feels like that to me, too." She wanted to rant, but Elizabeth drifted into her own thoughts.

"Everybody we loved, real people, killed for being at the wrong place at the wrong time," Elizabeth said. "It could have been any ship, any crew…" Another bun approached her mouth but stopped, and she pinched her eyes closed.

"What is it, hon?" Meriel asked.

"It couldn't have been just anyone. Only us."

"Why?"

"Mom knew about Home. Or almost. She was close and would have gone public with information she should not have had."

"The Alderson vid?"

Elizabeth nodded.

"I think they arranged it so we had to take that cargo."

"How do you know?"

"All the suppliers were new and aren't in business anymore."

"Fronts?" Elizabeth asked.

"Yeah. And steered the legit distributors away. We'd have gone bust without that cargo."

Elizabeth stared at the deck. "Damn. It's like the cheap novels; some thug burns down the family farm just because it's in the wrong place."

"Except no hero is coming to the rescue. The hero lit the torch. It's Alan Biadez, for God's sake." Meriel crossed her arms. "I didn't think it would feel this bad. It's like a kick in the chest. Harry keeps Biadez's poster in his cabin like he's a holo star."

"M, I know you look up to Biadez and the foundation, but they're bastards. I'll never forgive them for what they did to you. What they tried to do to us. The drugs. The separation. We were just kids. I'll bet that's why they cut Teddy out of the custody hearings. To keep us isolated. The foundation did that."

"Damn. They paid for the investigation and worked with the Troopers." Meriel paused and shook her head. "I saw the toys, Liz. Right where we left 'em."

"They told us they took them as evidence."

"Yeah, the bastards. That was just mean."

"They weren't trying to find evidence. They were hiding it."

Meriel sat up straight. "Oh, jeez! The Biadez Foundation knows how to contact all the kids. If he knows, then BioLuna and the Archtrope know too." Staring forward, she began to breathe rapidly, her eyes unfocused. Nausea gripped her, and she ran to the sink. She turned on the faucet and leaned over with her hands on the sides.

Elizabeth took her arm. "Breathe slow, hon."

"I can't help them." She slammed her palm on the rim. "Shit. The only people who *don't* know they're in danger are the people who can protect them."

"M, it's OK, we'll—"

"No, it's not OK. They're going to kill them, kill us." She trembled. "God, I never wanted to feel this way again." *It will all go away with the meds.* She grabbed the tube from the cabinet and collapsed to the deck. Closing her eyes, she gripped the tube until her knuckles turned white.

Elizabeth gasped. "No, M."

After a long pause, her hand relaxed and she looked at the tube. "I wanted the meds, Liz. When we were kids. I couldn't handle it. I'm sorry we drifted apart. But it was all too much."

Elizabeth smiled and cupped Meriel's cheek with her palm. "I know, Sis. But I don't care. I need you, all of you, not that zombie on the meds."

"Was I really so bad?" Meriel asked.

"Hon, you'd stare at the wall and drool."

"Really?"

"Well, almost."

Meriel rose and returned the tube to the cabinet. With her head down, she leaned against the bulkhead. "I brought this on us, Liz."

"What are you talking about?"

"They might have left us alone, but I stirred it up again. I screwed up. I hoped to keep us together like Mom wanted and have a normal life.

"Sis, we all read our own obituaries before we were fifteen. We're never gonna have a normal life."

"But now we're all targets."

"You can't blame yourself for this."

"If I'd left this alone, we might not be in danger now."

Elizabeth shook her head. "If you'd left this alone, we'd all be dead."

"You helped me, Liz. I couldn't have done it without you."

"Don't be dumb. I was ten and a basket case. Mom was dying."

"You didn't believe me?"

"That she was sleeping? No. I saw you trying to wake her and how scared you were. And later, you tried to hide it, but I knew you were hurt bad."

Meriel dropped her gaze, and her shoulders shook, but Elizabeth lifted Meriel's chin and looked her in the eyes.

"M, you still don't get it. You can't screw up with us. The older kids remember what happened back then. You kept going when we just wanted to sit and cry. They don't know what you had to do...with our folks; they don't want to know. But they know you did it for us, to protect us. They'd die for you."

"I won't let them."

"Yeah. But it's not up to you. We all know the life we have is a gift. No one says it, but we know, and you can't screw up after that." She took Meriel's hand. "I'll alert them, M."

"Tell 'em to go dark, hide."

"They're not gonna like it."

"They'll like dead even less."

"I recycled my link. What do you have here I can use?"

Meriel pointed to the comm console, and Elizabeth began to draft the messages. As she worked, she asked, "OK now, what else?"

"I warned the XO, and she alerted Cookie. I need to report to him."

"Worried about another *Princess*?"

Meriel nodded.

"What do you have here?"

"Suits and breathers are in the closet."

"What about weapons?"

"Two stunners here under the deck plates," Meriel said and tapped her foot on her hidey-hole.

"Nothing deadly?"

"Only the knife."

Her sister's concern was justified. A stunner would not kill an attacker; it would only knock him unconscious for a few minutes. Repeated use might cause seizures and permanent brain damage, but it would not kill.

"Cookie has the vests and lethal weapons," Meriel said. "Hard-suits are near the air locks." She paced her little cabin. "OK, you send the alert to the kids and their families. And we need copies of Moira's chip ready to sync with the outbound beacon. Nick should have one, and Jeremy, and Teddy. About two hours remain until jump. I'll report to Cookie and help with the security planning."

Elizabeth nodded.

"I'll stay on the link, so buzz me if you need anything," she said and left to meet Cookie.

In the passageway on the way to the galley, Meriel ran into John.

"Hey, Cookie mentioned you took two rations of food. I thought I'd stop by. We could snack and chat a bit."

She kept walking. "Sorry, there isn't time. I have to report to my security team now."

"Really, we need to talk. You mentioned your sister, and I—"

Mention of Elizabeth stopped her in her tracks, and she walked back to him. "Shhh. This is our secret, remember?" She looked around and behind them and whispered, "I stowed her away in my cabin. I had to. They'd arrest her and throw away the key. Maybe kill her."

He frowned. "Did you tell Molly?"

"I will, just not yet. Liz is still in witness protection, and this will just get them into trouble. I added her weight to the cargo to make the mass work out, but the center of gravity will shift a bit."

"Meriel, I need you to—"

"Please, John, I have to report. We may be in danger," she said over her shoulder and rushed away.

***

John shook his head as he watched her hurry away. Doc had not convinced him she was having delusions, but she was acting strange and had lied to him. He needed confirmation before helping her again.

Using an administration app, he checked utility use in her cabin, specifically water and lighting. Her lights had been on all day, but that might point to a defective motion detector driving the environmental controls. The record showed toilet use at the same time the roster reported her on duty. That would not be the first time someone returned to their cabin without logging out.

A red highlight on the effluents flashed. After a touch on the light, a graph of something called Aristopine appeared. Another touch and background material appeared: an antipsychotic, just like Doc said, and expensive. BioLuna was the exclusive supplier. The effluent monitors signaled that she took them on schedule. *So why would he say she skipped her meds?* He rubbed the back of his neck. *Nothing conclusive that she hid someone there. Well, there's one way to check for sure.* He rose and left his cabin.

***

Halfway to the security office, Meriel's link buzzed with notification that Doc Ferrell placed a flag on her cargo-rating card. A flag meant she couldn't work, and Molly would kick her off the boat, leaving her stranded on a station scrounging for a meal while she appealed. Meanwhile, her sister would be without help.

She called him immediately. "Doc, why is this flag on my card?"

"You're off duty until I clear you, Chief. Be in my office within five minutes, or I make it permanent."

"Doc, I'm working on something vital. Please, right after the jump."

"Five minutes."

"Please. Cookie's called me to a security alert."

"Five minutes."

Crap, I don't have time for this. But I need my work card, or we lose the Princess. *Well, we have two hours yet to jump. Only a few seconds with him, and then I'll talk to Cookie.* She sent a brief message to Cookie and charged into Ferrell's office.

"OK, Doc, so here I am." Eyeing a couch she would never lie down on, she sat in a chair opposite Ferrell across a desk. On it stood a pitcher of water and two glasses. Otherwise, the monochrome beige room appeared like a morgue, untouched by human character. *Just how human is this guy?*

"Chief, you've stalled for weeks now, and time is up. I clear you, or you're done on the *Tiger*."

"Does the XO concur?"

"I don't need her concurrence to put a medical flag on your card," he said without looking up. "Drink?" A flask materialized from a drawer.

Practical man, she thought. "No, thanks."

He pointed to the JCS medal on her necklace and turned back to his console. "You a believer?"

Taking a wire cargo tie from her pocket, she began to clean her fingernails. "Kinda. Just been busy."

"You're rated marine-three. That's a loaded weapon."

"You may be grateful for that." She checked the time. "You wanna talk? Then talk." She poured a glass from the pitcher and sipped.

"File says your psych was clear until the *Princess*. Tell me about it."

Curve ball. He wants a therapy session. "Not a chance, Doc. You read my file. Pirates. Cargo emptied, adults slaughtered. It's all there."

"That's your conclusion, not what you endured. You were a child."

"We were all children," she said, while concentrating on her cuticles.

"How many?"

A mild lightheadedness slowed her reply. *I should have eaten something with Liz.* "It's in the file. Six kids plus me and my sister…"

"And…?"

This is not why she had come, and she rose to leave. "Look, Doc…," she began, but the room spun, and she fell back into the chair. *This wasn't hunger.* "You bastard!" *Drugs. This will be bad.*

With the remnants of her self-control, she fixed the wire tie between her palm and the arm of the chair. Now, every squeeze would force an electric jolt of pain to focus her attention. *If he finds out Elizabeth is here, they'll turn the* Tiger *around and hand her over to murderers. Don't tell him about Liz or she'll die. Don't tell him about Liz…*

Rising, he stepped to her side of the desk and sat on the edge. "Sorry, Meriel. My responsibility is to this ship, not your privacy."

"Uh-huh," she said and closed her eyes. She was under.

"Open file, personal, Meriel Hope." Her files displayed on the active wall. "New entry, interview, time, ship, Ferrell, MD, attending. Begin."

He snapped his fingers. "Meriel. Meriel. Open your eyes, please."

With no concern for what might happen to her and only the need to do what was asked, she opened her eyes. The wire poking her palm reminded her not to mention her sister.

"Meriel, are you still taking your meds?"

She opened her mouth to lie, but the drugs removed all resistance. *Such a nice man. And so attractive.* "No."

"Why not?"

With a goofy smile, she tipped her head. "They make me forget things."

"Forget what?"

"Forget to care," she said.

"Don't you want to forget?"

She stared at his desk. "All the time. But I can't. I need to remember. They need me to remember."

"Who needs you to remember?"

"The kids." Smiling at the memory of Anita and Harry, her eyes closed and her head bobbed. Ferrell snapped his fingers again, and Meriel raised her head, her eyes unfocused.

"Tell me about the *Princess*, Meriel. The day of the attack."

"I don't want to."

"It'll be OK. You're safe here."

The drug urged her to tell him of her sister and the kids. *Oh God, I'll tell him.* She squeezed the arm of the chair and the wire cut into her palm. A white-hot flash of pain jolted her, but she still wanted to speak. *Why not tell him? I have to tell him.* Another squeeze and the wire dug into the meat of her thumb and argued back: *do not tell.*

"Come, Meriel."

She told him the whole story about how the claxon's wailing awakened them, and how her mother hid them in the maintenance hold and left them.

"Continue, please, Meriel."

"The ePod ejected and scared us."

"Who was inside?"

"I don't know."

"And then?"

"Mom returned and welded the hatch closed. She was hurt."

"Continue, please." His was the voice of God, a disembodied spirit who walked with her through that horrible day again. She re-experienced everything while he listened as no one ever had before.

Without hesitation, she told him about her most precious possessions, the pendant with the key and q-chip.

"May I see that, please?"

She took off the necklace and handed it to him. Pressing the end of the pendant between his thumb and index finger, he exposed the tiny gem of the q-chip. He tapped the chip on the desk near his console and studied it.

"What's on it?" he asked.

"I don't know. Nav coordinates and family vids. My mother said, 'It's all here.'"

"All what?"

"I don't know."

Bringing the chip closer to his console, he frowned. But instead of inserting it, he lay the pendant in the middle of his desk and spiraled the chain around it.

"Go on, Meriel."

"We got too cold and had to leave, and I cracked more lightsticks to see better…," she began, but in a flash, she returned to the hold, where they hid. She gasped; the image of her mother's ashen face was crystal clear.

The drug compelled her to speak. "My mom… died." When she said it aloud, her feet sank into a tar pit, and she could not move.

"I'm sorry to hear that," Ferrell said without the slightest trace of emotion, but his voice lifted her out of the pit. "Go on."

She wanted to stay and warm her mother's icy hands and wait for her to wake, as if she had simply fallen asleep. However, Meriel knew that was a wish, and they needed to leave the hold. They had to find warmth or they would all die.

It was all up to her. "I told the kids she was sleeping and would be OK."

The memory of her sister taking care of the kids appeared. "My…" but the painful wound in her palm scolded her not to talk about Liz. *He'll understand. No!* "Mom welded the hatch shut, so I went another way and…" The black cloud reappeared and blocked her memory. It terrified her, and she started to shake.

"And what, Meriel?"

Tears streamed down her cheeks. "I don't know. I can't see."

"Try harder. Your memory is fine."

"No!" She struggled with herself, not wanting to remember. "I shouldn't be here. I'm only twelve. Mama and Papa should be here, not me. I don't want to be here."

"Try, Meriel."

A groan escaped her lips. The black cloud would not lift, but she knew what lay on the other side. Her teardrops fell openly, and she could not speak.

Ten years ago, she had left their hiding spot and led the children to the alt-bridge, taking the shortest path. But when she turned the corner to the mess hall, a bloody arm lay in her path outside the infirmary. She asked her sister to hold the kids back while she checked. The bloody arm was connected to Penny's dad, but he was not breathing. When she glanced into the room, she cried out. There lay the entire crew, stacked up like cargo and bleeding.

"Oh, God." She blinked to stop the visions, but they still came. Even though she was old enough to tear down the black wall, she did not want to, because it hid the face of her father.

"No, Papa," she murmured.

Ferrell clapped his hands. "Meriel, wake up."

"Huh?"

"You're leaving the cargo hold. What's happening?"

"I'm with them. They don't want me to be here, to see them like this."

"Who?" he asked.

"Our parents."

"See them like what?"

"Broken. Hurt so bad."

"Go on, Meriel."

"I can't let the kids see them like this. But they'll freeze if I don't do anything." She remained quiet, drowning in a tidal wave of horrors. One by one, she examined each of the adults to check if they needed help, fully aware she was a child and did not know what to do. They were all dead, and she sat in the doorway and cried.

"Meriel, what's happening?" Ferrell asked.

"I tried to wake them. They're…all gone." She froze. "I shouldn't have to see this," she said aloud now, powerless to stop herself. "I'm only twelve. I need help. I shouldn't have to do this."

"What happened to the people?"

"They're…" She froze again, unable to speak of the carnage. "They're gone. It's just me, just us." Another jolt of pain reminded her not to refer to her sister.

"OK, Meriel, what do you remember next?"

Wishing for someone to aid her, the image of her Uncle Ed's wrecked face came to her instead. "Meriel, help me," he had begged in her imagination.

"Ahh," she groaned, and she clutched her arms to her chest and neck to cover her scars. "I don't know how."

"What's happening?"

"I…I got hurt," she said, dopey and exhausted. "I got this." She pointed to the edge of the scar on her neck.

"How did it happen?"

"I think it was one of the…things they used to hurt my folks." She closed her eyes. "A laser scalpel, maybe. I slipped on…on the blood into a table. It fell on me and…burned me from here…" she said, tracing the scar across her breast and stomach to the opposite hip, "…to here." Her pulse raced, and her breath quickened. "It hurt a lot."

"I'm sorry, Meriel. That must have been tough growing up."

Nodding, she held her left arm tight to her chest with her right hand. Tears fell again and a soft, "Yeah," was all she could manage. *He understands.*

"How do you feel now?"

"It still hurts." She wanted him to ask her what it felt like to grow up not wanting boys to look too close; to ask her why she could only make love in the dark. But Ferrell took notes and did not ask. Without the polestar of his voice, she was adrift again.

"What happened next, Meriel?"

Back on the *Princess*, she had locked the infirmary door and found an alternate route around it for the kids. And along the way, she closed the cabin doors before letting them pass.

"I led the kids to the alt-bridge."

"And then?"

Standing alongside her sister, she stuck the q-chip in the nav comp. The *Princess* came back to life. "We jumped to Enterprise Station."

"We?"

She wanted to tell him Elizabeth helped her, but she pushed her palm against the arm of the chair again. The wire dug deeper into her hand until she gasped.

"Are you all right, Meriel?"

"No."

Ferrell ignored her response. "Who helped you program the route?"

"My mom scripted a self-executing nav route."

He leaned over his desk. "Then you didn't need help jumping the *Princess*."

Meriel went silent and the black fog began to form again.

"Meriel, were you alone?"

"No," she murmured, but her memory was cloudy now.

Ferrell nodded. "How did you know it was pirates that attacked your ship?"

"I saw what they did. Normal people can't do things like that."

"Did you actually see any of the pirates?"

"No."

"Are you sure?"

"Yes."

He sighed and reclined in his chair. "What happened to everyone?"

"They're…gone," she said, and her vision blacked out again.

"What about the other kids?"

God, I'm so stupid. "They sent them away."

"Where are they now?"

The drug demanded she mention Liz, and to quiet it, Meriel dug the wire in deeper into her thumb. But she was becoming inured to the pain; the wire was losing its authority to focus her attention. She wiggled it and winced.

"Hiding. They're gone, and I can't be with them anymore." That was true, referring to the court order she violated every day of her life. "I want them with me again. I want us all to be back together on the *Princess*." True again.

"I'm sure you do." He picked up the pendant again and tapped the q-chip on the console while spinning it between his fingers. Interrupted by snoring, he glanced up to see her head on her chest and caught a twinkle of reflected light from the flask. It beckoned, and he complied.

***

John went to Meriel's cabin and tried the biolock. Hoping she would forgive him, he torqued the handle, and after a jerk, opened it.

He entered her little room and found it empty, but strewn with dirty dishes and food containers. This surprised him. Spacers tended to be neat and tidy, if not clean, because the smallest mass might become a projectile when gravity shifted and the deck became the overhead. He inspected the wall and ceiling panels for tampering but detected no trace of a stowaway.

A draft message remained open on her console describing what they had uncovered about the Treaty of Haven and the conspirators. It was addressed to a lawyer on Lander, and John wondered if that was the shyster Doc had mentioned.

Sitting on her bunk, he sighed and keyed his link. "M, real important I talk to you."

The claxon announced five minutes to jump, and he had to leave.

***

Meriel awoke to the sound of the claxon still groggy, as if she had jumped without boost. Her nightmare was fresh. She sat up to orient herself and squinted with a severe headache.

A jolt of pain shot up her arm when she moved her hand, which woke her completely.

How did I get in Ferrell's office? Then she remembered and sneered. His head rested on his hands next to an empty flask. The pendant and medal lay with her necklace in his hand. Standing, she scooped them up but rested a hand on the desk until her legs steadied.

"Hey!" she shouted, and he raised his head and blinked, still half asleep. She slapped him across the face so hard he almost fell off his chair. "Satisfied?"

He nodded as a red welt rose on his cheek. "I didn't know."

"Of course you didn't know. You think they're gonna tell my story on the net? How about vids, maybe, or a movie? Families would never fly again, and stations would die." She balled her fist to punch him, and he flinched, but she held back. "OK, weasel; did that information in any way help you assess my performance on this ship?"

"No, but—"

Her fist slammed on the table. "Then stay the hell outta my head! And stay out until I can get my family back together."

"I'm sorry, Meriel. You think the kids are still alive?"

In disbelief, she tilted her head. "Of course I do. Didn't you hear me?"

"It's not in your file. None of this is."

She looked away. "They didn't believe me."

"Show me. I'll give you a chance. Show me they are alive. Give me some proof. Anything."

"There's a court order, you slime ball, and I can't say anything."

"Then the *Princess*."

"My lawyer will—"

"A two-bit shyster hiding behind attorney-client privilege."

She took a chance he would not tell the Troopers. "I have messages, I can show—"

"From an anonymous proxy. You could have sent them to yourself."

How could he know that? Speechless, she scowled at him, and then lowered her head. She had nothing. The evidence she needed hid in her cabin, and she could not expose her sister until they jumped away from Etna. *Or is that a delusion, too?*

"After the jump, Doc. I can show you then," she said, but her stammer exposed her uncertainty.

He rubbed his cheek and regained his composure. "Sorry, Chief. If you're not back on the meds by the end of the shift, I'll have you restrained."

She stormed out, and the door slid closed behind her.

***

Doc Ferrell took another drink and rested his forehead on his palm. "What the hell have I gotten myself into?" After a long sigh, he stored the recording of the interrogation in case he needed to defend himself to Molly and the board of medical review. Then he began to dictate into Meriel's psych file.

"Hope, Meriel. Off medication and intractable. Interviewed under 15 ccs scapo-G: G selected to enhance emotional detachment. Subject questioned about traumatic experiences on LSM *Princess*. Unlikely her role was anything other than innocent victim and sole survivor. However, continuing severe psychosis with delusions of getting her dead family and ship back from the station lawyers. Holds on to delusions even under scapo. Fantasy maintenance seems to provide a structure for self-control. Without it, stability is in doubt. That structure also supports her impulse to rationalize deception in defense of her delusions, in which she is most certainly still engaged. Will enforce medication or restraint."

He pondered his link a moment as if waiting for a guilty verdict. Then, after attaching Meriel's interrogation, he keyed a message to an encrypted GRL.

```
To Kadvi:
Assignment complete. Hope has no
additional info re: LSM x2:88 or crew.
```

…which referred to Meriel's ship, the *Princess*.

Picking up the picture of the young girl, he smiled. "I'll be home soon, Asha."

***

Just a few feet down the empty passageway and around a corner, Meriel stopped and leaned against the wall, cringing with pain. She took her bloody hand out of her pocket. The wire tie had pierced a full inch into the muscle of her thumb. New tears fell as she extracted it slowly.

Staggering to the showers, she squeezed her palm to flush the puncture with fresh blood and wrapped her hand with a towel. She still needed to report to Cookie, and time was running out. And she still had to tell Molly about Ferrell's abuse and log a complaint.

The claxon sounded again, three minutes to jump. *Oh, crap! I must have slept in Ferrell's office. There's no time to reach Cookie now. I gotta find Liz.*

Rushing to her cabin, she bumped into John.

"Meriel, I still need to talk to you."

She glared at him. "You told him, didn't you?"

"Who?"

"You told Ferrell about Elizabeth, didn't you?"

"I only told him she was in trouble, that you debarked to help her."

"Dammit! You promised." She hit him in the chest.

He reached for her shoulders to calm her. "What happened? I was trying to help."

Knocking his arms away, she pushed him across the corridor into the bulkhead. "I don't need any more goddamned help!" she said with fresh tears in her eyes. *Damn, I can't trust anyone but family. But they…* "Liz," she murmured and raced to her cabin.

"Meriel, wait," he called as she turned the corner.

Cookie was not in his quarters or the galley as she ran past. *He's preparing, but preparing without me. He has no idea what he's up against. But do I?*

Her cabin was in the same clutter she had left hours ago, but her sister was gone. A quick scan for messages found one from Molly, who wanted to meet with her, and another from Cookie, telling her to link auxiliary security teams on Channel 3. Liz had left nothing.

She checked the hidey-hole, but it was empty as well, the warm-suit and a stunner gone. Just before running out the door, she paused. *Is Ferrell right? What's really behind the black cloud in my memory? Am I making this up? I lost the party favor from Harry's birthday and have no vids. Teddy and Nick are off the grid, ghosts as far as anyone knows. Liz is gone. I have nothing, no proof at all.*

Am I having daydreams again? Oh God, what if I really am alone?

As she leaned against the bulkhead, her eyes burned—there were no more tears left to cry. She slid down the wall until she sat on the deck, still holding the handle. Imaginings came unbidden of what else might have happened that horrible day on the *Princess*, of what else might be behind the black cloud she would not consider. Crushed by doubt, she stared straight ahead and yearned for the disorientation of the jump without tranq.

***

On the bridge, the crew made final preparations for the jump, waiting only for the communications beacon to complete synchronization. Captain Richard was at the helm, and Molly watched from the chair in her ready room.

She tapped her link. "Cookie, did you find anything in the malware scan?"

"No, ma'am. Something might be sleeping, but I found nothing to wake it."

"Hey, XO, here's something for you," Socket said and displayed the message.

```
   From: J. Conklin, Cpt., LSM Jolly
Roger
   Subject: Whereabouts of Doc Griffin
   Hi, Molly & Rich. Regarding your ex-
doc, immigrated to Moon-D. Now has an
address there in a luxury arcology.
Plans a vacation to Europa. I think
you overpaid him. By a lot.
```

"We didn't fund all that. Where'd he get the money?" the captain asked.

"That must have been some inheritance," Molly replied. "I guess it explains why he left in such a hurry."

"Beacon sync complete," Socket said.

"Begin jump count. Ten seconds," the captain said.

Her screen flickered, and the bridge lights and the consoles blinked and returned.

"Whoa!" Jerri said. "Did you see that?"

Molly's mouth dropped. "Abort!" she yelled. Jerri slammed her hand down on the big red button, but the jump program had already locked her out.

They jumped.

Chapter 10
Etna 320 Ort Cloud

Visit from a Black Swan

Molly's scope flashed white noise when she woke from jump.

"Too early," she said. When she switched to visual, it remained black without the nearby star of Etna.

She tapped her link. "Sergeant Cook to the bridge, ASAP. Chief Hope, report." Unsecuring herself from her chair, she rushed to the small-arms locker while the turmoil on the bridge reached her through the open door.

"Where are we?" the captain yelled. He hit the alarm claxon and toggled comm to PA. "All hands. Red alert! Prepare to repel borders. Pilot, jump as soon as it's safe."

"Where to?" Jerri yelled over the loud pinging, which rang the entire hull like a bell.

"Anywhere we can find our way back from. And I mean *anywhere*. Just get us out of here."

She raised her hands. "Sorry, sir. Nav locked me out."

Socket interrupted from the communications station. "Incoming EM, sir, and recent."

Recent meant close.

An explosion smashed Molly headfirst into the locker, knocking her down. Turning back, she glimpsed a big smoking hole a few seconds old and black-suited intruders storming the bridge. One of them grabbed Jerri by the hair, threw her off her chair, and stuck a device into the nav console. Nav came back to life, and the pinging stopped.

Before the blast door closed to isolate the bridge, a black-suit jumped through, but Molly shot him in the face before he reached her. Reaching her desk, she clipped the command-link to her pocket, and careened out the side door to the adjoining corridor.

Her feet lost traction, and she twisted midair. When gravity returned, it slammed her back on the deck unprepared. Returning to her feet with a hand on the wall for support, she staggered to the security assembly area only to find black-suits there as well. Using a different passageway, she retreated and headed for the weapons locker.

A pounding hum vibrated though the hull from the bridge behind her. She pressed her link against the bulkhead to identify the sound.

Her link replied, "Carbon delaminator. Used to repair or dismantle high tensile strength bucky-sheet laminates…"

"The blast doors," she murmured. "It's only a matter of time."

The sound reverberated through her body, tickling her cheek. She scratched it, and her hand came away red with blood. When she looked up again, the corridor tilted, and she fell again. "No thugs are gonna take the *Tiger* while I'm XO," she pledged.

Finding the locker empty, she stumbled to the alternate assembly area, hoping to locate survivors. But the world spun again, and she slumped against the bulkhead and fell onto her face.

***

Meriel knew they had jumped short: the disorientation was brief, and she did not feel stiff. And she knew they were in trouble when the pinging reached her. It was real now—not a nightmare. *Survive. Don't fold.* She wasn't frightened; she'd prepared for this for ten years.

From her hidey-hole, she retrieved the remaining stunner. The other weapon, and the warm-suit, might be with Elizabeth—if her visit was real and not another delusion. Grabbing the knife, she ran to the forward mess, the assembly area where Cookie should be waiting. *Thank God Cookie's here to lead the defense.*

The red alert blared over the intercom. Before Meriel could respond to Molly's call, the hull shook and an air leak whooshed.

That's them.

Grinding vibrations from the closing blast doors isolated the bridge and cargo sections. Her feet slipped from the deck as the ship lost gravity. Crouching in midair, she poised for its return; when it did, she landed on all fours. The *Tiger* still had power and pressure. *They want us to live, at least for a while.*

Before reaching the mess, a seductive voice appealed from the PA system.

"Attention. All passengers and crew of the *Tiger*. Please do not be alarmed. I am the envoy for a regional security team. Your vessel is known to carry dangerous fugitives, and we are concerned for your safety. The nature of the threat to you is quite serious and demands these drastic measures. Cooperate, and no harm will come to you. Remain calm and assemble in the forward mess hall for interviews. Any resistance will produce discomfort. Please, your cooperation will be appreciated."

The mess hall was the security assembly point. *They know our protocols.* But she had to take a chance someone from Cookie's team might make it to the alternate rally area at Cargo-C. She turned her link to Channel 3.

"Do not attempt a security intervention or resist in any way," the envoy said over the secure channel. "Again, we wish you no harm, but we are firm in our request for cooperation. We await your presence in the forward mess."

So they compromised security, as well. We have a mole onboard.

Another boom followed the pops of small arms and the hiss of laser fire.

She ran to Cargo-C but stopped at the door to look in. Instead of her team she found passengers kneeling with their hands over their heads. Behind them stood two armed men in black combat suits with blasters pointed at their heads. *Damn*. Cookie lay sprawled out bleeding from a head wound, and she could not tell if he was alive or dead.

In the doorway across the room, she spotted one of the auxiliary Marines, Lev, from her cargo crew. He appeared to be about to do something suicidal, so she used hand signals to call him off and tell him to meet in the corridor.

"They have our security protocols," she said.

"Lots of fares this leg. Could be anyone."

Meriel thought only of Ferrell.

Lev pointed his link to a camera. "Internal surveillance is off. Cookie secured the main pressure doors to slow down the boarding party."

"My link is dead."

"They're jamming it," he said. "Communication is down except for the PA."

"What about alt-nav?"

"Captain gave Cookie the command codes and... Say, you were at the briefing; you should know this. Where did you hide the weapons?"

She had no idea what he was talking about and raised her hands.

He grabbed her arm. "They're important, Meriel. Where are they?"

"What do you mean?"

Deep creases carved his brow. "When we rallied to Cookie, you wore a warm-suit, and he told you to secure the weapons."

"The weapons locker?" she guessed but wondered what else had happened before she woke in Ferrell's office.

He stared at her, then shook his head and turned away. "We're hosed," he mumbled.

Together, they searched each cabin directing survivors to the gym. With the main pressure bulkheads closed, that required using service accessways and hatches, just like when she was a kid. And at each turn, she wondered what else Cookie would do.

They rounded up only eight crew members, and she could not tell how many others aboard remained hidden. On the way to the weapons locker, they found Molly on the deck struggling to stand.

Meriel held Molly's shoulders. "Are you all right?"

"Dizzy. Need to keep my eyes closed, but I can think."

Together they helped Molly to the gym. There they found the other survivors, some in pj's and lounge gear, some drunk and cowering, and others dazed from tranq. Her relief at the sight of John surprised her, but not her contempt when Ferrell arrived.

"What happened?" she asked Molly.

"We couldn't stop the jump. It was like you told us. The bastards froze nav and breached the hull at the bridge. Crew is captive or…dead."

"Captive, I expect, until they find what they are looking for," Meriel said.

Ferrell cocked his head. "And what would that be?"

"Me. What I know. Was the captain on the bridge?"

"Yes," Molly said. "How did they get here so fast?"

"Short jump," John said. "Maybe just outside the Etna system: small sphere and easy to find. They ambushed us."

"I don't hear Sergeant Cook. Is he here?" Molly asked.

"Cookie's down, XO. Sorry," Lev replied. "Seems like he was a primary target."

"Where is the backup nav, Molly?" Meriel asked.

"Alt-bridge behind Cargo-C."

"Damn," Lev said. "Raiders are there."

"It's behind the rear blast doors. The pirates are trying to bust through them."

Meriel placed her hand on the bulkhead to feel the low vibration, and Lev nodded.

Molly unclipped her command-link and gave it to Lev. "You can open them with this."

"No," Lev said. "If we open them now, they'll rush us."

"Check the bridge crew."

Lev queued up a bridge camera on the command-link. The crew members appeared kneeling at their stations with their hands behind their heads. "They're alive."

After a quick smile, Molly passed out, and Meriel restrained her in case they lost gravity again.

Lev and Ferrell continued to watch the bridge camera. Ferrell's eyes widened, but he said nothing.

"Jeez, this guy must be ten light-years from a horse," Lev said.

"Huh? Let me see," Meriel said.

Lev flipped the link to display a holo of the back of a man who slapped a riding crop on his leg. "Crap. It's not a security team. That's General Khanag."

"This is bad," John said. "He's got a fleet."

A black-suit on the bridge viewed the same image on his screen and mentioned it. Khanag barked a command, and the link went dark.

The envoy spoke again. "To those of you who have not come forward, we are disappointed. We will take no action if your crewmate named Meriel Hope reports to the bridge. Again, we wish no one to come to harm and will let you go on your way with your fuel restored. However, our patience is running out."

Ferrell reached out his hand. "Give me the link."

She sneered. "Lev is senior security now. He should keep it."

With a squint, Ferrell raised his chin. "With the bridge crew down, I'm the ranking officer."

Lev frowned but nodded and handed him the link while Meriel stared in disbelief.

Following a deep breath, Ferrell spoke into the link. "This is Dr. Patrick Ferrell. I am the senior officer onboard. What is your intent?"

"We wish you well, Doctor, and all those with you. If you would, please, help us locate this Meriel Hope person so you can continue on your way. Spacecraft are fragile things, and additional damage would expose you to more danger." The view of the bridge and crew reappeared. "See? We have nothing to hide. They are all in good health."

Everyone remained unharmed, but a raider lay on the deck and blood dripped from a fresh cut on Socket's forehead.

"Let me talk to the captain," Ferrell said.

"As you wish."

"Captain, is everyone all right?"

In the image of the bridge, Captain Vingel turned to Socket. When she nodded, he turned to the camera. "We're OK, Doc. Restrained but OK."

"Captain, did you transfer the command codes?"

Meriel and Lev cringed and shook their heads.

The image vanished. "Now, now, Doctor, we're patient but not stupid. Be reasonable. As soon as we talk with your crew members, we'll be on our way."

Plural now: he said "members." She turned to Lev, who nodded.

The envoy continued. "Please, surrender yourselves at the Cargo-C area before our patience wears any thinner. We offer you amnesty and safe passage to Ross. That's next on your circuit, no? There's no need for any bloodshed. Your vessel is under our control, and there is really nothing you can do. We are humanitarians and respect all life. Please be assured you will be unharmed."

Meriel surveyed the survivors. Except for John and Lev, they all appeared scared and passive. She was shocked and unprepared for them to give up so easily.

"This is Dr. Ferrell again. We are caring for those injured during your rude introduction. Please give us a few minutes to treat them, and we will comply. Until then, we request a cease-fire."

"If you'd open the blast doors, we would be glad to assist."

"Your concern is appreciated, but you can understand why we must decline. A few minutes, please."

After a pause, the envoy replied, "Your request is granted. Do not exceed ten minutes."

Lev turned to Ferrell. "What are you doing?"

"We're going to surrender," Ferrell replied.

"You can't do that!" Meriel said and reached for the command link.

He yanked the link out of her reach. "It's over. We're outgunned, and they've secured the ship and cargo."

"You can't trust them, Doc," Lev said.

"They're lying. If they had complete control, they wouldn't need our cooperation. We have a chance." Those gathered around them grumbled with disbelief.

"Our only chance is to give up," said Alf Martin. "They're offering us our freedom and—"

Ferrell interrupted. "Meriel, they just want to ask you a few questions. Maybe if you—"

Her jaw dropped. "Are you kidding me? Sure, they want me, but they will not let you go. General Khanag is the muscle for the Archtrope's drug ring."

"This is piracy, Doc," Lev said, "and piracy doesn't exist, remember? They'll kill us for our silence."

With a raised eyebrow, Ferrel said, "Technically, they're privateers, not pirates."

"Technically, we'll still be dead," Meriel replied.

Alf raised his arms. "So, why didn't they blast us?"

"Too much debris. Too much evidence," she said. "They'll just point us at a big mass at one-g, and we'll disappear."

John interrupted. "They want to know what she knows first. What *we* know. And what we've told others."

She understood the "we" and nodded to him.

"People, we need to act," Lev said.

The envoy returned to the PA. "Come see us, please. We mean you no harm. Human life is so valuable, and we all wish to avoid unfortunate accidents."

Lev shook his head. "Accidents, huh. They'll kill us all. No witnesses. Cargo-C is one door from deep vacuum."

A warm-suit with a helmet walked up to them weighed down by a mesh duffel full of weapons and dropped them at Lev's feet.

"Ah, there you are…" Lev said but stopped. With arched brow, he turned his head back and forth between the newcomer and Meriel. Ignoring him, John took a blaster from the bag and ran through the safety drill like a trained soldier.

Meriel smiled at the newcomer in the warm-suit but blinked repeatedly to convince herself this was not a fantasy. *Now what would Cookie do?* She turned back to Lev. "We can do this. We're armed now. Tell them we can do this. It's not over. If we take the alt-bridge, we can jump away from the pirate ships and have the numbers on our side. You know I'm right. Tell them!"

Lev nodded, turned to the others, and held his hand over his head. "Listen. She's right. If we fight together, we can take back the ship. We have the weapons now. Only the boarding party is engaged until we're pacified. Until then, they'll keep the bigger vessels away. I can get a squad to the alt-bridge if we have a diversion."

"We can't leave the bridge crew," Meriel said. "If we engage them at alt-bridge, they'll just kill them."

"We can use the command-link to open the blast doors before they can do that," Lev said.

"Those doors are the only thing holding them back."

"This is madness," Ferrell said. "If we fight, we'll die."

She poked a finger into Ferrell's chest. "Listen, Doc. I'm not sure whose side you're on, but you don't understand yet. You're already dead meat as far as they're concerned."

"They're human beings; they won't kill us all," a passenger said.

"They only want you!" another shouted.

She lifted her hands and shook her head. "You still don't get it. Pirates don't set prisoners free."

Ferrell laid his hand on Meriel's arm. "Calm down, Meriel. You're irrational."

She yanked her arm away and snapped, "I'm the closest thing to rational you've got."

"You're delusional if you think three Marines can take this ship back."

"No, Doc. We've got four: Lev, Nobu, me, and my sister."

Ferrell gave her a gentle smile and lowered his voice. "Meriel, please, stop this fantasy. She's gone. Your sister and everyone else on the *Princess* died."

His words silenced her. *What if he's right? What if I am crazy, and all this is just another delusion? But if they follow him, we all die.* "No," she said with a weak voice and then a stronger one. "No!"

One of the passengers gasped, and another whispered, "She's the one!"

"She's the Jonah."

"Give her up."

"You hear them. We can't wait," Ferrell said and raised the link.

Before he could speak, the warm-suit trapped his hand in a wristlock, drove him to his knees, and took the link. The visor popped up from the helmet, to reveal a scowling Elizabeth.

"Who you calling dead?" she said, emphasizing each word with a poke to his forehead with her gloved finger. "Hey, Sis, who's the stiff?"

Meriel smiled. "He's the acting captain, Liz."

"Then frag him, and let's do this." Elizabeth slapped the link into Lev's hand. "Jeez, come on, girls, we're running out of time."

Ferrell stared up at her and squinted as if she could not exist, then turned his head to Meriel. "You can't—"

With a slight adjustment of her fingers, Elizabeth forced a wince and Ferrell became quiet. "Open your mouth again, and I'll break it."

"Eight minutes left," Lev said. "We can reach alt-bridge in one." He leaned over to her and whispered, "Not enough fighters. The bridge has three doors, Cargo-C has two. It's slaughter without more firepower."

She studied those gathered in the room—the young men, women, and parents who watched them, wondering what they would do. Biting her lip, she glanced to the exits.

Lev gripped her shoulder. "Cookie's not coming, Meriel."

She nodded. In the crowd she found Elliot Goodwin, who had taken the captain's advice and stayed onboard at Etna. He smiled at her.

"We can do this," she said to them. "We can take back the ship and save all our lives. But we need your help. Who will join us?" No one moved.

"I know you didn't sign up for this. You are not trained to fight, but I don't believe you want to die. If we resist, we can win our freedom. If not, you will die."

Alf scoffed. "They got no reason to kill the rest of us."

"Yes, they do," she said. "Khanag runs the organ-smuggling trade."

The crowd got quiet, and the arrogance vanished from Alf's face. Meriel picked up a blaster and clicked off the safety.

Lev tapped his wrist. "We only have a few seconds. Will you die without a fight?"

No one moved to help.

"We don't have to fight! We just have to surrender!" said one, while others grumbled.

This isn't working, Meriel thought and waved an arm for attention. As she walked over to a mother with a small boy, she softened her voice. "I understand your fear. If I had the power, I would arrange your passage on another ship, and you would be safe." She stood. "But that's not to be. If we do nothing, we will die and be forgotten like all the other ships that disappeared in the black."

Elliot Goodwin made his way to Lev, who gave him a weapon and instructions.

Meriel raised her voice. "If you will not defend yourselves, you will die. If your children live, they will be slaves, and no one will know to free them from their torment."

Three of the parents stood and joined Lev. He shook his head—still not enough.

"This is suici—" Ferrell began, but Elizabeth tweaked his wristlock again. "You, shut up. Dead, huh?"

"But if we defend ourselves, you can live free again," Meriel said, "and spend your days with your children by your side."

More parents joined, and she addressed the young adults. "Imagine what they will say about us few who escaped an entire fleet of vicious slavers and did so knowing how overwhelmed we were. Those who hear your story will wish they had been here with you to expose a hundred years of murder." She studied the rest who had not joined. "Choose now. Join us and live."

"But we are only a few," a passenger said.

"I survived the *Princess* with less. We can survive this."

The remainder of the young adults stood and went to Lev for weapons. He shook his head again; they still did not have enough fighters.

John took Meriel's arm. "M, listen. The humming stopped. They quit trying to break through the doors."

At the sound of John's voice, Elizabeth widened her eyes.

Meriel ignored her sister's signal. "Damn, they're leaving. They're gonna kill us."

"They lied about the time," Ferrell said.

"What did you expect?" Lev said. "Hell, I ain't giving up like this. Who's with me? Come now."

She held out her open palm. "Give me the command-link."

Lev hid the link behind his back and narrowed his eyes. "What are you doing, Chief?"

With a patient smile and a sigh, she tapped the intercom.

"This is Meriel Hope. I'll come. Just tell me where."

"No, M," Liz said. "You can't do this!"

Sighs of relief and mumbles of gratitude swept the crowd.

"Now, you're making sense," Ferrell said.

Meriel placed a finger on her lips.

The calm voice of the envoy echoed over the PA. "Ahh, that's the sensible thing to do. Come to the bridge, starboard blast door. Have the others disarmed behind you."

"Just me. Later you can talk to the others."

"As you wish. One minute. We'll be waiting. Open the doors now, please."

"I'll open them when I get there. But it will take me a few minutes."

"My, my, so distrustful. As you wish."

Meriel tapped the intercom to end her broadcast.

"Sis, don't do this," Liz said. "They'll kill us anyway."

"Meriel, no," John said. "We'll resist and—"

Meriel shook her head. "The only thing that will stop them from killing us now is my giving up. Here's what I have in mind." She took the command link and huddled with the volunteers.

The mother of a young boy tugged on Meriel's sleeve as she turned to leave. "Please, I can't abandon my children to join you," she said. "If there's any chance of them letting us go."

Meriel handed her a stunner. "They're lying." She turned and handed another to Ferrell, who rubbed his wrist. "And they lied to you about me."

He grimaced as though he'd been struck. "You trust me?"

"No. I trust you don't want to die."

He took the weapon.

"Protect them," she said and ran to join Nobu.

En Passant

With her hands over her head, Meriel walked toward the bridge blast door wearing her cargo vest and goggles, the command link held high in her right hand.

"That's far enough, Ms. Hope," the envoy said through the intercom. "Now, open the door."

She pressed the link and the pressure doors opened throughout the ship, but she kept walking toward the now-open door. A column of black-suits in helmets ran past her and around the corner into the corridor.

One black-suit with captain's bars and a face shield appeared in the doorway flanked by two helmeted raiders.

"Please stop, now." He signaled his escort to meet her while he backed away.

Reflected light twinkled from tiny canisters falling through the overhead vents in front of and behind her. Before they hit the deck, she pulled out two stunners from the back of her vest and took out the escorts who approached her. The flashbangs exploded, stunning the pirates. Protected by earplugs and goggles, Meriel remained unfazed and rushed to the door of the bridge to jam a cargo gaff into the open door. As she did, a slug sliced through the flesh of her shoulder.

Nobu and her squad caught up to her at the door, where she kept the pirates at bay with a stolen blaster. Three of her team stayed behind to restrain the fallen raiders. She had no expectation of winning control of the bridge and planned only to distract Khanag's men until John could jump the *Tiger*.

Nobu sprayed pulses into the room and peered inside. "They're reprogramming nav." He shot again to afford her a glimpse.

After a quick peek into the bridge, Meriel sat with her back against the bulkhead. She gave Nobu her rifle and holstered her pistol. "They can't leave anyone behind who can restore nav. They're gonna kill us." She took another quick peek.

The black-suit with gold bars on his lapels checked his link and stood behind Tim Brown, the ship's engineer, with a pistol to his head.

"Crap," she said, knowing he would execute everyone in turn. She closed her eyes for a moment, then leaped up. "Hey!" she yelled and waved her arms to draw his fire.

He ignored her, killed the engineer, and kicked him away.

Pulling the knife from her belt, she charged into the bridge. The officer stepped behind Jerri, but before he could pull the trigger, Meriel kicked the weapon from his hand and rammed him into the console. The other raiders held back for fear of hitting their officer.

"Shit, she's a friggin' mad dog," Elliot said, aiming for the pirates firing at her.

"Yeah, but she's *our* friggin' mad dog," Nobu said, armed a stun grenade, and leaped to help her.

The officer turned to her, and she recognized him as the captain in the vid with the Archtrope. In that split second of astonishment, he punched her in the face and pushed her away to give his men a clear shot. As she staggered backward, a direct hit from a pulse rifle threw her into the bulkhead near Nobu, and she fell unconscious.

The *Tiger* jumped.

Chapter 11
Free Space

Lethal Decisions

General Khanag scanned his fleet of ships from the bridge of his flagship. He paced impatiently while waiting for Captain Nurendra Khanag to dispose of their prey. As he watched, a hole swallowed the *Tiger* along with huge slices from the three vessels that had penned her in. Raiders and debris spilled into space from the gashes in their hulls, and he understood his son would never return.

***

John jumped the *Tiger* only a few AU away, capturing chunks of Khanag's ships in their jump field and dragging those pieces with it. The fraction of a second of disorientation gave Nobu enough time to throw the stun grenade. It exploded and knocked the black-suits and the bridge crew unconscious, bleeding from their noses. This gave the defenders time to restrain them. But the fighting continued.

Khanag's men still prowled the ship. Two of them found Ferrell and the noncombatants hiding in the gym.

"Please. I'm Dr. Patrick Ferrell. BioLuna will vouch for me. General Khanag knows this."

The black-suit laughed. "BioLuna is not here."

Ferrell's face twisted in a grimace. "It was all a lie," he murmured and raised his stunner.

"Imbecile," the raider said and shot Ferrell in the face, showering a mother and her child with blood.

As the raider watched Ferrell fall, a boy hit him in the face with a toy. He scowled and aimed his blaster at the child, but the mother shot the first pirate before he killed her child and the second before he killed her.

***

After Nobu and Alf finished tying up the dazed raiders, they freed the bridge crew, who left to secure the ship. Nobu kneeled by Meriel to see what he could do for her. Blood seeped from her nose, as he maneuvered his backpack to stabilize her head.

Alf poked him in the shoulder and pointed to the pirates. "What do I do with them?" All were awake now, including the officer with the gold bars who struggled in his bindings and snarled at him.

Nobu handed Alf a stunner. "Just watch them and make sure they stay here. Any trouble and drop them. But we want them alive." His link beeped, and he tapped his lapel.

"This is Elizabeth Hope. Where's Meriel?"

"She's down," he said.

"On my way."

When Meriel's name was mentioned, the pirate officer sneered.

Nobu placed his ear on her chest and heard a strong pulse and a weak snore. From the corner of his eye, he noticed Alf with the pirate officer and turned to see them talking.

"Leave him alone, Alf," Nobu said, but Meriel groaned and he turned back to her. He unbuttoned her shirt but stopped when he noticed the purple region on the left side of her abdomen.

"Brothers, hear my words," echoed over the PA.

Turning to the sound, Nobu saw the pirate captain speaking over Alf's link and smiling.

"We are lost and have no future in this world," the pirate said. "There is only one honorable action left for us."

"Shut him up!" Elizabeth shouted past him from the corridor.

Alf jerked the link away, but before he switched it off, the pirate shouted.

"Follow me to Paradise, my brothers!" The pirate bit down on something with an audible click. White froth drooled from the corner of his mouth, and he began to shake. "Subedei!" he sputtered and fell on his face, convulsing and coughing up bloody foam. Before Alf could stop them, the other black-suited captives followed their leader, and within a minute, all the remaining pirates onboard lay still.

Alf raised his arms and looked at Nobu. "He told me he'd order them to surrender."

"Idiot," Elizabeth said and kneeled at Meriel's side next to Nobu. "How bad?"

"Internal," Lev replied, which to spacers meant death unless they could find a surgeon.

Prey

The *Tiger's* first jump hid them from General Khanag's fleet. That distance gave them time to secure the ship and see to the wounded before they jumped again. Molly and the others were moved to the infirmary. But Meriel, her injuries too serious to be moved, remained on the bridge with Elizabeth.

The able-bodied crew labored in the ozone and smoke for another hour until the scrubbers cleaned the air. Outside the bridge, Lev jettisoned the umbilical and air lock that the pirates had used. Inside, the engineering tech completed the hull patch with composite buckysheets and a carbon welder. A few feet away, other crew members worked to restore the main bridge.

Cookie wore visualization goggles and lay on his back under the bridge's command console, analyzing an abstract depiction of their ship's memory. A grid displayed on the active wall with an orange scar running through it. "Here it is."

"How much is there?" Captain Richard Vingel said.

"Just a fragment of the virus that hijacked us is left. It burrowed in during the last beacon sync."

"What's it do?"

Cookie pushed himself out from under the console and sat upright, a thin line of blood leaking from the bandage on his head. "This piece just flashes an ID to triangulate our position, but it replicates."

"How bad?"

"Likely anything on the ship that communicates is infected."

"That means everything," the captain said. "Hell, my shoes communicate." He tapped the link on his wrist. "Comm, tell everyone to turn in their links."

Cookie waved. "And we'll need to check the coffee maker and toothbrushes."

"And sweep for anything with a network ping. All devices that were or are live are likely infected."

Socket responded through the link. "We can wipe them all, but we don't have firmware backups. They'll be dead."

"Oh well, back to the Stone Age. Any clue to the cause of the ringing?"

"The virus uses the jump fans as an antenna and pulses EM," she said. "If you're within a few AU, you light up like a quasar."

"OK, what about nav?"

"Khanag's goons deactivated the virus when they took the bridge," Cookie said. "I flushed everything but the raw code in backup, but I wouldn't trust our lives on it."

"OK, so we'll leave jump control on the alt-bridge until we can scrub it. Ready?"

Cookie nodded and pressed a switch, and the bridge consoles woke.

"Jerri, where are we?" the captain said.

"We're about a light-day from the point of attack," she replied." Khanag could never find our EM, even if we were broadcasting. John will jump us again in another few minutes."

"Acknowledged."

"Anything more we can do here, Sergeant?"

"No, sir."

The captain switched to the PA. "All senior ranks report to the bridge."

Soon a crowd appeared at the bulkhead doors. Cookie permitted only crew on the bridge, so passengers spilled into the corridor. Socket took her station between Jerri and the apprentice engineer.

"Where are we going, sir?" Jerri asked.

"Doesn't matter yet," the captain said. "Just run. They may be only one jump behind us. Alternatives? Let's hear 'em."

"We have enough fuel to hide for a while."

"But not forever. Our food is limited, and we have lots of passengers this trip."

"And Khanag knows it," Cookie said. "He and BioLuna combined can post a ship at every station and refueling point. There's nowhere to go."

"We can't just wander out here," Jerri said.

Elizabeth raised her hand. "Meriel needs help, sir. She can't wait."

The captain turned to her. "And who are you?"

"I'm Meriel's sister, Elizabeth Hope."

"You weren't on the passenger manifest. How did you get aboard?"

"Ah...Meriel rescued me from Etna."

"A stowaway? Rescued from what?"

"There was a fight, and I..."

"A fugitive?"

After lowering her gaze, she said, "Yes, sir."

"Do you have proof you are who you say you are?"

"I..." Elizabeth began, but shook her head.

The captain looked down at her. "Any reason I shouldn't drop you off at the nearest asteroid?"

Lev raised his hand. "She helped us save the ship, sir."

"And hid the weapons for us," Cookie added. "We couldn't have escaped without her help."

The captain turned to him. "Sergeant Cook, she's your responsibility now."

"Aye, sir," he said and walked over to stand next to her. "Meriel needs a doctor soon, or she'll die. Internal bleeding as best as we can tell. Doc was our only medical officer, and he's dead."

Elizabeth remained quiet but bit her lip.

The captain turned to Lev. "Corporal, check what we have in cargo that can provide some emergency medical assistance. Buzz me when you have it." He then turned to Jerri. "What's the nearest station?"

"Etna, sir. Then Procyon A, Luyten's star, and DX Cancri."

"They'll find us anywhere we go," Alf said, sweating and twitchy.

"We could send an ePod ahead to signal the beacon and flush them out," Socket suggested.

"What'll we do when they find out it's a decoy?" Cookie said. "We can't shoot back."

"How about the Troopers?" the captain said.

"We'll need to sync with a beacon to alert them we're in danger, and before we do, we're a target. They can destroy us and spin any story they want."

"That would be kind of hard, don't you think?" Alf said with a smirk and a blink.

Elizabeth glared at him and furrowed her brow. "Why would that be hard? They hid piracy for a hundred years."

Cookie spoke. "If we make it to a station, Elizabeth will be arrested—"

"She's a stowaway, Sergeant," the captain said.

"—and Meriel will be arrested as an accessory for evading the police."

The captain nodded and paced. "Other ideas?"

"We've got nowhere to run," Socket said.

"John may have some ideas, sir," Jerri offered.

"Ask him to join us."

"It's this bitch, Meriel," Alf said, unconcerned that he stood next to her sister. This time the slur in his voice from a recent drink was obvious. "She's the reason we're in this fix.

Why not negotiate and give her up while we still got some leverage?"

Jumping to her feet, Elizabeth stared him straight in the eyes. "Shut up, a-hole. She's the one who saved your worthless ass."

"Another word, Alf, and I'll confine you," the captain said.

"But she's—" Alf began.

Elizabeth interrupted him with an elbow to the face that knocked him into the bulkhead. He slumped to the deck, unconscious, and she returned to the conversation as if she had simply scratched an itch.

Captain Vingel narrowed his gaze and frowned at her. "That was my crewman. Sergeant Cook, restrain the stowaway."

Cookie took Elizabeth's arm. "Aye, sir."

Elizabeth tried to yank her arm free and protest. "But I—"

He tightened his grip. "Time to close your mouth, lassie."

"They might let us go if we're near a station with witnesses," a passenger said.

"It's too late now," the captain said. "We all know their secret, and we're all a threat to their security."

Elizabeth shuffled her feet. "We can go to Home."

"Where is that?"

She gave them the coordinates of TTL-5B3. The bridge crew groaned.

"Sorry, dear," Jerri said as if speaking to a child. "They're frauds. TTL-5B is a rock with a refueling depot."

"No, no. Transpose to the DX Cancri ecliptic. We're looking for TTL-5B3, not -5B."

"B3 makes it a moon, Ms. Hope," the captain said.

Elizabeth nodded.

"Pilot, try it."

Jerri tapped her console. A few seconds later, she raised her eyebrows. "Eleven light from Dexter? Behind a dust cloud?"

Elizabeth nodded again. "That's it."

"Well, I'll be damned. You can see it from Dexter Station. They call the system Jira-1, but I don't have an SDS for it."

John walked in, and Jerri whispered to him. "We—"

"Yes, you do," Elizabeth interrupted. "The survey is for TTL-5B. It's just that the designation and offset were misunderstood."

They all ignored John's raised hand.

"That's a long way on a guess from a fugitive, Ms. Hope," the captain said. "Jerri, do we know anyone who's been—"

John spoke up. "TTL-5B3? I've been there." He turned to Elizabeth. "Has Meriel been working on this?"

Elizabeth smiled. "So, you're John."

"What are you two talking about?" the captain said.

"That's the location for LeHavre and Haven," John said. "It's BioLuna's best-kept secret, and your cargo chief stumbled on it."

Elizabeth frowned. "I wouldn't say stumbled…"

Cookie raised his hand. "Wait a minute. How can you hide an entire star system?"

"We're not hidden. Everyone has the data sheets. They're on every website in the galaxy. They made fantasy movies about us, not very accurate, by the way. The only thing unknown was the orientation from DXC. BioLuna's been aggressively scrubbing sites because people were getting too close to the truth."

"Is this real, John?" the captain said.

"My kids are there."

"Why didn't you tell us this before?"

"I did. You weren't listening."

The captain crossed his arms. "If Khanag and BioLuna can be at every station, why not LeHavre?"

"They can. They guard the jump points with laser cannons to keep us in and discourage visitors."

"So why should we—"

"I know the coordinates of an unguarded jump point. That's how I got here."

"Where else can we go, sir?" Cookie added.

"Sir, John got us this far and is familiar with the destination," Jerri said.

The captain smiled. "Funny thing, John, but I'll bet we're already headed in that direction."

John rubbed his chin. "Yeah, kinda."

"We're dead if we drop back into known space," Cookie said.

With a patient expression, John replied. "Haven *is* known space. It's just that *you* don't know it." He turned to the captain. "They can repair the ship and nav at LeHavre, sir."

"Do they have Troopers?" Cookie said. "We need them to start forensics before repairs begin."

"No, only Marines, but we have lots of them. And legal offices for LGen Inc. with standing on Lander."

"Pilot, what will it take?" the captain said.

Jerri tapped her link. "Jira-1 is about six light-years from our current sphere. That's most of our fuel if we make it in one long jump."

"One long jump will be hard on Meriel," Cookie said.

The captain nodded. "And too risky. We need to jump to a familiar station, just in case."

She tapped the link again. "Five jumps to reach it, and we can still make Lander."

"Meriel may not make five jumps," Cookie said.

The captain's link squawked. "Lev, here. We've got a prototype of something called a Med-Tech packed up. Got no information about it."

"That's BioLuna tech," John said. "It can do minor surgery and life support. It's one of their better products."

Elizabeth brightened, and she crossed her fingers behind her back. "Can it fix her?"

He shook his head. "No, but it can keep her stable." He lowered his voice. "It can keep her alive."

"Haul it up here, Lev," the captain said.

Lev's voice came from the link. "If we open it, we own it."

"You can bill me," Elizabeth said.

"Roger that."

Captain Vingel turned to Jerry. "Pilot, confirm John's jump points. John, if you can figure out how to operate this Med-Tech device, meet Lev in the infirmary."

With a plan in place, the crew left for their posts.

The captain turned to Cookie. "Her coming aboard just before a hijack might be a coincidence, but she's not to roam free. Understood?"

"Aye, sir."

"Ms. Hope, your sister warned the XO an attack was coming. Do you know anything more about this?"

"Only what she told me, sir."

"How did she know they would come for her after all these years?"

Elizabeth sighed. "She didn't. She's just afraid all the time."

The Abyss

Status indicators beeped on the Med-Tech, which held Meriel in biosuspension. The infirmary lights, as on most of the *Tiger,* were dimmed to help the crew and passengers rest during the short breaks between repeated jumps. A minute later, she blinked and looked around to find Elizabeth sleeping in the chair on one side of the machine, and Cookie on the other.

"Good morning, lass." he said.

Meriel smiled, comforted by his presence. "Hey, I thought I wouldn't see you again."

"My head's my best weapon. How do you feel?"

"I can't feel anything, really. Where am I?"

"John calls it a Med-Tech. He says it kinda locks down your system so you can't hurt yourself more. I guess your head works, though. What else can you move?"

She squinted and her neck muscles twitched, then her right hand and arm moved. "I guess that's it. Is this permanent?"

"Until we find you some real doctors. Captain says we're heading for Haven, and they have the docs you need."

"Did Ferrell escape with Khanag?"

"No. Ferrell's dead." The crevasses between his eyebrows deepened. "Why would he leave with Khanag?"

"Never mind." Attempting to raise her head, she cringed with an ice-pick headache, and then glanced at him.

"Sorry I couldn't be in the fight with you," he said.

"I thought of you, of what you would do. I wanted you to save us."

"Us?" he said with a gentle voice.

"Me."

"Sorry, lass. I should have been the one taking the fire."

"You outthought them, Cookie. We survived because you gave the weapons to someone they didn't know was aboard."

Cookie shook his head. "I thought it was you."

"So did Lev."

He kissed her on the forehead. "You did fine without me. I'm proud to serve with you."

"So where are we? Where are we headed?"

"John's place. LeHavre Station."

"Really? TTL-5B3?"

"Yup. He knows an unguarded jump point."

"Is it safe?"

"It's the safest among the suicidal alternatives."

Meriel turned her head.

"What is it, M?"

"They won't stop, Cookie. They'll be coming back."

"Then after we patch up the *Tiger*, we'll find a safer place."

"There is no safe place."

"They're unlikely to invade a whole planet just to kill us."

"They invaded Haven before. Maybe we're jumping from the frying pan into the fire. Tell the capt—" Beeps and a flashing light interrupted, alerting them to the start of a new cycle of sedatives. "Wait, I have…oh, nuts…" she began to say but drifted back to sleep.

A few minutes later, John entered the infirmary. "Damn, did I miss her again?"

Cookie nodded. "Get some sleep. You're exhausted. Go on, I'll spell you."

"Thanks, but everybody's exhausted. I'll stay."

Cookie left, and John took the chair opposite Elizabeth. "Molly is up and around, M," he said to the sleeping Meriel. "And the Goodwin boy stopped by to see how you're doing. Oh, and Liz mentioned that little Eddie came by earlier to visit. He told her he threw his toy at the black-suit before his mom shot him."

He rested his hand on the outside of the cowl near her hand. "Meriel, you'll like Haven. You can run all day in the fields without stopping. Jira-1 is a yellow sun, like Sol, and you can feel the warmth on your skin. My dad told me when we first left Earth orbit, they called out, 'We're going home.'"

In her dreams, Meriel was a child again on the *Princess,* surrounded by the scents of wheat and jasmine as her mother described Home. And barely visible in the light of the Med-Tech's monitors, the sisters both smiled in their sleep.

***

The next morning, Elizabeth pushed the Med-Tech's cowl away so Meriel could speak with John. When Molly entered with the captain, Meriel turned to Elizabeth and squeezed her hand. She signed, "Trust only Cookie."

"John, too?" Elizabeth replied in sign.

"Only Cookie."

"I hope you are feeling better, Chief Hope," the captain said and displayed a message on the active wall. "I need the three of you to review this before I send it."

```
    To: UPI, AP, GCI, UNE Human Rights
Council, UNE Office of Internal
Affairs, United Planets Council,
Independent Station Alliance, Sector
28 Space Troopers…
    From: Anonymous
    Please find attached documents which
link BioLuna, Alan C. Biadez, and the
```

Archtrope of Calliope to an attempted
illegal takeover of the moon Haven
(Jira-1/B3) and LeHavre Station. (See
certificate of origin enclosed.)

Attachments include evidence linking
named parties in attack on the trader
LSM *Princess* (GCN 13442:88) and recent
hijack attempt and murders on LSM
Tiger (GCN 35521:316). Trooper report
filed. Please see legal counsel
PacifiCo (Pacific League of
Independent Traders).

Attachments: Interim Treaty of Haven

"This is above my pay grade," John said.

Meriel considered John's response for a moment and turned back to Molly. "I'm not sure about this."

"Keeping this in your pocket could be your insurance policy, M. Make them aware you have this, and it might restrain them from action."

She shook her head. "A weak hold. Biadez knows where all the kids are. If he ever took one of them, I'd fold in a heartbeat."

"What about justice for the murderers?" Molly said.

"Justice? Are you kidding me? We'll all be dead. I need to save my family, not warn people. These people have two fleets and rule a star system."

"M, they're coming for them and us anyway, we—" Elizabeth began.

John interrupted. "Bring them with us. Before this goes public, have all your kids sent to Haven. We'll protect them."

Meriel's mouth fell open. "All of them?"

He smiled. "Of course, all of them."

"But Haven is a little colony."

"It'll surprise you. We'll tell the Troopers about the threat to the kids as soon as we sync with the LeHavre beacon. The Troopers can retrieve them."

"Are we OK with this, then?" Molly asked.

John frowned. "The prime minister of Haven will need to approve this."

"John, you sure you can take the kids?" Meriel said with a knitted brow.

"Yup. Plenty of room."

"Then tell *your* prime minister I don't need his permission to send this. Your people have survived these killers; my family did not." She sighed and looked away. "Nearly all the people who know about them want to harm them." *And that's my fault.* "We have to make this public before Biadez rounds them up. We're little people out here. We need to engage forces equal to theirs: the UNE, media, public opinion. I want them to be the most watched-after kids in the galaxy. The only thing that will save them from harm now is if every trooper in the sector is keeping his eyes on them and keeping the bad guys away. We need the conspirators on the run so they don't have time to search for them."

"OK? So we send it?" Molly said.

Meriel turned to her sister. "Liz?"

"Sure," Elizabeth said, "but not this infogram. How about 'Powerful Conspiracy Targets Children for Death.' And post it to IGB and the independent news agencies before the politicians and big media can spin it."

Molly smiled. "You ladies are pretty young to be so cynical."

Elizabeth and Meriel glanced at each other and rolled their eyes.

"OK, M," John said. "It goes as soon as we can sync. They can impeach me. Oh, that's right; I don't hold an office."

"Yet," Captain Vingel said. "You bring down BioLuna, and the people will elect you to anything you want."

Meriel frowned. "I think they'll resist being brought down."

***

Captain Ceirniki's sleek FTL corvette was much larger than the UNE could provide, and one of the reasons he served in the mercenaries under Admiral Leung. The current mission offered more land on a habitable colony than a CEO on Earth, in addition to a bigger bonus.

Through the window of his immaculate ready room, the orange glow of Jupiter's crescent swept across his desk. There, a tiny yellow spot announced the person he had flown fourteen light-years to have a private word with. From the desk, a holo displayed a gaggle of men in business suits, each with their own link and conversation led by a middle-aged man walking at the apex—Cecil Rhodes, the chairman of BioLuna.

"What is it?" Rhodes asked.

Detecting a slight delay in the exchange, Ceirniki surmised the man he spoke to was currently on E3, Europa's geosynchronous station. "Good evening, sir."

"We want to move now, Captain. What's holding us up?"

"The admiral has a request."

"Good God, what does he want now?"

"Their capabilities are uncertain, and the admiral wants an edge. The Marine contingent is modest but well trained."

"Yes, I am aware," Rhodes said with contempt. "We trained them." He turned his head as one of the gaggle tapped him on the shoulder, then waved his hand and huddled with his team. A minute later, he rejoined Ceirniki. "Then what is it?"

"The admiral will not leave victory to chance, which is why you hired him. The GCE would help us."

Rhodes stopped. "We were assured your resources were adequate."

"They are, sir, but the Hydra would reduce the resources needed to support an extended siege in case—"

"Just in case you underestimated the resistance?" Rhodes said.

"Yes, but primarily to make the populace more tractable after our victory."

"Well, the Hydra is busy on Seiyei. You're the weapons experts. Build yourselves another one."

"No. That requires UNE R&D."

"Pres…our partner is now too public to open those doors for you."

"Can we borrow the one at Seiyei?"

"No," Rhodes said in a tone that implied *you moron*. "Without the Hydra, everyone will know it was your admiral's invasion and not a popular revolution. God, I dream of the day we can control information the way they can on Earth. What about fixing the one already on site?"

"It's still broken."

"Can the natives repair it?"

"No, their mil-tech is too primitive."

"Can *you* fix it?"

"Not without expertise we do not have."

"What if I could access that expertise?

Ceirniki paused. "How?"

"My sources say they found a technician, one of the original design team."

"I thought they all disappeared after the *Princess* massac… incident."

"Apparently not all. The fanatics are holding him."

Ceirniki scowled. "Damn. We have to bargain with the devil?"

"Yes," Rhodes said and laughed. "And you won't like the terms." He waved his flock to follow him. "I'll see what I can do."

The holo vanished, and Ceirniki touched his desk.

"Where to, sir?"

"The fleet."

Chapter 12
LeHavre Station, Jira-1 System

LeHavre Station—Inbound

Meriel blinked as the infirmary lighting woke her from another round of sedation. The bright lights told her this was a working shift after a long jump, and the Med-Tech darkened the cowl to shield her eyes.

Sitting by her side, Elizabeth smiled. "Hey, sleepyhead."

"Where are we?"

"Jira-1. Inbound to LeHavre. We passed the beacon, and Socket sent our messages to the kids and their families. The alerts to the Troopers are out, too."

"Now we wait."

Molly's voice came through the link. "Liz, take a look at this."

With a click, Elizabeth displayed the message on the ceiling.

```
IGB news flash ET/2187:112:11
Breaking. For immediate release.
Documents hidden for ten years
implicate BioLuna CEO Rhodes, the
Archtrope of Calliope, and unnamed
UNE/IS officials in the attempted
illegal takeover of a colony.
  These documents link the conspiracy
to a complaint filed in the Lander
Station superior court from
representatives of the L5 colonists of
Haven...
```

"Jeremy must have forwarded a copy of the material we sent him before the attack," Meriel said. "There wasn't enough time for him to learn about the raid on the *Tiger* yet."

"He must have been thinking like you were. Better that the law and the media pursue Biadez and Khanag before they can get to us."

The infirmary was quiet as Meriel reread the news and smiled.

"You need to forgive him, M."

The smile vanished as Meriel turned to her. "Did he talk to you?"

"No, but it's obvious. He's here all the time sitting with you, and you're distant."

She turned her head away. "You're not Mom."

Furrows etched her brow. "No, but maybe you need one. Are you mad at him?"

She remained silent.

"He loves you, M. He comes here every time he's off duty."

She nodded. "I saw him sometimes."

"He sleeps here."

"So do you, Liz."

"I'm family." Elizabeth raised her arm to show she was still secured to the Med-Tech. "And Cookie only gives me potty breaks. You didn't talk to John about Ferrell?"

"What can I say?"

"I know John hurt you, but I think he was just trying to help."

"We should pay for our own mistakes, but I paid for his."

"Is that it? You making him suffer because Ferrell was a shit?"

"He didn't trust me, Liz."

"Oh, so now Ms. 'I can skirt the law whenever I like' is all so trustworthy? You're acting like you're going to walk away from this like nothing happened, like you can just forget him because he brings a bad memory."

"I don't need his help."

Elizabeth's eyes narrowed. "Now you're pissing me off. You're talking like you're alone in the world, like you can do all this yourself."

"I've had to."

"Not anymore, Sis, not for some time now. Mom gave you the data chip but she told me to help you, so listen up." She took a breath. "You're a mess, and he's sticking with you. No one ever cared for you like this except a few of us. And you've never cared this much for any man. You give all us kids a mile but won't give him an inch. Don't blow this, M."

"It still hurts."

Elizabeth nodded and took her hand. "Don't wait too long, or the hurt will never go away."

***

Ellen Biadez took the tiny vial of brown liquid from the nightstand, pierced her little finger with the sharp end, closed her eyes, and sighed. Wearing only a silk nightgown banned everywhere in known space, she walked to the coffee table and lit a cigarette from a monogrammed gold case. She inhaled deeply and strolled to the window to watch the Martian sunrise.

It had been a long day of spinning the news and deflecting reporters' questions because of a spacer who had lived ten years longer than they had intended.

Along the frame, she drew her finger to increase the window's transmissivity and enhance the contrasts of red and black on the cliffs of the Ophir chasm outside. Another swipe of a finger and the deep moan of the rushing wind filled the room as the air heated by the rising sun rushed into the long canyon. Without thinking, she traced her initials on the pane in the reddish dust that seemed to coat everything: even the most exclusive apartments of Mars-6.

Behind her, a mobile replicator rolled up and gazed up at her with a childlike face, awaiting her wishes. She scowled at it with a curled lip. "Champagne. Two. Surprise me."

The robot complied by placing two flutes of vintage champagne on the table.

Her armlet buzzed. "What is it?"

From the link came a man's voice, "We found them."

She waited and sighed. "OK, where are they?"

"Haven."

"Crap. Can we get to her?"

"Not yet."

"What about her old ship. Can we destroy it?"

"They explored that option. We can't do that without taking a chunk out of Enterprise Station and lots of collateral damage."

The little robot's childlike voice interrupted. "Can I offer you something more, ma'am?"

Ellen ignored it. "How can I hurt her?" she murmured. The robot tilted its head in confusion. "Can we destroy her reputation? Discredit her in the media?"

The link replied. "We've still got drugs on her record. We can push that button anytime we want."

She rolled her eyes. "Then push the goddamned button, moron."

A man stirred in the bed behind her, and the reflection of the bed lamp glinted off her champagne flute. She tapped her armlet to end the call.

"You were stupid to listen to my husband and not deal with those brats more...decisively," she said. "Now our entire plan is jeopardized by one stupid girl who has no clue what she's gotten herself into."

He sat up and stretched his arms around the adjoining pillows. "Your husband is an influential man, and he is our partner in this."

"My husband is an idealistic imbecile." She threw her cigarette on the plush white carpet. When the little robot moved to extinguish and dispose of it, she eyed it with contempt. "At least you should have taken out that little bitch before she shot off her mouth."

"She was too public."

"You've been saying that for a decade. How public is she now, for God's sake? We planned the media blackout to last a year, and now it's been ten. This is costing us a fortune, and I'm sick of patching the leaks."

He scoffed and rose. "You worry too much. No media company in the galaxy will print the real story." Walking to the window, he picked up the other flute of champagne. "Forces are in place. Only a few more weeks now."

Another sneer crossed her face. "As I recall, you promised that before." She turned on him with teeth bared and poked her index finger in his chest. "And this time when your soldiers roll over the squatters, make sure they roll over her, too."

With narrowed eyes, he gripped her hand and squeezed slowly. Her expression lost its animal fierceness, and when she winced, he smiled and eased his grasp without letting go. Kissing her on the lips, he released her and walked to the bathroom.

She rubbed her hand and clenched her teeth. The earnest face of the mobile replicator waiting for her wishes nearby caught her eye, and she kicked it. Her smile returned as she watched the wounded robot leave to engage a functioning replacement, dragging a shattered arm behind it.

She could not tell him what she knew: that her husband, Alan Biadez, was feeling remorseful and preparing to expose their plans. If she did, her lover, Cecil Rhodes, the CEO of BioLuna, would kill them both before she left the room.

LeHavre Station—On Station

LeHavre was a gleaming white torus, mostly dedicated to research and development and transshipments from space to the surface. Since John had left on his last tour, the stationers had built a new appendage around the slender zero-g axis, a toroid with a simulated 1.15-g at the periphery and pods along spokes to provide ranges of gravity for physical therapy.

In the clinic on the third tier, a wrinkled old doctor, the genetic surgeon who had saved her life, supervised Meriel's recovery.

"Any pain?" he asked as he touched a spot near the telemetry patch monitoring her damaged organs. Graphs, anatomy schematics, and false color visualizations flashed along the active walls. Next to them a holo of the patch region appeared.

"Nothing. Can't we move this any faster?"

He glanced at her for a moment and pressed on the patch. "Now?"

"Yeah! OK, OK."

"Stand for me."

She took the forearm crutches and winced when the crutch padding rubbed the rashes on her arms, and she stood awkwardly. "This would be easier in a suit, Doc."

"Can't use any of those gadgets and gee-gaws," he said while making notations on his link. "Once you go on the gadgets, you never get off. If you wear a walking suit, the body adapts to the suit, your muscles atrophy, and you'll never be able to walk again without it. The choice is yours, of course, but you'll look like a grasshopper, and—"

"They have different styles—"

The doctor glared over his glasses. "And you'll be choosing a different doctor."

He waved the link above the patch, and a full-size, real-time holo of the inside of her body appeared beside them next to a head-up display of a console. With a wave of his fingers on the console's icons, the holo zoomed into the region near each of her injuries.

"Uh-huh." At his touch, the image shifted to regions of glowing green and blue highlighting the fractured ribs and contusions. Zooming to the orange glow around her ruptured liver, he used the console to adjust the genomics pump, and the region calmed to light chartreuse.

He panned to the area around the lumbar plexus and the damaged nerves above the thin staples in the rear of her pelvis. "Hmmm. Healing nicely. See here." White fibers ran in all directions from an orange region with an angry red center. "Raise your leg."

She complied, and a few of the tiny fibers lit up along with the red area.

"There," he said. "That's where we need to work now." He waved his fingers near the console icons. "Here's an archive from last week." A similar holo popped up, but the red region now extended well outside the field of view. "Lots of progress here." Another wave of a finger and the holo shifted back to real time. "We've got your gross motor skills back, but we want the fast twitch and fine motor skills engaged. Until the red areas disappear, we want you exercising. We want blood in there to help you heal and your nerves to keep signaling that region."

"What's that lime-green area?" she asked.

"That's some cell structure mods to strengthen your core while you heal. It'll help to avoid reinjury."

She scoffed. "What are the odds that I'll get reinjured."

"What were the odds the first time?"

Actually pretty good. "So, am I a genomorph now?"

"No, but they won't let you compete in the Olympics."

With a hand gesture, he invited her to sit next to him. "Your whole body must relearn how to work together. It's smart, but it needs time. Twenty years ago, you'd be in a suit or wheelchair for the rest of your life. Now you have the opportunity for a full recovery. You made the right choice. Stick with it awhile longer." Reaching into a drawer in the wall, he removed a small tube. "This is for the rash on your forearms." His face softened. "Now, what about the scar? Did you make a decision?"

She placed her hand on her breast where the pale slash crossed her body, the scar from the attack on the *Princess*. Through the disaster of the last ten years, it had grounded her in reality. It would not let her forget and would not let her hide.

When she wanted to forget what happened and believe those who told her the *Princess* massacre was a drug deal, the scar reminded her of the horror. When she dreamed of her life that might have been, the dreams of every little girl of a happy life, it woke her from those dreams. Every time, the scar was still there, along with the memory of how she got it, and where, and when. It blew all her dreams away and slammed her back on the deck. Only the drugs made the horror go away, but they made everything go away.

If the scar was gone, she could pretend it was different and rebuild the pretty fantasies. But if she did, the vicious monsters who killed her parents would still roam free to threaten them. And she would be crazy.

"I'm not sure anymore, Doc."

He nodded. "I understand. Take your time. Anything else?"

"Yeah, how do you do a kata with forearm crutches?" She held them up. "I look ridiculous. What can I do to speed this up?"

"Exercise." He touched the medallion on her necklace and smiled. "And pray."

After he left, she stood near the large window to a view of Haven. Her experience of planets was limited to burned-out husks and frozen shells that maintained human life only with grit and technical genius. Still she struggled to imagine life down on that brownish-gray surface. And her interest was not curiosity; she might have to live there.

The deadline to save the *Princess* had passed, and Jeremy had not contacted her. She would have to adjust to the reality that her ship was gone and she was stuck on LeHavre or Haven. Without the *Princess*, space would be closed to her unless she could relearn how to move around in variable-g. And how could she pay her way if she was crippled? If she didn't heal up quickly, she would need to requalify on a cruiser just to keep her cargo-five rating, which was not guaranteed. Stations can't afford idle people, and what would she do on the surface?

But Haven wasn't her biggest worry; she had not heard from the kids, and Khanag was still on the loose.

"Hey, Chief," Molly called from the door to the clinic. "How are you feeling?"

"I'm worried, Exec."

"The doctors say you'll heal in time," Molly said.

"No. I mean I haven't heard from the kids. Their ships went dark after we alerted them to the threat. I don't know where they are or if they're safe."

"The Troopers will find them," Molly said. "The League will make sure of it. Say, I'm writing a letter of commendation for Ferrell to console his family. You were with him. What can I tell them?"

"Sorry, did he actually do anything except die? I must have missed the commendable part."

"He's crew. I just want to say something nice to them."

Meriel sighed and rubbed her bandaged thumb. Ferrell's interrogation of her on the *Tiger* was still fresh and painful, especially the memory of him asking if she was OK, and her saying, "No." He had ignored her as if all the pain of dredging up her past in detail meant nothing to him—as if he dissected a butterfly while it still twitched. "Permission to be candid, ma'am?"

"Granted."

"Tell his family I'll piss on his corpse."

Molly raised an eyebrow. "My, you're grumpy. Got something more to say?"

Confused, Meriel peered at her. "He didn't tell you?"

"Tell me what?"

"He drugged me. That shit drugged me to snoop around inside my head—without consent."

"I warned him I'd kick him off the boat if he tried something like that. Why didn't you tell me?"

"There wasn't time." She turned to look out the window. "And then it didn't matter."

"Did he tell you why?"

"He said I was off the medication and dangerous around equipment, and well, dangerous all the time."

"Well, you are pretty scary sometimes. Were you off the meds?"

Meriel gazed down at her hands and pressed her lips together, feeling guilty about her repeated lies. "Yeah, but I really don't need them."

"How long have you been off?"

"Nearly seven years."

Molly nodded. "And you qualified for eighteen ratings and a logistics-five during that period. Yup, seven years would do it."

She paused to study Molly's face. "You know something. What is it?"

"The passengers claimed Ferrell mentioned something about BioLuna to a black-suit."

Meriel sneered. "Maybe he took them hostage rather than protected them."

"I don't think so. One of the mothers told me they shot him as he raised his weapon. She gave me a vid."

The vid displayed Ferrell's profile and his anxious appeal. "Please. I'm Dr. Patrick Ferrell. BioLuna will vouch for me and the passengers. General Khanag knows this."

Molly stopped the vid. "What do you make of it?"

"They knew him. Ferrell worked for BioLuna, and they partnered with the Archtrope. Khanag's people knew him."

"But they killed him. Jeez. So what do I tell his family?"

"I don't know. So maybe he wasn't one of the bad guys, but he helped them. Oh, right, that makes him corrupt. Let's see now, corrupt and unethical and unscrupulous. And, oh yeah, he died trying to save his own skin. Did I miss something virtuous there you want to tell them?"

"He's got a nine-year-old daughter."

"That's not my fault either."   She rose to begin her therapy regimen.

"I'll write up a formal complaint against him, Chief."

A tear rolled down her cheek. "Why bother? He's dead."

"Legal action against BioLuna."

Meriel shrugged and struggled with her crutches to maneuver to a bench by the window. After sitting, she threw the crutches down and watched Haven pass by outside the window.

Molly gathered the crutches and leaned them against the wall within Meriel's reach. "You hid her in plain sight."

"Who?" she asked, thinking Molly referred to Elizabeth.

"I got a message from Jeff Conklin. He told me the *Liu Yang* is on the impound dock at Enterprise with a hull breach and never flew. That's your ship, the *Princess*, no?"

Meriel nodded.

"I'm sorry, dear," Molly said and laid her hand on Meriel's shoulder.

Another tear traced her cheek, but she remained silent.

John peeked in from the clinic door. "May I interrupt?" As he walked toward them, he noticed Meriel wiping the tears from her eyes.

"Greetings, Pilot Smith," Molly said. "Excuse me, please, I'm on duty. Chief Hope, I'll consider your recommendation. Good day to you both."

"Exec, don't tell her about me. Or what happened, OK?"

"As you wish," Molly said and walked away.

John sat by Meriel's side. "You OK?"

"Yeah. Molly reminded me what a total scumbag Ferrell was." She returned to gaze out the window to Haven.

"It's gorgeous, huh?"

She nodded but wondered what he meant. "There's a lot of brown down there."

"More dirt than water, but even the vegetation looks brown from up here. The cultivated areas are hard to find from this distance. The settlements are those dots by the sea."

"What are the little white spots?"

"Clouds," he said and sat next to her. He tapped the window ledge, and a wireframe overlay appeared around the features of Haven below them. "Nowhere near as many as on Earth. Lack of rain is one of our major problems. The water cycle returns through ground water, and there is very little surface runoff." Sliding a finger along the pane, he zoomed the view. "See those long, white, oval shapes near the coast?"

She nodded.

"Those are cloud plumes from hyperbolic cooling towers and evaporation ponds. They humidify the air and cut the dust, at least downwind. It may take a hundred years to generate a regional water cycle, and decades before the dust storms and mud rains stop."

"Really? It rains?"

"A little. We can't let it rain too much, though. The native animals take their water from plants and aquifers. They'd drown in a puddle."

"Where are the domes?"

Moving his fingers along the window, the view panned east to show the interconnected hemispheres of domed habitats.

She smiled. "They look like soap bubbles."

"There are only a few. We lived on the L5 habitat for generations, and some still fear living outside. These were built as protection from the storms, but most of us live out in the open."

"Really, you can walk around without suits?"

"Yup. Jira-1 has just a little less UV and a bit more IR than Sol. Great for crops. We only need goggles for the dust. The big dome is the capital at Stewardville." Panning farther east, he pointed to rectangular areas of green. "Those are the farms."

"The clouds don't reach that far."

"Not very often. We use subsurface drip irrigation. It's all pretty primitive still. We don't have the infrastructure yet to support heavy industry," he said with a chuckle. "We've got all the data sets but can't build the replicators yet."

He shifted the view eastward. "See that jagged cut? That's the Johnston Rift. It's too rocky to farm but has the firmest soil. Great for transports." Sadness marred his face and his voice softened. "We fought off BioLuna's mercenaries heading for Stewardville there." He zoomed in to an assortment of shapes and green areas adjacent to the valley. "And that's our compound there."

"I think my mom would have liked it here," she said but frowned.

He took her hand. "What about you?"

"I don't know. I feel in control in space, prepared for anything, kinda."

"Haven is safer than the *Tiger*."

"Maybe. I've been dreaming about Home since I was a little kid. But this is real, and all so new." *Can I ever trust a sky to keep us alive?*

"What about us, M? You've been distant."

She turned away. "It still hurts, John."

"I'm sorry. I was only trying to help."

"That's what hurts. You didn't trust me to deal with it."

"You weren't honest with me, M."

"How could I tell you I've been breaking the law for a decade and thousands of court-order violations? And then aiding and abetting an escaped suspect and a stowaway? They'd drag you off the *Tiger* and arrest you if they ever suspected you knew any of that. You wouldn't see your girls for years." And she still didn't tell him the worst—a security breach on Enterprise that could imprison him for life if he knew. "I haven't been a good girl, John. It's dangerous for you to hang around me."

"You kept all that from me."

"I told you everything but the stuff that could get you shipped off to a mining colony." *Which doesn't leave much.*

He nodded. "And I'm sorry I didn't tell you more about Haven. Everyone is afraid immigrants will overwhelm us. It's not resource rich like Earth still is, and our ecosystem is fragile. No one thinks those coddled people on Earth or the stations can survive here. Farming is nothing at all like spacing."

The stationside hydroponics and all the spacers living on the ragged edge of survival came to her mind. "They might surprise you."

"You can understand why we need to be careful."

"Sure, John, but the word is out, and immigration will not be up to you anymore. You can't just shoot people if they land here."

He glanced up "Hmmm."

A punch to his shoulder expressed her thoughts. "You wouldn't."

"No. But some would. They prefer sheep to people."

"You told me enough. I just couldn't believe it. I've been hearing horror stories of the low-grav hellholes that people populate, and I thought you were putting a good face on a wreck." *Like I've been doing with the* Princess. "I guess I really didn't believe what my mom searched for was real. I thought if I told you what I knew, you'd think I was stupid or crazy."

He smiled. "Liz wasn't afraid."

"Yeah, she's like that. And people don't start off thinking she's crazy."

"I didn't make the connection either."

She took John's hand. "I didn't tell you everything. John, I'm sorry I wasn't honest, but I was trying to protect you.

"Funny, I thought I was protecting you."

You may not know how bad these guys really are.

"If we had fewer secrets, we'd be able to trust each other more."

She nodded and leaned into him, and he embraced her. "Yeah, maybe."

In the window behind them, Thor rose over the edge of Haven and illuminated them in the gas giant's blue and orange light. But Meriel looked over John's shoulder beyond the gas giant and moons to the stars beyond and frowned.

"I hope I'm better before they come again," she said.

"Who?"

"Nothing," she said, but the frown remained.

***

Three days later, Meriel walked to LeHavre's null-g axis where the crew and naval architects refitted the *Tiger*. The periphery was maintained at a full one-g artificial for the comfort of the residents and the discomfort of those like her on crutches. At the dry dock window she beeped Molly. A few seconds later, a space-suited figure tethered a carbon welder and pushed toward the air lock.

New EMP and laser cannons broke up the smooth lines of the *Tiger*, weapons intended to discourage General Khanag from more mischief. Ship designs would evolve once again from those most efficient for space trade to those most effective in averting piracy with the minimum mass and energy. Those without the equity to afford the transition would be uninsurable and grounded.

Behind her, Cookie approached and began to suit up for EVA. Under his arm he held a box labeled "Enterprise Cyber Security," Nick's company.

"I have our new firewall and sniffer, M," he said. "Wanna help?"

She smiled. "Do you know who ECS is?"

"My friends recommended them."

"You don't trust the Navy's version?"

"I expect the UNE will sneak some other spyware into our systems. I'm gonna scrub everything down to the fullerenes and—"

A crutch slipped out from under her on a puddle of condensation from the high ceiling, and he caught her before she fell.

"Damn these things."

He helped her manage her crutches and sighed.

"It's not your fault, Cookie."

He would not meet her eyes, so she reached up and kissed him on the cheek.

Molly exited the air lock, and he stood and saluted. "Permission to come aboard, ma'am?"

"Granted, Sergeant."

"The nav system is installed, Chief Hope," Molly said while removing her hard-suit. "Once the retrofits and Cookie's reboot are complete, we'll prepare for a shakedown run. You game to get into space again?"

She held up her crutches. "I won't be very good for a while, ma'am, but thanks."

Molly tapped the link on her gauntlet and a message appeared. "Oh, I think this message was meant for you."

```
     cc: M.Hope. Court-5 petition from
Pacific  League  granted.  Injunction
stays    transfer    of    title   GCN
13442:88. J.Bell Esq.
```

"That's the *Princess*, but why would I get a message from the League?"

"They don't have your address here. I contacted them. The League has standing on Enterprise. They are supporting your custody claim."

"But Jeremy is handling that, and I couldn't afford it."

"The League has deep pockets, Chief. I think Jeremy is on retainer for them now, which I gather earns him a much bigger office. If I read this right, they granted his petition to stay the forfeiture. She's still yours, for now."

Meriel sat, stunned at her good luck. "Why in the universe would the League do that?"

"Seems when you exposed BioLuna, they went on the defensive and ended the embargo on Haven. That's huge for the League. They may be incapable of gratitude, but see this as a bounty, a finder's fee for opening up this route."

"What can I say, ma'am? This is more than I hoped for."

"I'm the grateful one, Meriel. I'm sleeping with my husband tonight and not a memory. No one else did that for me. Oh, but the League offer has strings."

"Uh-oh."

"If the *Princess* is working again—"

"*When* the *Princess* is working again," Meriel said.

"OK. *When* the *Princess* is working again, they want a piece of your circuit. They made us the same offer."

"They want me in the League?"

Molly nodded. "They want to set up new routes with stops here. It's yours when you're ready."

"How big a piece are they asking for?"

"Tiny. They made the same offer to the *Tiger*."

"LeHavre isn't built for trade, ma'am."

"John said they're negotiating financing for a new station."

Meriel could not speak. The future her mother had hoped for was becoming real. Except…

"Did you hear anything about the orphans?" Meriel asked.

"No, dear. The Troopers are unlikely to announce that they are protecting them. Sorry. I'll let you know if I hear anything."

"Thank you, ma'am."

"Now I think you can help us again. Richard and I have a bet about how you kids could communicate for so long without anyone knowing. Some encryption scheme?"

"All our messages were over the public net in clear text. I don't know how it works. Nick sent us all an app. He told us it's obfuscation, like having your jigsaw puzzle mixed up with a billion other puzzles of the same color."

"How does it figure out which pieces to use?"

"That's his magic."

"Mil-tech?"

"They wish."

***

Thor had dropped below Haven's horizon, and the light from Jira-1 streamed through the corridor windows as Meriel approached Elizabeth's cabin. An eighth around the arc of LeHavre's torus was the closest they could billet her sister because of the station's dense population. The station was small, but that was still a long way to walk, and the forearm crutches rubbed her arms raw.

She raised her hand to knock on the partially open door but stopped at her sister's voice.

"No way," Elizabeth said.

"I want you back again, Liz, like it was." *That's Tommy's voice.*

"Damn it, shithead, we were kids. I told you not to complicate it."

Meriel's heart jumped. *Tommy's alive!* She leaned against the bulkhead, closed her eyes, and listened.

Tommy continued. "It wasn't that long ago, Liz, and we weren't kids. I'm not just some station sleepover."

"Whatever we had, it's over," Elizabeth said.

"Not for me."

"Drop it, Tommy. I don't want to be dragging your heart around the galaxy." She sighed and lowered her voice. "It was my birthday, Tommy." After a deep breath, she exhaled slowly. "You know I have a hard time sleeping on my birthday."

He paused before answering. "I know, Liz. Sorry. All of us have a hard time on your birthday."

"You know what I meant. Just drop it, OK?"

Meriel could not wait any longer. "Ahem," she said and walked through the doorway. "Didn't mean to interrupt."

Elizabeth had Tommy's image on the active wall, and both of them frowned. "Hey, Sis," she said and wiped a finger under her eyes. "Tommy's doing a flyby."

"Hi, M," he said.

"I'm so glad to see you," Meriel said. "I thought.... You're not gonna dock?"

"Troopers have us in tow. We're off to...well, they won't tell us."

"Did you bring your whole ship?"

"Yeah, that's something, huh? LGen has a contract for us, and the manager told us it's worth changing routes."

"So when are you stopping in?"

"Not sure. The Trooper commander said 'when it's safe' but didn't say when that would be." Tommy turned to mumblings behind him and then back to them. "Crap. I'm in trouble. My captain says I ain't supposed to be talking to you. Gotta go now. See ya."

"No, wait. What about Sam and the other kids?"

He frowned. "Don't know. Bye."

"Tommy, wait," she said, but his image vanished.

Meriel smiled and held Elizabeth's hand. "He's safe. Only five left. I was afraid that all..."

"I know. Me, too. How about a drink to celebrate?"

Meriel accepted the glass, and for the briefest moment, let the relief wash over her. "I overheard part of your conversation with Tommy. Something you want to talk about?"

"Absolutely not. How did the vidcon go with Becky and Sandy?" Elizabeth asked, referring to John's girls.

"They're dolls. Just darlings. Their nanny was there, too. Maddie is her name, a real sweetheart."

"You don't seem happy about it. Think he's got something going with the nanny?"

"She must be sixty years old, Liz."

"Oops. Then what's bugging you?"

"Your girls make me nervous."

"How come?"

"I'm a spacer," Meriel said. "They may be looking for a full-time mom. I don't want to break their hearts."

"Be careful there, about whose heart you don't want to break." Elizabeth dropped her gaze. "M, I think I figured out why the ePod ejected."

"Why?"

"Mom did it. To stop the pirates—or whoever—from searching for us."

"No, ePods need someone onboard 'em to launch."

Elizabeth nodded. "That's how she was wounded; trying to convince an uncooperative hijacker he needed a trip."

"They would have blown up the ePod."

"Sure. But it worked. They stopped hunting for us," Elizabeth said, and they hugged each other.

Her console blinked. "Incoming, M. Looks like a ship synced with the beacon." She waved her fingers to display the message.

```
APB-General Subedei Khanag (AKA
Steven Chen) and associates in
Draconian League ET/2187:134:7.10
   Detain subject on charges of
criminal piracy, murder, and
terrorism. Charges filed Lander
Station, ET/2187:134:6.4.
   Space Troopers, Lander Station.
```

"Here's another."

```
IGB news wire ET/2187:121:10.10
For immediate release. Merchant Ship
Tiger attacked by men under the
command of General Khanag associated
with the Archtrope of Calliope. See
Space Troopers Lander Station for
sample physical evidence and redacted
interviews. Criminal charges to be
filed on Lander Station.
General Khanag also implicated in
ET/2177 attack on family trader
Princess. Physical evidence ibid.
```

"Well, the pirates have no reason to come after us now," Elizabeth said, "except for vengeance."

"Vengeance is motive enough."

"But it's inefficient with a small return on investment. These guys are in business."

"Maybe it's about power, not money. And he's still on the loose. Check the news, Liz."

Elizabeth pulled up the local wire service.

```
GNN Top News Today: Spacer with a
history of drug abuse and delusions
brings scurrilous charges against the
most reputable members of Earth
society. Defamation charges have been
filed on Moon-3 and injunctions issued
to stop distribution of slanderous
lies.
```

"Ouch. Guess we need to scratch Moon-3 from our vacation plans."

"They're fighting back," Elizabeth said. "I wonder whose version will get traction."

```
"Independent News Network's story of
the hour: Troopers issue arrest
warrant for General Subedei Khanag for
two counts of piracy; one recent
attempt and one approximately a decade
```

```
ago. The general was unavailable for
comment. The Archtrope, the general's
mentor and spiritual leader, had this
to say…"
```

The video switched to a press conference with the Archtrope wearing ceremonial mitre and vestments. Alongside him stood a man in a well-tailored business suit. The suit spoke.

```
   "Certainly, if General Khanag was in
any way involved with attacks on
innocent civilians, we would support
the strongest of sanctions to assure
such events can never be repeated. We
believers are humanitarians and
respect all human life. However, the
general is a pious man and committed
to the peaceful teachings of our most
revered prophet. I am quite certain
any charges against him are specious
and will be dropped before the
investigation is complete, and his
good name will be cleared of all
wrongdoing. Thank you. His holiness
has nothing more to say."
```

While his handlers hustled the Archtrope away through a crowd of journalists and disciples, one reporter shouted after them.

```
   What about LeHavre? What do you know
about the Treaty of Haven and
attempted invasion of an occupied
colony?
```

The vid switched back to the news anchor, who continued the report.

```
"In a related story, the Archtrope
of Calliope has been named in a
decade-long conspiracy to invade an
independent colony called Haven.
BioLuna and an unnamed member of the
UNE Immigration Service have also been
implicated in the conspiracy."
```

"Well, the news is out," Meriel said.
"You understood that, right? General Khanag is missing."

```
"Breaking news: Today. Alan Biadez,
UNE president, announced his
resignation for unspecified health
reasons after less than a month in
office."
```

The video feed switched to footage of Biadez and his family boarding a shuttle. Reporters with vids and links surrounded them.

```
"…yes. Thank you. That is most kind.
I'll be staying with my wife, Ellen,
and our children on Calliope during my
recovery."
```

"Calliope. That's the Archtrope's turf."
Meriel shook her head. "Asylum with the thugs. That clinches it. I totally hate his guts."
The news feed and interview continued.

```
"…Yes, yes, my resignation is
immediate, and Vice Chairman Toyama is
now acting president, pending
confirmation by the General Assembly.
Thank you for your love and support
all these years—"
```

The voice of a reporter interrupted him.

```
"What about Haven when you were
Chairman of the Immigration Service?
What about the Treaty of Haven?"
```

Biadez's wife turned with bared teeth and shouted at the reporter.

```
"How rude! How dare you impugn the
honor—"
```

Alan Biadez elbowed his wife out of the way.

```
"No more questions now. Thank you."
```

"She knew about the treaty," Elizabeth said.

Meriel nodded. "They'll be busy running for a while. Now, what are BioLuna and Khanag up to?"

***

His corporate yacht lounged just off Etna Station as the crew prepared for a long jump. The onboard office was almost as spacious as his headquarters on Moon-1 but more tasteful and comfortable. Although the ever-changing sights through the room-length window were more spectacular than the moon, Etna offered no such entertainments, and he ignored it. On one window, a blue light blinked, and he waved his hand to receive the laser tight-beam.

"Your pack of dogs screwed up," the nondescript man said.

"They're not my dogs, Benedict."

"You should have engaged me sooner."

"Yes, yes. I was assured it was under control—my mistake. This bodes ill for our other joint ventures." Another blue light blinked, and he waved a hand to dismiss it.

"Sir?"

"Yes, I'm back. It's time for you to end this problem of ours."

"The news is already out, sir. Why risk more attention?"

"The fanatic is the face of this particular fiasco. We still have plausible deniability, and any connection to us is rumor and speculation. It's too late to stop this in any case."

"And the survivors?" Benedict said.

"That's on him, too. As for our immediate concern, we placed delusions and antipsychotic medications on her record years ago for just this eventuality. We can spin any story we want as long as she's not around to contradict us. But she is elusive."

"They don't sell tickets to Haven, sir."

"I'll find you a ride," said Cecil Rhodes, the chairman of BioLuna.

Chapter 13
Haven

Indigenous Species

The shuttle shook violently as it cut through Haven's atmosphere and jarred Meriel like nothing she had ever experienced. She closed her eyes and gripped the armrests so hard the veins in her hands bulged out.

"Jeez," she said. "Is your atmosphere made of rocks?"

"At this speed, yeah, pretty much," John said, pretending the drink in his hand might actually end up in his mouth.

The orange glow outside her window dispersed, allowing her a view outside. The torus and odd protrusions of LeHavre diminished, and the tan landscape of Haven changed to shades of green. As the ride smoothed, she stopped worrying about disintegrating on reentry and returned to worrying about other things she could do nothing about. She fidgeted with nervousness, having never been on a planet before, but even more nervous about John's kids. He had told her everything about them, and they'd had a video conference, but meeting in person would be different. They also had an extended family on Haven who might not be so welcoming. *It's only a visit*, she reminded herself.

When the shuttle had coasted to a stop, she struggled from her seat due to the increased gravity and unwieldy forearm crutches. The sunlight blinded her as she approached the escalator, and with her hands needed for support, she could only squint against the glare.

Approaching the portal, cheers caught her attention. Crowded around the gangway stood more people than she had ever seen in her entire life. "Why are they here?" *Are they all so happy to leave?*

"They've come for you, M," John said.

"Why?"

Still awkward on her crutches, she stepped outside the escalator. This was the first time she had ever been outside of a space vessel without the protection of a hard-suit, and without thinking, she held her breath.

Her vision cleared in the shade of the shuttle wing to disclose a carpet of red flowers, and above it the huge blue sky. Careful of the uneven ground, she checked the horizon for orientation, but it curved down, not up like on a station deck. To compensate for the perspective, she leaned forward too far and lost her balance. She reached for a handhold, which onboard would be only a few inches away. Instead, she found John's arm, but without the crutch to support her, she slipped and fell, smacking her head hard on the carpet.

John and Elizabeth knelt by her side and helped her to sit up.

"Are you all right?" he asked.

Meriel did not answer, but glanced up, disoriented by the riot of colors. The sun glared down at her through open space, a sky without a dome to hold the air in. New scents irritated her nose, but she could not scratch it. The crowd and noise all pressed in on her, and she began to hyperventilate. Dizzy, her eyes glazed over, unblinking.

"M, what's wrong?" John asked.

She stared at the sky and gripped their hands. "I don't…feel safe." *All those colorful blotches at the base of the big blue…dome. Oh my God, it's the horizon. There's no hull. I don't have a suit… There's no air… I don't want this!* She trembled, and the color drained from her face. All she could think about was her meds.

Elizabeth turned to him. "John, what is it?"

"She's frightened, Liz. Meriel, here, take my hand," he said, but she remained motionless, staring at nothing and breathing rapidly. "Hon, take my hand." He took her face in his hands. "Look at me. Trust me. This is what your mother wanted for you. Come take this step with me."

She nodded, and with his help, got to her feet while keeping her eyes on him. But a balloon escaped the hand of a child and stole her attention. Her gaze followed the balloon upward until the blue sky swallowed it and the terror returned. "Oh God!" Unable to breathe, she collapsed into his arms.

***

Meriel awoke still groggy in a dimly lit room. She had slept through the day and night unaware of her surroundings and without the low hum of a ship's engines and familiar hiss of ventilation. Instead, a soft breeze fluttered the curtains of an open window and brought with it the faint smell of wheat and flowers.

It was a room for children, large by ship standards, with drawings on the walls and clothing strewn everywhere. Two little girls shared the room with her, both as quiet as shadows. One of the shadows, John's younger girl, Becky, sat on a chair next to the bed, playing with a rag doll though regularly peeking at her. Sandy, the bigger shadow, leaned against a dresser and watched intently through her good eye. A patch covered her other eye with a fabric that matched the bow in her hair.

When Meriel blinked, Becky dropped her toy and took her hand.

"Hi, Merry."

"Morning, sweetie," Meriel said. "Oops! Excuse me, 'Galatia!'"

At the mention of her heroine, Becky sat up straight, beaming, and struck her fist across her chest in salute. "And this is my partner, Brucilla the Muscle."

"Hello, Merry L.," Sandy said.

"Hi, hon." Meriel held out her hand to invite her over.

Becky would not be interrupted. "Last night, Maddie told us you 'saved Papa's ass.' Is that the gift you brought us?"

"Quiet, Bru. She's still resting."

"I am very sorry I couldn't meet you at the dock," Meriel said. "I wasn't feeling well."

Sandy held Meriel's hand like a baby bird in both of hers. "Papa told the others at dinner you saved his life. We're real grateful. He said you saved all of them in that ship up there. We saw it from our telescope, all beat up and dirty." Even more softly but beaming, she added, "Papa said you were a hero."

"I don't remember much," Meriel said, "and none of that hero stuff. I'm just glad your father is home with you. Everything smells so different. Where am I? My God, is this Haven? Really?"

"Yup! You're here at our house, on our farm and in our room. You've been sleeping since yesterday. The shuttle left this morning, but Papa says you can stay with us as long as we look after you and don't disturb you and—"

"We take care of the pigs and the chickens and the goats, so we can be trusted, all right!" Becky said, tripping on her sister's words, "and we helped foal a pony just last week, too, and Sandy...oops, she fell asleep again."

The two girls whispered their leave and closed the door.

The room darkened with the setting sun while Meriel slept. When the door opened again, the curtains quivered and a little face peeked in. Sandy walked over to the bedside table and upon it placed a small tray with a bowl of soup.

"Maddie thought you might like something to eat when you wake up," she said and sat on the edge of the bed. "Merry, I..." She laid her hand on Meriel's and gently kissed her forehead as her mother once did.

"Thank you, Merry. I don't know what we would do without Papa. I know you're really nice by the way he talks about you. He kind of just smiles a lot and hasn't acted this way since Mommy...died. She used to spend time with us. Well, I guess we just followed her around 'cause we were younger then. We don't have many friends here. There are kids at the next farm, but it's too far to walk. Papa built us a little school to bring the workers' kids closer. Most of the people are older, and they're always busy. We work, too, but it doesn't seem as important as what they're all doing. They don't let us do much with Becky so young and me only twelve and with just one good eye. The doc says I need to wait until my brain grows up a bit before they can fit me with a prosth...a fake. I can see as well with one eye as they can with two, and I can shoot better than any of 'em. Maybe I'll get a cool bionic one that detects heat or figures distance or something." She glanced up for a moment and raised her eyebrows. "Oh, or maybe one that looks like a tiger or glows red when I'm mad."

After pausing for a breath, she sighed. "Becky and I talked it over, and we want you to stay, Merry L. We didn't ask Papa yet, but we want you here with us anyway. So we want you to heal up real fine. We want so very much to be your friends."

In the middle of her dream, Meriel heard a tiny fairy say, "We want so very much to be your family."

And she heard correctly.

**

General Subedei Khanag's flagship was small and fast, functional rather than comfortable. He sat in the command chair on the empty bridge, scrolling through holos of children working in the mines and organ recyclers. The stench of oil and urine in the mines had not left his nose, nor had the putrid stench of rotting food thrown to those in the pits. And the iron taste of blood from the fights and beatings had not left his tongue, because these were not the vids of children whose lives he had destroyed. They were his own memories of the Stim den on mining colony RF33, where his parents had sold him for drugs.

He rubbed his forearm. Tattoos covered the tracks of the needles and IVs that had delivered escape for a decade and resurrection more than once. Between his crimes and pleas for more Stim, he had prayed for salvation. The Archtrope of Calliope answered those prayers, plucking him from the mines and giving him a life with purpose: to carve out a utopia for the forsaken, like himself, and his son.

A high-priority message interrupted his thoughts. On the bridge in front of him appeared a holo of a bulky man in silk robes. He lay on a couch with a bowl of grapes before him while a beautiful and scantily clad woman massaged his shoulders.

Khanag bowed his head. "Arrangements are final, your eminence. All is in order."

The Archtrope waved the young woman away and leaned forward. "I am sorry for your loss, General."

"Thank you, my lord."

"Your son was a hero for our cause and worthy in our flock. She and the orphans will be his slaves in paradise for executing him."

"After I am through with them."

"Yes, your revenge is assured. You will stay a bit for the memorial service?"

"Yes. Thank you, your eminence."

"Private, of course, discretion is still necessary considering our…upcoming ventures. Speaking of which, you still hold the technician?"

"Yes."

"Show me."

Khanag snapped his fingers to a uniformed crew member. "Bring him."

"You've come far, Mouse," the Archtrope said.

A flinch dispelled the memories resurrected by his old street name. "Yes, Prophet. But recent events exposed what was hidden. Do we proceed?"

"Of course. There is a momentum to violence: an inevitability that, once begun, cannot be stopped. It is Sente. Delay is weakness."

Khanag nodded. "And what about the orphans?"

"Yes, exposure makes them expendable now. But they would be useful as converts. No?"

"Avatars would be more easily controlled."

"But we have a new future to offer them. I want their souls, not their images."

Khanag waved his hand to defocus the hologram. "Our guest arrives. We must be discreet."

His crewman entered holding the arm of a much smaller man.

"Ah, there you are. I hope the accommodations are to your liking, Mr. Matsushita," Khanag said.

"What about my wife and children?"

"Why, they are safe, of course. Do not fret."

"I want to talk to them."

"I'm sorry, Warren. May I call you Warren?" he asked but continued without pause. "You know it is impossible to speak to your family now. They're on vacation, at our expense. A treat for them for your assistance. They're perfectly safe. I will send you a vid. Now to business. You can repair our little prize now, yes?

"If you have the equipment I requested, yes, I can fix it."

"Wonderful. What about the controller?"

"I don't need it. I can operate it from the device itself."

Khanag smiled and opened his arms. "Excellent."

"And if I help you, the Archers will release my family?"

"Yes, of course, of course, not to worry."

Warren's face remained grim.

"The Haveners will not be able to fix it?" Khanag asked.

"No, they don't have the parts or the technology to make the parts." His eyes widened and he shuddered. "You'll never make it work without me."

Khanag's eyes narrowed for a moment before his smile returned. "Thank you, Warren. I must beg your leave now, but you will join me for dinner later, yes?" He waved his hand and dismissed him without waiting for a reply. When the technician was out of sight, he reengaged the holo.

The Archtrope reappeared. "He'll do. Proceed."

"Yes, Prophet."

***

After Khanag signed off and the holo dissolved, a man in a business suit stepped closer to the Archtrope: Edward Siede, Editor in Chief of GNN, the Galactic News Network.

"You still have the family of the tech?" Siede asked,

A new woman distracted the Archtrope. "Who?"

"The tech who helped build the Hydra. And his family."

"The admiral will have them soon—a trade for cooperation, a joint mission."

"You'll lose your leverage." His confident smile slowly faded to a squint. "No. That's not quite right. You have a different plan. You want Khanag on the surface."

The Archtrope nodded. "And his men. Our partners are powerful and interpret passivity as weakness. We must secure our own territory and some of theirs with which to bargain."

Pacing, Siede assessed him through narrow eyes. "You wanted the blockade ended. The *Tiger* publicity is in your favor. Did you foresee that failure?"

An animal grin crossed the Archtrope's face.

"Did you… make it happen to make this public?"

"Of course not. But no outcome is certain."

"But if the blockade is ended, then settlers will rush—"

"That will only guarantee our victory. The settlers will cower and bleat before wolves like Khanag."

Siede frowned and shook his head. "You should drop him, Jim. His fanaticism is dangerous."

"Ahh, betrayed by your ignorance again, my friend. Some people you cannot control with money or threats of death. The fleet is loyal to him. He is my champion, and I will have no other."

"But if he fails?"

The Archtrope dismissed the idea with a wave of his hand. "There are other gladiators and other coliseums. The galaxy is mine already, as is the future."

"For now. The *Tiger* story is getting legs. What will we tell them?"

"Your creativity is why we are such dear friends, Edward. Tell them anything remotely plausible. Anything but the truth." He took a bunch of grapes from a bowl and gazed at his harem. "Just keep repeating it."

"I fear this is bigger than we can contain."

"Our friends control the media and will never publish an...unflattering article." The Archtrope flipped a grape into his mouth. "We number their children in our flocks."

Siede sneered. "And you will return their husks for a large donation when they have outlived their usefulness. What will you do when there are no more people to steal from, when only the innocents are left for you to enslave?"

Slamming his plump hand on the table, he shouted. "They are never innocent; they are human. They are beasts who cannot control their lusts and must be..." He clenched a fist and closed his eyes, but calmed his voice. "They must be sated and guided for their own good." His eyes opened with a glare at Siede. "And mind your tone, or you may outlive your own children."

Siede's eyes widened, and he shuddered.

The Archtrope lightened the mood with a smile and open arms. "Now, now, Edward, my old friend," he said and clapped his hand on his associate's shoulder. "Not to worry. We are allies in this grand venture, no?" He opened his arms to free the robes from his forearms and exposed tattoos from the Stim dens: tattoos similar to those of Khanag. "What you speak of is in the future, and there are many entertainments yet to enjoy." Attendants moved to make him comfortable.

"Dismiss your whores, Jim. I'm not interested."

A wicked smile crossed the Archtrope's face. "They are not for you, infidel. Now, let's devise how GNN news will celebrate our coming victory and new homeland."

Songlines

"See, Merry, it's not like your stunners," Sandy said and adjusted the sight on the pellet gun braced against Meriel's shoulder. They lay side by side in the dirt with barefoot Becky close by, pretending to shoot at varmints with a strange device. Meriel took aim and fired a few shots.

Sandy continued with pride in her voice. "This has some kick, so tuck it into your shoulder more. And it takes a while to reach your target, so you gotta lead it a bit. You got a disadvantage with two eyes." She smiled and tapped her eye patch. "So you gotta forget your left one is even there."

Meriel shot until she could hit the clump of dirt she aimed for. "What about something heavier for the bigger animals?"

"Papa says that would likely kill 'em. They don't mean to hurt us usually."

Nearby, Becky secured the toy weapon under her belt in the small of her back and surveyed the landscape through narrowed eyes. Placing her fists on her hips, she struck a pose as if she had vanquished the wild beasts and restored the planet's proper order with children at the pinnacle of power.

"I read about that. Haven's food chain is orthogonal to humans."

Sandy struggled with the word. "Ortha...right. If they eat us, they get sick. But sometimes they forget when they get hungry, and they bite first. And the little ones like to collect shiny things."

"Yeah, like Mom's earrings," Becky said with a sneer. "Papa told us not to kill things just 'cause they're stupid, but no one wants to get bit. So they need remindin' we're not food, and we have to stop 'em from comin' back."

Meriel aimed at a lump that might have been an armored beaver, but a little hand over the gunsight spoiled her shot.

"No, no! That's not a varmint. That's Dumpy." After Becky's whistle, the beast waddled toward them. She held out some indigenous plant to tempt it, but right behind it stalked a bigger critter. "Now would be a good time."

Meriel shot and missed the critter, but the dirt plume from the ricochet scared it off. Handing the gun to Sandy, she rose to her feet. "What's the brown patch by the house? It doesn't look like the native plants."

"Papa calls it grass," Sandy said. "Every few months he plants it again, but it just turns brown. Then he kicks the ground and swears."

"Uh-huh." Meriel turned to Becky. "Hon, what's that toy you're playing with?"

She took the device from her belt and handed it to Meriel. "It was Mom's."

The gadget was a light-blue ring about twenty-five centimeters around with a black bar across the major diameter. The bar appeared to be a natural hand grip, fitted with a trigger and colorful buttons and sliders that could be manipulated individually by the fingers. An indented segment of the torus provided room for the wrist, which oriented the plane along the axis of the forearm.

"Mom left it in a bag with lots of stuff Papa says is dangerous," Sandy said. "But he says this is OK."

"What does it do?"

The girls shrugged, but Becky replied, "It doesn't do anything except buzz."

Sandy pointed to a tiny dot on the handle. "You push here, and it glows in the dark."

The device was well made and did not appear to be a toy. She squeezed the trigger and felt the vibration in her hand. Dumpy accelerated his waddle toward them.

"He likes it."

"Yeah, he thinks it's a girl...or a boy...or, I dunno," Sandy said.

Turning the device over, Meriel examined a long string of numbers and letters etched faintly along the inside circumference. They seemed vaguely familiar, and she squinted. "Sandy, do you know what these numbers—"

"Hey, stranger," a man's voice called from behind her.

She turned and raised her hand against the midday sun to see John approach.

"Shh," Sandy whispered. "Don't ask Papa about the grass, or he'll get mad."

Becky cleared her throat and stuck out her hand. "Ahem."

Meriel handed the toy back to her.

"For someone living in our house for weeks now, we don't spend much time together," he said and hugged her.

Little Becky frowned and returned her hands to her hips. "She's spending time with the other people who live here, Papa."

"You're sounding jealous, cowboy," Meriel said.

"A little. Maddie will be sleeping at her own place now that you're up and around. Maybe you could tuck me in at night, too."

"We'll see. Is lunch break over?"

"No. They turned the evaporators off. We'll need to shelter in the soil-processing facility."

"Not today," Becky said. She took Meriel's hand and hauled her to her feet. "She's coming with us."

He smiled. "Aren't you bored with her yet?"

"Nope," Sandy said.

As the girls led Meriel away, she turned to John with an expression that said, "What can I do?"

***

"Shush, now." The teacher quieted the class as Sandy and Becky ushered Meriel to the back of the classroom. On their way, they passed drawings representing the highlights of Haven's short history: the first landing, the first successful harvest, and the attacks by BioLuna. She slowed to view up-close the colorful pictures of spaceships and laser beams and bloody bodies. One of them depicted a damaged merchant ship bristling with weapons. *Fantasy*, she thought and then saw the title below—the *Tiger*—and she realized the wall was filled with the children's impressions of the recent attack by Khanag. *Not so different*, she thought, but noticed the silence. She turned to see the entire class, most of them barefoot like Becky, smiling at her. And to each side, Becky and Sandy beamed up at her.

Meriel blushed at the attention. "Oh, excuse me," she said and went to the back of the room while the girls took their seats.

"OK, class," the teacher said. "Remember, the best of your essays will be presented at the Harvest Fair next week." She checked her link. "Whose turn is it now? Eddy, please."

A young boy ambled to the front of the room and fidgeted with a link the size of a folder. "Our first years—"

"Is that the title of your essay?" she asked, while fiddling with a console on her desk.

"Yes, ma'am."

She waved her hand for him to continue.

"Our first years on Haven were a disaster. The FTL ships that brought us here broke down on the way, and the life-support systems failed. We had to leave for the surface, but we didn't know how to grow things here yet, because the dirt has too much copper in it."

"And why is that?"

"Well, they think an asteroid flew close by millions of years ago."

"A comet, dear. Haven life has adapted to it, but the copper is harmful if we don't remove it. Why is that? Class?"

Sandy raised her hand but spoke without being called. "Because Earth plants can't grow well nearby."

"That's correct. Continue, Eddy."

Rattling glass brought the kids running to the windows. Meriel followed and stood behind them as a wall of grayish brown—hundreds of feet high—crept toward them. The dust cloud stretched across the entire horizon, and within it, the occasional bolt of lightning flashed.

The teacher rapped on her desk. "Back in your seats, children. Show me your masks." They complied by holding up their goggles and handkerchiefs, as did Meriel. "Go on, Eddy."

"Well, they planned on harvests from the hydroponic systems within two years, but that didn't work. Two of the shuttles crashed trying to move them down to Haven. People got hungry." He played with the pad in his hands.

"Eddy, please."

"Ah...our leaders—"

"President Steward, God rest his soul," the teacher interrupted.

"Our leaders assigned hundreds of teams to different plots of ground to experiment with soil treatments and crop species to find out what would grow best. After a year they figured out more efficient ways to leach the impurities from the soil."

She peered at him over her glasses. "Eddy, do you know what 'leach' means?"

He blushed. "Ah, it's a little bloodsucker on Earth? My dad calls politicians leeches."

"No, dear. That's a leech, l-e-*E*-c-h. You mean l-e-*A*-c-h. Leach means to dissolve out by percolation through the soil, which is one of the steps in removing the selenium and copper. Leech and leach are homophones, words that sound the same but have different meanings. Continue, please."

"Lots of people helped by fertilizing the plants because the bugs here don't like 'em," he said. "The end of the second year was a good harvest. That's when they sent for animal embryos, and we had the first Harvest Fair."

He stopped, apparently done.

John had told Meriel a more complete story. The colony was not saved by the Council or the white-coated scientists who optimized nutritional output from the sophisticated hydroponics systems shipside. People got hungry, and while the leaders dawdled trying to figure out what to do, the colonists acted on their own. Thousands of technicians with calloused hands and dirty jeans with a feel for growing things—people more concerned with starving kids than control—left the ships for Haven and began experimenting. There, as with so many industries, science followed practice. The scientists were wise, collecting data and offering advice, but did not try to control the explosion of creativity. With so much experimentation, they quickly learned the simplest processes to remove the impurities.

The windows rattled again as the gray cloud reached the farm, and the schoolhouse shuddered from the wind and thunder. Dust seeped through the cracks around the doors in little streams and puffs, and Meriel felt the dryness in her throat. She smiled as the hair on her arm nearest the desk stood up due to the static electricity—a condition they would never allow onboard a spaceship.

"Thank you, Eddy," the teacher said. "Who's next?"

Amanda, a girl Sandy's age, strutted to the front. "My subject is farm animals."

"Go on, dear."

"The third year on Haven, our leaders sent away for animal embryos. Embryos are useless by themselves because there were no animal mothers here to develop them. So they also sent for replicator data sets to make artificial...wombs." Amanda blushed, and the class tittered.

According to John, when they placed those embryo orders, BioLuna knew it had lost its bet, and Haven would not die off but would survive.

Amanda continued, "They ordered embryos for all kinds of farm animals. They unfroze the cows, goats, and sheep first, and we'll judge the best of them at the fair next week."

The teacher rapped on her desk for attention. "How many of you have entered livestock at the Harvest Fair?"

Among the many children who raised their hands was Amanda. "They haven't defrosted all the species yet. The scientists are worried that some might not get along with the indin...indi...indigenous ones. For instance, the pets—"

The class erupted in excitement. "I wanna beagle!" one child cried.

"I want a rabbit!" shouted another.

The teacher spoke above the din. "That's what we worry about. As house pets, we love them, but dogs are exceptional hunters in packs. And rabbits can destroy an ecosystem."

"Like people, my dad says."

"But people have a choice; rabbit's don't. Please continue."

A fine mist clouded the schoolroom as Amanda continued her talk, but Meriel fell asleep in the midday heat with her head against the wall. Becky saw her and sat next to her until class was over for the day and the dust storm ebbed to a misty mud rain.

Meriel woke to pattering sounds from the schoolhouse roof and a tugging on her sleeve.

"Wake up, Merry L. Wake up!" Becky said. "Now's the time."

She opened her eyes to see Becky's big grin. "Time for what, hon?"

"Just come." She helped her to her feet. At the door, she dropped Meriel's hand and ran outside to join her sister.

With bare feet, the girls jumped in puddles and splashed in the mud, their hair matted and clothing soaked. The rain fell clear now and washed the dirt from the buildings until they shimmered. Some of the indigenous animals played in the water with the children, but Dumpy cowered under the schoolhouse stairs.

Sandy ran up to her with another smile. "Papa says it will be like this more often in forty years." She held out her hand. "Come, Merry," she said and led her outside.

Meriel stood in the warm rain, totally unaccustomed to so much water. Like spacers, Haveners conserved and recycled all their water, and this downpour was almost as strange to them as it was to her.

"Stand like this," Sandy said. With arms outstretched, she threw back her head, and opened her mouth. "It's like sparkles on your tongue!"

Lifting her face, Meriel felt the rain tickle her cheeks and forehead. Opening her mouth, she tasted the sweet water. The raindrops fell along her body and slithered down her arms and legs as if they were alive. She smiled and spun slowly with Becky on one hand and Sandy on the other, like she had never been a child.

***

Dumpy shivered beneath the schoolhouse stairs in the damp chill air after hiding all day. The children had left hours ago, but he had remained in his shelter, his eyes darting at every movement and flicker of light. His trembling subsided somewhat with the rain, but he still flinched at the occasional drops that fell from the eaves and lay in cold puddles in the yard.

After tensing into a crouch, he sprinted for John's farmhouse, dodged the puddles, and waddled up the stairs. He nosed open the screen door and ambled through the dark house.

A soft breeze blew through the windows and carried the scent of the two little ones, the only beings on the entire planet that had not threatened to kill him. Waddling down the hall, he looked for an empty space to hide and squeezed his nose through another door with a faint squeak. The odors of the two large ones drifted past him, and he froze as one of them sat up and pointed something at him.

***

The squeak bolted Meriel straight up in bed, her body covered in sweat and eyes wide with fear. Grabbing the stunner from the nightstand, she aimed at the small moving target in the doorway. But before her eyes focused, the shadow disappeared.

She scanned John's bedroom for danger, saw none, and let the weapon fall to her side with a slow exhale. Next to her, John turned in his sleep and flopped his arm on her lap.

The outside door was unlocked... With a gasp, she took the stunner and ran to the girls' room. There she found them sleeping and heard the soft purr of Sandy's snores.

A tremor within the pile of clothing strewn on the floor caused Meriel to raise her weapon again. She leaned over and lifted a pair of jeans to find Dumpy staring at her and shivering.

"I know how you feel," she said and dropped the pants. Sitting on the edge of Becky's bed, she laid the stunner in her lap and rested her head in her hands.

"What is it, M?" John asked when he entered the room.

"They're coming."

"Who?"

"Khanag. Biadez. All of them."

"How do you know?"

She shook her head. "I just feel it."

"Not tonight. You're safe here."

"No, John. I'm not and neither are you. Damn, they sent a whole fleet for Liz and me. What the hell are they going to do here?"

"It's not all about you, M. They can't all be trying to kill you."

"That's been a pretty good bet so far." She looked away. "I'm exposed here. There's too much land, and no way to see it all. Plenty of places to sneak up on us. God, I'm always jumpy and can't sleep."

"You belong here with us."

She shook her head again. "If BioLuna or Khanag or any of those creeps find me here, your family can get caught in the crossfire. Your farm is a big bull's-eye, and I'd be better off in space and a moving target."

"But they can't reach us here."

"Not now. Not yet. I'm safer on the run. And so are the girls if I'm not here."

"I'm not giving you up, M."

"I know," she said and kissed him.

"I don't want you to run."

"I need to go, John."

He put his arm around her. "Not tonight. After the fair, hon. We'll talk about it then. Now let's go to sleep. We're walking the fence tomorrow and need our rest."

She lay back in Becky's bed, and he sat in the chair by her side and held her hand. When she drifted off to sleep, Becky took her other hand and placed it on her heart.

***

Fritz Leung, admiral of the Arcadian Rangers, stood on the gold tee at the seventeenth hole, with a breathtaking view of Stillwater Cove. His scorecard showed fifteen over par for the course, and he anticipated winning a sizable bet from his partners. Adjusting his aim to accommodate the headwinds blowing in from the Pacific Ocean, he swung his club for a respectable hundred-and-sixty-yard drive down the holographic fairway.

This would be his last mission before retirement after nine successful campaigns in the Wars of Immigration, the latest in the Seiyei Expansion. It ran like clockwork now, and golf cut the tedium.

Unlike the fool who lost his forces at Haven a decade ago, Leung joined this battle with an unsullied reputation. A luxurious retirement at the behest of BioLuna awaited him rather than a meager apartment on Europa like the last idiot. He looked forward to a waterfront estate on Tranquility Lake on Luna 2, with excursions to Earth and lots of time to entertain the grandkids.

Admiral Leung had twenty-six ships in his assault fleet, each armed with space-to-ground missiles and lasers. Eight thousand mercenaries crowded those ships, along with atmospheric injection capsules and countless mechs and drones, all under the command of a seasoned officer corps. Their first step would be to take control of communications using the GCE, the Hydra, like at Seiyei Station.

A light flashed in the holo and he waved his club at it. "What is it, General?" he said and took a practice swing.

"I am sending the technician to you by shuttle," Khanag said.

"Thank you."

"Also, His Holiness the Archtrope sends his greetings and will join you at the capitol building in Stewardville after our victory."

He cringed. That was bad luck to count your chickens before the engagement has even begun. "Regards to the Archtrope and your…followers." He did not say what he really thought of Khanag's savages. "Remember—we lead. My ships need clear space when they jump in."

"Of course," Khanag said. "But please do not interfere when we arrive."

"Our nav is better than yours, General."

"We'll see, won't we?"

"And on the ground, keep your corsairs out of our fight. We don't want any friendly fire, do we?"

"Are we friendly now?"

"For the moment. Out." The admiral cut the connection and turned to his aide. "Bring the tech to me when he arrives."

After finishing the eighteenth hole, he swapped the holo of Pebble Beach to the view outside the ship. It was daylight here, on the far side of the gas giant, and the iridescent bands of light blue and orange gleamed in the sunlight. He could communicate with his fleet here, confident that radiation masked their EM.

"Sir," his aide said.

The admiral turned to his guest. "Ah, Mr. Matsushita, I hope your stay has been comfortable. The tools and parts you requested are in the shuttle waiting for you."

"You will keep your promise?"

"I'm an honorable man, and nothing like our…associates. You can speak to your family before you leave."

Matsushita fell to his knees and cried.

"There now, when your mission is over, you can join them. Are you ready?"

The technician nodded, but his back shuddered.

"We only need a few moments to…prepare the planet for your arrival," the admiral said and grasped the tech's shoulder. "Go now to your family." With a brief nod, his aide removed the technician.

The smile vanished from the admiral's face as a new guest arrived. "When will you deploy?"

"After the first wave and ordnance arrive, I'll finish the job our associates could not," said Benedict, the nondescript man.

***

Meriel sat with her back against the chuckwagon with Sandy snuggled under her arm and Becky asleep in her lap. Together they watched Thor set on the Western horizon and the stars that followed. Like John and the rest of the work crew, they were tired from the long three-day trek. Without it, the groundwater supply would remain uncertain and larger critters could sneak onto the farm through the gaps in the electric fence.

Much of the trek Meriel spent in the wagon so as to not slow them all down. Tomorrow morning, they would be home for the start of the Harvest Fair. And at the day's end, she would make her decision to leave or to stay, a decision she did not want to make.

"Do you know about the stars, hon?" Meriel said.

"Only to wish on."

"How?"

"Mommy said that everything that's made is made in stars, so wishing on 'em makes the wish stronger. Here, close your eyes and say after me.

> *"Star light, star bright,*
> *All the stars within my sight.*
> *Wish I may. Wish I might.*
> *Grant the wish I wish tonight."*

"That's it?"

"Yup. But then you have to cross your heart so the stars know you mean it."

Meriel did as instructed. "What did you wish for?"

"Oh, you can't tell your wish or the stars will forget."

"What star did you wish on?"

"Me? I wish on that big one there," Sandy said and pointed to a bright star to the South.

"That's Aldebaran, and the fuzzy patch there is the Pleiades. It's also called the Seven Sisters."

"Like Thor's moons."

"What, hon? I don't understand."

Sandy pointed to one of the bright unblinking objects in the sky. "Thor has eight moons, including Haven. We call the other moons our seven sisters."

Meriel grinned. "Well I'll be...," she murmured, thinking of her mother's nursery rhyme.

Sandy kept her eyes on Meriel. "Do you miss them?"

"Who?"

"I've watched you look at the stars, Merry. Are you going back to space?"

Perceptive girl. "I'm not sure, hon. I'm a spacer."

Sandy bit her lip and turned away.

"I talked to your father. It might not be safe for you to be around me."

"You're just saying that 'cause you want to leave."

"I don't think I would be a good mom."

"I don't need a mom. She's been gone a long time now, and no one could replace her anyway. I know Becky does, but that's only because she doesn't remember her much."

Maybe she does, and I won't match up. "I won't go away forever, hon. My family is coming here, and you are part of that. I'll always return."

"For them?"

"For you." She took Sandy's little hand. "You're like me when I was a kid. Strong. Full of ideas. And you love your little sister."

Sandy gazed at her with a smile. "Yeah."

They were silent for a while as a meteor arced across the sky.

"Merry, is space your home? Your song?"

"What do you mean, hon?"

"Like your home isn't a place but a journey."

"I don't understand."

"Our teacher told us about a place on Earth called Australia that's kinda like Haven—arid and has animals and people that don't live anywhere else. She said the native people don't have any place to settle down 'cause the land is poor and can't sustain them. But they have trails they walk over the course of a year or more." Sandy scooted over and between them drew an irregular shape in the dirt that returned to its starting point. "That was their route. And many tribes would walk the same land but have different routes." She drew other closed shapes that meandered back and forth and crossed each other. "And as they walked, they sang of the places they passed, the hills and the plants, their ancestors and the spirits. They called them songlines."

Meriel imagined tribes of people following Sandy's little fingers as she traced their trails in the dirt.

"You know them all, don't you?" Sandy asked. "All the stars."

She nodded. "Pretty much. One of the first things that spacers do when they arrive somewhere is to orient themselves to the stars and constellations."

"Tell me."

"Well, my first spacewalk was near Wolf 359. That's over there." A star hovered above the horizon, and she pointed to it. "That was the happiest day of my life, well, before I met you and your sister." She squeezed Sandy's hand. "My mom and pop were lost near Procyon. The *Princess* is docked there at Enterprise Station. Over there is Lalande 21185, close to where I met your father. That's behind Thor now, and you can't see it." Meriel took the fringe of Sandy's shirt between her fingers. "The Crab nebula glows a teal color like your sleeves."

"You make the stars real for me, Merry. That's your song. You just don't have a melody for it yet."

"My route could be my home?"

Sandy nodded and snuggled into her arms. "Just make part of it here with us."

Meriel hugged her and nudged Becky under her other arm so the three of them could stretch out. There they watched the last slice of Thor set with stories of the stars until Sandy fell asleep.

As Meriel drifted off to sleep, the memory returned of Liz and her sleeping in her father's arms after their adventure on the dino-sims. For the first time she realized what her father felt that day. "Oh, Papa," she murmured and tightened her embrace though the tears ticked her cheeks.

Chapter 14
The Tempest

Grace

"Psst, psst."

Meriel blinked. They were in the stuffy little country church where she had nodded off, tired from the prior long day and fitful sleep. She had spent the early morning primping Sandy and Becky for church and the Harvest Fair in dresses more elaborate and colorful than she had ever seen.

"Psst, psst." Little Becky stood next to her and tugged on her sleeve, signaling her to stand like her sister and the other parishioners. Meriel complied but gritted her teeth during the pastor's prayer for forgiveness. Becky brushed her arm for attention again and squinted to tell her to close her eyes. She did as instructed, but closing her eyes to pray was the reason she had dozed off to begin with. In another moment the service was over.

The girls took her arms and rushed her to the front of the line to greet Pastor Lee. This was the strategy they had developed to be first to the desserts on the lunch table, which the women set for the churchgoers. After finishing their sweets, they went to play with the neighbor kids.

"Hello, Ms. Hope." She turned to the voice, as a smiling pastor approached. He offered his hand to her, palm up. "May I bring you something from the buffet?"

"No, thank you," she said. Uncertain how to respond, she laid her hand on his and shook it.

"Was this your first time in church?" he asked and sat next to her.

She nodded. "I heard your sermon."

"You did?" He grinned. "I heard you snore."

From his steady smile, she inferred a tease rather than a complaint and smiled in return.

"I promise my message will be more enlivening next week," he said.

"It's not your fault. I'm not much good in church."

"You wear the cross."

She touched the medallion on her necklace. "This was my mom's. It's all I have left of her." *That and a junk of a ship that may never fly again.* "I don't know the rules in there."

He laughed with a deep, honest laugh. "It's not about rules, Ms. Hope. It's about this." He waved his arm to survey the church with families having lunch and the kids at play. "It's about living. People kind of lost that after thousands of years worshipping abstract things. It's really about the spirit, about what drives you, what keeps you going."

"I thought it was about our immortal souls."

"What does that mean to you, Ms. Hope?"

"Ah…I don't know."

"That's the problem. Soul became just another abstract concept. The Greek idea of soul and spirit came from observing real life. In Latin it's *anima*, like in animal. It meant the breath of life: what inspires us, what rouses us to action. Love drives it all: love for life, love of self, and love for others. And love is what JCS is all about."

"My mom told me the same thing." She turned to watch the girls at play.

"What's troubling you?"

"I have a problem loving others. Doesn't God say to forgive your enemies?"

"So you were listening. Yes, but it's not so simple as—"

She balled her fists in her lap. "Well, I can't forgive."

He paused. "I can't pretend to know what you endured, Ms. Hope."

She flinched in anticipation of "poor dear" delivered in a tone of pity, which did not come. "You've all had your own struggles here, and I'm not looking for sympathy."

"Our trials don't apply to you. Tests of the spirit are always personal. I do know that focusing on those who hurt you leads you away from life. We've heard your story, and—"

"Then you know I will never love them, and I can never forgive them." She clenched her teeth.

"They need God's grace, not yours, and all they have to do is accept it. But this is about you."

"Doesn't God command us to forgive?"

"More of a request, really, but you have a choice. It's not about submitting to God's will or obeying some instructions for being a good person."

"Then why?"

"Because God's concern is for *you*, Ms. Hope. Focusing on the pain distracts you from living a full life of your own. That doesn't mean opening yourself up to repeated harm by pretending it didn't happen. God doesn't ask you to trade your safety for your salvation."

"It says that in the gospels?"

He smiled. "I'm sure it's in there somewhere."

Meriel dropped her gaze and clenched her fists again. "Do I need to forgive before I can find peace?"

"You've been carrying this with you a long time, no?"

She nodded.

"I've seen you with John and the girls, Ms. Hope. You have love in your heart. Live fully. Peace will come in time. But don't forget; Haven is a frontier out here in more ways than one. Don't let your kind heart blind you to evil."

"Is that what JCS says?"

"No, that's what a country preacher says," he said, and she noticed the blaster at his hip blink to signal a full charge.

John walked up to them with plates of food in his hands. "Morning, sir."

The pastor rose and helped him with the plates. "Mornin', John." He turned back to her. "Well, Ms. Hope. I look forward to seeing you here again next Sunday."

She nodded and watched him leave, then turned to John. "You called him 'Sir?'"

"Pastor Lee. He's a colonel in the militia. I report to him. He lost his wife and two sons with Annie at Kilgore." Waving to the girls, John called, "Becky! Sandy! The fair is waiting."

Soon after they arrived, John left for a Grange meeting, leaving Meriel to navigate the fair with his girls. All day she marveled at the event, which was so big and crowded it seemed the entire planet attended.

The whole idea of a fair was foreign to Meriel. Spacers never had them; ships never stopped working and never stopped in the same place very long. Even if stations would permit so many spacers to assemble, there would be the problem of dock space and the likelihood of riots.

The bright colors she found were just as foreign. Spacers wore subdued clothing and reserved the primary colors to signal function and safety; only inside white-zone or a pleasure-cruise ship might a spacer find color for color's sake. But Haveners wore their brightest colors at the fair, though not in the same hues: reds on Haven were the yellow-red of sunset, not H-alpha, and greens were chlorophyll rather than O III. They blazed through the haze so vividly she teased John about being visible from space.

This was the annual day of thanks for the blessings God had given them. After a hundred years of just scraping by, the L5ers knew how to make the most of this marginal environment and made it bloom. They knew Haven was a gift that twenty-five billion other humans around the galaxy had not been given, and they shed blood to keep it.

With no experience of their parents' hardships, the young enjoyed themselves without reservation, as if this were their birthright. Their energy drove the crowd with the rhythm of a common heartbeat.

Throughout the fair appeared the familiar cross within an oval symbol of the Church of Jesus Christ Spacemen. Just as common, the spirals representing the Haven system appeared in brilliant colors quilted on bedspreads and drawn on everything from toys to farm machinery.

"Hey, M."

Meriel turned to see Elizabeth with Cookie and a young Marine lieutenant.

"Hey, sprites," Elizabeth said, and the two girls jumped to hug her and then attacked Cookie. She took Meriel's arm. "You look happy, Mom."

"I'm not their mom."

"Too late. They're not giving you a vote, Sis. You gonna stay?"

"Maybe. For a while longer."

"You love him, huh?"

"Yeah, but he needs to be with his girls."

"What about them?"

"I love 'em too, but I can't bring them with me."

"That's not what they need now."

"The *Princess* is our dream, Liz."

"I'm not sure I'm so ambitious, M. But I understand. You're twenty-two and just starting out. You know the kids aren't all gonna settle here."

"I know. Tommy and Sam are likely to renew their contracts, and Erik loves open space."

"And they won't all jump to the *Princess* when she's fixed up.

"Sure, but this will be an option for them. They'll have a place here regardless and a ship, if they want her. That's what our folks wanted."

Elizabeth nodded. "Penny just passed her medic-two exams. Turns out she's a genius." She caught her sister's quiet mood. "What is it, Sis?"

"I'm afraid I'll lose what I have here if I leave."

"And rightly so. But you can just freeze some eggs somewhere. The kids and I will pick out a papa for them."

"I'll pick out the father of my children myself, thank you very much."

"Well, you better do something to lock down John. Jerri is still on the loose, and Socket plans to take a long vacation planetside next week."

"I think she plans to vacation with Cookie."

"About time. Hey, M, I'm bored. Abrams here has offered to take us on a tour of Johnston Rift, where the Haven Marines train. Want to come?"

"He's cute," she said with another smile. "You found him, or he found you?"

"He thinks he found me and wants to winch me in."

"Cookie's your chaperone?"

"For a while. If I need him."

"What about Tommy?" Meriel asked.

"Old news, M. He just won't let it go."

"Don't break his heart."

Elizabeth shrugged. "Too late. C'mon. Bring the girls. Abrams says that it's nearly abandoned. Most of the Marines are here."

A frown crossed Meriel's face. "Really? They're not on duty?"

"Lighten up, girl. They lifted the embargo, and LeHavre will know if hostiles wink-in. C'mon. You can distract Cookie."

Her sister's gay mood dispelled her anxiety, and she smiled. "Thanks for the invite, hon, but John will be back soon. You go have some fun."

Elizabeth kissed her on the cheek and turned to wave. "See ya back home. I mean at the farm."

***

John returned from his meeting and found them a place on a ridge to watch the sun set. The girls had finally settled down, tired from playing with neighboring children. When he sat, Sandy sat next to him and leaned against his arm while Becky nestled into Meriel's lap.

"Little girls are blurry whirls," he said.

She nodded while weaving tiny flowers into constellations in Becky's hair. Becky aimed the toroidal device at native varmints and made the world safe for children again.

"John, Liz told me most of the Marines are here at the fair. I think you should tell Colonel Lee—"

John was agitated about something and did not hear her. "The girls came to me last night and asked me if you could stay with us."

Becky crossed her fingers and closed her eyes, while Meriel gazed at him with a soft smile.

He took her hand. "Darling, stay. We love you. There's nowhere else in the whole universe you're happier than here, and I can't live without you. Together we can make this farm work and quit our wandering. Meriel, I—"

Fireworks behind them interrupted his proposal, and they turned to watch. When the spectacle ended, the smoke cleared, and the spiral arms of the Milky Way rose at a shallow angle. The racket hushed to whispered sighs, and everyone stared with wonder.

There are worlds out there, uncounted worlds within our reach, where the future shines bright like here on Haven. These L5ers are spacers, and the night is space to them; life. They know our destiny is out there, calling us, but you can only hear it clearly from out here.

Meriel noticed Sandy walk to the hilltop a few feet away and lift her head to the stars in the direction of Aldebaran rising to the south. She murmured something and crossed her heart. Meriel smiled with a guess about what Sandy wished for and turned back to see John grinning at her.

Above them, stars twinkled extra bright within the rising galaxy and new pops announced a late round of fireworks. But this series was odd, with no rocket trail and fewer sparklers and streamers. The flashes extended to encircle the fairgrounds.

John's link flashed, and he checked it. "Time to go, kids. We've gotta move. Now."

"They're not fireworks, are they?" Meriel whispered.

He shook his head. "Wait here. I'll bring the wagon around," he said and took off at a run.

Unable to run, she watched the lights in the sky with the girls. Flares followed the explosions, but just before reaching the ground, they slowed. *Just like a Marine.*

John rode up in the wagon, and they got in.

"They're here, aren't they?" she said, and he nodded.

"Who's here?" Sandy asked.

"The bad guys."

Nemesis

Elizabeth sat in the backseat of Lieutenant Abrams's small Armored Personnel Carrier and viewed the same fireworks through the rooster tail of dust thrown up behind them. Cookie relaxed in front, appearing comfortably at home with a hand on the barrel of the EMP cannon mounted between the seats. The show ended, and she turned forward to the narrow dirt road lit by the terrain lights mounted above the windshield. Another set of explosions, closer to their position, rocked the jeep.

"Sonic boom. Those aren't fireworks," Cookie shouted. "More like drone capsules. Paratroopers will be close behind."

Abrams nodded. "They're heading for the Johnston Rift."

"They'll roll over John's farm on the way," she said. "We need to stop them."

"You're civilians here," Abrams said.

"You think they're gonna let us go just 'cause we didn't fight?" Cookie said. "We can help."

Abrams's link buzzed. "They've turned off the evaporators. Dust storm's on the way."

A squadron of flying drones streaked past and peppered them with small-caliber slugs. One of them hit Abrams in the leg, and their jeep skidded off the road. Three drones remained back while the others continued on their mission.

Elizabeth took his sidearm and knocked down one drone. A second shot nicked another, which spun and killed the third. "Like he said, we can help."

"The nearest bivouac is up ahead. Fort Bantu," Abrams said with a groan. "It protects this side of the valley. There might be a few who aren't at the fair. Follow this road."

After tightening a compression seal on Abrams's leg, Cookie gave him a shot of painkiller. Elizabeth took the wheel, and they sped away.

Drones, flying and crawling, flowed across the road toward the valley on their right. Before they could target the APC or avoid it, she plowed into them, leaving a trail of debris behind.

Cookie harnessed himself to the cannon, and his finger never left the trigger. "How much juice has this got?" he shouted.

"It's run off the fuel cells," Abrams yelled back. "As much as you need until the H_2 runs out. Then one last discharge."

The trio raced past most of the drones and spotted the lights from the base's guard shack less than a quarter mile ahead.

Abrams's link squawked, and he turned up the volume. "Evacuate Fort Bantu," the message said. "Missile defense sabotaged."

She stopped the jeep as they glanced up to see missile trails streaking toward their destination. "Crap! Where do we go now?"

Abrams responded with a snore.

Cookie shook him. "Where to, boss?"

"Turn right and straight on till dawn," Abrams mumbled with a wave of his hand and a laugh. He groaned, his head bobbing like a doll's.

Spinning the wheel, she gunned the APC. A half mile away, the missiles hit the base, lifting it—dirt and all—forty feet into the air where it exploded into flame. The shock wave hit them from behind, jolted them forward, and lifted the rear of the vehicle.

"Johnston Rift is to the right," Cookie said, as dirt and smoking debris fell around them. "Kilgore's on the other side."

Abrams nodded and pointed ahead. "Follow the drones."

Within a few hundred yards, they caught up to the drones heading to the valley, and Cookie turned the EMP turret to clear their path.

She sped through the obstacle course of mechanical debris, but the road dropped over the bank, exposing a mech crawler twice as large as their vehicle. The wheels lost traction, and the APC slammed into a leg of the crawler, flipped, and threw them to the dirt.

The crawler wheeled and fired lasers, slug throwers, and energy weapons in all directions. With one leg disabled, it hobbled over and inspected the APC with a sensor stalk. It detected a reflection in the mirror and opened fire again, leaving a smoking crater where the vehicle had lain.

Twenty yards away, Elizabeth whistled. The crawler's sensors whipped toward the unfamiliar sound, and she fired the last charge from the EMP cannon. The crawler collapsed in a heap with electricity arcing between its appendages.

Abrams signaled them to head to a bunker at the top of the cliffs. After stumbling on his first step, Cookie threw him over his shoulder like a toy and carried him up the trail. She followed, dragging her useless cannon.

Another crawler detected them, extrapolated their destination, and directed its firepower and that of the nearby drones to the bunker. The entire hilltop erupted in flames, and the mechs and drones returned to their primary mission.

***

John drove the horses through the darkness led by a tiny drone that flew ahead of them to illuminate the road. The open wagon lurched and bumped over the unpaved road, while the young girls held on in the rear-facing seat behind them. Around them, the stars outlined the native vegetation and twinkled with entry of drone capsules.

"Where are we going, John?" Meriel asked above the thundering hooves.

"To Grassley. The nearest militia staging area is there."

"What about the girls?"

He checked the sky again. "We dug caverns and tunnels for the non-combatants. They'll be safe there, and we can hold out for years."

"Why didn't you tell me before this?"

"I'm telling you now."

She frowned at his reply but understood his anxiety.

When silhouettes of the church and shop buildings appeared on the horizon against the spray of stars, John stopped the horses and turned off the drone.

Meriel put her hand on his leg. "Why are we stopping?"

"The lights are off. The lights are never off."

"What about the militia?"

"We're the militia." He stood to survey the area. "They must have deployed."

"Or never arrived."

John nodded. "This entrance will be sealed or compromised." He tapped his link. "The evaporators are off. We need to find shelter before the storm hits."

"Where can we go?"

He turned the horses north and flicked the reins. "Home. To hide. If Khanag is coming for us, our Marines know where we live."

"Khanag may know as well."

"We're not defenseless."

Explosions lit up the night sky to the northwest, and light beams cut through the smoke and flickered.

"That's Johnston Rift," he said. "They blow ice into the air to scatter the lasers."

She remembered that was Elizabeth's destination and tapped her link.

```
Heading to the farm. You OK?
```

He turned his gaze west, and when he turned forward again, she caught his creased brow.

"Why the look?"

"I don't see the defense of Stewardville yet. There should be the trails of rail-guns."

Small robots like spiders crossed the road ahead of them, heading for the valley. He ran over those in their path, but that did not stop the others. "Bugs. Drones."

She scanned into the sky "Is LeHavre defended?"

"Not well, why?"

"The orphans from the *Princess*. I don't know what they have up there to defend them and—"

"Let's defend ourselves first."

"—and that's our only escape route."

Floodlights illuminated the farm compound when they arrived, but that was normal for early evening when everyone celebrated at the fair. On the horizon, they could see the approaching dust cloud covering the low stars and rising galaxy.

"Sandy, Becky, get your pellet guns and dust gear," he said as he unhitched the horses and slapped them to run them off. Then he opened the barn door to let the sheep and goats free.

They entered a kitchen large enough to feed the entire work crew during harvest. The girls ran for their weapons, and he led Meriel to a locked closet. From it, he removed stunners for each of them, a shoulder-mounted rifle with a sniper scope, and a canvas duffle.

"Nothing bigger?" Meriel asked.

"Anything bigger and we'll blast each other."

"I'm not up to a fight, John."

"Don't worry, M. The Marines will be here."

Soon, I hope, she thought and inspected the rifle. "Slug shooter?"

"Pneumatic and hypersonic. No tracer rounds, no muzzle flash, no laser trail."

The girls returned with their pellet rifles and reported for duty with a vague salute. "By the windows," he said. "Shoot the drones and bugs flying or crawling. Anything bigger than a sheep, it's a mech, and you gotta hide. Got it?" They nodded and went to their post. As their rifles popped, he headed for the front porch for a view of the main road.

Meriel shook her head. "Paratroopers, John. They don't need a road." She led him back to the kitchen to survey the compound. "We won't be able to see much in a dust storm. Do you have proximity alarms? Something to tell us when they arrive?"

He smiled, reached into the canvas bag, and produced a small metal box with switches. From the bag he also removed two pairs of tiny goggles and gave one to her.

Her eyes narrowed. *What are these gonna do?* "What do you have up your sleeve?"

The rattle of the windows caught his attention. "OK, girls. Gear up and into the shelter, now. And take the stunners."

Becky took the toroidal device from her belt and gave it to Meriel as she passed. "I got ten, I'm sure."

Sandy frowned. "Then I must'a got fifteen."

"But yours were small," Becky said and stepped into the kitchen closet.

"No, they weren't!"

Just as the girls closed the door, the dust storm engulfed the compound with winds much stronger than the day in the schoolhouse. The wind blew the flying droids away, but the crawling droids simply dropped their center of gravity.

After pressing a button on the box, a holo of the entire farm popped up. Red dots moved toward the middle of the screen and approached a series of concentric circles. He tapped the side of Meriel's goggles and then his own.

The goggles cast a head-up display of the same dots, grid, and symbols shown on the panel but oriented to her field of view. Objects outside that range collapsed to the edges of her peripheral vision so a foe could not surprise her. Contrast enhancements glowed to highlight moving objects. It appeared she could see through the walls, since the sensor array was outside the kitchen,

Turning around to scan the front of the house and the road, no dots appeared. Instead, the dots headed for the farm from the rear and resolved into figures as they approached.

Without this tool, the dust storm would blind them. *This is Marine equipment, maybe better.* "Not defenseless, huh."

Static crackled in the air. Lightning flashed, and her goggles fogged momentarily to protect her eyes. After each flash, one of the red lights blinked and died.

She raised the toroid to John's view. "I saw the girls playing with this. What is it?"

"Dunno. It's from Annie's kit. She set up the defenses here. Took the bag with her on her last mission."

"To kill the Hydra?"

He nodded.

"What does it do?"

"Really, M, I don't know, and I don't care right now. Pay attention."

She set the device back on the counter but pondered it.

John fiddled with the box, and bright flashes beamed from the tops of the buildings. Attackers fired at the flashes, which allowed John's defense grid to confirm their locations and weaponry. Once identified, a concussion device, such as the one John had used at Wolf Station, exploded nearby. Following each blast, some of the dots on the panel turned still and gray while others reached the red line.

Another switch activated focused EMP devices and caused her hair to fluff. The EMPs made all electronic weapons and drones useless, but soldiers would still be alive and dangerous.

"Annie built these for the second attack by BioLuna," he said over the growling wind.

Some small devices exploded, and one red dot dimmed and disappeared. Every few seconds, yellow beams shot from the roofs, and other dots blinked out.

"Three-hundred-nanometer maser," he said. "The yellow tracers come from different locations to warn us. They won't see the source, but neither can we."

Most of the defenses were spent when a squad of drones crawled up and circled the farmhouse where they hid. Across the kitchen, an odd link beeped and blinked. She went to check.

```
From: S. K.
Please pick up.
```

She tapped the link and a holo appeared of a man in black uniform lounging on a bridge chair. It was General Khanag. Without thinking, she cringed and her stomach tightened. Struggling to focus, she closed her eyes and clenched her fists so tight her fingernails bit into her palms.

"Ah, there you are, Ms. Hope. You've given me great distress."

"What do you want?"

"Your mates from the *Princess* have remained elusive, so I have had to improvise." A slight delay in response implied his message originated from space. "Mr. Smith, your farm is surrounded, and our ordnance is set to destroy you. A well-fought defense, but in the end, it is inadequate to the task— like all the works of unbelievers. Your daughters cannot survive, Smith."

The link projected a picture of Sandy and Becky entering the closet. Another view of them joined the first. Then four, and then eight—one from each drone.

"You bastard!" John shouted.

"Yes, yes. They say that of all audacious visionaries. Your weapons are useless, Smith. We have many more corsairs than you have defenses. Witness."

One of the drones spun in the compound and set fire to the barn with laser blasts.

"OK, where do you want me?" Peering out the window she searched for a path to draw the attackers away, but the storm and lightning still raged. She turned back to the link. "I'll trade myself for them, of course."

Khanag laughed. "Oh, no, Ms. Hope, there is no chance any of you will escape. I wish you to see them die first, slowly. Like all of those close to you when they arrive."

"You're just a cold-hearted thug," she said.

John shook his head and signaled her to keep talking while he reprogrammed the control box.

"Hardly," Khanag said. "My corsairs and I value all life. The prophet tells us that ending a single life is like killing all humanity. Everyone should have the choice to accept his teachings and submit to his mercy. You were given the opportunity aboard the *Princess* ten years ago, and you declined."

"I was a child, and you didn't ask."

"Your parents chose for you, and they paid for their lack of vision."

"You tortured them."

"Ah, yes, my interrogation team. You've seen their work. I should rein them in, but they do enjoy it so. And they are effective."

"What did they tell you?" she asked and wiped away the tears to see the dots on her display move closer.

"I truly don't remember," Khanag said with a chuckle, "but like them, you declined. Now you are anathema and have less value than an insect I might grind under my boot."

Lightning struck nearby, and thunder followed almost immediately. Static crackled the air, and she touched the metal cabinet to ground herself.

She glanced at John, who tapped feverishly on the little keypad. *Stall*, she thought. "I'll convert. Without conditions."

"Ah, now you understand."

"I'll make it public and wear the veil. I'll be the most celebrated convert in history, your former victim, granting forgiveness. The pr... publicity will be invaluable," she said, avoiding the first word that came to mind: *propaganda*.

"Yes, useful. This was foretold."

"By who?"

"The prophet himself, the Archtrope."

"And the girls would be safe?"

John raised his index finger.

"There can be no conditions, Ms. Hope. They, like you, would be at the Archtrope's mercy. But he may be generous."

"You discussed this with him?"

"Of course, but your turning up alive after this incident would be…problematic." The holo vanished.

"Khanag?"

"I am grateful for our little conversation, Ms. Hope," he continued. "Had you died here without giving us a chance to record your voice and mannerisms, my mission would have failed. Your usefulness is at an end now, and your avatar will suffice. Let's see. Who dies first?"

"But you have to do what the Archtrope says!"

"Don't be silly. He is my spiritual guide, not my commander," Khanag said, but she could barely hear him over the howling wind.

John tapped a toggle on the box and showed it to her. "It's all wired to this now. But don't—" A bright-red spot distracted them, a spot that moved across his chest to his stomach. He dropped his gaze, and the spot exploded in blood. He lurched back and fell to the floor. Meriel grabbed a can from Annie's kit and sprayed a compress on the wound.

"Yes, he will die slowly with a stomach wound," Khanag said, "long before you. What a glorious day this will be. I will secure a home for my people and wreak my vengence."

Her question *vengence for what?* dissolved in her anxiety. "Please, spare the girls. I'll surrender to you," she said and caught the weapons box that slipped from John's hand.

"No, Ms. Hope. We're not done. Yes, I understand you would sacrifice yourself for them, even if you don't believe in our cause."

She fumbled with the box, trying to configure it. "Of course I would."

"You are much like me, putting your people ahead of yourself."

"My kids?"

"And my archers, as they are called. Like you, I am loyal to those I care for."

Two red spots from laser sights shivered on the closet door.

"You have no idea who I am, thug. Maybe you didn't get the message, but I'm not that helpless little kid who had to hide while you butchered my family and friends."

She hit a switch on the box. An explosion flared in the field, and the red spots disappeared.

He laughed. "Defiant to the last."

Five new red spots converged on the door.

"Damn you!" She hit two more switches. Four of the spots vanished, but ten new spots shone on the door.

"No, no, no," she muttered while struggling to configure the box and dropped it. The tart smell of ozone caused her to look up. Just above her head, a laser beam sliced through the kitchen walls toward the red spots on the door.

"Soon now," Khanag said.

"You're not hurting my kids!" She held the medallion of JCS on her necklace for a moment and closed her eyes.

"It's not up to you."

"Go to Hell," she said and hit all the switches on the box.

The lights and defensive weapons in the yard dimmed as a low rumble from the generator shook the kitchen. Sensing the weakened defenses, the mechs charged the farmhouse and climbed the porch. But they stopped and whirled their weapons at the sound of a metallic click from the yard.

A bright flash lit up the compound like a dockside construction site and cast her silhouette on the closet door. In that split second, the glare froze the dust in midair. The texture of the boards on the kitchen wall, the tear in the screen door, and the shadows of the mechs that targeted her impressed their images on her retina before her goggles could fog.

She turned her head and began to raise her arm to protect her face, and a millisecond later, the farm erupted in flames. The blast blew open the door and threw Meriel to the back wall.

***

Elizabeth, Cookie, and Abrams reached the rubble of the hilltop bunker as explosions lit up the sky over the range of low hills to the west. Flaming debris arched over the approaching dust cloud.

Her brow furrowed. "That's the direction of John's farm. Meriel and the girls are there. All that hardware will grind them up."

"Focus," Cookie said. "We'll not be able to help her if we die here."

Beside them, Abrams sat on a square of concrete and rocked back and forth, moaning with his head on his fists. He waved away her offer of another dose of painkiller.

"I can't fight on that stuff," he said.

She lifted her head to the sky, took a deep breath, and let it out slowly.

"You worried?"

"I have a friend up there," she said and turned to view the valley with them.

From the unrestricted outlook afforded by the bunker, they surveyed their situation. Below them, thousands of armed mechs and drones scoured the valley floor, but their only weapon, her EMP cannon, required a power source they did not have.

Cookie pointed to the laser trails above the dust cloud far to the west.

"That's Stewardville," Abrams said.

"If they're aiming for it, they're horrible shots."

"'cause of the shields."

"But you can't shield—" Elizabeth began.

Abrams interrupted. "It's not a barrier. It confuses the targeting computers. Like camouflage."

"They can't keep up that rate of energy use unless their aim improves," Cookie said. "Do we have a shield like that here?"

Abrams looked around the rubble. "Not anymore."

"Then what do we have to fight back with, sir?" Cookie asked.

Abrams aimed his link at a door in the side of the bunker, and a light changed color. "Push the button."

When Elizabeth did as ordered, a meter-thick blast door swung in to expose an arsenal with an assortment of ordnance.

Cookie placed his fists on his hips. "This I like," he said and walked over to an antique twentieth-century minigun, a small Gatling gun with six rotating barrels. He strapped the harness to his shoulders and slung the weapon in front of him.

Abrams grimaced and limped over. "You like that? Then you're really gonna like this." He hobbled over to a metal cabinet that held a laser gatler: a huge, but lightweight, weapon with shoulder straps and a series of ten tubes that rested on a hip. "The lasers run hot, and the focusing pipes warp, so we alternate them every hundred milliseconds or so. Capacitor is below us." He pointed to a thick cable.

"Oorah!" Cookie said over the roar of wind from the approaching storm.

Elizabeth pointed to another blast door at the opposite end of the armory. "Where does that go?"

"To the tunnels. They lead to caverns were we can hole up in a siege."

"They're fixed assets," Cookie said. "Easy to target."

"The tunnels are reconfigurable. They're traps. We hope they attack them."

Abrams tossed goggles and masks to them. "Here, you'll need these." He found another cable for Elizabeth's cannon, and the three of them set up their defense on the broken ramparts as the dust storm rushed toward them.

In the distance, the gray cloud swallowed everything in its path as it swept through the valley. The mechs vanished, but reappeared briefly when lightning burst within the storm.

Cookie turned to her. "Did you decide yet?"

"About what?"

"Bridge or Marines."

"Kinda busy now."

"You like it, or you don't. Now's the time, you know," he said.

"It's not about the fight, Sergeant. It's about the why. It's about the what for."

"Same thing."

"'Sides, I'm not much good with rules and orders."

After a nod, he glanced back to the valley. "Runs in your family." He turned to Abrams with eyes narrowed. "You mentioned holing up for a siege, sir. You expecting to lose?"

"No. But we could lose the battle on the surface for a while."

"How long is 'a while?'"

"Maybe two years."

"Living on rations in a cave will be hell. Especially for the children."

"We're planning on surviving, Sergeant. It shouldn't be anywhere near that long. The invaders can't keep up a siege with a fifteen light-year supply line. They need to win quick or leave."

Cookie nodded toward the rift. "Then what are they waiting for?"

Abrams scanned the valley again. "The techs to catch up." He struggled to his feet, flipped the goggles down, and adjusted the magnification.

"Why the look, sir?" Elizabeth asked.

"This isn't in our playbook. If they're heading for town, why didn't they land closer? Why are they committing so many resources over there at Kilgore?"

After zooming in on the area on his own goggles, Cookie sat back and exhaled slowly. "Where's the Hydra, Lieutenant?"

"Uh…what's left of it is in the complex. But it's broken, and we can't fix it. We tried for years."

Cookie pointed to a massive building overlooked by a hill. Behind it, drones gathered with unarmed technicians and grav-sleds loaded with equipment. "Is that it?"

She frowned. "Is that what?"

"The Hydra."

Abrams's jaw dropped. "Crap, it's in there. But it's broken."

"Yeah, so you said. They built it; maybe they can fix it."

"If they can, we're in trouble," He tapped his link, but his hands shook. He closed his eyes and tightened his fists.

Before he fainted, Cookie caught him. "You've lost a lot of blood, soldier. Better sit."

"Sorry," Abrams said.

Headquarters answered his call, and he told them of the activity near the Hydra. "Yes, sir." He turned to his team. "Seems they think they can use it. Our mission is here. Colonel Lee is on the other side. Our job is to pound them and thin out their forces so the infantry can move in."

"What else?" Cookie said.

Abrams nodded. "They're not telling me everything." He pointed to flashes above the dust cloud in the direction of the Capitol. "Stewardville is under attack from the south, but they're not surrendering." The valley began to stir. "Here they come."

Not just drones, but mechs and men on ATVs raced to the building housing the Hydra. Seconds later, the valley undulated with moving equipment.

Cookie turned on the laser gatler, and the armature spun up to a loud whine. They opened fire and so did soldiers in the bunkers across the valley floor. The sea of mechs and drones passing before them returned fire, and the battlefield filled with light.

Cookie stood atop the rubble for better shooting. The gun on his hip spat laser blasts, making the power cable glow with overcurrent and casting a giant shadow behind him. At his side, Elizabeth kept the drones away with the EMP cannon. All around them, ricochet blooms rose and concrete chips flew, shredding Cookie's pant leg and one scratching Elizabeth's cheek. With crossfire from the bunker on the opposite ridge, they thinned out the invading forces.

Roaring into the valley below them, the dust storm dissolved the invaders in haze and swatted the drones from the air. The goggles protected the defenders from the stinging grit, but still they could barely find their targets.

The heavy dust scattered the pulses from Cookie's laser gatler, forcing him to change weapons. He grabbed the minigun, returned to the wall, and sprayed the valley with slugs, shouting curses through the roar of the wind and scream of the minigun.

Lightning flashed brighter and more often, outlining individual targets within the murk. One bolt struck nearby and blew them off their feet. When their goggles cleared, a smoking hole appeared. Plasma arcs danced between the fluorescing ground and the twitching hulks of mechs in various stages of disassembly.

They turned their dirt-streaked faces to Abrams and pointed to the crater.

"Nothing to worry about," he yelled above the wind. "Bunker's insulated. Hell of a show, huh?"

Cookie shook his head and resumed strafing the valley.

The dust storm passed, and they continued to fire into the thick haze. When the minigun ran out of slugs, Cookie let it spin down and dropped it to the ground where the hot barrels started a blaze in the native brush.

"Feel better?" she asked.

"Much," he said and sat.

Abrams's link chattered. "They're getting overrun. That means suicide for the defenders."

Cookie grabbed a blaster and rose. "Let's go down there and help them."

"No," Abrams said. "Orders are to stick."

Elizabeth zoomed her goggles but could make out little through the murky haze. She switched to infrared and saw men entering the Hydra complex, and a few seconds later, the lights flickered and died.

"Crap, they're overrun," she said.

Even from far away, they could hear the shouts of "Subedei!"

"Damn," Cookie said. "Archers, too."

"They must have turned it on," Cookie said. "Can you still hear your HQ?"

"Affirmative. We're hardened. We thought they had another of these things and prepared." He pointed a thumb at the nearby laser line-of-sight transceiver. "There's only one thing we can't protect from it...."

A mech blew the LOS transceiver away, and Abrams frowned.

Their primary mission achieved, the drones converged on the defensive bunkers, and fire rocked their position again. Cookie spun up his laser gatler again, and Elizabeth recharged the cannon.

A quarter-hour later, the debris of hundreds of droids and mechs littered the slope in front of the bunker, but they did not stop. Just when it appeared the defenders would be overwhelmed, the attacking drones retreated. In that moment of peace, Abrams sat with his back against a broken slab of concrete while Elizabeth checked his compress.

Cookie stood to survey the battlefield and lifted his brow. "That's unexpected." He raised his head to the sky. "What's that one thing you can't protect from the Hydra?"

"The missile defense shield," Abrams replied.

Cookie pointed up. Through the clearing haze and blinking stars above them, missile trails headed their way, and space-based pulse lasers ignited the dirt around them.

Elizabeth grabbed Cookie's hand.

"Into the bunker! Now!" Abrams yelled.

**

Meriel awoke and felt the dry tenderness of the sunburn on her face from the explosion. She blinked to clear her eyes of the afterimage of the mechs and found the entire kitchen filled with smoke and haze. The storm had passed, and the wind subsided so that only the occasional pop or buzz from small-arms or laser fire broke the silence. All the windows were blown out, and the door groaned twice and crashed to the floor. Two knocks in reply to hers told her the girls were all right.

The compress on John's wound held, and she placed her ear to his chest to verify his breathing. She brushed her hand over his forehead, unable to do anything else without help. But this was the frontier, and there would be no help unless she brought it.

Cautious, she peered outside for an escape route. A dense, dirty fog blanketed the compound, lit only by the flash of laser. Toward the yard, the red lights of aggressors appeared on her goggles: the flying droids were back and looking for targets. She stepped outside, and they raked the porch with lasers. Grabbing the pneumatic rifle, she lay prone by the kitchen door.

Smoke and dust obscured everything, but the sharp outlines of threats appeared on the goggles. The riflescope synced with the display, showing her the exact positions of the hostiles and where her shots would land. Targeting the drones first, she picked off each new target that came into her field of view until she ran out of slugs.

Sweat clouded her vision, and she removed the goggles to wipe her eyes. But the goggles had cut deeply into the bridge of her nose, and her hand came away bloody.

The battle was not over, she knew. There were still soldiers and droids loose, any one of which could kill them. Without weapons or the strength in her legs to support her martial skills, she was an ineffective defense. But it did not matter if she were tired or injured; she was all that kept John and his girls alive.

While staying below the counter to avoid the droids, her search uncovered only slivers of metal and a board with exposed studs, which she hung on her belt. Annie's empty bag lay in the debris and under it Becky's toroidal device. Picking it up, she sat next to John with her back against the wall.

She held the device in her hand and pressed all the buttons in all combinations but produced only the familiar hum. Her link was dead and could not help her read or identify the numbers etched along the inside circumference. It glowed when she pushed the right button, but nothing else. Frustrated, she threw it on the floor and glared at it.

In the hazy dark kitchen, the light blue glow of the torus and black center bar reminded her of a cat's eye. She frowned and played with her pendant.

"It's all here," her mother had told her.

A cat's eye, like the one on the crate on the Princess. A minor detail from the nightmare she had relived thousands of times. She examined the string of numbers now clearly visible in the glow from the torus. *XE-M446-...Mil-tech. The same one I queried on Wolf. The Hydra?*

"Not a cat's eye, a snake's eye," she mumbled. *But how does it work?* Forgetting her need to hide, she snatched up the device again and banged it repeatedly on the floor. The banging brought attention she did not expect.

At the sound of creaking, she jammed the device in her belt, grabbed the nail-studded board and rolled next to the interior door leading to the front porch. A black-suited man appeared in the doorway, scanned the room, found John, and raised his blaster. With the edge of the board, she hit him in the back of the knee, between his calf and thigh armor, and he collapsed, dropping his weapon. Then she whacked him in the helmet with the nails, seized the blaster, and shot the next man who came through the door.

Another creak came from the porch, and she turned. A big shadow standing in the empty doorframe. The smoke cleared, and he stepped into the light—the nondescript man who had followed her on Lander and Etna—an assassin.

"Well, Ms. Hope, we finally meet," he said.

She pointed the blaster at him, but they could both see the charge light blinking yellow, and nothing happened when she pulled the trigger.

"It's over. Let it go." He raised his pistol, but she threw her weapon at him, and he lost his aim.

"You won't get away with this," she said while ducking under a counter.

"I've been told that before."

"What kind of man are you that kills defenseless women and children?" she asked, stalling for time to find a charged weapon.

"A professional." He blew off a corner of the counter that hid her, its slivers cutting her forehead. After reloading his pistol, he stalked her.

She threw a chunk of debris across the kitchen. When he turned to target it, she stabbed him in the knee with a shard of scrap metal and rolled away behind a cabinet.

"BioLuna and Biadez, they have everything. Why are they doing this?"

"You don't understand power, Ms. Hope."

All she had now was the device. She took it from her belt and gripped it to use as a club, but it beeped, and the buttons began to move without her pressing them.

"Ah, there you are," he said.

Glass crunched, and she knew he approached. Before she could crawl away, a head-up control set displayed from the device with jiggly lines and a logarithmic scale in Hertz written sideways. When she rotated her wrist to read the projection, it now extended above the cabinet.

"*Merde!*" he mumbled and shuffled toward her. She moved her finger to a visual area marked "Activate," and a virtual control panel appeared alongside a map she remembered from the view from space—the Johnston Rift and their farm.

Turning the corner, he pointed his pistol at her, but then realized what was displayed—trajectories moving toward their locale. He followed her eyes skyward through the holes in the roof and the dusty haze. There, missiles streaked toward the valley where Elizabeth and Cookie had headed, and their own position at the farm.

"You know what this is," she said.

He gazed at the missiles arcing toward them. "Of course."

"Then you know they plan to kill you, too."

"I'll meet you in paradise."

"That's not where you're going." She placed her finger near the only button on the display that seemed to make sense. "Jam-ALL."

Above them, the missiles veered off course. One landed in the farm compound and blew him off his feet.

***

On the active wall inside the arsenal, Elizabeth and her team watched the missile trajectories veer from their gentle arcs to aimless spirals. Missiles collided and exploded in the air. One exploded nearby and knocked the dust from the ceiling. In the valley outside, drones and mechs now stumbled, shooting at random targets. Crawlers attacked each other as well as the men who walked with them.

"That's a Hydra in action," Cookie yelled over the explosions. "Someone else is controlling it."

"Someone friendly," Abrams said.

Her link still buzzed with static. "How soon can I call my sister?"

"Dunno. Meanwhile, please remove the remaining invaders."

Cookie and Elizabeth left the bunker and picked up their weapons. Standing on the rubble of the bunker, they sprayed fire into the disoriented drones. When the valley lay motionless, they sat on the edge of the rampart and zoomed their goggles to survey the carnage. The only things moving on the opposite side of the rift were rows of enemy combatants on their knees with their hands on their heads. To the west, the tacks of rail guns and glow of ground-based lasers lit up the night. Behind them, Abrams lay snoring.

She sighed to break the silence and leaned against his shoulder. "Meriel told me about your niece. Sorry."

He nodded and patted her hand, but he remained silent and surveyed the wreckage.

"You sorry you missed the fight on the *Tiger*?" she asked.

"Damn straight." Standing, he held out his hand to her. "Now, let's go help your sister."
***

Meriel crawled out from under the debris of the missile blast. A yellow glare filled the kitchen, and she shielded her eyes. She peered over the counter as a space-based pulse laser ignited debris in the farmyard in a meter-wide swath. And as it passed the farmhouse, the killer's shadow emerged.

Broken glass crunched as he climbed to his feet and cleared a path toward her through the smoke and dust. "Come now, Ms. Hope."

"I saved your life. You owe me."

"You are my target, not my savior."

As he rounded the cabinet where she hid, she stabbed him behind his other knee.

"Arh!" he howled as he collapsed, clipping her shoulder with *fléchettes* as she scrambled away.

In a much more congenial tone, he said, "You and your friends can all survive this if you come with me now. All we want is your cooperation and your silence. It does not have to end badly."

"That wasn't Khanag's goal."

"He does not speak for us."

"Tell me more," she said to stall. *Why would he talk if he could kill me?*

"You know how powerful we are. We can take care of them and give them a good life. A life much better then you can ever hope to provide. We can open many doors for them."

Instead of his beautiful portrait, the door she imagined opened on Etna to a world of drugs and horrors inflicted on them as hostages for her silence. John would die attempting to free his daughters.

A revelation pushed out her despair. *He's just a few feet away, so if he could kill me, I'd be dead. He's crippled and can't reach me.* But she had no weapon and could not reach him either. She was out of ideas to save them.

"It can be better for you as well," he said. "I expect you've had a difficult time without these. Here."

After a rattle and a soft click, a small tube rolled toward her. Retrieving the tube, she opened it and turned it upside down. A pill fell into her hand—her meds.

"This must be very hard on you, Ms. Hope. Perhaps if you take your medication and come with me, we can make all this pain and confusion go away." More pills rattled.

He's right. I have nowhere to go, no place to hide, no way to protect the girls or John. She rolled the pill between her fingers. *Just one, and I won't care anymore and it will all be over.*

"They'll take care of us?" she said with a shaky voice and tossed the empty vial back to him.

"Yes."

"I'll come, but drop the gun."

"OK," he said.

Something hard clicked on the countertop. Using her link as a mirror, she checked around the end of the counter and then over the top. Behind the next counter, he leaned against the wall and supported himself with one hand, the gun laying in front of him. When he spotted her link, he raised his other hand, palm to her.

She rose slowly, unsteadily with one hand behind her and took a step toward him.

A creak drew their attention to the closet door, and they both turned.

"Merry, are you OK?" came a muffled voice from behind the door.

"Hide!" Meriel shouted and swung the board she hid behind her back.

He turned to her, and before her weapon completed its arc, he deflected it and punched her in the face with his free hand. The punch knocked her into the wall, and she slumped to the floor.

Past spinning stars and unable to move, she watched him pick up his pistol and fire at the closet until the door hung in shreds. With a stick as a crutch, he limped over to the door, which crumbled in his hands when he turned the doorknob. Beyond the shards of door lay only a hatch in the floor. He fired again, but the *fléchettes* merely pinged and bounced off.

Stumbling while trying to stand, she saw him lean over to open the hatch and aim his weapon into the widening gap. She threw the toroidal device at him and struck him in the shoulder. Before he could restore his aim and fire, a stunner buzzed and an airgun popped. He staggered backward, and the pistol fell from his limp right hand. With his other hand, he scratched at a pellet embedded in his bleeding cheek. Dropping the crutch, he reached down to pick up his pistol. While struggling to her knees, she grabbed a metal chair leg.

"Hey!" she called, and as he turned, she smacked the chair leg on the side of his head.

He fell to his side but grasped a pistol hidden in his sock. Becky flipped the stunner to her, and she fired point-blank. The assassin slumped and lay still.

Meriel crawled over to the closet and Becky. "Where's Sandy?"

"In the basement. She shot through the crack in the trapdoor and got some of the stun on herself. She's OK, just sleeping. Where's Papa?"

"He's been hurt."

Becky moved to climb out, but Meriel held her shoulders. "I'll take care of your papa, hon. You stay hidden."

Another creak came from the porch, and she turned. Two shadows stood in the smoky haze—one small, one huge, both with gigantic weapons.

"God, no." She raised the stunner with a shaky hand.

"Hi, Liz!" Becky said.

A wisp of breeze cleared the smoke and haze to disclose Cookie and Elizabeth standing in the empty door frame.

Flares in the yard illuminated the mud-soaked hair that hung over Meriel's sunburned cheeks and swollen eye. Elizabeth winced and ran to her. "Are you OK?" Meriel nodded, and Elizabeth helped her to her feet. "It's clear; M. Colonel Lee gave us a ride here. The—"

"Sandy needs help, Liz." She pointed to the closet and turned to Cookie. "John's down, Sergeant. Call for a medic. And tie up this garbage." She pointed to the unconscious assassin and black-suits, and then went to help John.

On the floor behind her, the Hydra controller became dark and still, just as she had found it hours earlier.

When the medics arrived, Meriel hobbled over to the assassin. Taking the pill from her pocket, she crushed it between her fingers and sprinkled the crystals on his face. She stunned him again and leaned against the counter.

Becky rose from the hatch and looked worriedly at the medics helping her father.

Meriel gave her the stunner. "I need your help, hon. Watch him, OK? If he moves, stun him."

"Is he the one who hurt Papa?"

"One of them."

Glaring, Becky turned and stunned him.

Meriel walked over to check John, and Cookie gave her a nod. She picked up the link and opened the channel to Khanag.

"You lose again, thug. If I'm right, they should have your position about now." She stopped and looked up through the bare rafters to see the beams of laser cannon and flashes of light in space. Abruptly, the connection dropped. Within the ribbons of laser fire, the explosion of Admiral Leung's flagship appeared as only a momentary flash.

Turning around, she noticed Becky stunning the assassin every few seconds. Each time, his body jerked.

"He keeps twitching, Merry. When do I stop?"

"Oh, a few more will probably do it."

"Easy," Cookie said. "We need some residual brain function for testimony."

Meriel and Becky frowned.

"Maybe just a few more."

Becky grinned and stunned him again.

The medics prepped John for removal to the field hospital nearby. To protect them from the muddy rain, Meriel and Cookie built a lean-to over the collapsed eaves of the porch. After the shelter was completed, they sat close to John and Abrams. Each of them felt the occasional drop of mud from the seams in the tarp.

Elizabeth carried Sandy from the storm shelter. Still groggy from the stunner's ricochet, she scootched over onto Meriel's lap and closed her eyes.

Smiling at her sister, Meriel wiped a drop of blood from the cut on Elizabeth's cheek. "You're not perfect anymore."

"I like it. It'll make a great story."

Meriel turned to Abrams. "You knew Khanag would be here?"

He wiped the dirt streaks from his face. "We figured they'd try again. When BioLuna dropped the embargo last month, we figured something was coming, something much bigger than Khanag."

"I thought they pulled back because of the charges against them," Elizabeth said.

He shook his head. "They withdrew for safety. Somebody there knew the plan."

"You didn't tell us," Meriel said.

Elizabeth laid a hand on her sister's arm. "He didn't know, M. He was surprised, too."

Meriel's eyes narrowed. "Was I the bait here?"

"No," Colonel Lee said as he walked into the makeshift shelter. "A magnet. A concentration of forces." Turning to Abrams, he handed him a flask. "You see the medic yet, soldier?"

"I'm next, sir."

"A medic should treat you as well, Ms. Hope," the colonel said. He pointed to the assassin. "Is that him?" Meriel nodded, and he waved his escort to take custody.

Becky pouted, but she laid the stunner in Meriel's open hand and snuggled under her arm.

"Is LeHavre still there?" she asked.

With a nod he said, "It's a little beat up inside, but the Marines were there. The Troopers came by, too. We don't have a defense treaty in place with the other stations, but they helped us anyway. Speaks well of 'em."

"These weren't pirates," Meriel said.

"No. They sent corsairs and commandoes here to the farm, but this was a full-scale invasion. The mercenaries and most of the mechs attacked the Capitol and the Rift. We didn't think Khanag's corsairs would come after you."

"Meriel did," Elizabeth said.

"Sorry we were too busy to help you. The intelligence team says craters and debris ring your farm for miles around. They're still extinguishing the brush fires. What did John have up his sleeve here?" he asked, but she shrugged.

"We were lucky," Cookie said. "All of us."

"No plan survives contact with the enemy," Lee said. "The Hydra is decisive in high-tech habitats like colonies or stations. The major purpose is to cut off life support. People give up pretty fast when they can't breathe."

Elizabeth scoffed. "Kinda hard to do that on a planet."

"Yeah. They thought it would be decisive. Turns out, we were pretty evenly matched. Another few hours pounding on Stewardville, and they'd have driven us into the caves like rats. Now that woulda been crap."

"But instead you took out their command structure?" Cookie said.

Lee smirked. "Well, yeah, there is that."

A medic called to them. "We're ready for you, Lieutenant."

Abrams nodded, and Elizabeth and Cookie helped him to the field surgeon.

Turning to Meriel, Lee lowered his voice. "You found the controller here with Annie's stuff?"

She handed the toroidal device to him. "How did you know?"

"A tech named Matsushita surrendered. He tracked the signal and turned it off. You're the only ones out here along this vector." He sighed. "Ms. Hope, BioLuna is in the dark about what happened here. It's to our advantage to keep it that way: keep them guessing; keep them thinking we're invincible and not just lucky. You will keep our secret?"

"Sure. They're wounded, but you don't think they're done, right? They're too strong, too well connected."

"Their strength is closer to home in Sol system, not way out here. We've got Troopers guarding the jump points rather than BioLuna now, so they're unlikely to hit us head-on again. I think they'll aim for an easier target."

"Like Chosho?"

He nodded. "And tau Ceti-4."

***

"Thank you," Meriel said and accepted a stack of blankets from a medic at the field hospital the Marines had set up near the farm. It was Colonel Lee who had expedited John's surgery and found them shelter and cots near John since Meriel had completely leveled the farm compound. And it was Colonel Lee who had ordered the medics to treat her. Now her face was coated in salve, except for the bandages on her forehead and dark glasses on her eyes. Her arm lay in a sling to protect her torn shoulder.

She limped back into John's recovery room. Cookie slept on the floor, while Sandy and Becky snoozed tucked under Elizabeth's arms. After covering each of them with a blanket, Meriel sat on a broken-down couch next to John's cot and held his hand.

As the rain pattered on the tarp overhead, she looked over her small family and played with the pendant on her necklace.

"It's all here," her mother had said. And it was: the nav program that saved them; the manifest that incriminated the conspirators; the way to Home; and the living history of everyone on the *Princess* in the vid galleries.

"Everything is here," Meriel whispered. *Everything except you and papa.* She looked to Sandy and Becky again and smiled. *You'd like them, Mama.*

Using the visor she had dug out from the rubble, she found a reference in *Galactipedia* to songlines and listened with her head resting on the back of the chair.

```
    The native peoples of Australia
    still walk their songlines, paths
    unique to each tribe or language
    group. While they walk, they sing of
    how the gods sang the world into
    being—the mountains, the streams, the
```

plants and animals, and all the
features of their world. Those songs
brought forth all the distinctions of
rock and food and poison that made
their home possible to live in. And
when the gods finished their songs of
creation, they taught their people the
songs and lay down and became the
landscape. For many thousands of
years, every time the people walk
their songlines, they sing their world
and their gods back into being.

That's like me and Liz and the kids. It's not a choice. And it's not intellectual. It's what we know in our hearts. I learned my songs as a kid and sang them to my sister and now to Sandy: the places, the smells, the feel.

And she knew more now. It's not just what you know, it's what you are drawn to, what you want enough to forsake the familiar. She gazed at Sandy and Becky again.

"It's good to see you like this," Colonel Lee said and sat next to her.

She smiled but then cringed as the dried salve stretched her burned cheeks and purple eye. "Really? Maybe I should try for this look more often."

"I mean happy."

Unsure of what he meant, she surveyed her team. "Yeah, like they were born to it."

"Not them. You with them. You're remembering what it feels like to be loved."

"I put them in danger."

"They're here for you. They made a choice."

"The girls didn't. I'm a danger to them."

"Perhaps. Living is not without risk."

Torchlight glittered in her eyes and the tears on her cheeks. "I'm afraid I'll disappoint them, and this will all fade away."

"Love is not without risk either, Ms. Hope." He sighed. "You dream of a life among the stars?"

Without speaking, she turned to him.

"I gathered you might be leaving."

"I need to protect them."

He nodded. "I understand. They will miss you. It's your decision, of course. But don't run away from them because you feel unworthy of their love."

She bit her lip.

He tapped behind his ear. "Command asked me to tell you that your friends will dock as soon as the repairs are completed."

"Friends?"

"The other orphans from the *Princess*."

Meriel's mouth fell open. "All of them?"

"All of them."

Meriel hugged him, and though her bruised face hurt and the dried salve cracked, she could not stop her tears.

"Hi, Pastor Lee," Sandy said, rubbed her eyes, and went to Meriel.

Meriel scooted over to make a place on the couch. "Hey, sleepyhead."

Sandy stretched out a hand to touch Meriel's cheeks but cringed and pulled it back. "Are you OK, Merry?"

"I'm wonderful, hon."

"How's Papa?"

"He'll be fine. He just needs to rest for a while."

Colonel Lee rose. "Well, I must visit the other injured." He smiled at them and turned away.

When he left, Sandy gazed up at her. "Becky and I heard what you told the bad guy on the link."

"What?"

"That we're your kids."

"You are. And nobody's gonna take you from me." She put her free arm around her and squeezed.

Sandy laid her head on Meriel's shoulder and closed her eyes. "Yup, that's what we heard."

Meriel leaned back and hugged her tight. With memories of dancing in the rain with Sandy and Becky, she smiled and slept without boost or meds or nightmares for the first time in ten years.

***

In the quiet of the field hospital that night, Meriel received a message.

```
From S. K.:
This isn't over, Ms. Hope.
Subedei
```

Chapter 15
Home

Spacers

One month after Haven repulsed the invasion, Meriel sat at the kitchen table of the rebuilt farmhouse covered in dust, with sweat streaking down her face. The white scar that crossed her tanned body showed clearly in the sleeveless shirt, but she took no notice. Instead, she pulled on her ear and stared at a link displaying a draft message.

They had worked a long day finishing the dorms, which would be their refuge away from their jobs as spacers. She and the neighbors had started reconstruction of the farm compound right after their victory, well before John was back on his feet. As soon as their ships docked, the orphaned kids from the *Princess* chipped in. Still, it took days to complete the roofing, and until then, they'd all lived in tarps under the shattered walls of the farmhouse.

That's when she moved out of Becky and Sandy's room to be more discreet. However, the two girls often stayed in the new dorms with her and the returning orphans.

She remembered what he had told them when they arrived. "Kids, these quarters are yours permanently. When you feel like coming home or on a vacation, there will always be a place for you here. Haven has citizenship papers for you and your fosters, and whatever happens, you will find safe passage here."

This would be her last day on the surface for a while. A few days earlier, Molly had returned from a dry run with Teddy's new nav system. At LeHavre, the *Tiger* prepped to leave on their new circuit, and she would join them: her first tour since the attack.

Behind her, John poured a glass of water from the new sink and took a drink. He dragged a chair next to her.

"Sorry for blowing up your lawn, hon," she said.

"Now you apologize?" he said and kissed her on the forehead. Leaning over, he scanned the message.

```
To: Asha Ferrell, Europa 2, 4456y
  I wish to express my condolences for
the loss of your father and wish he
could be there with you. I served with
your father on the Tiger and he helped
me. I had been struggling with the
loss of my own parents ten years ago.
Because of our conversations, I was
able to confront some very tough
issues, and I am grateful to him for
that.
  My sincerest sympathies for your
loss. If you need anything, please,
just send me a note.
  Best wishes,
  Meriel Hope.
```

John tipped his chair back and hefted a boot up on the nearby stool. "Did you forgive him?"

"Hell no, but that's his burden, not hers. Whatever she hears about him, she doesn't need to carry it all."

He nodded. "The orphans look comfortable here."

"Some will stay. The others will probably ship out when their contracts renew. We can all get posts on routes working LeHavre."

"What about you?" he asked, but Meriel did not answer. "Do you still love me?

"Of course I do, but I'll have a route as soon as the *Princess* is fixed up."

"You're not rated for captain."

She smiled. "I'm trying to recruit the Vingels when their contract on the *Tiger* is up for renewal."

"Familiar faces?"

"I trust them."

"You didn't invite me."

She took his hand. "We talked about that, hon. You need to stay with the girls. The ship and the kids are my dream."

"You willing to give me up for a dream?"

Meriel kissed him and smiled. "Now, why would I need to do that? Will you stop loving me if I'm gone for a while?"

"No. Of course not. But the girls—"

"Don't guilt me."

"I have to say it, M. They love you now. The only thing that will hurt them more than you leaving is if you don't return."

"I've always been honest with them, John."

"Those were just words. They're listening with their hearts."

"And you?"

"I'll be here. Just don't be too long," he said. "Hey, sailor, how about a little fun on your last night on shore leave."

She smiled back and leaned toward him. "Just what do you have in mind?"

***

The next day, John and Meriel waited in the farm compound for her hop to the Stewardville shuttle and LeHavre station, where the *Tiger* idled. It was another hot day, and the VTOL ferry stirred up little dust devils. Elizabeth and Tommy stood nearby, holding hands. Anita, Harry, Penny, and the rest of the orphans and fosters joined them to wish her off.

John took her hand. "When will you return?"

"Should be only a month or so Haven time. One circuit through the quadrant."

Becky and Sandy ran up to her and held her other hand.

Kneeling, Meriel removed a well-worn book from her duffle. "Here, girls. Keep this for me."

Sandy ignored the treasure and gazed up with wide eyes. "Come home to us."

"I'll be back soon. Don't worry," she said with a smile, but their frowns told her she had said something wrong.

Sandy stared at her shoes. "That's what Mom said."

But she could not keep her promise, just like my mother. She hugged them both tightly. "You two are a part of the most important thing in my life. Look around you." The girls turned to see all the orphans and their foster parents who had come to say good-bye. "This is our hub now, and I'll always return—to you and to them." She hugged them again. "They're new here and have no idea what life is like on a planet. Help them, just like you helped me."

Sandy accepted the book and brightened. "Sure, M. I can show them the sheep and the farm and how to muck out a stable, and Becky can teach them how to track varmints..." and she continued well after the ferry's engines drowned out her little voice.

Home

"Pass me a flex elbow," John said to Sam Spurell, Tommy's younger brother. Two weeks after Meriel had left for her tour, Sam furloughed on Haven with Harry and Anita. Together they relaid the drip irrigation lines torn up during the defense of the farm.

Sam burst a dirt clod with his pickaxe, bent over a pile of fittings, and threw one to John. "I heard they caught some smugglers dropping off illegals at Terni."

"That's on the other side of the sea."

He nodded and leaned on the pick handle. "They brought their own replicators and hydroponics, so the council will likely give 'em a pass.

"Nothing wrong with settlers. Did they bring any seed stock? Or embryos?"

"Dunno."

"Waste processing?" John asked, but Sam shrugged. "You know, it's always waste management that kills a settlement."

"It'll be another load on the ecosystem here."

"Yeah, but it may take a thousand years before it breaks down."

Sam pointed to a brown patch of failed lawn near the house. "You gonna replant that, too?"

He scowled. "Maybe. When's your tour?"

"Next week. Be gone two months." He hefted the pick over his shoulder and resumed digging the narrow trench for the irrigation lines.

"You coming back?"

He surveyed the field and compound. "You know, I think I might."

Becky and Sandy ran to John with Dumpy close behind.

"Papa, incoming," Becky said and handed him a link. She picked up a dirt clod and threw it at a critter skulking nearby. Sandy sat nearby watched Sam with a gentle smile.

John read the message. "They cleared the *Princess* crew of all charges, Sam."

Sam stood up straight. "Damn. Meriel did it. I never thought that'd happen. We'll get our ship back." He dropped the pickaxe and ran back to the compound. "Hey, Harry! Annie!"

"Wow. Merry's gonna get her ship," Becky said. "You think she'll give us a ride?"

John nodded. "As soon as they fix her up. But only if you're good, and when you're old enough."

"Merry did her spacewalk when she was nine and jumped a ship when she was twelve," Sandy said.

He frowned. "She told you that?"

She clasped her hands behind her back and traced patterns in the dirt with her toe. "Yeah."

John took her hand. "The *when* will be up to me, OK?" he said, and she smiled. "Say, what did Meriel give you when she left?"

"A book, Papa."

"Can I see it?"

"Sure," she said and ran back to the house for the book while John listened to the rest of the IGB news feed.

```
"On News of the Galaxy Tonight:
Piracy is not dead, according to a
special investigative report on the
LSM Princess. Surviving children from
the Princess disaster have surfaced
after ten years in hiding and are
expected to tell their stories. Sealed
court records have been opened that
document the tragedy of a deadly
attack. Just recently this attack was
linked to a conspiracy between the
UNE, BioLuna, and the Archtrope of
Calliope to invade a populated colony.
News of this attack was suppressed for
a decade to avoid panic among
independent traders.
    More after this message..."
```

Sandy ran back with the book. A slip of paper marked a dog-eared page.

> *"And once in an age, the arc of history bends around the wheel of one committed person...That person acts not from selfishness or the lust for fame but instead from love and commitment... He or she can live no other life and be fully human.*
>
> *"As if by God's hand, through that individual the forces of darkness are dispelled, and humanity is saved from the abyss..."*

John sighed, held the hand of each of his daughters, and walked with them to the hill to watch the galaxy rise. As they watched the stars, his linked buzzed with a message.

```
From M. Hope:
Circuit ended.

Coming Home.
```

Appendix

As If by God's Hand

From *The Diary of Neuchar de Merlner*, Europa, 2112
Verse 34: Nova Conta, Section 3
Comme Si Dans les Mains de Dieu (As If by God's Hand)

Once in an age, the forces of darkness align to bend the arc of history.

And once in an age, the arc of history bends around the wheel of one committed person who, acting from his or her own virtuous interests, changes the course of humanity: the child who raises the flag above the barricades; the mother who thrusts the picture of her murdered child before the dead eyes of the tyrant; the girl who refuses to deny her love for God even while her flesh burns at the stake—an individual who grips their shred of civilization with both hands and will not give it up.

Through the fidelity of that individual, the complex interrelationships constructed by the powerful to order society to their personal ideologies and selfish interests collapse under the weight of justice and moral right.

The light of their virtues burns throughout history, despite the fog of interpretation. When this light is observed, it needs no explanation. It is remembered though demagogues and armies strive to erase it from our hearts. Volumes are written to describe these single acts of faithfulness, and volumes are never enough. It is proof that humans are more than animals and God lives in each of us.

That person acts not from selfishness or the lust for fame but instead from love and commitment. "Hero" is a label bestowed by those of us who benefit from their virtues, not a crown they reach for. For that person, there is no other way. He or she can live no other life and be fully human.

As if by God's hand, through that individual the forces of darkness are dispelled, and humanity is saved from the abyss.

I assign to you the mission to be that person every day of your life in small ways with every breath you take, and someday you too may be the wheel around which history bends.

I assign this to you because civilization and freedom are not inevitable. Sometimes that person does not appear, and the forces of darkness consume everything, and civilization is lost for centuries.

Excerpts from Alan C. Biadez Address to the Copernicus Club

In Memorium: Remarks on the Anniversary of the Destruction of Brazil

[Introduction deleted.]

Throughout history, humans have lived on the brink of extinction. We have evolved on the razor's edge between starvation and annihilation at the whim of the unforgiving hand of nature and subject to the universe's existential lack of concern. We humans challenged nature's strong hand that once constrained our species, and we won. But we risk destruction by our own hand through overpopulation and overconsumption. In the last hundred years, the strong hand of man acting through the United Nations of Earth intervened to stop humanity's destruction of itself and our planet. As human beings who care for all Earth's creatures, this strong hand was necessary; we could do nothing else. We conquered the threats from Gaia and in so doing became her protector.

The sacrifice of personal liberty, the limitations of technological innovation, the strict regulation of how and where we live were all necessary to achieve this victory over ourselves; painful changes to be sure, but necessary for the common good.

But every act of good produces unforeseen consequences. As we found when Asteroid G-44 destroyed Brazil and the coastlines of the Atlantic, our single home on Earth leaves us vulnerable to even more severe threats from nature. To meet those threats, humans have seeded the stars.

Outposts of humanity cling to life in the stars, but only human life. Even the richest habitats cannot support self-sustaining ecosystems with diverse species. And our experiment living among the stars is still young. It is not yet clear whether these outposts can survive without roots planted firmly in the soil of Earth, the single planet that supports life. I implore us to change.

Earth is our home, but our future is out there. We must expand the quantity and diversity of Earth life on the colonies and stations to protect it from the whims of nature. We must affix anchors on other worlds and build ecosystems upon them that will support Earth life. We must make the stars our home. Humanity must rise to that challenge or suffer annihilation.

Join me, and let us populate the stars!

Glossary for Earthers

The authors have done their best to use the vernacular of Earthers in the event that unredacted editions of this work will be smuggled past the UNE censors. However, some distinctions common to spacers may be unfamiliar and we thus offer this brief glossary.

Arcology

A very densely populated structure or hyperstructure. Popularized by twentieth-century Earth visionary Paolo Soleri, who coined the term.

AU

Astronomical Unit. One AU is the distance from the Earth to Sol, or about 149-million kilometers. The speed of light is about 0.3 million kilometers per second, so it takes an electromagnetic (EM) signal about eight minutes to travel one AU. That's a huge distance!

Communications beacon

Physicists have not figured out how to send radio and other electromagnetic (EM) signals faster than the speed of light (FTL), so FTL ships consistently outrun their messages. Since information is often more valuable than mass, ships carry messages and news-storage systems that synchronize with beacons near stations. Ships resync on-board memory with these beacons every time they leave a station and enter a new system. Each ship that downloads to a beacon receives some revenue.

Cruiser

Mark IX Сила Грузчик, or Power Loader designed on a Russian colony near Bernard's Star. They are nicknamed "cruisers" because in English, the name sounds like "silly cruise-chick." Cargo handlers sometimes refer to themselves as cruisers, but the term is considered an insult if used by anyone else, especially when referring to a woman.

EM

Electromagnetic waves, like radio, TV, light, infrared, ultraviolet, gamma, and X-rays, which travel at the speed of light.

EMP

Electromagnetic pulse. A strong EM wave that essentially zaps all nearby electronics.

ET

Earth Time. A useful baseline for coordination in time. Loosely based on Earth Standard Time and the convenient assumption that there is one single time for everything in the universe. ET is useful in all astrophysical calculations and has nothing whatsoever to do with the timekeeping devices on each ship or mass. An exact correlation is very difficult over light-years because everything of interest moves at fractions of the speed of light. Navigation computers only have a useful approximation.

Floor and deck

Floor typically refers to the horizontal platform under your feet on a colony, moon, or planet with a stable gravity. Deck refers to the similar structure of a vessel. However, stationers think of their stations as stable and permanent and use floor. Spacers often refer to the deck on a station, which identifies them to stationers.

Grange

Voluntary organization of Earth farmers first organized in the United States in the nineteenth century. Earth agriculture became socialized by

2040 under UN regulations and land productivity has declined ever since.

Gravity well

A large mass that distorts space-time like a bowling ball on a trampoline.

ISA

Interstellar Sports Association.

Laws of Navigation

In common language these can be stated as (1) all positions are relative (there are no fixed reference points, only conventions); (2) everything is moving all the time; and (3) you can only know for sure where things were, not where they are. (0) Law 0 was included later to keep the math honest. Law 0: the arrow of time is unidirectional.

Light curtain

Archaic technology from early twenty-first century where an array of low-power lasers separated adjoining rooms with a translucent curtain of light. It replaced the modestly priced hanging beads found more commonly in environments with steady gravity. Light curtains were also less likely to become a choking hazard if gravity shifted or was lost.

Nav-Four

Navigator, rating-four. This designation refers to the skill level of a navigator as assessed by an independent agency. In this case, John's post is chief warrant officer of navigation. A nav-five rating would qualify him to be posted to pilot and senior navigator for the *Tiger*, but Jerri currently held that post. The post is different from rank, such as captain, commander, pilot, chief warrant officer, petty officer, or seaman. Rank and post are also different from skill level.

OOD

Officer On Deck. The OOD is the ship's officer in charge of the bridge during a shift and serves as the direct representative of the captain

Sphere of uncertainty

Sometimes just known as the sphere. When you jump, there is uncertainty in time and space about where you will end up. This is due to your lack of certainty of the positions and masses of everything along your path. This uncertainty is shown by drawing a sphere around a calculated destination. The second law of nav says, "Everything is moving all the time," so it is difficult to calculate precisely where you will end up, unless you know every mass and where it's all going. That's impossible to do without infinite compute resources. So there is always an uncertainty of where you'll end up, and that uncertainty can be shown as a sphere. It's actually more like a sphere with a hollow center because there is absolutely no chance you will hit what you aimed at. The sphere grows exponentially with distance, so shorter jumps have smaller spheres.

Suit

Warm-suit—emergency gear for an air leak. Warm-suits have a carbon mesh and an inflatable clear hood to allow the wearer to survive in a vacuum for a few hours. A rebreather and temperature control are built in. It will not last more than a few hours in a hard vacuum and is no protection against weapons.

Ten stages of a spacers' party

(1) uncomfortably shy and distant; (2) polite or coy; (3) friendly and engaging conversation; (4) double entendre, puns, and sexual innuendo; (5) loud and bawdy; (6) out of control, partial undress, drinking with your worst enemy; (7) looking for trouble; (8) finding trouble, confrontation/altercation; for large

parties, rioting; (9) nursing wounds; and (10) Soberall(TM), sleep, or rehab.

Tranq boost

Tranquilizers, called "tranq," are needed to overcome the long periods of disorientation during jumps. Tranq-boost is a stronger tranq that suppresses the imagination and memories, which can overwhelm during jumps.

UNE

United Nations of Earth. Intergovernmental organization of 804 nations, states, planets, colonies, and moons within the Sol star system dominated by planet Earth.

Wink-in

When an FTL object comes into your view, you have no sense of it before it physically arrives. That's because it is moving faster than the photons or EM radiation that tells you it's coming. When the FTL object arrives, it appears followed by its EM, and it looks like a weak flash or a wink.

XO

The executive officer or first officer is next in command to the captain.

About the Author

Ray Strong is an award-winning sci-fi author who lives in Northern California. Growing up, his passion for sci-fi began the moment he picked up his first book by Andre Norton and viewed Wernher Von Braun's "Man in Space." Those geniuses inspired Ray to study aerospace engineering and begin a career in high-tech industries. He has been striving to build the future ever since.

Personal Note:

Thanks for reading my book. If you enjoyed it, please take a moment to write a review at your favorite retailer.

Friend me on Facebook at:
  https://www.facebook.com/ray.strong.399
Follow me on Twitter:
  http://twitter.com/RayStrong8
Subscribe to my blog:
  http://impulsefiction1.blogspot.com/

Ray Strong

Made in the USA
Las Vegas, NV
21 January 2024